SONS
OF DORN

WHEN SCOUT S'TONAN looked back to the rise of the hill for the sniper, he could see that the Roaring Blade had shouldered his weapon and was now rushing down to join his fellow cultists in close combat with the Scouts. Most likely the lasrifle's power cells had drained before the sniper had been able to take another shot.

Taloc stepp[...]he line again, shiftin[...]by the fallen Vulpes[...]

The Roarin[...]ut any apparent tho[...]n narrowed his eyes and readied to take on the next attacker. They fought so much like the warrior-clans of his youth. But he was an Imperial Fist now, a proud scion of a heritage of strategic planning and mastery of defence. He would not act without thinking, without planning, but would out-think and out-plan his enemy, like any proud son of Dorn.

By the same author

DAWN OF WAR II

More Space Marine action from the Black Library

THE ULTRAMARINES OMNIBUS
by Graham McNeill
(Contains the novels: *Nightbringer,*
Warriors of Ultramar and *Dead Sky, Black Sun*)

THE KILLING GROUND
by Graham McNeill

COURAGE & HONOUR
by Graham McNeill

BROTHERS OF THE SNAKE
by Dan Abnett

THE BLOOD ANGELS OMNIBUS
by James Swallow
(Contains the novels: *Deus Encarmine*
and *Deus Sanguinius*)

THE GREY KNIGHTS OMNIBUS
by Ben Counter
(Contains the novels: *Grey Knights, Dark Adeptus*
and *Hammer of Daemons*)

SALAMANDER
by Nick Kyme

A WARHAMMER 40,000 NOVEL

Imperial Fists

SONS OF DORN

Chris Roberson

A BLACK LIBRARY PUBLICATION

First published in Great Britain in 2010 by
The Black Library,
Games Workshop Ltd.,
Willow Road, Nottingham,
NG7 2WS, UK.

10 9 8 7 6 5 4 3 2 1

Cover illustration by Hardy Fowler.

A CIP record for this book is available from the British Library.

ISBN 13: 978 1 84416 789 0

Distributed in the US by Simon & Schuster
1230 Avenue of the Americas, New York, NY 10020, US.

See the Black Library on the Internet at
www.blacklibrary.com

Find out more about Games Workshop
and the world of Warhammer 40,000 at
www.games-workshop.com

Printed and bound in the US.

IT IS THE 41st millennium. For more than a hundred centuries the Emperor has sat immobile on the Golden Throne of Earth. He is the master of mankind by the will of the gods, and master of a million worlds by the might of his inexhaustible armies. He is a rotting carcass writhing invisibly with power from the Dark Age of Technology. He is the Carrion Lord of the Imperium for whom a thousand souls are sacrificed every day, so that he may never truly die.

YET EVEN IN his deathless state, the Emperor continues his eternal vigilance. Mighty battlefleets cross the daemon-infested miasma of the warp, the only route between distant stars, their way lit by the Astronomican, the psychic manifestation of the Emperor's will. Vast armies give battle in His name on uncounted worlds. Greatest amongst his soldiers are the Adeptus Astartes, the Space Marines, bio-engineered super-warriors. Their comrades in arms are legion: the Imperial Guard and countless planetary defence forces, the ever-vigilant Inquisition and the tech-priests of the Adeptus Mechanicus to name only a few. But for all their multitudes, they are barely enough to hold off the ever-present threat from aliens, heretics, mutants – and worse.

TO BE A man in such times is to be one amongst untold billions. It is to live in the cruellest and most bloody regime imaginable. These are the tales of those times. Forget the power of technology and science, for so much has been forgotten, never to be re-learned. Forget the promise of progress and understanding, for in the grim dark future there is only war. There is no peace amongst the stars, only an eternity of carnage and slaughter, and the laughter of thirsting gods.

IT IS THE 41st millennium. For more than a hundred centuries the Emperor has sat immobile on the Golden Throne of Earth. He is the master of mankind by the will of the gods, and master of a million worlds by the might of his inexhaustible armies. He is a rotting carcass writhing invisibly with power from the Dark Age of Technology. He is the Carrion Lord of the Imperium for whom a thousand souls are sacrificed every day, so that he may never truly die.

YET EVEN IN his deathless state, the Emperor continues his eternal vigilance. Mighty battlefleets cross the daemon-infested miasma of the warp, the only route between distant stars, their way lit by the Astronomican, the psychic manifestation of the Emperor's will. Vast armies give battle in His name on uncounted worlds. Greatest amongst his soldiers are the Adeptus Astartes, the Space Marines, bio-engineered super-warriors. Their comrades in arms are legion: the Imperial Guard and countless planetary defence forces, the ever-vigilant Inquisition and the tech-priests of the Adeptus Mechanicus to name only a few. But for all their multitudes, they are barely enough to hold off the ever-present threat from aliens, heretics, mutants – and worse.

TO BE A man in such times is to be one amongst untold billions. It is to live in the cruellest and most bloody regime imaginable. These are the tales of those times. Forget the power of technology and science, for so much has been forgotten, never to be re-learned. Forget the promise of progress and understanding, for in the grim dark future there is only war. There is no peace amongst the stars, only an eternity of carnage and slaughter, and the laughter of thirsting gods.

PROLOGUE

In the exercise hall deep in the heart of the Imperial Fist strike cruiser *Capulus*, Captain Taelos swung his blade through the air in a two-handed grip, eyes closed and thoughts racing. For most of the ship's day he had been in the hall, going through the various forms and movements set down in Rhetoricus's catechism of the sword. Ever since he'd been a mere neophyte, to perform the sword-forms had been for Taelos a meditative act, one which in even the most stressful and demanding of circumstances helped him order his thoughts and centre himself, pushing away distractions and focusing on the essential matter at hand.

It didn't seem to work for him any more.

Long centuries before, Rhetoricus had codified the Rites of Battle by which the Imperial Fists guided their actions. Surpassed in the Chapter's estimation only by Primarch Rogal Dorn himself, Rhetoricus had near the end of his life distilled all he knew of combat and conquest, of weapons and warriors. In the resulting work, *The Book of Five Spheres*, Rhetoricus detailed the strengths and limitations of all of the potential weapons in a warrior's arsenal, but reserved his greatest praise for the sword, which he considered the most perfect close-combat weapon ever devised by the mind of man.

'The soul of the Imperial Fist can be found in his sword,' Rhetoricus had said. 'When the odds are innumerable against you, and there is little hope of victory, still a holy warrior with a sword in his hand can prevail, if his intent is righteous and pure.' Ever since the days of Dorn, it was seldom that a battle-brother of the Imperial Fists ever stepped onto the field of battle without a sword in his fist or at his hip, and it was not unusual to see an Imperial Fist facing the enemy with nothing but his own trusted blade in hand. In the undertaking on Malodrax, which Taelos recalled all too well, Captain Lysander stood against the Iron Warriors with a sword as his only weapon, until he finally reclaimed his master-crafted thunder hammer the Fist of Dorn and was able to scour the servants of Chaos from the planet with hammer and blade.

Captain Taelos cherished the words of Rhetoricus, finding in them the clarity of thought and purpose that had guided him through campaign after campaign, on countless worlds over the long years. In the forms of the sword laid out in *The Book of Five Spheres* Taelos had always found the answer to any question that arose, if he would only first discover the still centre of his being and listen to the lesson which his blade whistling through the air was trying to communicate to him.

But now, try as he might, all Taelos could hear were his own thoughts racing through his mind. And when he closed his eyes, he couldn't discover the still centre of his being, but could only see replayed across his mind's eye the landscape of Nimbosa.

The memory of his last undertaking still burned in Taelos's mind. He had been tasked with protecting the Imperial envoy to the tau sept of T'olku, with both envoy and escort given instructions to commence protracted negotiations which would delay the tau from launching their main offensive on the contested world of Nimbosa. The delaying tactic failed, despite the best efforts of Taelos and the envoy, and the full weight of the tau forces led by Commander Brightsword fell on Nimbosa before the Imperium's forces had arrived. Not a single human colonist survived the assault, down to the youngest child.

When the Imperial forces arrived, Taelos and the Imperial Fists 2nd Company fought alongside Marshal Helbrecht's Black Templars in the bloody campaign to retake the world. The Imperial forces strove valiantly, but paid heavily for every victory won. At the Massacre of Koloth Gorge, a number of

Imperial Fists and a detachment of Imperial Guardsmen were caught in a narrow gorge by Brightsword, and subjected to a three-hour slaughter in the crossfire. The Guardsmen, and many of the Imperial Fists who fought alongside them, were lost in the action.

Taelos himself had been badly injured, and another Imperial Fist had been forced to step forwards and take command of the 2nd Company. Had the gene-seed of the Fists not lost the Sus-An Membrane millennia ago, and with it the ability to enter a state of suspended animation, Taelos would have been rendered insensate and unconscious by the severity of his wounds; as it was, he remained fully conscious throughout the aftermath at Koloth Gorge, aware of each and every Guardsman and Astartes who had been lost under his command.

His injuries had been painful, to be sure. But for the first time since he had been a neophyte, Taelos had been unable to find the healing power of the pain itself. He could not find what the Imperial Fists' Liturgy of Pain called 'the healing, purifying scalpel of the soul'. Taelos knew that pain was the wine of communion with heroes, and yet he could not seem to allow himself to fully embrace it. Like all Imperial Fists, he had been taught as a neophyte that pain was a lesson that the universe teaches us, and yet the only lesson he could glean from his own injuries was that of his own failure. He tried to see his pain as a golden astral fire, the quintessence of a dedicated existence, and yet he found himself looking upon his pain not as 'philosophic vitriol', in the words of the Liturgy, but as *punishment*.

Taelos knew that, if any deserved punishment, *he* did. First he had failed to avert the tau offensive, and as a result he considered the death of the human colonists in their millions as his responsibility, and his alone. But then to have lost so many men and Marines in the attempt to retake Nimbosa was in Taelos's eyes all but unforgivable.

It was long months before Taelos fully recovered from his injuries, by which time the Nimbosa campaign was over and the 2nd Company had returned to the Chapter's fortress-monastery, the massive ship dubbed the *Phalanx*. Presenting himself to the Chapter Master of the Imperial Fists, Taelos had but one request.

'A WARRIOR PILGRIMAGE?' Chapter Master Vladimir Pugh had thundered, all those months ago. 'Explain yourself, Captain Taelos.'

'Chapter Master,' Taelos had answered, lowering his gaze in deference, 'I can see no other way to atone for the loss of the human colonists of Nimbosa whose lives I failed to protect, and for the loss of our own battle-brothers who fell in the subsequent campaign.'

Pugh fixed Taelos with a hard stare. It was said amongst the Imperial Fists that their Chapter Master could take the full measure of an Astartes in a glance, and that nothing short of an exhaustive mental probe by a Librarian could uncover anything which had not been revealed by a single appraising look from Pugh. It was this facility, many in the Chapter believed, that made Pugh so adept at selecting the right Fist to promote to any given command, or to which battle-brother to entrust a critical mission.

Taelos had gone before the Chapter Master in the hope that Pugh's appraising stare would find him worthy of the boon he requested, and that he would be given leave to pursue his warrior pilgrimage, and so find atonement at last. It was rumoured that Master Pugh had excised his own taste buds, centuries before, in penance over the loss of one hundred and seventy Marines under his command in one terrible action. Taelos hoped that if anyone would understand the need for atonement, it would be the Chapter Master.

Taelos had hoped in vain.

'And do you consider your own needs to be of greater importance than those of your Chapter, brother-captain?'

'No, Chapter Master,' Taelos was quick to answer.

'Do you consider your own desire for atonement of greater significance than your service to the Emperor, greater even than the well-being and continuation of the Imperial Fists themselves?'

'No, Chapter Master!'

Pugh nodded once, slowly. 'Good. Then you should be pleased to learn that there is still a service you can provide to Chapter and Emperor. The Imperial Fists' numbers have been sorely depleted in recent actions, the Nimbosa campaign only one amongst many, and the Chapter is in dire need of reinforcement. We require, in short, aspirants.'

Taelos knew that it had been some time since a recruiting mission had been dispatched from the *Phalanx*. Had the Imperial Fists possessed a home world, like some Chapters, they could have culled the likely youth from among the population, a simple matter of expediency. But the Imperial Fists had no home except their fortress-monastery and the ships of their fleet. The Chapter followed the wishes of Primarch Rogal Dorn, who had famously said that he desired 'recruits, not vassals', and who had wanted nothing of the responsibilities that came with having a home world to maintain. Instead, the Imperial Fists recruited from any number of inhabited planetary systems, visiting them in turn every few generations.

'You are to take command of the 10th Company,' Pugh continued, 'and lead a recruitment mission to scour the nearby systems for suitable aspirants. The strike cruiser *Capulus* has been prepared, and stands ready for your use.'

Taelos remained silent. The previous captain of the 10th Company had only recently fallen in battle, his loss a significant blow to the Chapter. The posting was a single honour for any Imperial Fist, to be entrusted with the Chapter's very future.

But Taelos found it difficult to see the honour, now.

As captain of the 2nd Company, Taelos had led undertaking after successful undertaking, always bringing greater glory to the Chapter, and to the primarch and Emperor in whose name they fought.

But that had been before Nimbosa. Now, he was being taken off the front lines, and given command of the 10th Company. Certainly the task of training and educating new Space Marines was a worthy one, but in Taelos's eyes training Scouts was simply not the same as leading a company of battle-brothers into combat.

Taelos understood. He would not be allowed to seek atonement and peace on a warrior pilgrimage until his service to the Chapter was done. He could not help but look at his new command as a demotion, however, and the Chapter Master's indictment of Taelos's actions on Nimbosa.

'Is there some problem, brother-captain?' Pugh broke the silence, eyes narrowed.

'No, Chapter Master,' Taelos said firmly. 'Orders received and understood.' Taelos balled his right hand into a fist and crashed his arm against the Imperial aquila emblazoned on his chest plastron, the Chapter's salute.

'In the name of Dorn,' Chapter Master Pugh said, returning the salute.

'And Him on Earth,' Taelos finished, providing the antiphonal response.

CAPTAIN TAELOS LOWERED the point of his blade to the floor of the exercise hall, and slowly opened his eyes. The sword-forms were failing him, again. If it was not memories of Nimbosa that haunted his thoughts, it was the recollection of the *aftermath* of Nimbosa that occupied his attentions. Neither the focusing agent of pain nor the meditative solace of the sword had proved sufficient to guide him back to the still, silent core of his being.

'Captain?' came a voice from the doorway.

Taelos turned to see Veteran-Sergeant Hilts standing in the open door. 'Yes, brother-sergeant?'

'You had wished to inspect the aspirants at their training, sir?' Seeing Taelos nod, Hilts continued, 'They're ready for you now.'

Taelos returned the blade to the rack, and followed Veteran-Sergeant Hilts out of the exercise hall and down the corridor.

'This is not your first recruitment mission, brother-sergeant,' Taelos said as they walked along the passageway. 'How would you rate our crop of candidates?'

The veteran-sergeant was thoughtful for a moment before answering. 'There are a few among them who may go on to join the brotherhood of Dorn.'

The captain nodded, considering the response. They were months into the recruitment mission, with more months yet to go before they would finally return to the *Phalanx*. Once they rendezvoused with the fortress-monastery ship, it was Captain Taelos's duty to present a cadre of new-minted neophytes to Chapter Master Pugh, ready for the rigours of initiation.

'Through here, sir,' Veteran-Sergeant Hilts said, and opened a wide doorway on the passageway wall with a touch.

Captain Taelos stepped through the doorway onto a balcony, and looked down at the youths gathered on the floor below. Aspirants from a dozen different worlds, they were being led by another veteran-sergeant in the first rudimentary exercises of the sword-forms, learning the basics of the Imperial Fists' art of the blade.

'Their progress is satisfactory, brother-sergeant,' Taelos said. 'You and your fellow Scout sergeants honour your posts.'

Hilts and the other veteran-sergeants clearly understood the honour that had been bestowed upon them, to help train the next generation of battle-brothers. And the opportunity to lead the 10th Company was that much greater an honour. But while he knew it was his duty to lead the recruitment mission, both to Chapter and to Emperor, Taelos could not help wishing that the mission would soon be at an end, and the Chapter once more at full fighting strength. Then, and only then, might the Chapter Master at last give Taelos leave to depart on his warrior pilgrimage.

'Thank you, Veteran-Sergeant Hilts,' Taelos said, turning and heading back out into the corridor. 'Keep me posted on your ongoing progress.'

Captain Taelos walked back down the echoing corridor of the strike cruiser, alone with his thoughts. Once he set out on his Pilgrimage, Taelos would spend what remained of his life in hunting down and destroying any and all enemies to the Imperium. He would give all that he was, and all that he would ever be, in cutting a bloody swathe across the heavens in the name of primarch and Emperor, in remembrance of all the battle-brothers of the Imperial Fists Chapter who had fallen on Nimbosa. Alone, armed only with bolter and blade, Taelos would face xenos and traitor, heretic and daemon, until finally the sheer numbers of the enemy overwhelmed him and he fell, never to rise again.

Perhaps then, when life had fled and his hearts had beat their last, might Taelos finally silence the ghosts that haunted his thoughts.

PART ONE

'The soul of the Imperial Fist can be
found in his sword.'

Rhetoricus,
The Book of Five Spheres

CHAPTER ONE

FROM THE DECK of the caravel anchored off Eokaroe's western shore, with the red moon of Triandr hanging directly overhead, it seemed as if a baleful red eye was peering down upon the island, painting the silhouette of its mountains and forested hills in a muted chiaroscuro of crimson and black. On all sides the rest of the fleet rode at anchor, and from the topmast of each the noble ensign of Caritaigne fluttered listlessly in the mild evening breeze.

Jean-Robur du Queste, standing by the railing at the caravel's forecastle, dimly recollected from his childhood religious instruction that Triandr's moon was in Caritaigne traditionally considered in some phases to be the eye of god, and in others was thought to be instead the eye of god's Dark Twin.

Never a dutiful student, though, at least in any pursuit but the art of the blade, du Queste could not for his life remember which eye was which. Was god looking down upon the island, and turning his favour towards the fleet of Caritaigne warships anchored off her western shore? Or was this instead an infernal gaze, cast longingly at the souls of Caritaigne's enemies who would soon be sent into its dark embrace?

It did not occur to Jean-Robur to imagine, even for the briefest instant, that any signs or portents in the heavens might foretell anything but victory for the forces of Caritaigne. The alternative was simply inconceivable.

Still, though this would be Jean-Robur's first battle, he couldn't help but be somewhat bored with the whole affair. He understood little of the importance of this island of Eokaroe in the ongoing struggle, and cared even less. He was looking forward to testing his blade against the enemy forces, to be sure, but was more interested in the choice of wine at the victory celebrations afterwards than in the combat itself.

'What troubles you, *Mamzel* du Queste?' came a mocking voice from behind him. 'Afraid?'

Jean-Robur bristled, and turned to see Benoit Vioget, surrounded by his braying pack of sycophants. A distant cousin of Jean-Robur's, Benoit was only a handful of years his senior, but had lorded the brief difference in age between them since the expedition had left the shores of Caritaigne, months before.

'It's as I said,' Benoit said to his companions. 'The little woman pisses herself with fear at the thought of tomorrow's battle.'

The other young men scoffed, laughing at Jean-Robur's expense. He knew that few of them would have the courage to openly mock a son of one of Caritaigne's noble houses, had his cousin Benoit not called the tune. And not just out of fear that casting aspersions on a young noble might hinder their own chances of advancement at court.

'I tire of your gibes, cousin,' Jean-Robur answered, his tone pure acid. He paused, and then chuckled. 'Though I can almost forgive you calling me a woman, addressing me as "mamzel". Your repellent features clearly suggest you have no real experience with *actual* women, and likely wouldn't recognise one if they disrobed before you.'

That garnered a few chuckles from the crowd, though sharp glances from Benoit to his friends quickly stifled any laughter.

'I still say you are a rank coward,' Benoit spat, jabbing a finger at Jean-Robur. 'You may step lively at the salles d'armes back home, but put you up against the enemy and I wager you'll soil yourself and run crying for mama.'

A few of Benoit's friends laughed, but seeing Jean-Robur's hand stray to the handle of the falchion sheathed at his side, most began to exchange uneasy glances. Not yet blooded in battle, Jean-Robur was already considered one of the most promising young fencers in all of Caritaigne, and in the last few years he'd already won more duels than fencers more than twice his age.

'You are a braying ass, Benoit,' Jean-Robur snarled. He drew his master-crafted falchion part-way from its scabbard, the blade glinting reddish in the moonlight. 'Call me a coward but once more, I dare you, and we shall see whether I can do more than merely "step lively".'

For the briefest moment, it seemed as though Benoit might take up the gauntlet Jean-Robur cast down, taking a half-step forwards and reaching towards the hilt of his own sword. But after one of his companions placed a hand on his shoulder and whispered a word in his ear, Benoit demurred, giving Jean-Robur a mocking half-bow.

'Please accept my *apologies*, Monsieur du Quest,' Benoit said, voice dripping with oily mockery. 'I certainly had no intention of giving *offence*.'

With a final dismissive glance, Benoit turned and led his companions aft, away from the forecastle, leaving Jean-Robur alone.

The young duellist sneered at his cousin's back, and let his falchion slide back into the scabbard. He turned to face the dark silhouette of the island. At least the morning would bring the possibility of a real challenge, and even if it didn't he would still have won his spurs in combat, and would never again have to hear the foolish jests of his cousin and those like him. And once Jean-Robur's falchion was sated on the blood of Caritaigne's enemies, then Jean-Robur would sate himself with a few sacks of wine. He just hoped it was worth the long voyage, and the months spent away from the comforts and vices of home.

AT THAT MOMENT, on the eastern shores of Eokaroe, the forces of the feudal lords of Sipang had already beached their landing craft, and by the crimson light of the moon above were girding themselves for battle.

Zatori Zan held the blade of his tachina in one cloth-wrapped hand, carefully running a fold of paper along the cutting edge with the other. He'd already cleaned and oiled the blade, then dusted it with whetstone-powder, and was now honing the edge to a razor's keenness. It was unnecessary, of course – he'd cleaned and sharpened his sword every day of the journey west from the islands of Sipang, and the blade was already sharper than any razor could have possibly been – but still Sipangish tradition called for the warrior-elite to observe certain rites and rituals on the eve of battle, and Zatori had never been one to disregard tradition.

He was not yet one of the warrior-elite himself, of course, even though he carried a warrior's blade; he was instead a squire to a battle-monk with years of indentured servitude to go until he earned his freedom. Still, Father Nei was a fair master, and treated Zatori well. And he had not simply instructed Zatori in the art of combat, granting him the rare licence to carry a tachina, but had taught his young squire everything he needed to know about proper etiquette and decorum, all that he would need to go on and take his place among the warrior-elite in the service of the Sovereign of Sipang.

Zatori was ambitious, and dreamed of one day being called to the Royal Court itself, perhaps to serve in the Sovereign's personal Honour Guard. But even if he died with the morning's first light, he knew that he would fall having done his duty, to sovereign and country. Zatori did not know if he would ever see his father again, in *this* life at least, but if he did ever encounter the man again Zatori planned to thank his father for selling him into a battle-monk's servitude. He had already travelled farther and seen more than any lowborn son of a goat-herder should have dared to dream.

Or perhaps it was that a goat-herder's son should not dare to dream at all, and as a warrior's squire it was an allowable luxury. Even so, Father Nei frequently scolded Zatori for being too often lost in his own thoughts, mind filled with dreams of ambition and the promise of future glories.

Zatori was lost in just such imaginings, his hands methodically polishing and sharpening his tachina's blade without any conscious direction, when he felt a tap on his shoulder, catching him unawares.

In an instant, Zatori reversed the bare blade of his sword, taking his tachina's long handle in a two-handed grip and rolling to the side, sweeping the point of the blade up and behind him in a precise arc. He had reacted without thought, as unconscious a motion as the movement of his hands mindlessly sharpening the blade, thoughts as pure as an uncarved block.

Father Nei regarded the swordpoint that hovered less than a hand's width from his chest, and then with a widening grin tapped Zatori's tachina aside with a quick parry from the same walking staff that had tapped Zatori's shoulder only a moment before.

'Not bad, Squire Zan,' the battle-monk said, nodding slowly, expression flat and unreadable. 'Not at all bad.'

Zatori stifled a proud smile, and slid his tachina back into its sharkskin scabbard. Lowering his gaze, he dipped his head in an abbreviated bow. 'Master.'

'Of course,' Father Nei went on, face still expressionless, 'had you not been lost to wool-gathering and idle fancy, you'd have heard my approach and never been surprised at the feel of my cane on your shoulder.' The battle-monk's eyebrows knit together, his gaze narrowing. 'What if I had been one of the island's barbaric natives? Or worse yet, some decadent son of the Caritaigne oligarchy creeping up on you with murderous intent?'

Zatori's cheeks stung with shame. 'I beg forgiveness, master. I fail you, but shall endeavour–'

Father Nei silenced him with a quick motion of his hand. 'Enough. It is sufficient that you understand your failing and resolve to improve. I need not hear endless self-recrimination.' A faint smile tugged the corners of the battle-monk's mouth.

'Now, as you are sharpening your already-honed blade – again – I can only assume that you have my arms and armour prepared and ready for the coming conflict?'

Zatori nodded eagerly, and then pointed to the collection of sheathed blades and pieces of lacquered armour neatly stacked a few paces away. The forces of Sipang had come ashore with nightfall, but had not armoured themselves before reaching land for fear that the weight of their armour, even as relatively light as their lacquered leather, might drag them beneath the waves should one of the boats have the misfortune to capsize. Now the forces gathered together by moonlight, unwilling to give away their positions by lighting fires, and prepared to march with the morning's first light against their ancient enemies, the servants of Caritaigne.

This island of Eokaroe was simply the most recent battleground between the two powers, of some strategic significance in the ongoing war but of more symbolic importance than anything else.

'Observance of the rites of battle is commendable,' Father Nei said, nodding towards the scabbarded sword at Zatori's side, 'but sharpen that sword much longer and it will be whittled away to nothing.' The battle-monk studied his young squire closely. 'I trust you will not disappoint the faith I showed in bestowing that blade upon you?'

If the island of Eokaroe was of mere symbolic importance in the ongoing struggle, for Zatori Zan the coming battle was of considerably greater significance. He had engaged in minor skirmishes before, but this would be his first contest of note, and the first in which he carried a warrior's sword – a sword already honed sharper than any razor.

Zatori straightened, chin held high. 'I will endeavour not to disappoint.'

Father Nei nodded, then held out his hand, motioning for Zatori to hand the sword over. For a moment, Zatori wondered if his answer might not have given some offence, with his master deciding at the last moment not to let his squire go to battle armed with a warrior's blade after all. Instead, though, the battle-monk held the tachina up before him, fingers brushing the emblem of the holy duality worked into the circular hand-guard that separated blade from hilt.

'May you cleave always to the principle of the Sacred Duality,' Father Nei intoned in prayer, eyes half-lidded, 'and may this blade act as a lodestone to lead you down the Path of Balance between light and dark.'

The battle-monk opened his eyes, and handed the sword back to his squire.

'Remember all that I have taught you, Squire Zan,' he said, laying a hand on Zatori's shoulder in an almost fatherly gesture. 'Keep your wits about you and you will prevail. And remember above all that it is not ambition or glory that should drive you, but duty.'

'Yes, master,' Zatori said.

Father Nei smiled. 'Now come, help me on with my armour. With any luck you and I will celebrate our victory tomorrow, and if we do not, then perhaps we shall serve together again in another life.'

As THE FORCES of the two great Triandrian powers massed on either side of the island, another force was gathering unseen in the dark forests at the island's heart. Neither the Caritaigne nor the Sipangish armies had given them much thought, but if the warrior clans of Eokaroe were successful in their plans, the two great nations would soon learn to respect and fear their prowess.

The islanders had dwelt in the forests and hills of Eokaroe longer than memory stretched, since the days when their myths told them that two great warriors had led the People to this world from the stars. Eokaroean legend told how the People had been divided one group against another when one of the two warriors had betrayed his brother, and brought ruin and evil into the world. Only among the Eokaroeans had the true faith of the Great Father in the Sky been preserved, and for the untold generations since that time the warrior clans had remained steadfast, abhorring any contact with the fallen and faithless wretches who occupied the other lands that lay beyond the ocean's waves.

The purity of the Eokaroeans had not come without a price, the islanders had learned to their sorrow in recent generations. The faithless who dwelt beyond the waves had prospered in turning from the Great Father, though their souls had shrivelled in the bargain. But while the Eokaroeans did not possess ships that could sail over the waves as fast as bird's flight ahead of the wind, nor did they possess cannons capable of propelling great hunks of metal through the air, still the warrior clans were proudly defiant.

For long years had the two great faithless powers sent emissaries to Eokaroe, to beguile the clan chiefs and lure the Eokaroeans to their respective cause, but the warrior clans had remained resolute. Now, the two faithless nations intended to seize the island by force, fighting each other as if the home of the faithful were merely some bauble that they could wrest from one another's grasp.

Neither side would claim their prize if the warrior clans had any say in the matter.

Taloc s'Tonan held his ironbrand in a two-handed grip, raising the sword's blade to the heavens in silent homage to the Great Father in the Sky. He had worn the ironbrand at his side since before he was as tall as the sword was long, but its blade had never yet tasted an enemy's blood. The ironbrand had not yet earned a name, or brought favour to the son of Tonan or to the clan. Taloc begged the Great Father in his thoughts that the coming dawn would change all that.

Taloc's father and the other warrior chieftains of Eokaroe's principal clans were still in council, though the council firepits were unlit and cold. In former times the warrior clans would have gathered in this season to hold the tourney, a fierce contest of martial skills in which young warriors competed to determine the standings of their clans for the coming year. The clan whose champion won the day would rule the island until the following spring, and any champions who had lost their lives would be mourned by all Eokaroe as the very flower of manhood.

Taloc had only been of an age to vie with his cousins for the chance to be the clan's champion since the previous summer, once he was past his thirteenth year, but had been denied the chance to test his mettle when the chieftains had decreed that there would be no tourneys until the faithless had been driven back to their homes beyond the waves.

In the ceremonies that marked the beginnings of each year's tourney, the boys who had come of age since the last spring were put to the test, and their manhood recognised if they won through. With no tourney, and no manhood tests, Taloc was still technically just a child, despite his years.

When the chieftains finished their council, they could call together the warriors to receive the benedictions of the shamans, who would anoint them with oil and ash, and beseech the Great Father in the Sky to protect them in the coming battle.

With the sun's rise, the two great armies of Caritaigne and Sipang would clash on the green fields of the Eokaroean lowlands. One by one the faithless would fall to sword and cannon and musket, their numbers gradually depleting. Those who remained to fight would be drained and spent by their exertions, the long battle taking its toll.

When the faithless combatants were at their weakest, the faithful warrior-clans of Eokaroe would emerge from the forest's shadows, blessed and rested and ready to fight. They would drive the invaders from the island, back into the sea and fleeing towards their distant homes across the numberless waves.

And then Taloc's ironbrand would have earned a name, and the son of Tonan would at last be a man. Even if he lost his life in the attempt, Taloc s'Tonan would die a man with a named sword in his hand.

THE MORNING'S FIRST light was greeted by a dawn chorus of birdsong from the innumerable species which nested in the upper branches of the island's trees. Sunlight spilled like molten gold over the waves to the east, and drove back the night's darkness to ever-shrinking pools of darkness in the inland forests.

The armies of Caritaigne splashed ashore on the western beaches, while the forces of Sipang moved into position along the eastern approaches. And in the shadows, the warriors of Eokaroe lurked unseen, their villages emptied and the women and children sent to the highest points of mountain and hill to await their salvation.

In moments, the Battle for Eokaroe would begin.

And if any noticed that one of the evening's stars still shone brightly over the southern horizon, growing brighter by the instant, they paid it little mind.

JEAN-ROBUR DU QUESTE advanced, falchion in hand. Ahead of him at the vanguard marched his uncles and their fellow officers, proud scions of the noble houses of Caritaigne. On either side of Jean-Robur were his cousin Benoit and the other young men who had seen combat a bare handful of times at most, and who considered that their meagre experience made them hardened veterans. Behind them followed the pikemen and musketeers and grenadiers, nearly all of them the sons of landless families who lacked titles or holdings of their own, and who had turned to soldiery as the only alternative to lives of backbreaking labour or crushing poverty.

Striding from the white-sand beaches into the morning cool of the island's forests, surrounded by his brothers-in-arms and following in the footsteps of decorated knights like his uncles, Jean-Robur felt a swell of pride. It was only fitting that he was here, now, at this hour, about to prove to all and sundry that he was a true son of Caritaigne. This was his birthright, and his due. Jean-Robur knew that he was a virtuoso with the blade, as his many bouts and duels had attested, and once he had won his spurs in honest combat against the heathen foe, he could return to a life of ease and comfort in Caritaigne. He would draw his falchion to fence and to duel, but would never again have to leave behind the comforts of home, if he so chose.

So far they'd had no sign of the enemy's ground forces, though they knew from the reports of fast-sailing cutters who had sailed ahead of the Caritaigne fleet that the Sipangish had made land-fall shortly before the Caritaigne had arrived. The two fleets were too evenly matched to face one another on the open seas, or so Jean-Robur had been told, and even so what did it profit them to gain a victory on the seas if the enemy forces were already on land?

In the grey predawn hours, he had been forced to listen to the expedition's commander addressing the force, warning them all that theory seldom matched practice, and that combat was not the same as contests in the salles d'armes or duels in the avenues of Caritaigne. Their enemies were not gentlemen, and might not observe the same rules of etiquette that governed their actions back home in Caritaigne. What was more, the commander insisted, circumstances might not always allow a level playing field, and it would only be those com-batants able to adapt to realities in the field who would win the day.

'Keep careful note of the path, Mamzel du Queste,' Benoit called over to Jean-Robur, leering. 'You'll need to know the way back when you run fleeing in terror.'

Jean-Robur replied with a rude gesture, but didn't deign to speak. Continuing on, he thought back to the morning's speeches, and the endless litany of instructions and exhortations they'd received. Jean-Robur had paid little attention to the old man's droning. Rules and etiquette and level fields be damned, Jean-Robur was convinced that with a sword in his hand he was the equal to any who might stand against him.

The birds whose incessant chattering had filled the morning air had finally fallen silent. The Caritaigne vanguard was just stepping onto a wide, green field, large enough to swallow the entire royal palace of Caritaigne. There was a scrum of movement on the clearing's far side, indistinct grey figures that milled to and fro like carpenter ants.

'You see?' Benoit called out to his friends in lusty tones. 'The Sipangish are even more fearful than Mamzel du Queste, and huddle at a distance afraid to face us.'

His friends joined in with Benoit's guffaws, laughing at the expense of Jean-Robur and the enemy alike.

Jean-Robur was about to retort when he heard a sudden cracking sound, like a sharp peal of thunder in the near distance. He turned to his cousin, just in time to see Benoit dissipate from the waist up in a fine red mist.

'Mortar fire!' one of the Caritaigne officers yelled. More peals of thunder split the air, and Jean-Robur could feel vibrations travelling up his legs from the ground. 'Take cover!'

The ordered ranks of Caritaigne nobility broke into confusion as they went to ground, making room for the musketeers and grenadiers – commoners all – to come to the forefront and return fire. Once they had laid down suppressing fire, the officers, swordsmen and pikemen would advance to close with the enemy.

Jean-Robur huddled behind the bole of an ancient tree, waiting for the order to advance, the image of his cousin's smirking face exploding to mist and viscera fixed in his mind's eye. The avenues and salles d'armes of Caritaigne suddenly seemed very far away.

It was nearing mid-morning, and the wide field which had been green at first light had by now been transformed into a quagmire of mud and blood and gore. The two great armies had exchanged their initial volleys of mortar and musketfire, and then closed in a chaotic melee that ranged from one side of the clearing to the other.

Zatori Zan stuck close by as his master and the other warrior-elite slashed their way through the enemy, tachinas flashing like silver lightning in the bright island sun. Though the forces of the Sovereign were well equipped with firearms, Sipangish tradition held that such weapons were base and crude, and not fit to be carried by the storied warrior-elites. And so mortar and musket, cannon and carronade were reserved for the rank and file infantry, lowborn soldiers with no honour to stain. Warrior-elites like Father Nei and the others went into battle armed only with their blades, as was right and fitting.

'For the Sovereign!' shouted one of the battle-monks as he drove his tachina's blade straight through the neck of a Caritaigne soldier, the point protruding a full arm's length out the other side. Zatori studied the battle-monk's technique as he removed the tachina by forcing it sidewise in a flat arc, slicing out through the flesh and gristle of the Caritaigne's neck, leaving the man's head to flop to the other side like a dead fish dropped onto a dock. The exposed bones of the dying man's neck vertebrae shone white for a moment, then were subsumed beneath a tide of crimson as the Caritaigne's heart pumped its last lifeblood out through the severed arteries.

'Squire Zan! Attend!'

The voice of Zatori's master shouting at him shook him from his reverie. He'd been too easily distracted by thoughts of form and technique, and by the chance to finally see the effects of the blade on living human bodies. Such distraction could easily get him killed on the field of battle, Zatori knew.

'Coming, master!' he called back.

Father Nei was standing over the body of a fallen enemy, his tachina in his right hand and his left hand staunching the flow of blood from a wound on his right shoulder. The fallen Caritaigne had managed to drive the point of a pike into the joint between two segments of lacquered leather armour, and the resulting wound was bleeding freely.

'Here,' Zatori said, sheathing his own tachina – which had so far remained unblooded – and drawing a length of bandaging from the pouch at his waist, along with the makings of a poultice. 'Allow me to–'

'No.' The battle-monk shook his head, and Zatori could not help but notice that his master's cheeks seemed bloodless and drawn. 'No time for that. Simply apply the styptic, and quickly!'

Zatori stifled a grimace, and pulled the vial of greyish powder from the pouch. As soon as he pulled the stopper his nostrils stung from the faintest scent of the stuff, and he hoped he got none on his own bare skin.

'Quick now!' Father Nei urged, tightening his grip on his tachina's hilt with his right hand while blood continued to seep through the fingers of his left.

'Yes, master.' Zatori lifted the open vial. 'Your hand?'

Father Nei pulled his hand away, and as quickly as he was able Zatori liberally dusted the battle-monk's shoulder with the contents. Most of it powdered his master's armour or drifted away on the breeze – the few bare granules wafting into Zatori's eyes being sufficient to bring stinging tears streaming down his cheeks – but enough reached the wound within to do its work. Father Nei hissed in pain as the styptic powder caused the ragged edges of the wound to violently contract, all of the severed arteries and veins sealing themselves shut.

It was as effective a treatment as cauterising a wound with an open flame, and about as painful.

'Come along,' Father Nei said through gritted teeth, pausing only a moment to wipe clean his bloody hand on the fabric of the fallen Caritaigne's tunic. 'The battle continues. And it is time for you to join the fray.'

Zatori returned the first aid equipment to his belt-pouch, careful to fit the stopper securely in the vial of styptic, and then followed his master, drawing his own tachina and muttering a quick prayer to the Duality.

'Grant me strength and a keen blade, and allow me victory or an honourable death, whichever pleases the balance.'

TALOC S'TONAN AND his brothers remained hidden in the shadows, watching the two faithless powers clashing in the great field. The Sipangish had enjoyed an early advantage, but as the morning wore on the Caritaigne had taken up fortified positions to the north and west, holding them in reserve while the bulk of their forces joined in the melee and then rotating out elements as they became wounded or incapacitated.

Taloc's nameless ironbrand had been in his fist since morning's first light, and he ached to rush onto the field of battle waving his sword overhead, to shout defiance at these faithless wretches for daring to defile this holy place. But the decision to attack rested with the chieftains, and like the other warriors of his clan Taloc looked to his father, Tonan, to give the sign to move. So far, Tonan had remained silent and immobile, carefully studying the battle unfolding before them.

When Tonan finally spoke, it seemed to Taloc as though these were the first words ever spoken, the first words of any true importance at least, and that all other utterances up to this point had been mere preamble, generations of throat-clearing before the truly significant words were given voice.

'Soon, my brothers,' Tonan said simply, his voice scarcely above a whisper. 'Soon.'

Taloc tightened his grip on the ironbrand's handle, and drew a deep breath into his lungs. When the moment came, and courage was needed, he would not be found wanting.

UNSEEN BY ANY in the field or in the forests, the star which had outlasted the night still hung over the southern horizon, growing larger with each passing moment.

But it was no star, no distant sun that hung in the heavens. It was a vessel, and carried holy warriors from beyond the stars.

'The population is divided into nation-states, brother-captain. Two predominate, in their own tongues called "Caritaigne" and "Sipang".'

Two of the holy warriors peered down at images of the planet taken from high orbit, gauging the prospects.

'And they war with each other, brother-sergeant?'

'Yes, brother-captain. The conflict between the two has raged for generations. But not since its earliest days has the war touched the shores of either nation. Instead the battles play out on the few independent states not yet under the yoke of one country or the other.'

'Such as this one.' The holy warrior reached out a gauntleted hand and pointed towards the irregularly shaped emerald island set against the sea of crystal blue. The data which scrolled across the display indicated the number of troops now massing on the island, the largest concentration of military forces currently gathered on the planet.

'Exactly, brother-captain.'

'Well, then.' The holy warrior paused, considering. 'There should be sufficient candidates gathered for a cull, I would think. Wouldn't you, brother-sergeant?'

The other holy warrior straightened, nodding in reply.

'Prepare the Thunderhawks. We are going hunting.'

CHAPTER TWO

ZATORI ZAN FOLLOWED close on his master's heels as the veteran battle-monk sliced his way through the enemy forces, felling one Caritaigne after another. He had accompanied Father Nei on a number of skirmishes since first becoming the older man's squire, but never before had he been granted the opportunity to see his master unleash his skill against so large an enemy force. It was truly a sight to behold.

Father Nei seemed completely unencumbered by the lacquered armour he wore, moving with the same supple grace and agility which Zatori had seen him display in the simple robes of the sparring hall. For his part, Zatori was still somewhat unused to the weight of his own armour on his shoulders and arms, even as light as it was, and found that he was always forced to compensate for its effects on his own movements.

As a squire, Zatori was charged with assisting his master in combat whenever necessary, whether by tending his wounds as he had already done, or by making any repairs needed to Father Nei's armour on the field of battle, or by alerting his master to any unseen threat. But of all his responsibilities, it was this duty to cover the battle-monk's back that sent a thrill up Zatori's spine. In melee combat such as this, squires were instructed to prevent any enemies from approaching unseen from behind while their masters were engaged with other combatants. Traditionally squires were required merely to alert their masters with shouts of warning, but wielding a warrior's blade in his hands meant that Zatori would never be content merely to cry out an alarm.

Father Nei's blade was darting back and forth before him like a hummingbird, parrying the crude lunge of a Caritaigne officer, then reversing the blade's motion to slice back across the officer's forearms. The Caritaigne howled in pain and fury, head thrown back and eyes squeezed shut in agony, and Father Nei ended his suffering by neatly lopping the man's head from his shoulders in a single stroke. Then, before the officer's decapitated body had even begun to fall to the ground, Father Nei shifted slightly to the left to meet the onrushing attack of a Caritaigne pikeman intent on goring the battle-monk on the end of his pike. Father Nei spun the point of his tachina in a tight arc around the tip of the pike, turning it aside in one smooth motion, and then skewered the pikeman through the belly with his tachina's gracefully curved blade.

So intent was Zatori on studying his master's technique that he almost failed to notice the Caritaigne swordsman rushing towards Father Nei from behind. The battle-monk, turning from the fallen pikeman to another opponent, could not from his vantage point see the swordsman's approach.

Years of training and instinct impelled Zatori to shout out a warning, so that Father Nei could turn and address the swordsman's attack. Zatori knew full well that the battle-monk would have no difficulty in fending off his present opponent and dealing with the onrushing swordsman at the same time. But if he cried out an alarm, Zatori would be denied the chance to wield his own tachina in single combat, and he would remain simply another squire lugging poultices and bandages in his master's wake.

Raising the point of his own tachina, grimly silent with his lips pressed firmly shut, Zatori rushed forwards to intercept the Caritaigne swordsman before he came within striking distance of Father Nei's back.

IT WAS A struggle for Jean-Robur du Queste to avoid being overwhelmed by the tumult around him, and he was only barely succeeding. In the confusion after the traditional exchange of firearms volleys between the two sides, as the forces of Caritaigne had charged to meet the enemy in close-quarters combat, he had lost track of his uncles and the other members of his unit in the smoke and noise and confusion. He'd fallen in with a group of Caritaigne officers, none of whom he'd seen before, and had little choice but to follow along with them as they battered their way through the enemy forces.

Though he did his level best to maintain a stalwart demeanour, he was certain that he could not completely hide in his expression the disorientation he felt. He was, simply, unsure where he should be, or what he should be doing. There were enemies aplenty against whom he could raise his falchion's blade, but he found himself completely unprepared for the scope of the chaotic battle.

In single combat with another fencer, whether in a duel upon the avenue or in a supervised bout in the salles d'armes, Jean-Robur knew precisely what actions were required of him in any circumstance, exactly when to lunge, to parry, to riposte. But in this frenzied melee, with friend and foe on every side, he scarcely knew which way to face. He would find himself confronted by a Sipangish soldier with spear in hand, and before Jean-Robur could address himself to his opponent and bring his falchion en garde, another Caritaigne would have shot or stabbed or clubbed the spear-bearer and suddenly Jean-Robur would find yet another Sipangish rushing at him from another angle.

He had not sheathed his blade since leaving the treeline behind, but so far had hardly used it. On occasion he'd had the opportunity to batter away a Sipangish thrust, but his parries had been artless, crude manoeuvres, displaying none of the skill in which he normally took so much pride. And as yet his falchion had not tasted enemy blood, as before he could riposte after each of his clumsy parries the Sipangish had already rushed away like frenetic hounds to attack another foe. Jean-Robur felt ineffectual and graceless.

The Caritaigne officers he followed had managed to clear a space some dozen paces wide, arranging themselves in a defensive ring with their backs turned towards one another, facing outwards. Jean-Robur had lingered in the midst of the ring at first, hoping to get his bearings, but when one of the officers was felled by Sipangish musket-fire, the officer to his right turned to see Jean-Robur hanging back.

'Hurry, boy!' the officer yelled, pointing to the gap in the ring where the fallen officer had previously stood. 'Take it!'

Tightening his grip on his falchion's handle, Jean-Robur had hurried towards the gap in the ring, stepping over the body of the fallen man, and taken up a position halfway between the officers on either side. Now he stood ready, shoulder to shoulder with the Caritaigne officers against the enemy.

A Sipangish swordsman came rushing towards Jean-Robur, shouting a war cry in the heathen tongue of Sipang, and at last Jean-Robur felt that he was on solid footing. The Sipangish whirled his sword overhead, the long curved blade flashing in the morning sun, and Jean-Robur slid his left foot back and planted his right foot forwards, turning to the side to present as narrow an approach to the enemy as possible. His left arm bent up at the elbow with the left hand hanging loose for balance, and with his right hand he raised the tip of his falchion, prepared to meet the enemy charge.

The Sipangish did not stop at sword's length to make his first attack, but continued to run headlong towards Jean-Robur, screaming all the while, his long curved sword a blur in his hands. Jean-Robur blinked, momentarily taken aback. It was *suicide* to rush straight at an opponent's blade, as every instructor in the art of the blade would agree. And yet here was an enemy swordsman rushing straight at Jean-Robur's falchion with seemingly no concern for his own safety. Jean-Robur could handily skewer him on the point of his falchion, but with the forward motion of the Sipangish there was every chance that Jean-Robur himself would fall to the long curved blade of the enemy before his own falchion dealt a fatal blow.

Involuntarily, Jean-Robur took a step backwards, flinching before the mad rush of the enemy. And in that single step he discovered that his footing was not so solid as he had hoped. Just as he shifted all of his weight off his right foot and onto his left, he ran into the motionless form of the fallen Caritaigne officer whose place in the ring he had taken. Knocked off balance, he toppled backwards, legs up and backside down, and landed flat on his back on the dusty ground with an audible thud, knocking the breath from his lungs.

Jean-Robur looked up, expecting to see the Sipangish sword arcing downwards to end his life at any moment, but was relieved to find the Sipangish swordsman spitted on the pike of a Caritaigne pikeman who had rushed at him from the side. Struggling up to his feet, Jean-Robur chanced to look to the right and caught the eyes of the Caritaigne officer to his right giving him an appraising look.

'Damnation, boy!' the officer swore.

Pushing to his feet, Jean-Robur felt the sting of embarrassment on his cheeks. He had vague memories of one of his instructors mentioning such a tactic, designed to throw an opponent off their guard in melee combat, but as it had seemed to have little utility in the avenues and salles d'armes the younger Jean-Robur had not given it much of his attention.

'Take your place, boy!' the officer barked, motioning towards the gap in the ring. 'You can rest when you're dead.'

Cursing under his breath, and sparing time for a discreet kick aimed at the fallen Caritaigne officer's head in repayment for the tumble, Jean-Robur took his position. He scowled, and swore that he would not be caught out so easily again. The next Sipangish he faced would fall, and no foolish tactics or stratagems would do them any good.

TALOC S'TONAN AND his brothers had remained in the shadows of the forest for as long as they could, unseen by any of the combatants on the wide field before them. But as the morning wore on, the melee had drifted nearer and nearer to their hiding place, and as midday approached it seemed unlikely that they would be able to remain concealed for much longer. His father Tonan, chieftain of the clan, had begun exchanging hushed whispers with his closest advisors, calculating the risks of attempting to remain hidden versus charging onto the field of battle before their carefully orchestrated plans allowed.

At strategic locations all throughout the forests lining the great field, Taloc knew that the other warrior-clans were occupied with similar deliberations. The plan of attack devised by the council of chieftains had called for the Eokaroean clans to remain concealed until one or the other of the two great faithless forces were all but defeated, and then to burst from hiding and fall upon the victor, who would be so depleted from the struggle that they would be unable to resist the Eokaroeans' might.

As the battle had unfolded, though, it was clear that neither side was weakening as quickly or as completely as the warrior chieftains had hoped, and as things stood it would likely be well into the afternoon before the strength of the faithless had ebbed sufficiently to ensure an Eokaroean victory. If the warrior clans were to take to the field too soon, with the strength of the faithless not yet waning, the superior numbers and weaponry of the invaders on both sides could threaten to overwhelm the Eokaroeans entirely.

However, worst still for the warrior clans if they were to be discovered by either the Caritaigne or the Sipangish while still in hiding, encumbered by the close-growing trees on all sides, where a barrage of incendiary fire from the invaders' cannons might serve to wipe out all of the warriors of a clan in a single attack.

As the melee raged ever nearer to their place of concealment, Taloc's father seemed to come to a conclusion. He rose up from a crouch, and motioned to the other warriors of the clan who were arrayed through this section of forest. Keen ears straining to listen, the brothers of the clan gripped their ironbrands in anticipation, ready to follow the chieftain's orders, whatever they might be.

'Now!' Chieftain Tonan called out to the others, raising his own sword Lightning high overhead. When he had been a young man in the tourneys, his ironbrand had earned the name on account of the quickness with which Tonan had slashed and hacked, knocking all competitors' blades aside as quick as a flash from a storm cloud. Now Lightning flashed again, and seemed to be eager to bite deep into faithless flesh. 'The hour is upon us! Attack, my brothers, and drive the faithless invaders back into the sea!'

Taloc lifted his head and let forth the deepest, most guttural martial call that he could manage, answering the beastly roars from his brothers on all sides. And then, ironbrands swinging in two-handed grips, the Eokaroeans of Tonan's clan burst from the shadows, throwing themselves into the melee beyond.

JEAN-ROBUR DU QUESTE held his place in the defensive ring until a superior force of Sipangish swordsmen crashed into the ring's far side, and suddenly their defences were broken. The ring splintered, becoming first a ragged bowed line as a handful of their number fell to the Sipangish blades, then breaking into ever-smaller segments as more of their fellow officers were cut down. Ringed together, back to back as they had been, the Caritaigne had succeeded in standing firm against the previous Sipangish onslaughts, but having lost their cohesion when faced with a party of even greater numbers the Caritaigne were unable to withstand this newest attack. Perhaps if enough of them survived they could reform into a smaller defensive ring, but for the moment Jean-Robur and the officers were left to fend for themselves.

Jean-Robur found himself alone, cut off from the others, and only now realised that he had never learned any of their names. All around him on the ground were sprawled the dead and the dying, Sipangish and Caritaigne alike, and the air was filled

with the stench of acrid smoke, the coppery tang of
spilled blood and the noxious odour of human
waste as the corpses on all sides voided their bowels
in death's final embrace. Jean-Robur's eyes stung,
and with the bright island sun directly overhead he
was forced to squint in the glare. With his left arm
shading his eyes, his right hand holding his falchion
before him, Jean-Robur turned to one side and then
the other, trying to find any familiar faces, or at least
any who bore the armour and ensigns of Caritaigne
that he might join. But the only Caritaigne he saw
was as isolated as he was, and busy holding off
Sipangish attacks.

A short distance off he saw the officer who had
stood beside him in the ring, his sword dancing in
his grip as he struggled to ward off the thrust and
blows of an older Sipangish swordsman. The
Sipangish had his back turned to Jean-Robur, and in
that instant the young Caritaigne saw an opportunity to blood his falchion at last.

Students in the salles d'armes of Caritaigne were
taught never to stab an enemy in the back. Lowborn
soldiers might employ such techniques, Jean-Robur's
instructors had told him, but it was poor etiquette
not to allow one's opponent the opportunity to face
one's attack head-on.

'Etiquette be damned,' Jean-Robur said in a low
voice. He sneered, raised his falchion and advanced
towards the Sipangish swordsman's back.

* * *

ZATORI ZAN EXULTED in the feeling of the tachina leaping in his hands. He parried away the lunge of the Caritaigne swordsman, then danced back out of the reach of the dagger in the swordsman's other hand. Then, as the swordsman shifted his footing, Zatori slashed down with his tachina, coming within a handbreadth of slicing into the swordsman's forehead before the Caritaigne blocked the blow with a cross made of his sword and dagger held overhead. Sparks flew from the edge of Zatori's sword as he whipped his tachina back against the Caritaigne's crossed blades, and then Zatori fell back into a ready stance, preparing to try again.

Zatori's heart swelled with pride that his mastery of the blade was equal to the challenge of facing such a strong and skilled opponent. That he had not yet managed to do more than nick the Caritaigne swordsman's shoulder and cheek with his tachina merely meant that he had not yet divined the proper technique, but the fact that Zatori had so far succeeded in blocking or parrying all of the Caritaigne's own thrusts and attacks meant that Father Nei had taught Zatori well.

Thinking of his honoured master brought Zatori up short.

Since the moment Zatori had closed with the swordsman intent on attacking Father Nei from behind, he had not kept track of the battle-monk's movements. Considering that his sacred duty in combat situations was to remain by his master's side and serve his every need, the fact that Zatori had no clear idea at the moment just *where* Father Nei was did not speak well of his service. He could have simply shouted out a warning to the battle-monk, and let Father Nei deal handily with the swordsman, but Zatori had wanted to enjoy the thrill of combat himself. If his absence meant that some harm were to befall his master…

The panic on Zatori's part was momentary, but the Caritaigne swordsman saw an advantage and pressed the attack. Flipping his dagger end over end in the air, the swordsman caught hold of the blade, then threw it in a spiralling arc directly at Zatori's head. Zatori saw the blade spinning towards him, and scarcely managed to duck out of its way before it could drive point-first into his head. As the thrown dagger continued flipping harmlessly past his ear, though, Zatori was unprepared and off-balance when the swordsman rushed forwards, swinging his sword over his shoulder like a club, bringing it slicing down towards Zatori's exposed neck.

Zatori reacted on pure instinct, the muscle-memory of Father Nei's long hours of martial instruction taking hold. Rather than trying to regain his balance, as his opponent might expect, Zatori instead allowed gravity to overcome, and fell straight back towards the ground. As the Caritaigne's swing whistled harmlessly through the space Zatori had just vacated, Zatori thrust his tachina forwards and up as he fell backwards and down. The point of Zatori's tachina drove into the

Caritaigne's left hip, and red arterial blood came fountaining forth when Zatori pulled the blade back out.

As the Caritaigne fell howling to the ground, clutching the crimson bloom on his hip, Zatori sat up, looking from one side to the other for any sign of Father Nei.

There! Zatori spotted his master in close combat with a Caritaigne officer, a few dozen paces away. True to form, Father Nei was easily besting his opponent, who was already on his last legs. In perhaps a moment or two, but little more, the battle-monk would deliver the fatal stroke, and the officer would fall.

Only then did Zatori see another young Caritaigne swordsman, rushing at Father Nei from behind, a naked blade in hand and murder in his eyes.

'Master! No!' Zatori shouted, struggling to rise to his feet. But by then it was already far too late.

As TALOC S'TONAN rushed the unsuspecting faithless nearest the forest's edge, he tried to imagine what sort of name the day would win for the ironbrand in his hands. Perhaps something that could refer in some fashion to his father's blade Lightning? Of course, at the moment there were *other* considerations that should have occupied his attentions.

The two armies had clearly not accounted for the disposition of the island's warrior-clans as their battle had raged across the field, and as the brothers of Tonan's clan raced towards the nearest of the combatants shouting blood-curdling war cries, the Caritaigne and the Sipangish seemed at first hardly to take notice.

'For Eokaroe!' Taloc shouted, as he swung at the nearest of the faithless, paying no heed whether it was a Sipangish or Caritaigne. He felt the edge of his nameless ironbrand bite into the flesh of the faithless's unarmoured shoulder, hearing the satisfying *thunk* of metal against meat, but experienced a momentary bout of panic when the ironbrand's blade seemed to become lodged in the bone beneath. The faithless looked back over his shoulder, shouting in surprised agony, and fixed wide and frightened eyes on Taloc as the young Eokaroean wrenched his ironbrand back and forth to pull it loose from the bone. Blood sprayed in a fine mist as the blade finally pulled free, and as the faithless reached up in a futile attempt to staunch the flow, Taloc stabbed forwards and drove the ironbrand halfway to the hilt into the soft tissue of the man's back. The faithless collapsed to the muddy ground as Taloc yanked the blade free, bile and viscera pouring from the wound.

Taloc had felled his first enemy. Teeth bared like a mastiff protecting its territory, he felt strangely unsatisfied by the moment. Was it that he had not actually faced the faithless in combat, braving an enemy's blade being the act that would have earned Taloc the distinction of manhood? But what did it matter that Taloc had struck the man down from behind? This was no tourney, where the champions would observe the protocols of tradition, each declaiming his name and his ancestry before approaching one another to close in single combat – these faithless were not champions or respected opponents, but were instead little more than vermin to be eradicated. Such degenerates did not deserve the observance of protocols, and could be struck from behind or unawares with as little hesitation as one would behead a viper who had slunk its way into an infant's crib.

Taloc pushed such thoughts from his mind. He would have ample opportunity to brave an enemy's blade before the battle was through, he had little doubt.

Glancing around him, he saw that the other warriors of his clan had also cut down faithless combatants, at least one Caritaigne or Sipangish fallen for every one of Taloc's brothers who had taken to the field of battle. But while the Eokaroeans were able to score easy hits against the faithless in the attack's first rushing instants, it would not take the main body of the Sipangish and Caritaigne armies to discover that a third force had taken the field, and to respond accordingly.

Taloc turned to see one of the faithless rushing towards him with some manner of long spear in his hands, though whether the attacker was a son of Sipang or of Caritaigne he had no way of divining.

Remembering all of his father's lessons, Taloc leapt to one side just as the spear's point traversed the space he had previously occupied, and then swung his ironbrand down with full force at the haft of the spear, hoping to cut straight through and sever the metal spearhead from the wooden shaft. But the spear's shaft was reinforced with metal, and when Taloc's ironbrand connected it rebounded with a clash of metal on metal that rang through the noisy din like the sound of a distant thunderbolt.

The shock reverberated back up Taloc's arm, jarring his teeth and causing his vision to jitter, but as the faithless turned the spear's point on him, Taloc found himself thinking of thunder, and of Lightning. The young Eokaroean felt as though he were moving in slow motion, as if he was trying to run while completely submerged in clinging mud, as he saw the spear being brought to bear.

'Ware the spear!' shouted the gruff voice of Taloc's father from somewhere off to his left. In the next instant, the spearman was spitted on the point of Tonan's Lightning, Taloc's father scarcely out of breath from having raced over to his son's side.

Taloc felt himself synch back up with the speed of the world around him as his father turned to regard him for the briefest of instants.

'Don't lock your elbow when striking a blow, son. Your flexed arm will absorb the impact.'

And with that, Tonan turned and met the charge of another faithless's attack.

Taloc nodded, needlessly, and followed in his father's wake. 'Thunder,' he said beneath his breath. Then he smiled, and added, 'Thunderbolt.'

ZATORI BURNED WITH rage and shame in equal measure – rage at the cowardly attack of the young Caritaigne who had struck down his master, shame at having failed to stick by the battle-monk in combat as was his duty.

In the time it took Zatori to cover half the distance to where Father Nei had been attacked from behind, the battle-monk had already slumped to the ground, bright blood mixing with the mud and the dust beneath him. By the time Zatori reached the battle-monk's side, his master's face was already wan and bloodless.

It was clear that the wound was a fatal one, and that while Father Nei still lived, it would not be for long.

'Sacred Duality, no!' Zatori grabbed hold of his master's shoulders, teeth gritted as though the pain the battle-monk felt were his own.

Father Nei's eyes fluttered open, and his gaze locked with Zatori's.

Numb with shame and rage, awash in sympathetic pain as he imagined the agony of his master's wounds, still Zatori could not help hoping for some final pearl of wisdom from the battle-monk's dying lips. Some final admonition that Zatori could carry with him always, or a plea for vengeance on his murder that could spur Zatori in

slaying all of the Caritaigne on Eokaroe in holy retribution. Any final utterance that could connect
him to the man who had come to mean more to
him than a father, and who had taught Zatori everything that he truly needed to know.

Instead, eyes locked with his squire and pupil,
Father Nei was suddenly wracked by a fit of body-
shaking coughs, pinkish foam flecking the corners
of his bloodless lips. The battle-monk convulsed,
violently, and when the coughing fit passed, so had
Father Nei's life. Sightless eyes rolled up in their
sockets as the battle-monk's head fell back to the
ground with a sickening thud.

There would be no final moment of connection,
no final lesson from master to student. Only death
and blood and pain, and in its wake the lingering
rage and shame.

Zatori forced his hands to release their vice-like
grips on the dead man's shoulder, and then raised
stinging eyes on the confusion around him. His
gaze sought out the one whose hands had taken his
master from him, the one whose cowardly blade
had spilled Father Nei's lifeblood.

There he was, only a dozen paces away. His sword
still stained with the battle-monk's blood, the decadent Caritaigne was standing close with a pair of
Caritaigne officers, one of whom was sporting a
grave wound on his arm.

Zatori surged to his feet, and only then realised
that he'd lost track of his tachina somewhere along
the way. Perhaps he had dropped it in the mad

scramble to reach his master's side? Could it still lie
back on the ground where he had fallen after the
Caritaigne swordsman's attack? He could not say.
But there at his feet was Father Nei's own tachina,
lying discarded in the dust.

Snatching up his master's fallen sword in a two-
handed grip, Zatori set his jaw. Then, with a final
glance at the body at his feet, he started running
towards the murderous wretch, a sudden thirst for
vengeance burning deep inside.

JEAN-ROBUR DU QUESTE stood with the two officers,
one of whom was bleeding freely from a deep cut
to his sword arm. It appeared that the three of them
were all that remained of those who had stood
together in the defensive ring.

Now that Jean-Robur's falchion had tasted
enemy blood, he felt surer of himself, better orien-
tated on the field of battle. To be sure, his fencing
instructors would have turned up their noses at his
disregard of etiquette, but Jean-Robur was still
standing and the accursed Sipangish had fallen.
His instructors could keep their damned etiquette,
Jean-Robur thought, but he would rather keep
alive.

The three Caritaigne were still formulating their
next course of action through the confusion when
Jean-Robur heard an angry shout from close by, and
looked up to see a young Sipangish soldier rushing
towards him, waving a long curved sword overhead. Jean-Robur saw the rage that distorted the

Sipangish's face. He appeared to be racing right towards *him*.

Jean-Robur raised his falchion, confident in his ability to fend off the artless attack of a Sipangish youth no older than himself, but in the final moment before the Sipangish closed the distance between them the circumstances took a sudden turn. When the raging Sipangish youth was near enough for Jean-Robur to see the whites of his eyes, a dozen or more newcomers burst onto the scene with ear-splitting shouts.

The newcomers were a barbaric rabble, some of them dressed in little more than loincloths and breeches, nearly all of them naked from the waist but for the crudely wrought metal jewellery that adorned virtually every neck and wrist among them. Their hair was long and lank, tied back in plaits, and their chins were plucked hairless and smooth. Pale blue eyes against skin the colour of purest porcelain, except where it was discoloured by garish tattoos, and each of them wielding a long, simply forged sword of bare iron.

'Islanders!' one of the Caritaigne officers yelled, raising his own blade, but a moment too late. One of the barbaric tribesmen tackled the officer to the ground, like a lion bringing down its prey, and then battered the side of the officer's head with the pommel of his crude iron sword.

Jean-Robur glanced back in the direction from which the enraged Sipangish had been approaching, but all sight of the Sipangish youth had been lost by the sudden appearance of the barbarous islanders. Jean-Robur had little time to wonder what had become of him, though, as he was quickly forced to fend off the attack of yet another of the islanders, only barely managing to avoid being dragged down by a lion's-leap attack like his fellow Caritaigne.

Dancing out of the barbarian's path, acting only on instinct now, Jean-Robur swung his falchion and pressed the attack.

TALOC S'TONAN AND his brothers fought their way through the mass of combatants, howling war cries all the while. More than a few of his brothers had fallen to the blades and firearms of the Sipangish and Caritaigne forces, but Taloc was filled with the holy fire of righteousness, and fought on, undaunted. The men of their clan had been joined by the scattered remains of several other warrior-clans, and they now fought together as one. Young men who in other years might have faced each other in the contests of the tourney, fighting for the glory of their respective clans and to win names for their ironbrands, now battled side-by-side against the invaders, all distinction of family and clan forgotten. They were all merely Eokaroeans now, facing a common foe, and would remain so until the last of the interlopers had been pushed back into the sea.

A screaming came from overhead, and for an instant Taloc thought that one of the larger cannons had been discharged in their direction, sending a huge chunk of metal doom flying through the air towards them. He glanced up, and saw that something was indeed flying towards them through the air. But it was nothing that had ever been fired from any Triandrian cannon.

JEAN-ROBUR LOOKED UP as the screaming grew ever louder and higher in pitch. Descending from a cloudless sky were a number of strange objects – three, four, perhaps more, and each of them easily as large as the caravel that had brought Jean-Robur from Caritaigne. They were like stylised birds, perhaps, or the streamlined sculptures sometimes employed as ships' figureheads.

Mouth hanging open in bewildered amazement, Jean-Robur followed the objects with his gaze. As they lowered gracefully down to earth, the combatants on the ground below were sent scrambling to get out of the way, and to avoid being crushed beneath.

From his scarcely remembered instruction, Jean-Robur could dimly recall ancient stories of messengers from god riding such vessels down from the heavens. But such things didn't really *exist*, did they?

WHEN THE FIRST of the craft opened, Zatori Zan fought the urge to kneel in devotion. Surely these could be nothing but the divine chariots referenced in the ancient legends of Sipang, which carried holy warriors between the stars.

Then a giant figure emerged into the light, its face and form completely hidden within an enormous suit of armour, golden yellow and trimmed with jet-black. Behind it followed another, then another, and then another. More and more of the giants in armour descended from the open hatches onto the field, dwarfing even the tallest of the combatants.

Zatori was brought up short, mouth gaping and eyes widening with wonder.

So the ancient legends were true! And these giants in gold *must* be those same holy warriors, from beyond the stars.

Zatori felt his mind reeling with the revelation, but as he looked from one golden giant to another, his eyes tracked across the field, and he saw what effect the descent of the divine chariots was having.

As tumultuous as the battlefield had been, the arrival of the giant warriors in gold threw everything into confusion. Some of the combatants threw down their weapons and dropped to their knees, praying for deliverance. Others turned and fled, shrieking like children frightened by a ghost story.

Other combatants, though, saw the chance to use the confusion to their advantage, turning their blades against enemies overwhelmed by the arrival of the divine chariots. He saw Caritaigne slashing at Sipangish who knelt to pray, and Sipangish clubbing down Caritaigne who fled in terror.

The ancient legends might be true, and demigods might now be walking the earth, Zatori realised, but he still burned with the righteous fires of vengeance. Whatever else happened, he would avenge Father Nei.

CHAPTER THREE

Zatori Zan knew that if he wanted to avenge the shameful murder of his master he could not hesitate an instant. The question as to whether these *were* the holy warriors of legend, and if so whether the legends might not have presented the *full* story of their nature, would have to wait for another time… if there was to be any other time.

He'd already lost sight of the young Caritaigne who had murdered Father Nei even before the arrival of the armoured giants, when the horde of barbaric islanders had rushed onto the scene. Now one of the older islanders, face and arms shadowed by the ink of ancient tattoos, stood before Zatori with a simply forged iron sword in hand, teeth bared and fearsome. Zatori raised his tachina in a defensive posture, taking calming breaths in through his nostrils and out through his teeth, finding his still centre and waiting for the proper time for action.

The older islander, who from the relative finery of the ornaments at his neck and wrists was a figure of some stature in island society, did not utter a word. He seemed hardly to notice the golden giants who were striding towards the centre of the battlefield. Instead, the islander rushed forwards with his iron sword swinging in a deadly arc at Zatori's bare head.

Zatori shifted his weight to one foot, raising his tachina with the blade parallel to the horizon in a blocking motion. The islander's iron sword slid with a shower of sparks off the tip of the tachina. As Zatori repositioned, swinging his sword's blade in an overhand arc aimed at the islander's right shoulder, the islander danced back a few paces, out of range of the tachina's point. Then, lightning-fast, the islander lunged forwards, driving the point of his iron blade directly at Zatori's midsection, and only by leaning to one side like a tree in a high wind and whipping his tachina around in a blocking manoeuvre was he able to avoid being skewered on the end of the islander's sword. As it was, the shock of the impact of the tachina against the iron sword was so strong that it reverberated up Zatori's arms, buzzing his teeth in his skull.

Though the islander was easily three times as old as Zatori, he had the strength and speed of a much younger man. It would be no easy thing for Zatori to defeat him, and each moment that passed only increased the possibility that the young Caritaigne would move too far away too quick for Zatori ever to locate him again. Even assuming that Zatori's skill with the blade was equal to the task of overcoming the islander – which at this point was far from a certainty – the delay could mean that Father Nei would be left unavenged.

Zatori was already forming a silent prayer to the Sacred Duality in his thoughts when the solution to his problem presented itself, in the form of assistance from an unexpected quarter. Before the islander was able to renew his attack, there came from a short distance off to Zatori's right a sound like distant thunder or the crump of a mortar round, then another, then another.

Chancing a quick glance to his right, Zatori saw that one of the armoured giants was walking past, the sounds he had heard the thunderous impact of each mighty footfall. The armoured giant seemed to have taken no notice of Zatori and his islander opponent, his attention on another corner of the melee, but his path was carrying him near enough to where the two combatants stood that they could see the full glory of the giant's size. Towering over all of the other combatants, in gleaming yellow-gold and jet-black, the strange figure was like a living engine of war, face completely hidden behind an inexpressive helmet.

Zatori immediately pulled his gaze back from the giant to the older islander before him, resolving to find time to dwell on the strangeness of the armoured giants only after his fire for vengeance had been quenched. But as he turned his attention back to the islander, Zatori saw that his opponent was not so quick to look away from the giant. For just that brief instant, the islander seemed finally to take notice of the golden giants, and stood transfixed by the sight of the huge armoured figure stomping by, eyes wide in bewilderment or disbelief or simple shock. In another instant, Zatori knew, the islander might well recover himself and renew the attack, so if Zatori was to use the momentary distraction to his advantage he would have to act now.

Without pausing an instant to reflect, Zatori speared the blade of his tachina forwards into the islander's chest, the razor-sharp point sliding between ribs as easily as an oar through water. Zatori did not stop until the tip of the tachina extended a full handspan out the islander's back.

As Zatori drew out the blade, the islander looked at the blood freely flowing from the cut in his chest with a slightly puzzled expression on his face. Then he lifted his head and looked Zatori in the eye.

Zatori's face was as inexpressive and unreadable as the armoured giants' helmets when he met the islander's shocked gaze. There was nothing of pride or glory in this act for the young Sipangish squire, only duty and obligation. He did not exult in the islander's death and defeat, and why would he? The islander was an obstacle on Zatori's path, one to be swept away in the observance of responsibility. Zatori did not hate his opponent, but was cool, methodical and calculating, just as his master had taught him to be. Detachment and duty, the two pillars of the Sipangish warrior-elite.

But when he finally faced the young Caritaigne who had murdered Father Nei? Then, perhaps, Zatori might not remain so impassive and detached...

TALOC S'TONAN STOOD rooted to the spot, watching the metal giants make their way through the confusion.

He could not help but remember the story of the two great warriors who had led the People to this world from the stars, loyal servants of the Great Father in the Sky who ruled over all. In the stories, one of the two great warriors had turned against his brother, and his betrayal had brought evil into the world. Were the Eokaroean legends true, and did such great warriors still sail between the stars? Had the successors of those two great brothers finally come to this world to finish the work begun in time out of memory? Would the faithless be brushed aside, and the Eokaroeans who had retained the true faith of the Great Father in the Sky finally be restored to their proper place of glory?

Taloc still puzzled over the nature of the giant invaders as he turned to look behind him, just in time to see his father Tonan in close combat with a young warrior who Taloc took to be Sipangish. Tonan appeared ready to spit the young Sipangish on the tip of the ironbrand Lightning when one of the armoured giants passed less than a half-dozen paces away. Taloc watched as his father and the Sipangish followed the giant's movements with their eyes, but while Tonan was still distracted by the giant glittering figure, the Sipangish suddenly and without warning drove his long curved blade into Tonan's chest halfway to the hilt.

'Father!' Taloc screamed, knowing that even if his father could hear him, no shout of warning or support would do any good.

Taloc raised his nameless ironbrand high overhead, and cried vengeance on the Sipangish faithless. The Sipangish didn't look in Taloc's direction, but suddenly looked with eyes narrowed in a steely gaze at something out of Taloc's line of sight and then took off running in pursuit.

As for the armoured giants, they continued on through the crowd, seeming to take no notice.

JEAN-ROBUR DU QUESTE suddenly wanted to be anywhere but on this blasted island, and his chances of winning his spurs be damned. What did it matter if he never earned the privileges of a fully blooded son of Caritaigne if in earning those privileges he died here on this godforsaken island? And as overwhelmed as he'd been by the tumult and confusion of the melee only a short while before, the arrival of the strange armoured figures

in their flying craft had pushed him into whole
new realms of disorientation and disbelief.

To Jean-Robur's surprise, though, he found that
the mysterious giants did not particularly *frighten*
him. The other combatants – Caritaigne, Sipangish
and islanders alike – were mostly running in confusion from the giants, or else frozen to the spot
and watching their thunderous advance across the
field like terrified rabbits making like statues in the
underbrush in the hope that a passing wolf will not
notice them. Jean-Robur was somewhat bewildered
by the new arrivals, to be sure – his conception of
the world was simply not big enough to allow for
the existence of such beings, and their appearance
was forcing him to reconsider what he believed to
be possible – but there was nothing of fear in his
reactions. Rather, he was *annoyed*, since the
armoured giants had made a royal mess of the
battle, and the chances of a Caritaigne victory
seemed suddenly more remote than ever.

At this point, it seemed like the whole trip was
hardly worth the effort, and he'd have been better
off staying home in the first place. At least then he'd
have been able to sleep in his own bed by night,
and would have his choice of the finest vintages to
drink by day.

The armoured giants moved through the melee as
though they were searching for something, but just
what it was Jean-Robur wasn't sure. He'd caught
sight of one of the giants some distance off stopping
in front of a young Caritaigne infantryman,

pointing some sort of small object – or device? – at the soldier. The infantryman, with more courage than sense, raised his musket and aimed its barrel at the giant's head, defiantly. The giant did not lash out, but bent and regarded the infantryman. With the distance that separated him from the scene, Jean-Robur could not make out what the armoured giant said as it addressed the infantryman, but he could feel the reverberations of the giant's voice in the bones of his chest.

The infantryman seemed to consider something for a moment, and then bowed his head and threw down his musket.

Amazingly, the armoured giant turned and stalked away, with the infantryman following close behind!

Had the soldier been bewitched? What had the giant said that caused the infantryman to throw down his weapon and follow him?

From behind him, Jean-Robur could hear an angry voice shouting, and glanced over his shoulder to see a young Sipangish warrior rushing towards him and waving a long curved sword in the air. For the briefest moment, Jean-Robur thought that his question about the armoured giant's intentions would remain unanswered, and then he turned back to see that an answer might be at hand, and much sooner than he would like.

One of the armoured giants was walking directly towards Jean-Robur.

* * *

ZATORI RACED TOWARDS the place where the young Caritaigne who had murdered Father Nei stood. His throat was raw from shouting out his cries for vengeance, but Zatori didn't let that silence him. He continued on, jinking left and right as other combatants blundered into his path in their frenzied attempt to escape the giant warriors, or to fell at least one more enemy before the strange visitors from the sky seized them.

More than a few were clearly not above using the distraction of the giant warriors to their own advantage, just as Zatori had done. Still, he was secure in the knowledge that at least he had stabbed the barbaric islander while standing face-to-face, and not struck like a coward from behind. There was no shame in taking advantage if an opponent glanced away in the middle of a contest. At least, that was what Zatori kept telling himself, though a small voice he tried to ignore kept whispering in the back of his thoughts that perhaps he was *not* so different from the Caritaigne murderer, after all.

The Caritaigne had turned at the sound of Zatori's cry of vengeance, but was now turning back towards the armoured giant making right for him. Zatori poured on speed, not wanting to arrive too late to kill the Caritaigne himself. What if the armoured giant were to strike the murderer down himself? Then Father Nei's death would not be properly avenged, the sullied honour of Zatori's master not properly restored. And *that* Zatori would not allow.

* * *

TALOC COURSED AFTER the Sipangish faithless who had killed his father, as if he was pursuing a boar through the island's forests with blade in hand. As they had on countless hunts before, his senses had narrowed to a tunnel centred on his prey, his attentions completely focused on the task at hand, everything else not only ignored but for the moment all but nonexistent.

But this was no ordinary hunt, and this was no boar that Taloc pursued. The quarry that now raced ahead of him, seeming not even to notice Taloc's pursuit, had the blood of Tonan on his hands. And while the Eokaroeans did not fight for privilege like the Caritaigne, or fight for honour like the Sipangish, they understood too well the concept of blood-debt, and the value of a life for a life.

The life of Taloc's father had been ended by this Sipangish faithless, and so the task of ending the killer's life fell to Taloc. It was no different than the burden that would be Taloc's had it been an errant boar who had felled Tonan in the hunt. It was a debt of blood, plain and simple. Eokaroeans measured the glory of a clan by the deeds of its warriors, and were a blood-debt to go unanswered it would besmirch the clan's reputation.

Taloc's attentions were not so focused, though, that he was able completely to disregard the giant devils that had fallen from the sky. But what did it matter why the devils had come to the island, whether to bless them all or to kill them? Taloc would die easily, and with a clear conscience, if he first repaid his father's blood-debt by killing the Sipangish faithless. And then, even if no one living ever knew it, Taloc's unnamed ironbrand would have earned a name for itself, and he would die with the newly christened Thunderbolt in his hands.

JEAN-ROBUR WATCHED THE inexorable approach of the armoured giant, the huge sword in its massive gauntleted hand crackling with energy. His fist tightening around the handle of his own falchion, Jean-Robur's thoughts raced, trying to devise a way out.

But there was no way out. There was nowhere to run. With madness and confusion on all sides, it was unlikely Jean-Robur could get very far even if he did try to escape, and despite their massive size and heavy armour the giants were able to move surprisingly quickly, so the giant stalking towards him would likely catch up before Jean-Robur was able to take more than a dozen steps.

Jean-Robur's emotions were numb. He felt like an observer inside his own head, viewing his surroundings at a step removed. He found himself thinking briefly of the taste of a glass of vintage wine he'd sampled months before, and the whisper kiss of silk sheets against his bare skin, and all the other sundry pleasures he'd left behind in Caritaigne and that he would now never know again. He would meet his end, here on this distant and barbaric island, and would never enjoy the privilege and status that his spurs would have afforded.

But if he were to die, so be it. He would show the shade of his cousin Benoit and all the braying fools like him that Jean-Robur du Queste was every inch a man. He would give no enemy, whether Sipangish or islander or unknown giant come from the stars, the satisfaction of seeing a proud son of the house of du Queste unmanned by fear. He would not beg for his life, but would face his death bravely and without fear.

Jean-Robur raised the point of his falchion, squaring his feet in a ready stance. Once again he heard from behind him an angry voice shouting in the incomprehensible and guttural tones of Sipang, but he paid it no mind. He readied himself for a duel he knew he could not win.

But though his every rational impulse told Jean-Robur that he had not the slightest chance of defeating so large and powerful an opponent, nevertheless did his darting eyes seek out any possible advantage. He might fall before the armoured giant, but Jean-Robur was not about to go down easily.

ZATORI RAISED HIS master's tachina overhead, teeth bared, and shouted out once again his cry for vengeance.

'Murderer, prepare to taste vengeance! With this blade I shall restore the honour of the one slain by your cowardice and treachery! Your blood shall assuage the spirit of the dead!'

But this time the Caritaigne murderer did not even seem to notice Zatori's shouts of anger as he approached. Before, at least, the Caritaigne had glanced in his direction before turning dismissively away, but now the murderer just stood fast, facing the armoured giant that was now only a half-dozen steps away.

Zatori was almost within striking range of the Caritaigne's back, while the murderer focused his attention on the armoured giant.

'Turn, murderer, and face justice!' Zatori shouted, now only a few paces behind the Caritaigne. But the murderer did not turn, either not hearing Zatori or not caring.

Zatori knew he could strike the Caritaigne down in a single blow, before the murderer even knew the attack was coming. But even as hungry as Zatori was for vengeance, and to remove the stain from Father Nei's sullied honour, still Zatori found he couldn't bring himself to stab an opponent in the back. Not even one who had himself used such a cowardly attack. To defeat the Caritaigne dishonourably would do nothing to cleanse Father Nei's honour, but would only stain it further.

If the Caritaigne murderer would not turn and face Zatori, there was only one alternative, though it pained Zatori to consider it. He would help to defeat the murderer's opponent in honourable combat, and then demand that the Caritaigne face him.

Taking several long strides to the right, Zatori came abreast of the Caritaigne – well beyond the reach of the Caritaigne's blade, in case the murderer chose to launch a treacherous attack at him in these final moments – and raised his tachina towards the armoured giant. The Caritaigne did not acknowledge his arrival, but only glanced in his direction for the briefest of instants, with no more attention than he gave to casting his gaze on the ground underfoot, or the proximity of the nearest bodies and wreckage around them – Zatori was just another factor in the immediate environment, but the real enemy was the armoured giant.

The chances of the two young swordsmen defeating the massive figure seemed remote to say the least, whether or not it was a holy warrior they faced. But if Zatori died, it would be with his own honour intact. And if he were unable to restore the sullied honour of Father Nei, then he would have to attempt some redress from the land of spirits. Zatori hoped that his master's spirit would understand.

Taloc watched as the Sipangish halted a few paces behind a Caritaigne swordsman, shouting a challenge whose words Taloc could not comprehend but whose general meaning was unmistakable. But when the Caritaigne refused to turn, the Sipangish bafflingly refrained from attacking, and instead took up a position to the Caritaigne's right, evidently intending to fight against the giant at his enemy's side.

Taloc did not believe for an instant that any mortal could stand against one the massive sky-devils, even two mortals fighting side-by-side. But while his father's blood-debt demanded to be paid, Taloc could not help but admire the courage the two enemies displayed in standing against so unstoppable a foe. These two faithless were exhibiting the kind of bravery that Eokaroeans sang about in song, the kind of heart that earned untold glory for a warrior's clan and a name for a nameless ironbrand. Cutting down the Sipangish who had killed his father would pay Tonan's blood-debt, to be sure, but how much greater the glory Taloc could bring to his clan and to his father's name if he were to stand bravely alongside these faithless against one of the unstoppable invaders from the sky?

And if the three should prevail, against all hope and reason, and defeat the sky-devil? Why, Taloc could simply take payment on his father's blood-debt then and there, and kill the Sipangish with his own ironbrand.

Taloc paced ahead, veering to the left of the Caritaigne, opposite his Sipangish quarry, and raising his ironbrand turned to face the sky-devil's approach.

It was *possible* they could defeat such a giant. It hardly seemed likely, though, so Taloc resolved not to let it worry him. More than likely they would all meet their ends at the point of the sky-devil's crackling blade, and then their respective blood-debts would fall on the shoulders of others to pay.

* * *

CAPTAIN TAELOS OF the Imperial Fists stopped a half-dozen paces away from the three Triandrians standing in a line. In his right fist he held the handle of his power sword, energy coruscating up and down the blade's edge like heat lightning. In his left hand he held an auspex, that pinged faintly like the sound of raindrops hitting the still surface of a pond. The giant raised the device, pointing it first at the Eokaroean warrior, then the Caritaigne duellist, then the Sipangish squire. Seemingly satisfied with what he found, the giant clipped the device to a hook at his waist, and regarded the three young men for a moment, his own expression hidden behind his armoured helm.

'Come on, what are you waiting for?' shouted Jean-Robur du Queste in the liquid sounds of Caritaigne, waving his falchion impatiently.

'Hurry if you would please, stranger,' Zatori Zan said calmly in the language of Sipang. 'I have a matter of honour that must be addressed.'

'For the glory of the clan of Tonan!' called Taloc s'Tonan in the strident tone of Eokaroe. 'And for the glory of the Great Father in the Sky!'

None of the three Triandrians could understand one another, but it hardly mattered. Captain Taelos was fully versed in all the languages of Triandr, thanks to linguistic implants via hypno-conditioning onboard the Imperial Fist strike cruiser *Capulus* while still en route to the planet.

But though he was conversant in all the planet's tongues, when he addressed the three young swordsmen before him, Captain Taelos first spoke Imperial Gothic, the common language of the Imperium of Man.

'I greet you in the name of the Emperor of Mankind, who sits in undying glory upon the Golden Throne on Holy Terra itself.'

The three Triandrians clearly did not understand the captain's words, but from their expressions it appeared that they found the sound of them hauntingly familiar.

'You have been examined, and found worthy of a signal honour.'

The three Triandrians exchanged glances, none of them able to puzzle out the captain's meaning. Then, without a word being exchanged, the three turned their attentions back to Captain Taelos and raised their blades defiantly against him.

Taelos laughed, a sound like the rumbling of distant thunder.

'I admire your spirit, and I salute you,' he said in the language of Eokaroe, then in the tongues of Caritaigne and Sipang.

The three Triandrian swordsmen seemed startled to hear the familiar sounds of their native languages rumbling from the captain's helmet.

'I come to your world seeking recruits, not vassals,' he said in each language in turn. 'I offer you the chance to join a noble brotherhood of warriors, and to live a life you cannot even dream is possible.' He raised his sword before him, point towards the heavens. 'You will travel beyond the stars, and see sights you can scarcely imagine.'

The three swordsmen slowly lowered their weapons. Captain Taelos knew what choice they would make. But it was important that it be their own decision.

'Come with me, and I will make you more than mere men. I will make you holy warriors – Sons of Dorn!'

CAPTAIN TAELOS USHERED the three swordsmen to the nearest Thunderhawk, taking the blade from each as they clambered tremulously onboard. Sergeant Hilts was already there, supervising the loading of the candidates.

'It would seem a successful cull,' Taelos said, his gaze scanning the battlefield, and his battle-brothers escorting young warriors in small groups to the gunships.

'Nearly two thousand, at last count,' Sergeant Hilts replied.

'Good,' Taelos answered. 'With luck, perhaps a few of them will survive the trials.'

Hilts nodded in reply. 'We should get a few neo-phytes out of this crop, I would expect. And maybe some of them will even make it to battle-brother.' He gestured to the three Triandrian blades the captain held in his fist. 'Starting a collection, sir?'

Taelos looked from the veteran-sergeant to the blades, thoughtfully, but didn't reply.

PART TWO

'Pain is the wine of communion
with heroes.'

Rhetoricus,
The Book of Five Spheres

CHAPTER FOUR

Captain Taelos stood at the railing of the command dais onboard the strike cruiser *Capulus*. Having only returned from the planet's surface, he was still encased in full gold power armour, a gauntleted hand on the hilt of the power sword sheathed at his side. Only his head was bare, and as he cast his narrowed gaze about the command deck, he could feel the faint touch of the ship's recirculated air against his naked flesh.

All around him dozens of servitors operated the innumerous controls that governed the ship's systems and processes, making ready for the moment which was fast approaching when the *Capulus* would break orbit and leave Triandr behind. In another few generations, perhaps, the Imperial Fists would return to this remote world to cull the population once more for potential recruits, but for the moment it was of no further interest to the Chapter.

The long months of Taelos's current recruiting mission were finally nearing an end. When the *Capulus* next left realspace and translated into the empyrean, the Navigator would guide the ship through the warp's insane geometries back to the Chapter's fortress-monastery, the *Phalanx*. Taelos would present to Chapter Master Pugh a cadre of neophytes, and perhaps then Taelos would be granted permission to pursue his warrior pilgrimage.

Of course, that thin hope was predicated on the notion that any of the current crop of aspirants had the mettle to pass muster as neophytes in the first place. And that remained to be seen.

Captain Taelos was shaken from his reverie by the sound of heavy footfalls approaching the command dais, and turned to see the approach of a trio of figures.

First came Librarian Borgos, in robes of golden yellow that set off the somewhat sallow cast of his skin. His nose was long and slightly curved like a raptor's beak, and on his cheeks were the same sort of criss-crossed duelling scars worn by Taelos and most other Imperial Fists, badges of honour earned in the Arena Restricta. And above those white-scarred cheeks, Borgos's eyes were milky-white and sightless. Combat injuries had claimed Borgos's vision long decades before, but unlike other

Astartes who found themselves in his position, the epistolary had refused augmetic implants. Instead, he chose to use other senses to guide his way through the world, his psychic abilities perceiving far more than merely mundane sight could ever see. And any opponents on the field of battle who thought that his blind eyes made him any the less capable of wielding the force sword that hung at his hip soon learned the error in their reasoning.

'Greetings, Librarian,' Taelos said, inclining his head in an abbreviated nod.

'Captain,' Borgos said simply.

Next came Apothecary Lakari. On his back he wore the portable narthecium he carried into combat, though the chances of encountering an enemy onboard the strike cruiser were all but nil. Taelos had once asked the Apothecary why he carried the portable narthecium while onboard the *Capulus*, when the ship's Apothecarion contained a full-scale narthecium, to say nothing of housing every other tool and treatment required for the healing arts. Lakari had looked at Taelos as though he had begun suddenly to spout gibberish, and calmly explained that one could never predict when injury might befall an Astartes, and that it simply paid to be prepared.

'Apothecary,' Taelos said, nodding in Lakari's direction.

The Apothecary responded only with a quick glance in Taelos's direction and a brief nod in return.

Last came Chaplain Dominicus, his face hidden behind a silver death's-head mask, his coal-black armour encrusted with the ribbons and scrolls of countless purity seals. Around the Chaplain's neck hung his rosarius, an amulet depicting an Imperial aquila, wings outstretched, with the icon of a black fist emblazoned on its breast – not merely a symbol of the Ecclesiarchy, the amulet incorporated a force-field generator, and served to protect the body as well as the soul. In the Chaplain's hands was his crozius arcanum, a skull-headed staff that served Dominicus both as staff of office and as power weapon of choice.

'And the Emperor's blessings on you, captain,' Dominicus said, lowering the skull-head of his staff in benediction.

'The Venerable Dorn keep you in his graces, Chaplain,' Captain Taelos replied. He then turned to regard the others. 'My thanks for responding to my summons. I wanted to let you know that we have completed our business on Triandr, and will presently begin the journey back to the designated rendezvous with the rest of the fleet.'

'I trust that your journey planetside was a success, captain?' Librarian Borgos asked, head tilted slightly back and sightless eyes trained on the empty air before him, his voice so quiet it was scarcely above a whisper.

'The Thunderhawks returned to the *Capulus* with bellies filled with recruits,' Taelos answered, 'just over two thousand young Triandrians in all.' He paused, a slight smile tugging up the corners of his mouth almost imperceptibly. 'Though whether that number represents "success", I suppose, depends largely on *your* findings.' He glanced from the blind eyes of the Librarian to the Chaplain's silver skull-mask to the bare face of the Apothecary. In a sense, the captain's fate rested in the hands of these worthies, as they would be responsible for the exhaustive examination of the aspirants in the months-long journey back to the *Phalanx*. And if too many of the aspirants were found wanting, the *Capulus* would be despatched on another recruiting mission, and Taelos's hopes to seek atonement on a warrior pilgrimage would be once more put in abeyance.

'I have reviewed your preliminary scans,' Apothecary Lakari said, 'and the results are promising.' The captain and the other Imperial Fists who had gone on the recruiting mission to the surface of Triandr had performed preliminary physical examinations by auspex, as they had on more than a dozen worlds before, returning to the strike cruiser only with those candidates who fit the physical profile. But the examinations which the Apothecary would employ in the coming weeks and months would be considerably more robust, and could potentially find defects and incompatibilities undetectable by a standard auspex.

Like the recruits culled from the worlds already visited by the *Capulus* on this recruiting mission, the aspirants selected from the planet below were all young men between the ages of ten and fourteen years, all of suitable phenotype and morphology. Any potentials who had been beyond the age of fourteen had been left behind, deemed as already too fully grown for the successful administration of an Astartes' implants, which required that the recipient's body still be in the process of development. And while an auspex could do a basic scan of tissue compatibility, there was the possibility of variation on the genetic level that could still result in implanted organs failing to develop properly, which could only be identified in cellular-level examination in a fully equipped Apothecarion.

'A surface scan of the incoming Thunderhawks betrayed no trace of warp-taint in the minds within,' Librarian Borgos said in his whisper-quiet voice, 'but infection by the Ruinous Powers can often be insidious and difficult to root out. Individual examinations will be required to confirm that there are no hints of taint or other mental weakness among them.'

As important as physical compatibility was in an aspirant, mental suitability was of equal importance, if not greater. Of the implants, the catalepsean node and occulobe could only develop to a fully functional condition under the stimulus of hypnotic suggestion. If the recruit's mind proved to be resistant to hypno-conditioning, there would be no point in proceeding. Fortunately, among the first procedures performed on the aspirants upon their arrival to the strike cruiser was the force-teaching of

Imperial Gothic by means of hypno-casques, and if the aspirant emerged from the process still unable to speak and comprehend the Imperium's common tongue, it was a sure indicator that the more sophisticated hypnotic techniques employed in implantation would likewise fail.

'This feudal world of Triandr has been too long out of contact with the Imperium,' Chaplain Dominicus said with evident distaste, his voice sounding distant and cold from behind the silver death's-head. 'These raw recruits will know little of the Imperial Creed, and even less about the proper worship of the God-Emperor. They will need rigorous instruction if they are to join the ranks of the Chapter's neophytes.'

Tissue compatibility tests and psychological screening would over the coming days and weeks weed out those recruits unsuitable for implantation. And then, the examinations complete, Chaplain Dominicus would indoctrinate those who remained in the Imperial faith, and introduce them to the adoration of Primarch Rogal Dorn.

'Agreed, Chaplain,' Taelos replied, 'and I can think of no one better suited to the task.'

Dominicus's eyes regarded Taelos in silence from behind the silver mask for a long moment, and then the Chaplain nodded.

'Unless any of you have concerns to address?' Taelos paused and then, when the three responded only with silence, continued. 'Then I see no reason to tarry here any longer. We can be on our way, and rendezvous with the *Phalanx* that much sooner.'

Chaplain Dominicus raised his hand in benediction, and Taelos and the others waited in reverent silence. 'Oh Dorn, dawn of our being, be with us, illuminate us.'

Taelos closed his eyes, and solemnly intoned, 'Ave Imperator.'

JEAN-ROBUR DU QUESTE was convinced that he had died on the field of battle in Eokaroe after all, and that he was now suffering the torments of the damned in the perfidious domain of the Dark god.

Perhaps, he thought, he should have paid more attention to his religious studies. And taken a little better care of his immortal soul, at that.

But convinced as he was of his deceased condition, Jean-Robur did not *feel* like an ethereal spirit, his essence shorn of its gross material form. Admittedly he had not been the most attentive student of religious theory in his childhood in Caritaigne, but he didn't remember anything about ethereal spirits being able to *bruise*, or to *bleed*. And while he understood that the torments of the damned were meant to be unpleasant, he hadn't really considered that they would *hurt* so blasted much.

Of course, on reflection there was much about his current circumstances that did not quite align with Caritaigne traditions. There had been nothing in the hymns he'd been forced by his grandparents to memorise that had mentioned the half-man/half-machine monstrosities with needles for fingers and clamps for hands that now poked and prodded him from all angles. To say *nothing* of the smaller man-machine hybrids that were engaged in shaving all of the hair from his head and body with razor-sharp blades.

Jean-Robur's last clear memory before waking up to this hall of mechanical horrors had been of the interior of the strange craft that had fallen from the sky. He and a pair of others, a Sipangish and a barbaric islander, had been trundled onboard, and then rendered unconscious by a quick spray from a nozzle of a cloyingly sweet-smelling gas. Jean-Robur had rousted once while still in the craft, only to find the interior crammed so full with bodies that they were stacked like cordwood ready for the fire. He tried to scream, but no sound emerged, and when he tried to move he found his limbs completely immobilised. Jean-Robur had lost consciousness again almost immediately, and when he opened his eyes again it was to find himself here, in red-tinged darkness.

The lights had grown brighter as figures emerged from the shadows with strange clanks and wheezes, and it was only then that Jean-Robur realised that he'd been stripped naked and bound to some sort of hard, smooth surface that was as cold as metal against his bare skin. His first thought was that it was a dining table, and that the strange creatures of flesh and metal were coming to feast on his living flesh, but after they bared their blades and needles and clamps and went to work, Jean-Robur considered whether the table might not be the sort that could be found in an operating theatre, instead.

Jean-Robur tried to scream, but just like when he'd awoken on the flying craft, no sound emerged. He could open his mouth, but it was as though his vocal cords were frozen.

He could not move his head to either side, too. The only part of his body over which he seemed to have any control were his eyes, which he could swivel in their sockets, and open and close the lids. But all he could easily see of the strange space was the circle of light immediately around him, and the mechanical men bent over the table. If he strained his eyes as far as they would go in their sockets to the right or to the left, he could just barely make out another circle of light in the near distance, and another group of man-machine hybrids hunched over another table, and the impression of another naked form beneath the needles and clamps and blades. But the only sounds he could hear, no matter how hard he strained his ears to listen, were the clatter and snip of the clamps and blades, and the unsettling wheezing of the man-machines' movements.

Whenever the needles slid into his skin, whenever the clamps pinched back a hunk of flesh, Jean-Robur screamed silently at the searing pain. If he was *not* an ethereal spirit, and was still among the living, then the only consolation he could see was that his torments would not be endless, and that his body would eventually succumb. He would die, and his pain would at last be at an end.

Later, in the weeks and months to come when he would think back to those first waking moments onboard the *Capulus*, when he imagined that he would soon see the last of pain, Jean-Robur could do nothing but laugh ruefully at his naïveté. He did not even dream in those early hours that the pain was only *beginning*.

Zatori Zan had long since given up struggling, and sat bolt upright in the metal chair, his arms and legs securely fastened by thick straps. Despite himself he shivered, though whether from the fears that he could not completely suppress, or from the chill of the cool air against his naked and freshly shaved flesh, he could not say.

He had endured the long hours – days? – of torture upon the metal bench, when the strange creatures of commingled flesh and metal had poked and prodded him, taking blood and tissue samples with their long needles and cruelly sharp blades. Immobilised and rendered mute as he was, Zatori had not even attempted to cry out in pain as they inserted metal probes into his every orifice, everything from long snaking coils to metal rods to others in shapes even stranger still.

And when it seemed that he could bear it no longer, and he would either pass out from the pain or lose his senses entirely, the mechanical men had withdrawn. Zatori had been left alone on the bench, for how long he couldn't say, until finally a towering figure loomed over him. This newcomer was dressed in a blinding white hue instead of the golden yellow and jet-black of the giants who had come from the sky. And this one's face was not hidden behind a helmet, but his head was bare, with a thin stubble of white hair on his crown and eyes that were not entirely unkind.

The towering figure in white carried a metal tube in his hands, and for a brief terrifying instant Zatori had assumed that he was about to undergo further examination. But then he saw that there were lenses of some clear material set in either end of the tube, and buttons and switches along its length. The giant in white armour raised one end of the tube to his own eyes, and then trained the other end on Zatori. Was the tube some sort of spyglass, as used by seafarers on the waves? Did its lenses render it capable of scrutinising Zatori in ways beyond the scope of mere sight? Perhaps. How else to explain the fact that the white-armoured figure used the lensed tube to peer into Zatori's eyes, the lids pinned back by massive gauntleted fingers, or into his ears, or his open mouth. Zatori felt himself a piece of livestock being inspected by potential buyers, like the war-horses he'd seen his former master Father Nei obtain at auction.

It was that realisation that gave Zatori his first inkling of what was happening to him. The machine-men who'd subjected him to their needles and blades were not the daemons that plagued the dishonoured dead in the land of spirits, as he'd originally assumed. And Zatori was not being tortured and tormented for his failings in life, either. He was being *examined*, and *evaluated*. But to what end, and by what criteria?

An answer was not forthcoming. Still rendered mute, whether by the sweet-smelling gas that had incapacitated him in the flying craft or by some other treatment at the hands of the machine-men, Zatori was not even able to give his question voice. But after completing the examination with the lensed-tube, the figure in white armour had spoken to the surrounding shadows in words that were somehow familiar but no less incomprehensible, and a pair of machine-men emerged back into the circle of light. The bounds which pinned Zatori to the bench were removed, and the pair of machine-men lifted him and carried him bodily a short distance to an upright metal chair.

From the high back of the chair, suspended on a metallic coil, was an inverted-bowl-shaped object that appeared to be a helmet of some sort. Zatori was deposited in the chair, his arms and legs strapped in place, and then the machine-men retreated while the figure in white armour stepped forwards to regard him once more.

Again the figure in white armour addressed him, and again Zatori could almost puzzle out the words' meaning, hearing the echoes of the ballads which told of holy warriors who travelled in their divine chariots between the stars.

The white-armoured figure seemed to pause for a moment, almost as if awaiting some response from Zatori. Then he closed the distance to the chair, reached up to take hold of the inverted bowl suspended from the cord, and then lowered the helmet-shaped object over Zatori's head.

Zatori could feel the sudden kiss of the cold metal against his hairless scalp. And then in the next instant Zatori's entire world was consumed by an endless universe of pain.

TALOC S'TONAN FELT as though his mind would burst. His thoughts raced, blanketed in confusion as new words and concepts crowded together.

As the sky-giant in white armour lifted the metal bowl from his naked scalp, Taloc realised with a start that he knew that it was not a bowl, but a 'hypno-casque'. And the massive figure who loomed over him was not a sky-giant, but a member of the Adeptus Astartes: a Space Marine.

The Astartes spoke to Taloc again, as he had when first placing the hypno-casque on his head, but this time Taloc found that he could understand the Astartes' words, though he knew for a certainty that it was not the Eokaroean tongue he was hearing.

'If the procedure was successful, you should now be fully versed in Imperial Gothic. Respond verbally to confirm that you understand what I am saying.'

Taloc's tongue felt thick and useless in his mouth, and he realised that he had not spoken since he had shouted a challenge to the sky-giant – to the *Space*

Marine – on the green fields of Eokaroe. He opened his mouth tentatively, then closed it again.

'Don't worry, the effects of the paralysing agents on your vocal cords have been disabled, and you are now free to speak once more.'

'W-where am I?' Taloc said in Eokaroean.

'In Imperial Gothic, please,' the Space Marine replied with some impatience, 'to confirm the efficacy of the cognitive implantation.'

Taloc swallowed hard, and felt concepts and words shifting in his brain. It was as though a whole new set of signifiers and labels were being overlaid atop his conceptions, and that with the slightest effort he could shift his way of thinking away from the old paradigm and to the new. Taloc could not help but be reminded of the day when his father first introduced him to the Mysteries, the sacred teachings of the Great Father in the Sky, which were not spoken of openly, but communicated in secret to children once they approached the threshold of adulthood. From that moment forwards Taloc's mind had undergone a change, and as he looked at the world around him – sky, land, sea, and stars – he had found that once-familiar things had taken on new meaning, an unexpected significance.

'Where am I?' Taloc said again, this time employing the new words which were still settling into place. 'Who are you? Why am I here?'

The Space Marine nodded once, seemingly satisfied, and then began removing the straps which bound Taloc to the chair.

'You are onboard the Imperial Fists strike cruiser *Capulus*. I am Apothecary Lakari of the 10th Company. You are here to be examined further, and your suitability for implantation procedures measured. Does that answer your questions?'

Strike cruiser – the meaning of the words bubbled up from somewhere deep in Taloc's mind, a ship of war that sailed between the stars. *Apothecary* – a word combining the Eokaroean concepts of 'healer' and 'midwife', but not one who aided women giving birth to babies, but who aided young men in giving birth to their own transformed selves. *Company* – a concept greater than 'clan', signifying a host of warriors who did not share bonds of blood or family, but instead were linked by the genetic legacy each of them carried, seeds passed down from a single great warrior of the past.

And *implantation* – the concepts associated with this word in particular were confusing to Taloc. It suggested living bodies being cut open and things being buried within in order to improve it, but in Taloc's experience cutting open bodies was an act designed to injure a living body, and even to kill it. He found the discrepancy difficult to reconcile.

The last of the bounds removed from the chair, the Apothecary straightened up and took a step backwards.

'Stand,' he said simply.

'I… I…' Taloc began, questions racing in all directions through his head like birds scattered from trees by the noisy arrival of a clumsy hunter.

Apothecary Lakari's face remained immobile and set, his expression as impassive and unreadable as the helmets which had hidden the faces of the Space Marines who had descended on Eokaroe.

'Stand,' he repeated, the slightest trace of impatience creeping into his tone.

Taloc glanced down at his naked form, at his arms and legs which had not moved of his own volition since the Space Marine in gold had battered the ironbrand from his hands and trussed him up like a prize boar being readied for the roasting spit.

'You have been imparted a knowledge of Imperial Gothic to facilitate the remaining examinations,' the Apothecary said, as though by rote. It seemed that the Space Marine were reciting a formalised chant, and Taloc found himself wondering how often Apothecary Lakari had said these same words to other young men seated in that chair. 'You now understand fully the spoken commands you are given, and are expected to comply. If you refuse to follow instructions, you will be dealt with accordingly.'

Though the Apothecary's tone remained level and emotionless, Taloc could not mistake the hint of menace behind the words themselves. Without delaying any further, he pushed off the metal chair and onto his long-disused legs, his knees shaking somewhat at the unexpected strain after being left idle for so long a time.

Apothecary Lakari regarded Taloc for a moment before continuing. 'The examinations so far carried out by the servitors' – *servitors*, a word signifying the terrifying, strange amalgamations of man and machine who had tormented Taloc upon the metal slab – 'have been rudimentary, meant to eliminate those candidates with physical defects, deformities or other unsuitabilities which may have somehow remained hidden to an auspex's readings.' *Auspex*, the handheld devices the Space Marines carried, which with his newfound vocabulary still unpacking as it encountered each new word, Taloc now understood were machines capable of gathering data about their surroundings.

'A considerable number of your fellow aspirants have been eliminated as candidates for implantation already, and there is every chance that you will yourself be eliminated in the coming, and more rigorous, examinations. Be warned, though, that compared to the relatively simple procedures already performed on you by the servitors, some of the tests that will follow can involve considerably greater degrees of pain.'

Pain – a new word for a very familiar concept.

THE FIGURE THAT loomed before Zatori had the same milky-white eyes as the blind beggar-woman who had spent her days on the front steps of the temple in the village in which Zatori had been born. Above the lined and weathered face, the cheeks marked by ancient white scars, was a golden skullcap much like those worn by the holy scholars of Sipang. Robes fashioned of cloth-of-gold hung from the figure's shoulders, rustling gently in the slight breeze through the chamber.

Zatori stood stock straight in the centre of the chamber, naked flesh chilled by the same faint breeze that rustled the golden robe and caused the flames burning in the censers and thuribles suspended overhead to flutter and wave like flags flapping in a high wind, smoke wreathing the rafters which arched high above their heads. And though Zatori was relatively certain that the white eyes before him were sightless and dead, still he could feel the pressure of the blind man's regard, as though Zatori were being studied by senses beyond the five granted to mortal men.

Of all the Astartes whom Zatori had encountered, on Eokaroe and here on the *Capulus*, this blind man was undoubtedly the most terrifying. Zatori's stomach clenched in knots, and he began to wonder whether he had made a seriously grave mistake in agreeing to come to the stars.

'Relax yourself, child,' the blind man said, his voice sounding older than the ice-capped mountains of Sipang themselves. 'The Apothecary has begun the long process of examining your body, and it falls to me to examine your mind.'

Zatori was still not accustomed to the fact that his mind could immediately comprehend the words his ears heard. Ever since Apothecary Lakari had removed the hypno-casque from his head, whenever he heard a new word for the first time it was as though a hidden door in Zatori's mind was unlocked, and understanding that he'd not previously realised he possessed came flooding into his thoughts.

'Hidden doors,' the blind man said, a faint smile playing around the corners of his thin mouth. The sight of that smile sent pinpricks of terror creeping up Zatori's spine. 'A more apt metaphor than you may realise.'

Zatori realised with a start that he had not spoken those sentiments aloud, but had kept them harboured in his thoughts. But how did he know…?

'I can hear your thoughts,' the blind man said, answering Zatori's unasked question. 'That is how I know. I am Librarian Borgos, epistolary of the Imperial Fists Librarium, and I am a psyker. In your culture, one such as I might be called…' The Librarian paused for a moment, lids fluttering over his eyes, and Zatori could feel something touching his mind lightly, like the wings of a butterfly brushing momentarily against an outstretched fingertip. '…a "dreamstealer", I believe?'

Zatori regarded the blind man with renewed interest. He'd heard stories about dreamstealers since early childhood, of course, as every Sipangish had, but he'd dismissed them as mere fancy, like green-skinned monsters and daemons from beyond the sky. To think that there might *really* exist individuals who could reach into a living mind and draw forth thoughts and dreams like a child pulling forth a speckled koi from an ornamental pond...

'Thoughts are often slippery,' Librarian Borgos said with a faint smile, 'and as difficult to hold.'

Zatori suddenly felt even more exposed than ever, his mind laid as naked and bare as his shaven flesh. Had he not seen the proof of it for himself, he'd never have believed it was possible. 'What... what do you want with me?'

'If your thoughts are like fish swimming beneath the surface of your mind,' the Librarian answered, 'there are other things that can lurk in the farther depths, hidden beyond the light of your conscious mind, so deep that you yourself might never suspect they were there. The material reality we inhabit – planets, stars, moons, and the empty space in between – is but a surface, beneath which stretch unplumbed depths. This region above which we float is known by many names – the immaterium, the aether, the empyrean – but perhaps the most fitting name is the one most commonly employed – the *warp*.'

The word conjured associations in Zatori's mind, doors unlocking and meaning flooding his thoughts. *Warp* – a twist, a bending, a perversion of the mind, a distortion of reality.

'The warp is like the reflection of our world in a broken mirror,' Borgos continued, 'a horrifically shifting domain in which the laws which govern our material world are twisted and perverted. And though mankind has learned to exploit this dark mirror-realm to our advantage, harnessing the ability to traverse the warp bodily and reduce to a mere fraction the time needed to travel from one point in our material world to another, this advantage comes at a terrible price. For the presence of a living mind, in either realm, can attract the dire intelligences which make that place their home, drawing them like moths to a flame.'

Zatori was reminded of the chilling stories he'd been told as a child, of the daemons who dwelt beyond the sky.

'Once a mind has been touched by the warp, it is forever after susceptible to those dire intelligences. You consider the unpacking of implanted knowledge in your thoughts as "hidden doors", but the analogy is even more apt when considering the taint of warp and Chaos. You might never be aware that such a door existed until it opened, and the Ruinous Powers came streaming out.'

The blind Librarian reached out a hand and brushed fingertips as cold and dry as parchment paper against the skin of Zatori's forehead.

'Those who are called as aspirants by a Chapter of the Adeptus Astartes must be thoroughly screened for such taint or stain. Eternal vigilance is the price we pay to ensure that we do not unknowingly invite vipers into our home, who might rise up and poison us when we least expect it.'

His fingertips still pressed lightly against Zatori's forehead, Borgos closed his blind eyes, and took a deep breath.

'As Apothecary Lakari has already begun the process of probing deep into your flesh for any defect or weakness, so must I begin the process of probing deep into your mind, seeking any sign of the touch of Chaos in your thoughts. Still your body and mind. And if some warp-taint *should* be found, rest assured that your remains will be disposed of promptly.'

Before Zatori realised the full implication of the Librarian's words it was too late, and he felt Borgos's mind already closing around his like a fist around a sword's handle.

JEAN-ROBUR DU QUESTE felt as though he'd been naked for days. And for all he knew, he realised, he *had*. Naked and hairless as a puppy just squeezed from some bitch's hindquarters, searching weak-eyed for mother's teats. The injections and infusions he'd received while in Apothecary Lakari's tender care had staved off any effects of thirst and starvation, come to that, so at least he didn't have hunger pangs to go along with the pin-pricks and needle-tracks which marched up and down his goose-pimpled flesh like the footprints of an army of ants. But if he could only get *clothed* again then the maddening strange circumstances in which he found himself might not be so difficult to take.

The sessions with the blind man who'd introduced himself as Borgos had mercifully ended a short while ago, and Jean-Robur had been ushered out of the Librarian's smoke-filled chamber as

another naked puppy was escorted in. It seemed
that the 'mind-reader' had failed to find any stain in
Jean-Robur's thoughts – at least any stain of the
'warp', that is, since it would not take a very profi-
cient mind-reader to find stains of *other* sorts in the
young Caritaigne's disordered thoughts.

Jean-Robur had been escorted by man-machines
– by *servitors*, his new-found facility with this Imperial Gothic insisted – to a great hall, an enormous
echoing chamber of hard curves and strong lines.
Entering the hall, Jean-Robur felt like a gnat crawling into a grand palace, scarcely worthy of notice.
The sounds of his footsteps were swallowed by the
vast space, and the hall seemed draped in a respectful silence, like a church or a graveside service.

Already gathered in the hall were a little under a
dozen other youths, all of them as naked and hairless as Jean-Robur, watched over by a pair of
towering Space Marines in armour coloured golden
yellow and trimmed in jet-black. It was difficult to
say without uniforms and other bits of identifying
fashion, but from their skin-tones and the shapes
of eyes and noses and such, it seemed to Jean-
Robur that the other youths were more or less
equally divided between sons of Caritaigne,
Sipangish and barbaric Eokaroean islanders. If all
of them had been infused with a knowledge of
Imperial Gothic as Jean-Robur had, he reasoned
that he could simply *speak* to any of the others if he
so chose – but when one of the others opened his
mouth to speak, a sharp bark from one of the Space

Marine ordered them all to remain silent. Not that Jean-Robur really felt he had much to say to the others as it was. What did they have to discuss, after all? 'What sins did *you* commit in your former life to merit ending up here?'

After Jean-Robur was deposited with the others, a final Triandrian youth was escorted to them, leaving their number at an even dozen. And for a long while the twelve of them just stood there, bare feet cold against the smooth metal floor beneath them, each boy's arms wrapped around his chest and sides as much for a sense of security as for any warmth the position afforded. All the while the pair of Space Marines stood watch over them, arms at their sides, faces hidden behind an inexpressive helmet.

Jean-Robur wondered where the rest of the youths captured on Eokaroe might be, as there were easily two or three times this number stacked in the sky-craft that had carried him into orbit. And there had been perhaps a half-dozen of the craft on the green field of battle, as well, and who knew how many others landing at other spots around the planet. Hundreds of youths could have been captured, perhaps even thousands. But if so, why were only a dozen gathered here? Were the others being held in other halls, or perhaps still being tested by Apothecary or Librarian?

Then another Space Marine approached, encased in gold like the first two, though this one's armour incorporated various emblems and ornate honours that set him apart from the others. And unlike those who had stood watch over the dozen pups, this one had removed his helmet, and approached with his head bared and face exposed.

It took Jean-Robur but an instant to recognise the face of the Space Marine that had defeated and captured him on Eokaroe, along with the Sipangish swordsman and the barbaric whelp. Jean-Robur wondered now what the giant had said to the bound and helpless combatants, before the sweet-smelling gas had robbed them of their senses.

Following close behind the bare-headed Space Marine was a trio of servitors, each carrying a large vessel of some sort, but though the vessels were open at the top, from his vantage point Jean-Robur couldn't see what was held within.

The pair of Space Marines who had stood watch over the dozen youths stepped aside deferentially as the bare-headed Astartes joined them, taking up positions a pace behind and to either side. It was clear that Jean-Robur's estimation of the bare-headed Space Marine's standing based on his ornate heraldry and decoration had not been unfounded.

The bare-headed Space Marine glanced over his armoured shoulder, and motioned for the trio of servitors to approach. Then he turned back and regarded the dozen naked youths gathered before him.

'You will each step forwards and take an article from each of these three receptacles.' When none of the dozen youths moved, the Space Marine narrowed his gaze and barked, 'Now!'

Jean-Robur and the others rushed forwards, gathering around each of the three vessels as orderly as possible and reaching inside. From one Jean-Robur pulled a long rectangular strip of golden-coloured fabric, from another a waist-length shirt with three-quarter sleeves, and from the third a pair of ankle-high black boots tied together on a notched belt.

'Now dress yourselves,' the bare-headed Space Marine ordered. 'Tunics first, then use the belt to secure the loincloth in place, then the boots.'

The dozen youths glanced at one another in evident confusion, but after some brief experimentation all of them were able to get into the clothing without too much difficulty. It was hardly Caritaigne cotton and silk, Jean-Robur decided, but it was better than nakedness.

While Jean-Robur and the other youths were dressing, the bare-headed Space Marine exchanged a few quiet words with one of the other two, who then departed quickly on some errand.

'That's enough,' the Space Marine said as the now-clothed youths settled back into order. 'Now, I am Captain Taelos of the Imperial Fists 10th Company, Chief of Recruits. You twelve have been granted the honour of being accepted as aspirants to the most respected Chapter of the Adeptus Astartes, the scions of Primarch Rogal Dorn himself. The rest of those gathered by the recruiting mission on your world have been found wanting, by one measure or another, and have been removed from your ranks.'

None of the dozen spoke. Some of them even hesitated to breathe.

'We are now en route to rendezvous with the Imperial Fists' fortress-monastery, the *Phalanx*, and in the time our journey takes you will be tested further, in mind, body and spirit. Those who survive the coming examinations will be granted the greatest honour of all, and accepted as neophytes to the Imperial Fists.'

The voice of Captain Taelos boomed, reverberating even in an enormous hall large enough to swallow all lesser echoes and sounds.

'The way forward is difficult, and while many are called, few are chosen. If you survive, though, you will be transformed in a crucible of pain and fire into a sublime being, a living extension of the Emperor's will and a divine instrument of justice and vengeance. You will become battle-brothers of the Imperial Fists, welcomed into the brotherhood of Dorn, to serve Chapter, primarch and Emperor. You will be given the opportunity to lead a life of pure duty and service, and to one day die with honour and pride on the field of battle.'

Jean-Robur glanced to the youths on either side of them. Their oddly familiar faces wore rapt expressions, commingling respect and fear, and it was only then that Jean-Robur realised that he himself was wearing just such an expression.

'Today you are mere humans, little more than children. But if you show courage, and strength, and win through the trials that you will face, you will become something more than merely human. You will become proud Sons of Dorn!'

CHAPTER FIVE

ZATORI ZAN COULD feel the hatred burning within as
though it were a literal flame, a conflagration that
engulfed his insides and clouded his thoughts with
dark, black smoke. Though shorn of all body hair
and now clad in different clothing, the person
standing next to him was, without a doubt, the Caritaigne swordsman who had treacherously
murdered his master Father Nei with a cowardly
attack from the rear. With the pair of giant Space
Marines facing them, Zatori knew that he could not
yet give in to his thirst for vengeance, but as soon as
their attention was diverted he would strike.
Already his fingers clenched into vicious claws at
his sides, and he could almost feel the meat of the
Caritaigne's throat beneath his hands as he imagined choking the life from his nemesis.

119

This Captain Taelos still faced the dozen young men who'd been taken from the fields of Eokaroe, but as soon as the eyes of the Space Marines were off them, Zatori planned to put Father Nei's spirit to rest, and to send the ghost of the Caritaigne murderer off to the land of the spirits to meet its own well-deserved damnation.

'You will live by certain rules aboard this vessel,' Captain Taelos was saying, his voice booming through the empty air. 'And those who cannot abide by those rules will suffer the consequences.'

TALOC s'TONAN COULD scarcely contain himself. Only a short distance away, on the far side of the familiar-looking youth whose colouration suggested Caritaigne ancestry, stood the Sipangish who had bested his father Tonan on the field of combat. Tonan's blood-debt demanded that Taloc take the life of this Sipangish at his first opportunity. Without an ironbrand in his grasp, though, Taloc knew that he would have to accomplish the task with his bare hands. He would first need to get the Caritaigne in-between them out of the way, and from the looks of the two Space Marines who faced them, Taloc felt certain that any of the twelve youths gathered in the chamber who stepped out of line would be dealt with quickly and, to all indications, harshly. He would need to wait for the right moment to strike, or else Tonan's blood-debt might remain unpaid.

In his thoughts, Taloc rehearsed the motions he would use, the blow to the Sipangish's nose with the heel of Taloc's hand to disorient his opponent. And while the Sipangish dealt with his broken nose and the flow of blood from his nostrils, Taloc would follow with a blow from the hard back of his forearm against the Sipangish's glottis, crushing the windpipe and cutting off his air supply. Then, assuming he had not yet been stopped and he was able to get his hands into position, he would simply wrench the Sipangish's head around on his shoulders, snapping the Sipangish's neck and ending his life in one swift movement.

If it all went according to Taloc's plan, the Sipangish would not even have the opportunity to react, much less flee from the attack.

But for the moment the two Imperial Fists were still keeping their eyes on the twelve, and the bareheaded Captain Taelos was still talking.

'Aspirants will conduct themselves as befits candidates for acceptance into the ranks of the Astartes,' the Imperial Fists captain went on. 'Neither fraternisation nor aggression will be tolerated.'

JEAN-ROBUR DU QUESTE was still mourning the loss of his body hair when Captain Taelos left off talking as the Space Marine he had sent on an errand returned, dragging another tunic-and-loincloth-wearing youth. This youth, though, was not as freshly shaven as Jean-Robur and the rest of the dozen Triandrians, but had a short fuzz of rusty-brown hair growing from his scalp, at least three or four weeks worth of growth. And the brassy colour of his skin did not resemble in the least the pale hues of Caritaigne, his reddish hair nothing like the smooth black hair of Sipang, and his dark green eyes were nothing like the pale blue eyes of the barbarians of Eokaroe.

Jean-Robur had almost got to the point that he could accept that the Imperial Fists had come to Triandr from beyond the skies. The massive ship and its mechanical monsters were proof enough of that, to say nothing about the helmet which distilled strange words and concepts into the wearer's mind. But the realisation that the rust-haired, brassy-skinned youth before him was from another world, too, was more difficult to take.

Perhaps it was that the larger-than-life Astartes *looked* like they belonged to some other sphere than the mortal world Jean-Robur had known all of his life, and fit in well enough with the stories and legends of the distant past that Jean-Robur had heard as a child. But this youth was no larger than Jean-Robur, no more visibly powerful, and did not appear to have at his disposal technologies and knowledge far beyond the grasp of any Triandrian. But his strange coloration and unusual features suggested that he *was* from another world, and no branch from any family tree that had taken root on the world of Jean-Robur's birth.

So taken aback was Jean-Robur by the startling realisation of the newcomer's otherworldliness that he didn't at first pay much attention to the fact that the rusty-haired youth was being dragged bodily behind one of the Space Marines. But then Jean-Robur noticed the expression of defeat, deep-seated fear and simmering anger on the brassy-skinned newcomer's lean face. And though the newcomer did not appear to be resisting – and really, Jean-Robur wondered, what *would* be the hope of an unarmed mortal youth struggling against the impossibly strong arms of one of the armoured giants? – it was clear from the newcomer's face that he would rather be anywhere but in this chamber, being dragged before Captain Taelos in the full view of the dozen Triandrians.

'Here is an example that you should all fix in your minds,' Captain Taelos said as the youth was thrown to his knees by the Space Marine escorting him. 'Remember this moment when you contemplate any action which is not in accordance with the rules of this ship and this Chapter.'

CAPTAIN TAELOS SCARCELY glanced at the aspirant who cowered on the deckplates before him. Less than four weeks had passed – four subjective weeks, at least, as several of them had been spent in transit through the warp, and as such any attempt to determine an absolute measure of the amount of objective time to have passed was not even worth contemplating – since the youth had been among those culled from a feral world visited only twice before, long centuries ago, by an Imperial Fists recruiting mission. This youth in particular had been selected from among the tribesmen by Taelos himself, and the captain had harboured hopes that this aspirant might well go the distance, and be welcomed as a neophyte by the Chapter on their return to the *Phalanx*. But then recent events unfolded which made clear that the aspirant did not meet the Imperial Fists' standards of discipline and self-control. Nor, for that matter, would the aspirant be granted the opportunity to gain any discipline he might currently lack.

Once a candidate proved themselves unsuitable, for any reason, the risks involved with keeping them on through the initiate stages – whether motivated by the vain hope of improving them or in an attempt to somehow eliminate the flaws or by an act of sheer desperation – were simply too great. Once unsuitable, always unsuitable, and so the Chapter was always quick to winnow undesirables from the ranks of aspirants.

'Listen well,' Taelos said, his gaze fixed on the dozen Triandrians before him, his expression set and unreadable. 'No aspirant may behave aggressively towards any other, or goad another into acting aggressively against them. Any such disruptions will not under any circumstances be allowed. Those who transgress against this simple precept will be dealt with severely.'

Taelos raised a gauntleted fist, and extended a single finger at the wretch kneeling before him, green eyes lowered to the deck-plates, shoulders hunched in an attitude of defeat but with defiance still radiating from him, teeth gritted and bared.

'This one has been amongst the hopeful candidates since before the *Capulus* reached your world, and he has already passed examinations which you twelve have yet to face. He is a fine physical specimen with a keen mind who likely would, if he were to survive the implantation procedure, make a fine addition to the Imperial Fists Chapter. However, though he fits both the physical and psychological profiles required to become a neophyte, and is free from any taint of warp or mental instability, he nevertheless is completely unsuitable, and will not be afforded the honour of becoming an Astartes.'

Taelos scanned the dozen Triandrians with his gaze, monitoring their facial expressions, their gestures, even the non-verbal expression of their postures and slight hand movements. He studied and noted all that the aspirants were telling him without the youths ever realising they were communicating a thing.

'This unsuitability has nothing whatsoever to do with his fitness to fight, or the keenness of his mind to grasp strategy and tactics. No, this aspirant is being expelled from your ranks because he lacks self-control, and cannot bring himself to follow the simple orders and precepts handed down to him.'

The aspirant glanced up to the side, his eyes falling on Taelos's face for the briefest of instants. The captain saw in those green orbs a momentary spark of rebellion, the fires of anger still burning somewhere behind the irises. Not deigning to strike a blow, Captain Taelos merely swung one of his massive booted feet forwards a fraction of an arc, the tip of the boot striking the aspirant's midsection without sufficient force to injury, or even bruise, but with enough of an impact to knock the rusty-haired aspirant off his knees and send him sprawling across the deckplates on his side. Taelos knew that any respect the Triandrian dozen might have harboured for the still-defiant aspirant would waver and wane as they saw him lying so indecorously on the ground like a discarded rag.

'This one before you,' Taelos went on, 'this *wretch*, attacked one of his fellow aspirants in the dormitory. The assailed did not survive the assault, his injuries being too grave and too sudden for mending. By ending the life of another aspirant, the assailant has cost the Imperial Fists one potential neophyte who might one day have gone on to join the ranks of the Astartes, and become a proud bearer of the gene-seed of Rogal Dorn himself. As though this transgression was not insult enough to the Chapter, the assailant's actions force us to expel him from your ranks, as well, and thus have his actions cost the Imperial Fists not merely one potential neophyte but *two*.'

Taelos paused for a moment, for effect.

'This one no longer belongs among you. He is not now worthy to wear the gold armour of the Imperial Fists, nor will he ever be. Instead, he is to be reduced in status to a Chapter serf, and banished to the bowels of this strike cruiser. There he will tend her engines for the rest of his natural life, and if the Techmarine so wills it perhaps he will continue to serve the ship and Chapter as a servitor even after death claims him.'

Taelos motioned to the battle-brother who had escorted the wretch from his place in the holding cell a few moments before. 'Brother-Sergeant Hilts?'

'Yes, brother-captain?'

'Escort him to the enginarium deck, and deliver him to Techmarine Phaestus with my compliments.'

'At once, brother-captain,' Sergeant Hilts answered, smashing his arm against his armour's plastron with his hand clenched in a fist, then raising the fist in the Chapter's salute before crashing it once more against his chest.

Taelos turned back to regard the new candidates before him.

'Learn from this one's example. His chances of becoming an Astartes are over. Your chance still lies before you. Will you seize it, and join our brotherhood? Or will you allow it to slip through your fingers? The choice is yours.'

ONCE THE SPACE Marine sergeant had unceremoniously dragged the ousted candidate away, the captain dismissed the assembled aspirants, and ordered the other Imperial Fist in attendance to escort them to their dormitory. Taloc could not help noticing that the expelled candidate, who had managed to maintain something resembling a steely resolve while hearing the captain recite the doom that had befallen him, had when being dragged away lost all composure and restraint. Tears had flowed from the dark green eyes, leaving snail traces down the youth's cheeks, and as he was taken away from the chamber and out of the Triandrians' sight, the expelled aspirant had screamed until he was hoarse, his harsh shouts like the dying cry of some wounded animal. While the Triandrians were being led away through another corridor which branched off from the chamber, Taloc could still hear the faint echoes of the poor wretch's distant cries, as faint as leaves rustling by night in trees overhead.

Perhaps the blood-debt of Taloc's fallen father would need to remain unpaid for a time yet. Though he knew little of the horrors and hardships that awaited any transgressors in the strange depths of the engineering section, Taloc was certain at least that he was in no hurry to sample them for himself. He would bide his time, and wait for an opportune moment to strike his father's killer when such a fate would not as a result be his.

THE FINAL PLAINTIVE wails of the youth being dragged to a life – and afterlife, perhaps? – of laborious servitude were still dying in Zatori's ears as they approached the dormitory, and seemed to Zatori to echo the dishonoured cries of his late master in the land of the spirits. But for the moment it appeared necessary for Father Nei's death to go unavenged, and his murderer to remain unscathed. Though he was unsure how Sipangish notions of honour might judge the strict discipline of the Imperial Fists strike cruiser, he knew enough to be certain that he would do his master's spirit little service if he failed to kill the Caritaigne murderer outright, and in the failed attempt got himself packed off to the ship's underbelly. He would need to wait for the perfect opportunity to strike, when he could be sure to end the Caritaigne's life without the slightest possibility that the company Apothecary might mend his injuries. Only then would he feel free to put Father Nei's spirit to rest. If after accomplishing his revenge honourably Zatori's fate was to be consigned to the hardships of the engineering section for the rest of his days, or even the rest of eternity, so be it.

THE SPACE MARINE threaded a course through the massive strike cruiser with Jean-Robur and the other Triandrians following close behind. They walked down corridors longer than the longest boulevards in Caritaigne, through halls that would have easily contained the largest warships that sailed on the seas of Triandr, and in and out of chambers not only large enough to contain the entire royal palace of Caritaigne, as the battlefield of Eokaroe had been, but practically large enough to contain the whole of the island of Eokaroe itself.

Finally, when Jean-Robur thought for certain that they must either reach the ship's end or his mind would burst from the vain attempt to fit the sight of it all within his skull, the Space Marine stopped before a large metal door. Wide enough for two members of the Adeptus Astartes in power armour to walk in abreast without brushing the frame on either side, as tall as three Astartes standing atop one another's shoulders, the door opened easily with a single touch from the Imperial Fist, swinging noiselessly on its hinges. Whether the door was simply superbly balanced, or the strength of the Imperial Fist in armour was even greater than Jean-Robur had anticipated, or both or neither, Jean-Robur could not say.

Though dwarfed by the grandeur and scale of the areas of the strike cruiser they had passed through to reach this point, the door was still on its own merits a massive thing to behold, far larger and grander than anything Jean-Robur had seen in his years on Triandr. But for the entire door's massive size, the room which lay beyond was unimposing and sedate by comparison. Longer than it was wide, the chamber was roughly the size of the grand hall in the Caritaigne royal palace, which Jean-Robur had visited only on rare formal occasion when his ties of family required he make a brief appearance. And if its size might have impressed him before his perspective had been widened out of all proportion by the rest of the *Capulus*, the room's fixtures and finishing were nowhere near so impressive. Along either long wall were arrayed beds every few paces, really little more than rude cots that were – somewhat distressingly – the

same dimensions in width, length and breadth of the coffins which rested within the du Queste family crypts. Aside from the cots, of which there were some hundreds in all, most of them apparently untenanted, there was a row of long tables which ran lengthwise in single-file along the spine of the room, with benches on either side, fashioned of some dull-finished metal with which Jean-Robur was not familiar.

When the twelve Triandrian aspirants entered through the now-opened door, there were already several dozen youths inside, perhaps as many as a hundred. All of them were wearing the same belted tunics, loincloths and boots, marking them out as fellow aspirants, but from the varying degrees of hairlessness – some with their pates barely shadowed by a dusting of newgrown hair, others with a crop hanging in a shag over their foreheads and the tops of their ears – it was clear that some of these other candidates had only been onboard the *Capulus* for a short time, while others had been on the strike cruiser for considerably longer.

And if Jean-Robur had found it difficult to wrap his mind around the idea of a single native from another world that was roughly his size and age when he looked upon the aspirant that Captain Taelos was consigning to the netherworld of engineering, his mind threatened to explode out from the confines of his skull on first seeing the rest of his fellow aspirants. For here there were other youths not simply from another world, but seemingly from *dozens* of worlds. The riot of skin tones covered everything from the pale white of bleached bone, to the deep red of Triandr's moon, to the brown hues of polished oak, to the inky black of a moonless night, and all values in between. And the amazing variation of facial and body features! Everything from noses short and fat to long and thin; faces round or pointed; small ears and large; long, dexterous fingers and short, muscular digits. But for all their variability, Jean-Robur felt at first glance as though there were some indefinable quality in common with all of them, some fire burning in the eyes, perhaps, that bespoke a sense of resolution and stamina that most of the men Jean-Robur had encountered on Triandr had seemed to lack.

Was it this light burning inside that Captain Taelos and the other Imperial Fists had seen inside Jean-Robur and the others brought up from the surface of their home world? Had the Imperial Fists been seeking that same fire on recruiting missions to other worlds, as well, perhaps on dozens of planets stately circling distant stars somewhere out beyond the curtain of night?

If so, and this inner fire was the quality which the candidates shared which made them attractive to the Chapter, it was clear that it was a fire which could be extinguished, as evidenced by the poor wretch trundled off to the engineering section.

Despite the strangeness of his circumstances, though, and the somewhat bewildering fact of humans living upon far-distant worlds, and ships capable of travelling between the stars, Jean-Robur was not terribly discomfited by his experiences. Since he'd accepted that he was *not* dead and suffering the torments of the damned, but was rather alive but in circumstances that he'd never before dreamed to be possible, everything else about the current state of affairs had been relatively easy to accept. His principle concern at the moment, as things stood, was that his stomach growled with hunger.

The Imperial Fists Chapter had culled a group of potential candidates from the world below, deeming that these thousands might be worthy of being inducted into the ranks of the Adeptus Astartes. Well, Jean-Robur had *always* considered himself worthy of special recognition, of being singled out from the herd of such peers as his cousin Benoit Vioget, marked out for a position of privilege. Was it so strange that holy warriors from beyond the stars should mark him out as being just as worthy of recognition and privilege?

And the fact that all but a dozen of the thousands of Triandrians brought to the *Capulus* had in the end proved unworthy in one way or another did little to dampen Jean-Robur's sure conviction that he deserved any honours and accolades coming his way. After all, wasn't he among the dozen who did *not* prove to be unworthy? And wasn't that proof enough of his special quality?

Surely, Jean-Robur was convinced, he would breeze through whatever examinations and initiations awaited them. And in short order he would be a proud member of the Imperial Fists, with all of the rights and privileges appertaining thereto, without any unnecessary pain or hardship.

That was what Jean-Robur believed. He would soon learn, however, to his dismay and disappointment, that he was entirely wrong.

'...AND WHEN NOT otherwise engaged, you will remain here in the dormitory, your barracks for the remainder of our journey,' the helmeted Imperial Fist was saying, his voice somewhat distorted by passage through the helmet which hid his features. 'These are the rules of conduct that have been laid out for you. Any deviance from these rules will be dealt with accordingly, and without mercy. Better that you should break now, and prove yourself unable to continue with the initiation, than to fail later, whether in the process of implantation which precious organs might be wasted on you unnecessarily, or later when you take to the field of battle as a Scout, where failure on your part might additionally mean the loss of your fellow Scouts, the veteran-sergeant who will command you, or even the battle-brothers who you will follow into battle.'

The Space Marine paused, and swivelled his helmeted head back and forth, his hidden gaze taking in the dozen Triandrians who still clustered near the entrance to the dormitory chamber.

'Are any of you unclear about the rules of conduct as they have been explained to you? Do any of you require additional clarification?'

None of the twelve newest additions to the ranks of the aspirants spoke up, but remained silent and still, eyes on the Imperial Fist.

'Then you will be expected to comply. Deviate, and disciplinary action will follow.'

The Space Marine stepped closer to the open door.

'You have until the next watch to rest and refresh, at which point the examinations will continue.' Pausing at the doorway, the Astartes' helmet swivelled to the other hundred or so aspirants in the dormitory. The offspring of far-flung outposts of humanity, natives of hive worlds, feudal worlds, feral worlds and even some void-born sons of far traders – they represented all of the many-faceted aspects of the Imperium of Mankind, all of the far-flung children of Terra, whose God-Emperor it was the sacred duty of the Imperial Fists Chapter to defend. From among these hopefuls gathered here, it was hoped, might come the next generation of Sons of Dorn.

'I will leave you now…' the Imperial Fist began, and then saw one of the new Triandrians gesture for his attention.

'When we will eat?' the young Triandrian said in Imperial Gothic before the Space Marine had even had a chance to respond, his tone haughty.

The Space Marine, still standing in the doorway, stepped back into the room. Perhaps it was too soon to hope that these aspirants might one day become Imperial Fists, at that.

'I will restate the pertinent rules, Aspirant du Queste, but only this once. Aspirants will not address their superiors unless invited to do so, under any circumstances. Nor will aspirants address one another in the presence of a superior, without explicit permission to speak. Failure to comply will earn the offender disciplinary action, up to and including time spent within the pain-glove.'

The aspirants who had already been onboard the *Capulus* for some time, and had seen the pain-glove in operation, involuntarily recoiled somewhat, many of them backing a step away from the Triandrian who had spoken up, as though proximity to his offence might earn them the same discipline.

'That is all. I leave you now, and in short order you will be taken before the Chaplain who will instruct you, in advance of the next round of examinations.'

With that the Space Marine stepped back through the open door, which he then closed behind them, leaving the aspirants alone in the dormitory.

ZATORI ZAN NARROWED his gaze angrily at the Caritaigne who had murdered Father Nei, who he now learned was to be addressed in this place as 'Aspirant du Queste'. Zatori glared at him, imagining all the myriad ways in which he might end this 'Jean-Robur's' life – crush his windpipe between his hands, break his neck against the hard edge of one of the metal benches, punch him hard in the nose with an uppercut to drive the bone up into his brain – but knew it would have to be done in an honourable way, as defined by the culture of Sipang, so as to put Father Nei's spirit to rest, and in a situation in which there was no chance that the Caritaigne might survive or that Zatori would be stopped or apprehended before the deed was done. And while he stood considering all of the factors leading up to his hotly desired revenge, Zatori was startled when the Caritaigne turned and looked him right in the eye with an expression of indignant outrage on his face.

'To damnation with his talk of pain-gloves and discipline and all that!' the one named du Queste snarled. 'Especially since he didn't even answer my question!'

It was clear to Zatori that Jean-Robur did not recognise him as the Sipangish who had cried out vengeance on him. It was equally as clear that Jean-Robur did not expect any response in particular from Zatori, but was simply venting his anger and looking to the young Sipangish as a convenient target.

Even so, this Jean-Robur continued to glare at him, eyes narrowed and brow furrowed, as if he demanded *some* satisfaction.

'I...' Zatori began, unsure what to say to his hated enemy.

He was saved from having to compose any meaningful response by the arrival of another aspirant with yellow hair that looked as fine as cornsilk, who put his hand on Zatori's shoulder in a companionable gesture and came to stand beside him, smiling into Jean-Robur's outraged face.

'Meal period is in a short while, friend,' the newcomer said with a smile. 'A little patience and your appetite will be sated.' He paused, and his smile widened somewhat. 'Admittedly, it will not be the *best* fare you've ever tasted, but with any amount of luck it will not be the *worst*, either.'

Jean-Robur turned his gaze from Zatori to this interloper and sneered. 'And who are *you*, to so freely address a stranger as "friend"?'

The yellow-haired aspirant extended his hand, thumb up and palm perpendicular to the floor, as though he expected Jean-Robur to grasp it. 'My name is Aden Kelso, but everyone here just calls me "Aspirant Kelso". I'm from the planet–'

'I have little interest in learning which world you call home, "Kelso",' Jean-Robur answered icily, 'which is no doubt some strange and alien place which I will never have need nor occasion to visit. I'm only now getting used to the idea of other human worlds out there, so please don't bore me with your *biographical* details.'

'Well…' the one named Kelso replied, looking a little confused. He began to draw back his hand, on his face an expression suggesting disappointment.

Perhaps it was the fact that his hated enemy was being needlessly cruel to this yellow-haired aspirant that drove Zatori into action. Or perhaps it was the memory of seeing a young girl, like Zatori a fellow

low-born Sipangish, being treated poorly once by a rich and overfed merchant who'd had one too many cups of rice wine. That girl had worn just such an expression as this Kelso now wore, one that commingled hurt feelings and confused bewilderment. Zatori felt the overwhelming urge to come to the aid of anyone who wore such an expression, and to ally himself to anyone poorly treated by this accursed Jean-Robur.

'Well met, Kelso,' Zatori said, reaching over and taking hold of Kelso's hand. 'I am Zatori Zan, former squire to the master warrior-elite Father Nei, and I am from the island of Sipang on the world called Triandr.'

Kelso smiled, and tightened his grip around Zatori's hand. 'Well met, indeed, friend Zatori. One day we may find ourselves on the field of battle together, and it would serve us well to have a friend at our sides, yes?'

Zatori nodded, returning Kelso's smile with a faint grin of his own. But he could not help glancing over at Jean-Robur. Already the Caritaigne had lost interest in the discussion and thrown up his hands in disgust as he went off in search of someone else to whom he could complain about his hunger.

Taloc s'Tonan watched the Sipangish faithless talking to a pair of aspirants, one of them with strikingly bright yellow hair of a hue Taloc had never seen before. When the Sipangish who'd bested Tonan turned and clasped hands with the yellow-haired aspirant, the third aspirant in the huddle broke away and came towards the place where Taloc stood.

Taloc could feel the weight of his father's blood-debt pulling on his shoulders, and he stared at the back of the Sipangish faithless's head, imagining breaking it open like an egg against the hard floor beneath their feet.

'Hold, stranger,' Taloc said, motioning towards the Triandrian who stalked in his direction. It seemed strange to address a faithless in a shared tongue, much less one who had invaded the sacred places of Eokaroe, but the knowledge of Imperial Gothic which bubbled up through Taloc's thoughts made possible communication that would at any earlier time in his life have been impossible. 'That Sipangish you addressed a moment ago. What did he say?'

Close to, Taloc could see that this was a Caritaigne, the same one he'd stood beside while the Imperial Fists captain had addressed the new recruits. When he heard Taloc's question, the Caritaigne aspirant quirked the slightest of sly smiles.

'Well, I find I prefer "stranger" to "friend" under the circumstances.' Then, seeing Taloc's confused expression, he added, 'The Sipangish bastard just spoke his name and provenance, as if any cared to hear it, and then went back to yammering with that yellow-haired ray of sunshine.' He paused, put a hand on his stomach and added, 'Gods above, but I'm hungry.'

'His name,' Taloc asked, 'what is it?'

The Caritaigne thought for a moment. 'Zato, I think? No. It was Za*tori*. That sounds right.' He shook his head, grimacing slightly. 'I suppose it's too much to hope that you might answer a question for *me*, now.'

Taloc kept his expression stony and unreadable, but gave a slight motion with the fingers of one hand, as if waving something towards himself. *Ask me*. It was then that he saw the door open at the far side of the dormitory hall, and the first of the hunched shapes trundle in.

'When are we going to get to *eat*?' the Caritaigne demanded, petulantly. 'I'm *starving*!'

Taloc merely pointed past the Caritaigne's shoulder, and said, 'Now.'

The Caritaigne turned, and saw the line of servitors carrying trays over to the row of tables, twists of steam curling up from the contents. To Taloc's nostrils was wafted a smell that, while it seemed bland and unrecognisable, was still enough to make his mouth begin watering. He could not identify precisely what the trays contained, but knew immediately what it was – *food*.

The Caritaigne turned back and gave Taloc a grin. 'Now *that's* what I call a prompt answer!'

As the Caritaigne headed off to take his place at the table, along which the aspirants with stubble and locks were already congregating, Taloc turned and glanced in the direction of the Sipangish faithless who had killed his father.

'Zatori,' Taloc said under his breath in a voice scarcely above a whisper. 'I name you nemesis. Perhaps not now, and perhaps not soon, but one day you will pay my father's blood-debt. This I swear.'

Then Taloc's stomach growled audibly. The blood-debt would wait, he knew. For the moment, there were more pressing concerns. It would do his father no good if he starved to death.

THE MEAL WAS, as Jean-Robur had been warned, fairly uninspired. It was, in fact, bland and all but tasteless. Still, it was warm and filling, and when it was done his hunger was gone. The fact that he could not identify any of the constituents of the meal itself was a matter he chose not to dwell upon.

After the aspirants had finished eating, the servitors cleared the empty trays away, and clanked and wheeled their way back out of the dormitory and out of sight.

The twelve Triandrians had eaten in silence, so intent were they on sating their gnawing hunger – how long *had* it been since they had properly eaten, and not been sustained by the fluids poured and pumped into them by the Apothecary's needles and tubes? It was not until Jean-Robur's tray was picked clean that he noted that the other aspirants, those whose heads were shadowed with stubble or with ragged locks, were almost as silent, hardly speaking or even making a sound. Was it something in their various cultures which drove them to dine in silence? Or perhaps a trait they developed in their time onboard the *Capulus*?

It was not until they were taken before the Chaplain that Jean-Robur got his answer.

After the servitors' exit, Jean-Robur considered stretching out on one of the cots and getting some sleep, when the great door at the head of the dormitory swung open once more. When the doorway was completely open and unobstructed, a Chapter serf strode into the room. The aspirants were ordered to gather together, and then were escorted through the ship to a hall where a towering figure waited on a massive rostrum.

Encased in coal-black power armour, from which countless ribbons and scrolls fluttered in the slight breeze, and with his face hidden behind a mask fashioned in the shape of a silver skull, the figure stepped forwards to the edge of the rostrum with footsteps that echoed like thunder, punctuated by the tap-tap-tap of his skull-topped staff.

'I am Chaplain Dominicus,' the towering figure announced, his words booming like the voice of a thunderstorm. 'The Emperor's blessings on you, aspirants, and the Venerable Dorn keep you in his graces.'

All around him the aspirants who had already been onboard when the Triandrians arrived bowed their heads in respect, averting their eyes from the Chaplain's silver death-mask.

'You are here to begin your instruction in the proper worship of the Emperor, to be familiarised with the rudiments of the Cult of Dorn, and

introduced to the noble heritage it may one day be
your privilege to carry forward.'

The Chaplain's gaze passed over the faces of the
assembled aspirants.

'First, an instructive lesson, and then we will
adjourn to the chapel where you will each be introduced in turn to the pain-glove, which will aid in
clarifying your thoughts. Now, those of you who
come from worlds who have not lost their connec-
tions with Holy Terra may have heard of the
Column of Glory, the tower of rainbow metal near
the Emperor's own throne room which is embedded with the armour of the valiant Imperial Fists
who gave their lives selflessly in the defence of the
Emperor during the dark days of the Horus Heresy.
What you may *not* have heard are the details surrounding the battle, or the ways our fallen brethren
exemplified our Chapter's absolute and uncontested mastery of siege warfare...'

The Chaplain continued on, but Jean-Robur's
attentions were elsewhere. What *was* the pain-glove?

Jean-Robur's imagination filled with thoughts of
gauntlets fitted with spikes and blades, or vices, or
needles and barbs. The Chaplain continued to talk
about the glorious history of the Chapter and its
primarch, Rogal Dorn, but Jean-Robur heard none
of it. His thoughts were only on the pain-glove.

CHAPTER SIX

WHEN THE CHAPLAIN called on Jean-Robur du Queste to step forwards, Jean-Robur could not help but feel that it was an ironic bit of justice. So often he had transgressed the rules in Caritaigne and never been caught, and here he was the first to be put in the pain-glove? And not as punishment for any transgression, but simply to help him 'focus his thoughts'?

Jean-Robur du Queste was to be the first of the Triandrian aspirants to spend his time in the pain-glove, which the Imperial Fists used not only as a disciplinary measure, but also as a routine part of their training and initiation. All of the aspirants would take their turn in the nerve-searing pain-glove, as Jean-Robur learned when the Chaplain explained the ways in which the Chapter viewed the device as an aid to focus and meditation. But knowing that he would not be the last to be subjected to the treatment did not make him any more eager to be the first.

* * *

THE FULL RANKS of the aspirants onboard the *Capulus* gathered in the chapel, arrayed in ordered rows on hard and unforgiving metal pews that ran from one end of the nave to the other. Chaplain Dominicus stood at an altar positioned at the apse, between two great pillars upon which were positioned holy images, on the left an icon of the God-Emperor fashioned in gold, on the right a representation of Primarch Rogal Dorn carved from alabaster. A heavy fug of incense hung over the massive chamber from the censers positioned throughout the chapel, and the golden light which streamed through the faceted panes of the ornate windows high overhead glinted off particles of dust which floated lazily through the air, causing them to flash and sparkle momentarily like miniature stars in the far distance.

'Since our earliest origins,' Chaplain Dominicus declaimed, 'we Imperial Fists have found strength in meditation, and focus in pain.'

The death-masked Chaplain paused, and touched a runic stud embedded in the altar before him. Immediately before the altar was what appeared to be a circular pattern of tiles, with spiralling arms radiating out from the centre. With the sound of machinery grinding away somewhere far below their feet, the spiralling arms began to twist, and a hole appeared at the centre of the pattern, growing gradually larger and larger.

'Scripture teaches that Rogal Dorn once resisted the pain-glove for seven days until at last he was gifted with a vision of the Emperor. Presented with the sure and certain knowledge that the sublimed master of us all still watched over humanity from the Golden Throne, our noble primarch ordered that the VII Legion should symbolically enter the pain-glove, and thereby transformed and clarified by its purifying fire the Imperial Fists emerged from the other side as a Chapter of the *Codex Astartes*.'

The hatch which had been hidden in the patterned tiles continued to iris open, until with a sound like a weary and laboured sigh it finally came to a halt, revealing the mouth of a shaft as wide as a Space Marine in power armour, that descended from the golden light of the chapel into pitch darkness below.

'So too do each of us enter the pain-glove as mortal humans when first brought within the compass of the Imperial Fists, and through the clarifying fire and pain of initiation emerge eventually transformed into superhuman Astartes.'

With another sigh, though one of lamentation and not of laboured weariness, a steel framework began to rise from the mouth of the shaft. It was a gibbet, a roughly cubical scaffolding of metal rods, from which was suspended what appeared at first glance to be a representation of the flayed skin of a grown man. With legs and arms and torso fabricated of a transparent material threaded with a network of needle-thin silvery wires, it lacked only a head and the tops of the shoulders to make it fully man-shaped.

'The pain-glove,' the Chaplain continued with an increased degree of reverence in his voice, 'is an all-encompassing tunic of electrofibres suspended in a steel gibbet. These electrofibres interact directly with the nerves in the supplicant's flesh, sending excruciating pain signals to the brain without causing any physical harm to the body itself. The stimulation produces the same sensations as being burned alive, but with no actual damage being done... to the flesh, at least. The supplicant is kept conscious throughout the process, while waves of pain wash over him, but there are limits to the body's ability to process such intense sensations of pain, whether real or stimulated. There comes a point at which the nerves become so burned out by the stimulation that they continue to broadcast the pain signals to the brain, even after the pain-glove is removed. A supplicant who reaches this state will suffer irreversible insanity, awash constantly in a never-ending torrent of searing pain for the rest of their days.'

The Chaplain pressed another rune stud embedded in the altar, and the framework of the steel gibbet expanded, stretching the fabric of the pain-glove and widening the opening where the head and shoulders would be. Then the gibbet slowly lowered back into the shaft, until the mouth of the pain-glove was level with the surrounding floorplates.

'Aspirant du Queste, step forwards.'

Rising from the metal pew where he sat with the others, Jean-Robur walked forwards, coming to a stop at the edge of the circular hole in the floor.

'Disrobe, aspirant,' Chaplain Dominicus ordered, pointing to Jean-Robur with the tip of his staff.

With evident hesitation, the aspirant removed his belted tunic, loincloth and boots. When he had done, he stood naked, hairless and exposed, at the edge of the shaft.

'Drop into the pain-glove, aspirant.'

Jean-Robur swallowed hard, his hands tightened into fists at his sides, and then stepped off the edge of the floor. He dropped straight down like a stone falling to earth, and then the transparent Glove caught him. With a sound like a sigh of regret, the framework raised back up above the floor, closing as it did, so that the stretched fabric of the pain-glove retracted, tightening and settling around the curves of Jean-Robur's body.

'Aspirants!' Chaplain Dominicus called out to those assembled in the chapel. 'Hear now the words of the Liturgy of Pain.'

The Chaplain lifted his arms at his sides, his staff held high overhead.

> *'Pain is a lesson that the universe teaches us.*
> *Pain is the preserver from injury.*
> *Pain perpetuates our lives.*
> *Pain is the healing, purifying scalpel of our*
> *souls.*
> *Pain is the wine of communion with heroes.*

Pain is the alembic which transmutes mere mortal into immortal.'

The Chaplain turned to his left, and pointed his staff at the alabaster statue of Primarch Rogal Dorn atop the right-most pillar.

'Turn your face to the image of Rogal Dorn, aspirant. You must learn to focus past the pain, and to strengthen your link with our primarch.'

And then Chaplain Dominicus pressed a final button embedded in the altar, and the pain-glove was at last activated.

THE PAIN-GLOVE felt to Jean-Robur like an unending eternity of agony. From the first moment that his nerves were set afire by contact with the electrofibres, it was as if he were consumed by actual raging flames. So intense was the sensation of burning that Jean-Robur could almost smell the bitter tang of scorched flesh, and could easily imagine his skin darkening and bones cracking as the fire transformed living tissue into char and ash. But even through the excruciating agony he remained completely awake and fully aware, the mechanism of the pain-glove preventing his brain from shutting down in the face of such overwhelming sensation.

And through it all, Jean-Robur's eyes were fixed on the alabaster countenance of Rogal Dorn, primarch of the Chapter and progenitor of the gene-seed that all Imperial Fists shared. Jean-Robur felt as though he were adrift in a sea of molten fire, swamped by tidal waves of pain, and yet here remained a constant and steady guiding light to lead him safely to the other side. Like a beacon on a shore, lighting the way for wayward ships at sail, the pure white image of Rogal Dorn showed Jean-Robur the way through the pain.

For year after endless year, it seemed to him, Jean-Robur hung within the grip of the pain-glove. But while the electrofibres and opiate-blocks would not let him grow accustomed to the searing pain, each passing moment as fresh with torment and agony as the first shocked instant, still Jean-Robur kept his eyes on the idol of Rogal Dorn.

Pain is a lesson the universe teaches us, he remembered the Chaplain reciting. *Pain is the alembic which transmutes mere mortal into immortal.*

Jean-Robur would learn this lesson, he swore to himself and to the cold and flawless features of the primarch. He would learn this lesson, survive the purifying fires of this alembic, and emerge on the other side the stronger for it. And he would go on to survive the coming examinations and initiations, the implants and the operations, and take his place among the Adeptus Astartes. And he would not do so for the same reasons that he had laboured to win his spurs on the field of battle, when he had gone to war to earn the privileges due a blooded son of Caritaigne; he would win through because the alternative was a life of miserable servitude, at best, and death and dishonour, at worst.

He would grit his teeth and accept the pain as his due, and would be the better for it.

Already an eternity had passed though, Jean-Robur thought. Surely the excruciation of the pain-glove would soon be at an end.

ZATORI ZAN AND the rest of the Triandrian aspirants had been seated on the front pews, closest to the altar at the apse of the chapel. On one side of him sat a Sipangish youth he recognised from the battlefleet that had sailed to Eokaroe, and on the other sat the Eokaroean tribesman who had stood beside Zatori when they had dared face the Imperial Fist captain on the battlefield.

Watching his hated enemy writhe in the pain-glove, Zatori felt a mix of emotion. On the one hand, he found some satisfaction in seeing the murderer receive such well-deserved pain; on the other hand, though, and knowing full well that he himself would soon be subjected to the same treatment – perhaps *his* would be the next name the Chaplain called? – Zatori could not help feeling some faint stirrings of sympathy for the young Caritaigne.

Now the Chaplain reached forwards and pressed a stud on the altar with a gauntleted finger. Then, as Jean-Robur slumped in the transparent grip of the Glove, Chaplain Dominicus pointed his crozius at the aspirants closest to the steel gibbet, which happened to be Zatori and the Eokaroean sitting beside him.

'Aspirants Zatori and Taloc,' the voice of the Chaplain echoed through the Chapel. 'Step forwards and assist Aspirant du Queste in removing himself from the pain-glove.'

With a quick glance at the Eokaroean tribesman beside him – Taloc, the Chaplain had said – Zatori rose from the pew and stepped to the edge of the opening in the floor. Then, as the framework opened slowly like the skeletal petals of some strange metal flower, stretching the transparent fabric of the pain-glove, Zatori and Taloc reached in and each took hold of one of Jean-Robur's arms. With the Caritaigne hanging limp between them, the two aspirants lifted him clear as the scaffolding and the now-empty pain-glove retreated back into the shaft underfoot, and with a whisper the hatch began slowly to iris shut again.

The three Triandrians stood before the Chaplain, with Taloc and Zatori keeping Jean-Robur between them from collapsing in exhaustion onto the floor.

'So it should always be with the Imperial Fists,' the Chaplain announced. He leaned his staff against the altar to free his hands, and then raised his right hand balled in a fist. 'The one hand clenched in a fist, to strike your enemies.' Then he raised his left hand, palm out and fingers outstretched towards the aspirants as if offering aid. 'The other hand held out to your brother, to share your strengths.'

He paused, and regarded the assembled aspirants.

'Aspirant Zatori,' he intoned solemnly. 'Step forwards and disrobe.'

And so it continued.

IN THE DAYS and weeks that followed, as the strike cruiser *Capulus* made its sure and steady way through the insane topographies of the warp, each of the aspirants took their turn in the pain-glove, many of them more than once. Brief encounters to help focus the mind, almost like jumping in and out of a freezing lake in an instant to clear their heads, and longer excruciations to discipline those who had strayed from the path, lengthy baptisms of pain to guide them back to proper conduct.

The examinations continued, as Apothecary Lakari sampled and studied their bodies all the way down to the cellular level in search of any taint of mutation, while at the same time confirming that they were strong enough to survive the implantation procedures that would follow once they reached the *Phalanx*.

Having been psychically screened initially in their first hours onboard the strike cruiser, each of the aspirants were subjected to ever more invasive and lengthy probes as Librarian Borgos dug ever deeper into their minds, past conscious thought and down into the subterranean levels of impulse and urge that the aspirants themselves knew nothing of, searching for any sign of corruption or weakness.

And the Chaplain continued to gauge their warrior spirits, questioning them on hypothetical scenarios, testing them to see how much they retained of the Chapter Lore and Imperial Dogma he had already doled out to them. Those who failed to recall the proper rites and rituals employed in the worship of the God-Emperor, or who could not recite the rudiments of the Cult of Dorn, found themselves marked out for additional time in the pain-glove, to allow the pain to improve their memories.

Not all of the aspirants passed each of these tests, of body, mind and spirit, and as day followed day the number of cots occupied in the aspirants' dormitory began to dwindle as the failures were quietly and without ceremony winnowed away from their fellows. Among the aspirants, in rare moments of rest and privacy, there were whispers of these unfortunate failures being used for experimentation, or transformed at once into half-man-half-machine servitors without even the luxury of first spending a lifetime of backbreaking labour as a Chapter serf.

And every day that passed brought them that much closer to the rendezvous with the fortress-monastery *Phalanx*, when the fittest among the aspirants would be welcomed as neophytes of the Imperial Fists. What waited them in the initiation period that followed, though, the aspirants were not entirely sure, and lacked the courage to ask.

'FOR TEN MILLENNIA,' Captain Taelos said, pacing back and forth before the assembled aspirants, his voice booming through the hall, 'the greatest threat to the continued existence of the Imperium of Mankind has not been any of the xenos hordes which have harried at our heels, but those sons of humanity who have turned their back on the God-Emperor on his Golden Throne and embraced the vile worship of the Ruinous Powers. Since the days of Rogal Dorn himself have the Traitor Legions waged their Long War against He whom they once served. Those who were once our brothers-in-arms are now the twisted and hate-filled disciples of Chaos, intent on overrunning the galaxy and despoiling all that the Imperium has accomplished. It falls to us of the Adeptus Astartes to see that they do not succeed.'

He paused at the edge of the rostrum, framed by the holy image of Dorn which hung from the wall behind him.

'The Imperial Fists are, above all, a brotherhood, bound by bonds of loyalty and duty. It is for this reason that we are committed to defeating those who have broken their covenant with the Emperor, who have betrayed their honour and turned their backs on the Imperium.'

TALOC S'TONAN LAY on his coffin-shaped cot in the dormitory, eyes half-lidded, wishing sleep would come. But exhausted as he was, he was somehow too tired for slumber, and so instead lay awake, muscles aching and thoughts racing.

It was only beginning to sink in for Taloc that he would in all likelihood never see the green forests of Eokaroe again, nor would he ever again be in the company of his uncles and cousins in the shadows of the island's great peaks. More than that, he would never again wield his ironbrand, which had been wrested from his hands on the battlefield by Captain Taelos of the Imperial Fists before the blade had ever earned for itself a name.

It occurred to Taloc that, in the strictest sense, he would never in fact become a man, denied the tests of the tourney and the battlefield alike, never to win the recognition of his warrior-clan that he had at last attained the status of manhood. If he survived the training and implantations that awaited him on the *Phalanx*, as they had been explained to the aspirants by their superiors onboard the *Capulus*, then he might one day be fortunate enough to join the ranks of the Adeptus Astartes, becoming a superhuman engine of war, but there would always be some small part of his mind that considered himself still a youth, denied the validation of his clan.

Taloc's head ached with the glut of information that had been forced into him over the previous weeks, both the knowledge that had been implanted by frequent sessions under the hypno-casque, and the lessons he had received verbally at the hands of the Chaplain, captain and sergeants. The knowledge gained through the former – basic concepts of science and technology and biology and interstellar cosmology and more implanted directly into his subconscious – had allowed him to better grasp the substance of the latter – histories of primarch and Chapter and the Imperium, introductory surveys on the nature of humanity's variegated enemies – but still Taloc found it difficult to digest all that he had been taught.

Opening his eyes, Taloc lifted his head fractionally off the cot and glanced from one side to the other. The number of aspirants had dwindled in the weeks since they had left Triandr behind, and where a hundred or more cots had been occupied in the first days Taloc had spent in the dormitory, now there were a bare few dozens of cots in use. Taloc tried not to dwell on what might have become of the other aspirants, including the few Eokaroeans who had been brought with him from Triandr. None of them had been of the warrior-clan of Tonan, but they had been kinsmen of a sort to him, and he had drawn some comfort from their presence. Now, he was the last of the Eokaroeans in the dormitory, and there was every chance that he would never again hear the language of his forefathers spoken aloud.

Only two other Triandrians beside Taloc remained among the ranks of the aspirants, for that matter. The Caritaigne named Jean-Robur, who seemed more concerned with his comfort and appetites than he did with the strangeness of their circumstances. And the Sipangish named Zatori, who held the blood-debt of Taloc's father Tonan.

Taloc had learned the names of few of the other aspirants who had already been onboard the *Capulus* when he and the rest of the Triandrians had been brought to the ship. Given the frequency with which the other youths suddenly disappeared from their ranks, removed for one deficiency or another, at times it seemed hardly worth the effort of establishing any kind of contact with them. He had become somewhat familiar with a bare handful of them – Kelso, Rhomec, Fulgencio, Valen and a few others – but had not engaged in anything like meaningful conversation with any of them.

But while Taloc's head throbbed with the knowledge that had been crammed into it, his muscles ached from the torturous examinations to which the aspirants had been subjected. Once their basic tissue and cellular compatibility had been established, their bodies were subjected to extensive examination to ensure that they had the proper resilience and capacity for healing necessary to survive the implantation procedures. Endurance tests followed, endless hours of running and lifting and bending, to measure their capacity for muscle growth and flexibility. After several weeks of this regimen, Taloc felt that there was not a muscle in his body that had not been strained or prodded, not a nerve that had not been plucked and jangled.

And then there was the pain-glove. Taloc had erred in protocols and procedures several times in recent days, minor infractions all, but onboard the *Capulus* even the most minor of infractions resulted in time within the Glove. And when he felt that he had just recovered from his disciplinary excruciations in the Glove, it was time for him to undergo his regularly scheduled meditative sessions, though thankfully for lesser periods of time and at lower pain settings. As it was, it seemed that scarcely a day had passed that he had not been subjected to the searing fire of the pain-glove, but Taloc had to admit, if only in silence and to himself, that each time he plunged into the mess of electrofibres he was that much more capable of enduring the pain. Each time he was able to retain more of his focus, to marshal more of his wits and his will, and when he emerged from each session he was less debilitated than he had been the previous time, better able to stand on his own feet without collapsing from the exhaustion of his overloaded nervous system.

Taloc closed his eyes again, though he knew it was too late now to consider sleeping. In moments, a line of servitors would come into the dormitory through the far door, carrying the aspirants' morning nourishment, and then the training and examinations of the day would begin. Already the lights set in the ceiling far overhead were beginning to brighten, cycling slowly from the near-complete darkness of the ship's night to the bright illumination of the ship's day, like the rising of Triandr's morning sun in miniature.

As a child, Taloc had been taught that the sun which shone by day was a symbol of the Great Father in the Sky, who had sent humanity untold ages ago to live in the forests and mountains and plains of Triandr. The red moon which shone by night waxed and waned in symbolic representation of the struggle between the two great brothers of ancient legend, warriors who fought in the Great Father's name until one of them betrayed his brother and turned his back on the Great Father in the Sky.

Lying in the lingering gloom of the dormitory, thoughts racing of their own accord, Taloc could not help hearing echoes of those Eokaroean beliefs in the histories he was being taught by the Imperial Fists – the God-Emperor of all humanity, presiding over the Imperium of Mankind from the Golden Throne on Holy Terra, His empire protected by the holy warriors of the Adeptus Astartes. And the story of the Traitor Legions, who turned their backs to the God-Emperor and their brothers-in-arms, siding with the ruinous powers of Chaos against humanity.

Taloc had been raised to believe that only the warrior-clans of Eokaroe had preserved the true faith of the Great Father in the Sky, remaining steadfast while the faithless wretches of the lands beyond the waves fell from grace and strayed from the path of righteousness.

Had the teachings of his grandfathers been true, at least in part? Were the beliefs of Eokaroe an echo of true history, and were the Great Father in the Sky and the battle between the two warrior-brothers themselves dim remembrances of the God-Emperor and his Great Crusade, of the Space Marine Legions and the Horus Heresy?

Taloc was no shaman or scholar, no expert in tales and traditions, but it certainly seemed a possible explanation. But if so, did that mean that Taloc might one day be a great warrior like those brothers of legend? It seemed ironic to think that he, who would never become a full man in the eyes of the Eokaroeans, would instead be elevated to the level of the more revered figures in his people's traditions.

Eyes still shut tight, with the realisation of this paradox Taloc's thoughts began to slow, his mind and jangled nerves slowly beginning to calm.

His aching muscles relaxed, and as he fancied himself as a great warrior of legend, Taloc could feel himself slowly sinking into slumber.

Darkness swallowed him, and Taloc drifted off to sleep.

And in the next moment, the clank and rattle of the servitors bringing the morning meal wrenched him back to full wakefulness. Rubbing his eyes, Taloc sat up and swung his legs over the side of the cot.

Tomorrow, perhaps, he thought, I will sleep.

'THE IMPERIAL FISTS are the uncontested masters of siege warfare, able to fortify and defend any site against all enemies,' Chaplain Dominicus declaimed, leaning heavily on the altar, 'and in recognition of this Rogal Dorn had been charged by the Emperor Himself with fortifying the Imperial Palace on Holy Terra. But you have not yet been told how this led inexorably to a great schism within the ranks of the Legions. Among his many worthy attributes, Primarch Rogal Dorn was always truthful, no matter the circumstances. And when Horus once proclaimed that Perturabo of the Iron Warriors was the greatest master of siege warfare in the Crusade, Primarch Fulgrim of the Emperor's Children called upon Dorn, asking in jest whether even the defences of the Imperial Palace which Dorn had constructed were proof against the Iron Warriors. Dorn, truthful to a fault, answered that his defences were proof against *any* assault, so long as the fortifications were intact and well manned. Hearing this, Perturabo flew into a rage, hurling imprecations and a stream of unfounded accusations at Dorn.

'The wedge thus driven between the primarchs grew ever wider, with neither Legion again serving in the same campaign. And when Horus led his treacherous vanguard against the Emperor, Perturabo and Fulgrim were at his heels, while Dorn and his Imperial Fists remained steadfast at the side of the Emperor. Now the Iron Warriors and the Emperor's Children serve the ruinous powers, and would seek to despoil all the works of man, while the Imperial Fists stand resolute in the Imperium's defence. But as Rogal Dorn himself taught us, there is *no* place that an Imperial Fist cannot fortify and defend against all enemies, including the galaxy itself!'

ZATORI ZAN SAT in rapt attention as Captain Taelos introduced to them the Rites of Battle as laid down in centuries past by the honoured Imperial Fist, Rhetoricus.

'Long before the primarch of the Ultramarines, the honoured Roboute Guilliman, formulated the *Codex Astartes*, the battle-brothers of the VII Space Marine Legion were governed by traditions of honour and discipline handed down from the most ancient traditions of Terra itself. Those first Imperial Fists revered the purity of the blade, and regarded the sword as the noblest of all weapons. Founded on Terra itself, the VII Legion inherited from the ancient Terran warrior-cults a tradition of honour duels, ritual combats that bound brothers together through the giving and receiving of honour.'

Zatori felt a frisson of recognition, remembering the combat ethos of the warrior-elite that he had learned from his master Father Nei, and the veneration with which the swordsmen of Sipang had always regarded their tachinas.

'But while the adoration of the blade and the tradition of honour duels has been with the Imperial Fists since earliest days, in the estimation of most within the Chapter it was not until Rhetoricus codified the Rites of Battle that the accumulated wisdom of our noble traditions was finally distilled into one text. In the sacred pages of *The Book of Five Spheres* did Rhetoricus record all that he knew of weapons and war.'

Taelos drew the massive sword which hung at his side, holding the blade upright before him, the tip pointed towards the vaulted ceiling high overhead.

'Rhetoricus teaches us that the soul of the Imperial Fist can be found in his sword. And it is for this reason that Imperial Fists seldom if ever go to battle without a blade at their side. But it is not only into battle that an Imperial Fist carries his blade. Onboard the fortress-monastery *Phalanx*, and in the strike cruisers and larger ships of the Imperial Fist fleet, can be found the Arena Restricta, sacred halls hung with ancient and storied blades, temples dedicated to the worship of the sword. And upon that hallowed ground, battle-brothers draw their blades against one another, their feet secured in blocks of gleaming steel, while their brethren sit in solemn witness from above. We duel to settle a dispute, or to prove the strength of one proposition against its counter, or merely to test the mettle of one battle-brother against another. And though the wounds inflicted in the honour duel are seldom fatal, it is rare to find an Imperial Fist of years who does not bear somewhere on him the badges of honour won in the Arena Restricta.'

Captain Taelos reached up a gauntleted hand and brushed a metal-shod fingertip against the criss-crossed scars that marked his cheeks.

'Not until your implants have taken hold and your muscles have completed their accelerated growth will you be introduced to the art of the blade as practised by our Chapter,' the captain went on. 'And many of you who had some experience with the use of swords in your previous lives may well have to unlearn what you have been taught, if your former skills prove a hindrance to gaining true proficiency in the art. But while you will begin to practise the sword's art while still neophytes, and as Scouts will even have the privilege of carrying a blade into battle if the circumstances demand, only full battle-brothers of the Imperial Fists are allowed to step into the duelling blocks of the Arena Restricta. Not until you have gained the final implant, and the Black Carapace lies beneath your skin to bind you to your holy power armour, will you be allowed to participate in an honour duel. Any aspirant or neophyte who raises a blade against his brother until that time does so in contravention of Chapter precepts, and will be summarily stripped of standing and rank.'

Zatori glanced to his right, across the hall to where Jean-Robur sat on a hard metal bench between a pair of other aspirants. Could this honour duel be the solution to Zatori's dilemma? A way to put the spirit of Father Nei to rest without sacrificing his own honour – to say nothing of his *life*? But if it was, it would be a solution long in coming, as there were many years remaining until Zatori would take on the Black Carapace. And it would mean that he could not make a move against Jean-Robur until that time. Worse still, Zatori could only accomplish his ends if both he and Jean-Robur survived the implantation procedures and any combat missions on which they might be sent as Scouts, and both lived long enough to be welcomed as full battle-brothers of the Imperial Fists.

So be it, Zatori thought, turning his attention back to Captain Taelos, giving no outward sign of the plans he was formulating aside from a slight narrowing of his gaze, as if in deep thought. I will wait to take my revenge, and the vengeance will taste no less sweet for the delay.

Zatori did not notice the island warrior Taloc looking in his direction with a similarly thoughtful narrowed gaze.

'THE HALLMARK OF an Imperial Fist is discipline and self-control,' Sergeant Hilts said, standing with his hands clasped behind him before the serried ranks of aspirants. 'Allowing unchecked impulses to govern your action, or succumbing by giving into desire, is the path to excess, which is one of the principal doorways to Chaos. Whether fighting alone or in formation with your brothers-in-arms, it is imperative that an Imperial Fist at all times remains conscious of his actions and their effects, that he follows the orders which have been issued to him, and that he not make any rash or ill-considered action. Your enemy, however, will be aware of this, and will be forever tempting you to abandon your discipline and control and act in a thoughtless and inopportune manner. But the Space Marine has the faith and resilience to resist such temptation.'

JEAN-ROBUR DU QUESTE stood at attention alongside the other aspirants in the cavernous assembly hall of the strike cruiser *Capulus*. Before them on a dais stood Captain Taelos, flanked on one side by a pair of veteran-sergeants, and on the other side by Librarian Borgos, Apothecary Lakari and Chaplain Dominicus.

There were only twelve aspirants now, their number winnowed from the hundred or so of a month or more ago to the dozen deemed most suitable to continue with the initiation process. On either side of Jean-Robur stood the only other Triandrians to have made it this far, the barbaric Taloc and the calculating Zatori. Around them stood the sons of mining worlds and hive worlds, of agri-worlds and death worlds. A dozen youths thoroughly vetted, sampled, tested and examined, who had been found to be without any physical defect or mental aberration which would prevent them from beginning the long process which would gradually transform them from human into superhuman, from mere mortals into Adeptus Astartes.

'From this moment forwards,' Captain Taelos said, his helmet under his arm and his scarred-cheeked face bare to the world, 'you are no longer aspirants, no longer candidates. From this moment onwards, you are neophytes of the Imperial Fists Chapter.'

The twelve youths had received enough instruction from their superiors that they knew better than to respond, in word or movement, unless ordered to do so. Instead, they stood silently at attention like a row of graven statues, their arms rigid at their sides and their eyes fixed on the captain before them.

'The ease and tranquillity of the previous weeks are now at an end,' Captain Taelos continued. 'Be advised that the comfort and relaxation of your time as aspirants is no more, and that the life of a neophyte is one of constant toil and testing.'

If the newly-minted neophytes found any irony in the fact that the month of torment and torture they had just endured, straining their minds and bodies to the limit, was being described as 'comfort and relaxation', they gave no outward sign of it. For his part, Jean-Robur could only suppress a shudder, imagining what the coming days held if what the captain said were true.

'The *Capulus* has re-entered normal space,' the captain went on, 'and is now in final approach to rendezvous with the rest of the Imperial Fists fleet. In short order, we will dock with the fortress-monastery *Phalanx*, and you twelve will be presented to Chapter Master Vladimir Pugh himself. When you boarded this ship, whether voluntarily or under duress, you were the sons of distant worlds, far-flung outposts of humanity, each with your own language and culture, your own identities and traditions. You now share a common language, and what is more you also share a common culture – that of the Sons of Dorn – and a common tradition – the proud history of the Imperial Fists. Even more important, though, you now share a common identity. As neophytes, you are taking your first steps towards becoming members of a most respected Chapter of the Adeptus Astartes. But as recruits, you cannot be coerced into accepting this proud destiny. You must choose it for yourselves.'

Captain Taelos raised a gauntleted hand and held it palm-outwards towards the twelve youths. Dressed identically in belted tunics, loincloths and boots, and all of them now with shorn hair atop their heads, the former aspirants were of varying colouration and facial features, but still they had come to resemble one another in some ineffable way. Though this one had a lean face and this one a round one, this one fine hair and this one coarse, they still could have passed as brothers. Perhaps it was the inner fire that burned in the eyes of each of them, the same that Jean-Robur had noted. Perhaps their faces and features were different, but in some more substantial way their *spirits* were the same.

'If you would accept the destiny being offered to you,' Captain Taelos said, hand still stretched out towards them, 'take one step forwards, and you will then accompany me onto the *Phalanx*. If you cannot accept, remain standing, and a place will be found for you among the Chapter serfs on this strike cruiser.'

Keeping his gaze fixed ahead, Jean-Robur immediately took a long stride forwards. Then, planting his feet together, he stood once more at attention.

Captain Taelos nodded once. 'Look to your right and to your left,' he ordered.

Jean-Robur glanced to one side and then the other, at the former aspirants who stood in a neat rank with him, Taloc on one side and Zatori on the other.

'All twelve of you have taken the first step together,' the captain said. He tightened his outstretched hand into a gauntleted fist. When he spoke again, his voice grew gradually louder and louder, the echoes of his words booming back from the far corners of the hall.

'May the Emperor and primarch grant that you all take the final step together, as well.'

The captain lowered his helmet over his head, and then drew his sword. With the handle of his sword in his right hand, and his left hand curled into a fist and held overhead, he shouted the final words as loud as a battle cry.

'May you emerge transformed by the crucible of pain as battle-brothers of the Imperial Fists!'

PART THREE

'The craftsman, in his work, must comprehend
measurements and design, and have a mastery of
each of the tools at his disposal. In the same way,
the warrior must comprehend tactics and strategy,
and master each of the weapons in his arsenal.'

Rhetoricus,
The Book of Five Spheres

CHAPTER SEVEN

THE DAYS ONBOARD the *Phalanx* began early, after just four hours of rest period. The Scouts of the 10th Company, joined by those neophytes who had not yet been inducted into the combat ranks, mustered in the fortress-monastery's immense cathedral. There they were led by the company Chaplain Lo Chang in renewing their oaths to the God-Emperor. Any battle-brothers not currently away from the fortress-monastery on an undertaking also gathered in the cathedral, even those under the treatment of the Apothecarion for injuries sustained in battle. That morning, there had been nearly six full companies of Imperial Fists gathered to hear Chaplain Chang invoke the name of the primarch and to entreat the continued support and guidance of the Emperor.

'Oh Dorn, dawn of our being,' the Chaplain had intoned, reciting the words of the Primarch's Prayer, 'be with us, illuminate us.'

After the prayer service came the morning firing exercises. Each of the Scout squads adjourned to one of the *Phalanx's* many firing ranges to hone their marksmanship. Though the Chapter revered the blade, even the most traditionalist and romantic of Imperial Fists readily admitted that close combat was not always the appropriate tactic to employ, and so neophytes were required to gain proficiency in ranged weaponry before ever being inducted into the ranks of the Scouts. And in particular they were expected to attain mastery over the bolter, holy weapon of the Adeptus Astartes, bringer of the Emperor's own divine retribution.

Even after the neophytes had been inducted into the Scouts, and sent into combat situations to gather intelligence or assist in a support capacity for the battle-brothers of the Chapter, there continued to be the constant emphasis on improving their skills and proficiency. After all, if the full battle-brothers of the Imperial Fists participated twice daily in firing exercises, why should their junior brethren be any exception?

After two hours of firing exercises, the Scouts moved to one of the myriad of exercise halls in the fortress-monastery to engage in five hours of battle practice. For the past weeks the Scouts of Squad Pardus had engaged in live-fire exercises along with the Scouts of Squads Vulpes, Luscus and Ursus. Wearing their full

combat Scout armour, the squads had been divided
into two teams and set against each other in mock
combat, with the intent of the exercises being not
only to drill in various tactics, but to gain essential
practice in coordinating action between elements of a
fighting group when out of line-of-sight, using voxed
exchanges to establish the position and movement of
one's teammates. Today, however, Sergeant Hilts had
announced that Squad Pardus would be drilling
alone, and rather than working on cooperative tactical
exercises, they would be sparring one-on-one,
practising the art of the blade – albeit with blunted
practice swords instead of combat weaponry.

As heavy as combat blades were, though, the
blunted practice swords were designed to be even
heavier, so that the Scouts would become
accustomed to the greater heft and, in overcoming
the weight, be that much more agile and lithe with
combat weaponry on the battlefield.

'Mind your blade's angle of attack, Scout Zatori,'
Sergeant Hilts called out, hands clasped at the
small of his back as he watched the bouts progress.
'From that position the arc-path of your blade
could be too easily parried by a simple upswing of
your opponent's sword. And Scout s'Tonan,
remember that there is a difference between striking and hitting. Your movements should be
conscious and deliberate, not merely forceful.'

When battle practice finally reached its end, the
Scouts would prepare to adjourn and hear the midday prayer for an hour, and would then gather with

the rest of the 10th Company in the Assimularum where the Chapter serfs would serve the midday meal. Then the day would continue on as it always did, with more prayers and more training, indoctrination in the hypnomats and study in the scriptoriums, more firing exercises and rituals, before finally returning to their dormitories to rest for four hours before rising and doing the whole thing again. The routine onboard the *Phalanx* seldom deviated, nor had it for millennium after millennium.

But for the Scouts of Veteran-Sergeant Hilts's Squad Pardus, their routine would eventually be abandoned, and what the coming days would hold none of them would be able to guess.

IT HAD BEEN some four years since the neophytes had boarded the *Phalanx*, and with the blessing of Chapter Master Vladimir Pugh had begun the lengthy initiation of the Adeptus Astartes. Four years of surgical procedures and chemical treatments, near-endless hypno-conditioning and long indoctrination sessions. The neophytes had now undergone all but one of the implantation procedures, with sixteen organs added to their young bodies. Neophytes of other Chapters would have been implanted with eighteen organs by this stage of the initiation process, but in ages past the Imperial Fists had lost the Sus-An Membrane, the 'hibernator' that allowed other Astartes to enter a state of suspended animation, and the Betcher's gland, the 'poison-bite' that allowed Space Marines of other Chapters to spit corrosive venom. But as Rhetoricus had written, the Imperial Fists did not bemoan the loss of these two abilities. The Imperial Fists used what talents and abilities that remained to mercilessly crush their enemies.

With the sixteen organs successfully implanted and deemed to be functioning properly, the neophytes had been inducted into the Scouts, and sent onto the field of battle in support positions. Already the Scouts of Squad Pardus had participated in several expeditions, though they had not yet seen much of actual combat, and were still untested in battle.

But though their actions had been largely limited to reconnaissance and surveillance operations, with only limited engagements with the enemy and then for only brief encounters until the battle-brothers of the Chapter had arrived to take charge, not all of their squadmates had survived. Scout Kelso had fallen in an undertaking on the planet Tunis, for one, though he was honoured in death by the Chapter, his name entered into the rolls of the fallen dead. But still more of them had perished before ever becoming Scouts, when their implants failed to develop properly, and their metabolisms raged out of synchronisation; the memory of the last hours of those unfortunates was still fresh in the minds of all the neophytes, months and years later, as their fellow neophytes either lapsed into endless catatonia or burned themselves out in fits of irrepressible hyperactivity.

The neophytes would remain Scouts until the time that they had at last proven their valour and skill on the field of battle, at which point they would be marked out for the seventeenth and final implantation procedure. Only when the Black Carapace was implanted beneath their skin, the subcutaneous membrane allowing their internal organs to interface directly with the holy power armour with which they would then be entrusted, would they finally be elevated to the exalted level of full battle-brothers and take their place among the combat companies of the Imperial Fists Chapter.

Four long years of hypno-conditioning to aid them in weathering the emotional fluctuations as their bodies struggled to integrate and initiate their new organs. Long years of chemical treatments to aid the body's acceptance of the implanted organs, while the implants were constantly monitored for any sign of imbalance or corrupt development. Four years of physical training to stimulate the implants and test their effectiveness, and of indoctrination in the hypnomat and hypno-casque to train their minds to function at peak efficiency, learning to control their sensory and nervous systems to degrees unthinkable by normal humans.

Four long years of initiation – four years that would soon come to an end, as the Scouts of Squad Pardus faced the final challenge, and either proved themselves worthy of bearing the mantle of the Black Carapace, or perished in the attempt.

SCOUT DU QUESTE sat on his haunches along the base of the wall, towelling off his face and neck with the towel he'd taken from the brass railing that ran around the room's perimeter. Like the other members of Scout Pardus, he was dressed in a sparring chiton of cotton dyed golden yellow, which left his arms and legs bare and free to move. Having finished his most recent bout, he sat with the other Scouts and watched while Veteran-Sergeant Hilts put Scouts Zatori and Taloc through their paces.

With the loss of Kelso in the recent mission on Tunis, there were only eight Scouts remaining in Squad Pardus under the command of Veteran-Sergeant Hilts. Besides the two Triandrians sparring at the centre of the hall, two of the other Scouts stood limbering themselves up a short distance off, Scouts Valen and Sandor, readying to take the next turn under the sergeant's watchful gaze. The other three members of the squad – Rhomec, Fulgencio and Jedrek – sat in a ragged line along with Jean-Robur, bruised and weary after their own recent bouts.

'I didn't hurt you *too* badly, did I?' Scout Rhomec asked with an exaggerated sneer, leaning over and indicating Jean-Robur's right shoulder with a jerk of his chin. 'Need to scurry off to the Apothecarion to have that looked at, do you?'

Jean-Robur returned Rhomec's sneer with one of his own, and shook his head curtly from side to side. 'I scarcely felt it, I'm sorry to say. Perhaps next time you'll do some real damage?'

Rhomec only chuckled in response, and straightened back up, leaning his head against the cold stone of the wall and burying his face in the towel, to mop up the sweat that still streamed from his pores.

Before he'd been culled by the same recruiting mission that had snatched Jean-Robur, Rhomec had been a pitfighter in a hive-world circus. Scarcely out of childhood, not yet fully a man, Rhomec had become a champion gladiator, his weapon of choice the chainsword.

As neophytes none of the Scouts had been given the privilege of fighting an honour duel in the Arena Restricta yet, so alone among them Rhomec bore the scars of single combat, cruelly jagged lightning-shaped marks that zigzagged up from the corners of his mouth towards each ear, trophies earned in his childhood when he had not yet learned to dance back out of the reach of his opponent's chainsword.

Climbing up from either corner of his mouth, the scars gave Rhomec the appearance of always grinning widely, even when he scowled and frowned in anger. His comical-seeming appearance was somehow fitting, considering the somewhat cruel streak of humour that ran through the brutal young ex-pitfighter.

Jean-Robur had lied, of course. The wallops he'd received from Rhomec's practice-blade in the shoulder and upper arm, though Sergeant Hilts had castigated the ex-pitfighter about his poor technique, had bruised Jean-Robur to the bone. And though his implant-augmented metabolism had quickly repaired the damage, knitting broken blood vessels and restoring vigour to the impacted flesh, Jean-Robur could still feel the impact of each and every strike, like some kind of muscle memory that kept replaying in his mind the pain of the ex-pitfighter's attack.

Before Jean-Robur and Rhomec's bout had been the brief contest between Scouts Fulgencio and Jedrek. On first impression, the two Scouts could not have seemed more dissimilar. Fulgencio had been born in the vast interstellar voids, far from the works of man, while Jedrek was the son of a fisher-man sailor on an ocean world which knew neither land nor shore, but which was encircled entirely in seas. Fulgencio had been tall and lithe when he had first been recruited, his body elongated in the man-ner typical to those who grew up in low-gravity environments, while Jedrek had been short and stocky, with a sailor's muscled forearms and fingers quick with ropes and knots despite their stubby length. But after the years of initiation, as waves of hormones had lengthened and strengthened their bones and gradually built their muscles to the peak of physical perfection, the two had grown to simi-lar statures and proportions, though Fulgencio still somehow gave the impression of being supple and lithe, while from Jedrek somehow emanated a sense of stalwart solidity. And though one had been born in the starless void and the other on the trackless waters, they had come to realise that they were both the proud sons of far-voyaging sailors, of a sort, though their fathers had sailed on very different seas. In the years of their initiation, the two had become as close as brothers. But like brothers in blood, though either of the two would defend the other against all comers, refusing to hear any unfounded comment or criticism of his fellow sailors'-son, the two often bickered in bitter disagreement, squabbling over minor points of order that others would scarcely have even deigned to notice.

At the moment, the two were arguing over whether or not Scout s'Tonan's most recent attack had exemplified the technique that Rhetoricus in *The Book of Five Spheres* had called 'striking without thought or form', or had been as Sergeant Hilts suggested an example of mindless 'hitting'. Overhearing them, it hardly seemed to Jean-Robur to make much difference whether one struck without thinking because it was a technique to catch one's opponent off-guard… or because one simply *forgot* to think – but to the two sailors'-sons it seemed a matter of the gravest significance.

From the walls of the exercise hall echoed the sound of metal against metal as Scouts Taloc and Zatori again and again brought their blunted swords crashing together, punctuated every few moments by the low but carrying voice of Veteran-Sergeant

Hilts commenting on their form, praising this attack or criticising that parry and block.

Watching the bout, Jean-Robur could not help but admire the precision of Zatori's attacks. There was an economy of motion to the Sipangish's movements that wasted nothing, employing only the effort and energy needed to move the blade to this particular point in space, to strike that particular point on his opponent's body. But at the same time, though Taloc's movements were less disciplined and refined, there was a ferocity and power to his strikes and blows that Jean-Robur had to envy. At times the Eokaroean seemed like a force of nature unleashed upon the sparring hall, whipping his practice sword around like a broken branch caught up in a cyclone, battering at his opponent from all angles and all sides.

When the two of them faced off against each other, Zatori with his gaze narrowed in concentration, Taloc with his pale blue eyes wide and crazed, it sometimes seemed as though the Sipangish were competing in a courtly competition for points and pride, and that the islander truly intended to do his opponent real harm.

How strange then, Jean-Robur reflected, that when Zatori sparred against *him* that the Sipangish did not fight with narrowed concentration, but instead with a wide-eyed passion that suggested he wanted nothing more than to see Jean-Robur broken and bloodied before him.

* * *

'REMEMBER THE WORDS of Rhetoricus, Scouts,' Sergeant Hilts called, his voice as measured and steady as a tolling bell. 'When fighting another human, you must become your opponent. Put yourself in your opponent's place, and think from *his* point of view.'

Scout s'Tonan seethed through gritted teeth, pale blue eyes wide and glaring at the calm and composed features of Scout Zatori. From the sound of Zatori's laboured breathing, though, Taloc could tell that the Eokaroean was growing as wearied from the bout as he was. The two neophytes stood a pace apart from one another, their practice swords held at the ready, each waiting for the other to make the next move.

'Remember, too, the principle of releasing deadlock,' Hilts went on. 'When you find yourself in a deadlock, with no progress being made, you must *immediately* change your approach. The victor will be he who is the most effective in choosing which is the correct tactic to use.'

Unbidden, the image of his father Tonan came to Taloc's mind. After four years of indoctrination and initiation, though, the Scout found it difficult to recall the exact features of his father's face, the precise colour of the old man's eyes or the pattern of the tattoos that marked across his pale skin. Sometimes Taloc would lie awake at night during the rest period, trying to piece together a complete picture of the man who had so dominated his childhood, but try as he might Taloc could not refrain from mixing elements of Rogal Dorn in with his father's features, or Captain Taelos as he had looked when he had snatched Taloc from the life he had known, or even Veteran-Sergeant Hilts who had ruled over Taloc's days and nights in the months since he had become a Scout. But while his mental image of his dead father was hazy and incomplete, still the memory of Tonan's death burned in Taloc's mind, and still did Taloc feel the weight of his father's blood-debt burdening his shoulders.

Also, Taloc remembered too well that he had chosen not to take payment on his father's blood-debt on the battlefield of Eokaroe, but had instead opted to stand with the two faithless invaders against the interlopers from beyond the sky. That decision had altered the course of Taloc's life, and when it became clear that he could not end the life of the Sipangish faithless onboard an Imperial Fists ship without ending his own life as well, he had opted to bide his time. He knew that he had only to wait until both he and the Sipangish were invested as full battle-brothers of the Imperial Fists and then he could challenge Zatori to an honour duel, and in the duelling blocks of the Arena Restricta finally put paid to his father's debt of blood. But four years on and it seemed as though that day would never come, and Taloc grew quietly more and more impatient.

In the normal routine of the Scouts' day, Taloc was able to keep his hunger for violence against Zatori in check, hidden beneath the shell of discipline and self-control that he had learned from his superiors in the Chapter, burying his desire to kill deep in the core of his being.

But today, when Veteran-Sergeant Hilts put a blade in his hands and set him against Scout Zatori in a bout, it had not mattered in that instant that it was merely a blunted practice sword, or that this was merely a sparring match and not a life-and-death duel. In that instant, all of the pent-up resentments had come bubbling forth, and when Hilts had signalled the bout had begun, Taloc could hear the voice of his father echoing in his head, demanding that his blood-debt, long overdue, now be at last paid in full.

And so while Hilts commented and critiqued, and Zatori studiously parried and blocked, Taloc suddenly acted as if he had forgotten all that he had ever learned of the art of the blade, and went on the attack like a man possessed – which in one sense, at least, he was. Taloc was a man possessed by the fading memory of his dead father, and by the imperatives of the warrior-clan that he had left behind.

'Desist,' Veteran-Sergeant Hilts called, clapping his hands together. 'Scouts, bow to your opponent and…'

Before Hilts could complete his instructions and order the two combatants to retire to the corners of the room, Taloc surged forwards, ignoring the fact that Zatori had stepped back and lowered the point of his practice blade to the floor.

Taloc's blunted blade whistled through the air, aimed directly at Zatori's head. The Sipangish didn't have time to raise his own sword to block, or to duck out of the way, or even to cry out.

Though his thoughts were clouded by his sudden inchoate rage, Taloc knew that when his blade struck Zatori's head, at this speed and force, it would be the Apothecarion for the Sipangish.

In the eyeblink-short instant that remained before Taloc's heavy practice sword smashed into the size of Zatori's head, Hilts collided with Taloc, knocking the Eokaroean to the ground and sending his practice blade clattering across the tiled floor of the exercise hall.

Taloc scrambled to jump back to his feet, bleary and muttering, 'But how–'

'Stay down,' Hilts ordered, standing over the fallen Scout.

Though clad only in a sparring chiton himself, arms and legs bare, and lacking the carapace armour he typically wore, Veteran-Sergeant Hilts was still a battle-brother of the Imperial Fists, a proud warrior of the Adeptus Astartes with more than a century of combat experience. Though the muscles of the Scouts' augmented and engineered bodies were nearly the equal of Hilts's own, at least in theory, they lacked his expertise and experience, his agility and his innate speed. The fact that he could cover a span of six paces before Taloc could complete two should have come as no surprise to any of them. *Should* have come as no surprise, but Taloc was clearly caught flat-footed.

'Five minutes in the pain-glove,' Veteran-Sergeant Hilts said in calm, measured tones, 'for failing to stand down as ordered. Then report to Apothecary Lakari for a check of your adrenals. You might need a reinforcing round of hypno-conditioning.' Hilts paused, glancing from the supine Taloc to Zatori and then back. 'Now stand.'

As Taloc climbed to his feet, his pale cheeks burned red with embarrassed shame. During the implantation stages of the initiation process, neophytes often fell afoul of severe emotional fluctuations, as their already belaboured bodies struggled to cope with the new organs introduced to the system. Sudden rages were a frequent occurrence among neophytes in the midst of those stages, and frequent sessions in the hypnomat were prescribed by the Apothecary as a matter of course. But to be a full Scout, supposedly with all but one of his implanted organs functioning at full efficiency, was to Taloc a shameful indignity, a sign that he was not as developed and progressed as his brethren.

Of course, Taloc reasoned, better that Hilts ascribe his murderous rage to an imbalance of his bodily humours, than to suspect that Taloc had truly wished his fellow Scout harm. And there was the fact that Taloc could not say with any degree of certainty that his rage had *not* been influenced or enflamed by such an imbalance, for that matter.

'My apologies, veteran-sergeant,' Taloc said in a low voice, bowing from the waist with his hands at his sides. 'I accept discipline with humble shame.'

Hilts nodded. 'As you should. Now, off the floor, the both of you.' He turned to the pair who stood waiting to spar in the next bout, practice swords in hand. 'Scouts Valen and Sandor, take the floor.'

As BATTLE PRACTICE drew to a close, and the Scouts prepared to enter the ablution chambers, to don once more their tunics and boots before proceeding to midday prayers, a Chapter serf came to the exercise hall with a data-slate for Veteran-Sergeant Hilts.

As Valen and Sandor caught their breath, and mopped their sweaty brows and necks with towels and joined their squadmates along the wall, Hilts studied the data-slate with his characteristic speed and concentration. Then he handed the slate back to the Chapter serf without a word, and turned to address the eight squadmates before him.

'It seems we have a change of routine,' Hilts said, clasping his hands behind his back once more, his habitual stance when addressing the squad. 'From the ablution chamber you are to proceed directly to the armoury, where you will don your full Scout armour and be issued with bolt pistols and blades. We will muster at 12.30 hours in the departure bay.'

A few of the Scouts cocked eyebrows at the announcement, but none of them gave voice to their curiosity over what the change in their routine suggested, or whether they were bound for some undertaking or action. They knew it would mean a session in the pain-glove were they to speak out of turn, and after their four years of initiation there were none of them foolish enough to speak without being first given leave.

Even so, the fact that they hesitated in following the sergeant's orders was, in itself, suggestive of the curiosity that was burning within each of them.

'Why do you delay?' Veteran-Sergeant Hilts asked needlessly, a barely detectable trace of humour laced through his evident annoyance. 'Dismissed!'

Leaving their sodden towels and practice swords scattered on the tiled floor for the Chapter serfs to address, the Scouts of Squad Pardus hurried from the exercise hall in tight-lipped silence, their minds racing with thoughts about what might lie ahead of them.

WITH TIME TO spare before 12.30 hours was chimed, Veteran-Sergeant Hilts and the eight squadmates of Scout Squad Pardus emerged through a massive hatchway into the cavernous departure bay.

Like all of the neophytes in the squad, Scout Zatori wore the gold armour of the Space Marine Scout. It was not the power armour worn by full battle-brothers. Instead, the Scout armour was simpler, more light-weight and quieter in movement, with a greater freedom of motion, but in exchange not nearly so formidable and durable. Formed of thick plates of carapace armour that were capable of stopping a slug projectile, the armour offered no motive power or strength enhancement, and perhaps as importantly left the wearer's head bare and unarmoured. Each of the Scouts had a bolt pistol holstered at one hip, and a combat blade hung at the other.

Unlike his battle-brothers in their suits of power armour, Veteran-Sergeant Hilts wore the same carapace armour as the Scouts he commanded, and like his subordinates in Squad Pardus, Hilts's head was bare. At Hilts's left hip hung a power sword, at his right was holstered a bolt pistol.

Scout Zatori had been in the departure bay only a handful of times in his four years onboard the fortress-monastery *Phalanx*, most of them in the last few months either departing on or returning from an undertaking under the command of Veteran-Sergeant Hilts. But even though he'd seen the departure bay several times before, each time he entered it was for Zatori like the first time, and he was all but completely overwhelmed by the sheer size and scale of the place.

Though he knew intellectually that the *Phalanx* was a mobile space station the size of a small moon, bristling with towering spires and buttresses, living onboard the fortress-monastery it was a difficult fact to hold in mind. Certainly while meditating in the Solitorium, that long starlit gallery that ran along the base of the fortress-monastery where the naked stars glinted through high lancet windows of stained armour-glass, one was always conscious of the fact that the *Phalanx* was surrounded on all sides by the cold void of the vacuum. But even given the majestic dimensions of the chapels and cathedrals, the Assimularum and Scriptoriums, it was too easy when living onboard to forget the sheer immenseness of the fortress-monastery. It was easy to imagine oneself living in a large city, perhaps, or a gigantic temple structure on some planet.

When one stepped into the departure bay, though, one was immediately reminded not only that they were in a space-borne vessel, but that the *Phalanx* was far more than merely immense or gigantic – it was *gargantuan*.

On the other side of the bay, so far away that the sight of it hazed with the distance, were the bay doors which opened out onto the cold vacuum of the void, before which were arranged Thunderhawks, shuttles and other such craft in their hundreds. Overhead, hanging from the rafters that were barely visible from the deck, hung decommissioned aircraft and space-faring vessels of the Chapter, preserved and displayed in honour of past victories, and of those who had fought and died onboard them.

It was said that the departure hall was so large that it had developed its own microclimate, separate from the artificial environment which prevailed throughout the rest of the fortress-monastery, and that there were strains of avian life-forms, roosting up in the rafters and onboard those ancient and honoured craft hanging from them, that had evolved into entirely novel forms and physiologies over the millennia, unseen by human eyes.

On a somewhat more human scale, though still towering over the Scouts who walked beneath, were arranged on the walls battle trophies from past victories, and enormous murals depicting famous battles from the annals of the Imperial Fists. There were ancient weapons and armour that dated back even as far as the Great Crusade, preserved eternally and displayed here reverentially after age finally robbed them of their use, each one of them carrying a provenance as long and celebrated as that of the Chapter itself.

Fluttering slightly in the pressure differential between the departure bay and the hatches which led to the corridors, there hung immense banners, each of them easily as wide as four Adeptus Astartes in full power armour standing abreast, and more than twice as tall. There was one for each of the battle companies of the Imperial Fists, each bearing the heraldry and litany of the company in question. Surmounting them all was an even larger Chapter banner, golden yellow and trimmed in jet-black and blood-red, on which was inscribed 'VII' – remembering the Chapter's origins as the Emperor's VII Legion during the Great Crusade – and the word 'Roma' – referring to the Imperial Fists' earliest battle honour, which now existed only on a ceramite icon which itself was considered too precious and valuable even to put on display in the Inner Reclusium of the *Phalanx* – and finally the icon of the black fist grasping a red thunderbolt, beneath which was scrolled the legend 'Sons of

Dorn'. There were several Chapter banners, but only one of them was put on display at any given time, rotated out at regular intervals in recognition of important actions and significant victories. It was perhaps a testament to the long lifespan of the Chapter itself that in all the four years Zatori had lived onboard the *Phalanx* the Chapter banner had not yet been changed out, which suggested that all of the great victories the Chapter had won in the time since had not risen yet to the level of a 'significant victory'.

The Scouts of Veteran-Sergeant Hilts's Squad Pardus were not the only ones to be summoned to the departure bay, it was immediately clear. As Hilts led them to their place alongside the neophytes of Scout Squads Vulpes and Ursus at the rear of the assembly, Zatori could see on the auto-reactive shoulder plates of the nearest Space Marines the markings and heraldic colours of both the 1st and the 5th Companies, at least. There were more than a hundred Imperial Fists gathered in the departure bay, battle-brothers and Scouts, arrayed in serried ranks facing the nearest end of the bay. Every eye was directed at the balcony which rose above the hatches through which Squad Pardus had entered, and as Zatori and the others took their places, a hush fell over the already-quiet assembly.

Scout Zatori raised his eyes to the balcony in time to see a group of worthies trooping into view. First came Captain Taelos of the 10th Company, the commander over all of the Chapter's Scouts. Next came Captain Khrusaor of the 5th Company, his golden-hued power sword at his hip. Then followed Darnath Lysander himself, First Captain of the Imperial Fists, Master of the 1st Company, Overseer of the Armoury and Watch Commander of the *Phalanx*. On one arm was his massive storm shield, and in the other hand he carried his master-crafted thunder hammer, the Fist of Dorn. Zatori had been given the rare and great privilege of seeing Captain Lysander charging into battle on Tunis, and cherished the memory like a treasured heirloom.

After the three captains had taken up position on either end of the balcony, Captains Taelos and Khrusaor on one end and Captain Lysander on the other, Librarian Franz Grenstein and Chaplain Lo Chang emerged into view side-by-side. Both Librarian and Chaplain wore force swords in scabbards slung at their waists, and both had cheeks nicked white with the crisscrossed duelling scars typical of the Imperial Fists, though Chaplain Chang's cheeks were further marked by crater-like wounds he had gained when his power suit's helmet had been shattered during a fire-fight, leaving him with a visage like the face of a meteor-scarred moon.

As the Librarian went to stand a few paces to Captain Khrusaor's left, Chaplain Lo Chang stepped towards the balcony's railing and extended his hands towards the rafters, lowering his eyes in an attitude of prayer.

'Oh Dorn, the dawn of our being,

Lead us, your sons, to victory.'

The Scouts and battle-brothers assembled below echoed the words, lowering their eyes to the deck plates. Then, when Zatori raised his gaze again and saw that Chaplain Chang had stepped aside to stand to Captain Lysander's right, he could not help but feel a small twinge of relief. The litany that Chang had recited was one of the shortest in the liturgy of the Imperial Fists. As honoured as he was for any opportunity to hear the Chaplain speak, Zatori was thankful that he would not have to listen to one of the much longer litanies before learning why they had all been called together.

He did not have much longer to wait. After the way was cleared, and the Chaplain and Librarian had taken up positions with the captains to either side, Chapter Master Vladimir Pugh himself strode onto the balcony.

Stern-faced, lips down-turned in a perpetual scowl, Chapter Master Pugh was clad in a gleaming suit of artificer-armour, forged by master craftsmen and nearly as ancient and honoured as the Chapter itself, festooned with purity seals, votive chains, ribbons and scrolls. Behind his head rose an iron halo, which even in a deactivated state seemed to crackle and coruscate with the powerful energy field contained within. A cloak the colour of new-spilt blood hung from Chapter Master Pugh's shoulders, and his left hand rested on the hilt of the master-crafted sword which hung in its scabbard at his waist.

Chapter Master Pugh raised his right hand in a fist, then crashed the arm across his armoured chest, then raised the fist on high again, saluting the Space Marines gathered before him.

'Imperial Fists, Proud Sons of Dorn, your Chapter Master greets you!'

As one, the battle-brothers returned the salute, crashing their fists and forearms against their chests, and then raising their arms overhead.

'Hail Chapter Master Pugh, First Among the Imperial Fists!' the assembled battle-brothers shouted in near-unison.

The Scouts, who had seldom been invited to partake in this traditional exchange of honours with their Master, whom they saw at all in only the rarest of circumstances, trailed fractionally behind the movements and words of the battle-brothers before them, closer in time with the echoes bouncing back off the nearest walls than to the original utterances. But the Scouts were not castigated for the delay by their sergeants, and so Zatori had to assume there were allowances made in such situations for neophytes.

Chapter Master Pugh lowered his arm and regarded the assembled Imperial Fists before him for a long moment before continuing.

'Imperial Fists, I greet you in the name of the primarch, Rogal Dorn, father to us all. Today you are to be given the opportunity to win glory in Dorn's name, and to bring honour to the Chapter he founded.'

Pugh turned and motioned to Captain Lysander, who stepped forwards to address the assembled. As he watched the captain move to the front of the balcony, Zatori fought the temptation to glance to his left and right, stifling the curiosity to see how his fellow Scouts in Squad Pardus were reacting to this. Were *they* to be sent on an undertaking with these veteran battle-brothers?

'The *Phalanx* and the rest of the Imperial Fists fleet,' Captain Lysander began, 'has been on a slow approach to the outer reaches of the Segmentum Obscurus for the last few years, on our long patrol, and as such we are now the nearest Imperial force to the Imperial world of Vernalis, whose rulers have sent an urgent request for assistance. Vernalis has recently seen an incursion by Chaos forces of a largely unknown composition and size, which have put the population in peril and threatened the Emperor's hold on that area of space.'

Captain Lysander rested an armoured hand on the balcony's railing, and passed his gaze from one side of the assembled to the other.

'It falls to us to defend Vernalis, and to scour the stain of Chaos from the face of the planet. To that end, Task Force Gauntlet has been commissioned, a mixed force whose primary objective will be to retake Vernalis, to eradicate any Chaotic presence and to secure the world against future invasion. I will command Task Force Gauntlet, and will be joined by Captain Khrusaor and elements of the

5th Company, and Captain Taelos along with several Scout squads of the 10th.'

Captain Lysander nodded towards the far end of the departure bay with a barely noticeable movement of his head.

'The strike cruiser *Titus* is currently docked with the *Phalanx*, fully fuelled and ready to depart. You are to proceed immediately to your designated berths onboard the strike cruiser and depart within the hour. Your Chapter and your brothers will await your return, wreathed in glory and crowned in victory.'

Captain Lysander stepped back while Chapter Master Pugh took his place at the forefront once more. His expression still as dour and stern as ever, Pugh reached his right hand down to his left hip, and drew the sword scabbarded there. He held the blade out over the railing, the point towards the distant bay doors like a needle pointing unerringly to magnetic north, aiming the way forwards for the assembled task force.

'Primarch-progenitor,' Chapter Master Pugh shouted, his voice echoing in the cavernous bay.

The battle-brothers below all drew their blades – chainswords, power swords, naked adamantium – and raised them overhead, returning the salute. A beat behind, Scout Zatori and the rest of Scout Squad Pardus did the same, drawing their combat blades in salute, while the Scouts of Squads Vulpes and Ursus on either side did the same.

'To your glory and the glory of Him on Earth!' Chapter Master Pugh finished, even louder than before.

As one voice with a hundred throats, the assembled Imperial Fists shouted the antiphonal response. And this time, the Scouts were right in time with their elder brethren, shouting in unison.

'Primarch-progenitor, to your glory and the glory of Him on Earth!'

CHAPTER EIGHT

THE SCOUTS' FIRST glimpse of the surface of the planet Vernalis came by moonlight, as they disembarked the Thunderhawks that had brought them down from the strike cruiser *Titus* which hung in low orbit above the world. Their boots crunched on the rocky shore of a beach, which rose up from the edges of an ocean whose glass-smooth surface stretched out to the eastern horizon. In the near distance, just north along the ocean's shore, rose a huge structure of some kind, and though they could see little of its detail, they could clearly see the bright lights which twinkled merrily on towers and steeples, and the brilliantly bright yellow flames that danced atop the tallest spires. But for a sour, somewhat acrid scent which wafted on the warm night breezes, it was an idyllic scene.

The smell triggered a scent memory for Scout du Queste, and he found himself remembering the faery stories his grandmother had told him as a child. Though he knew better, he could easily imagine this place to have been a page torn out from one of those tales and given life, the structure secretly the palace of some fey queen, with elegant ships sailing somewhere out there on the black waters of the seas, carrying treasures back from some distant lands on the far side of the world.

But when the sun rose a short time later, Task Force Gauntlet prepared to move out from the drop-point, the Scouts got their first clear look at their surroundings, and the faery tale scene of the dim-lit night gave way to the harsh and unforgiving reality of the daylit hours. And all that they had learned in their briefings en route from the *Phalanx* were given concrete and unavoidable form.

The name of the planet, Vernalis, meant 'springtide' in some ancient and forgotten Terran tongue, or so they had been told, a time of new life and green growth. But it was clear at first light that nothing was growing on Vernalis, and that nothing ever would again. Perhaps the name had been some bit of hopeful magic on the part of the original settlers from the Imperium, a fervent wish that the mere act of naming might change the nature of the world? Perhaps it had been a reference to a time in the planet's unimaginably distant past, when it *had* supported life? Or perhaps it was with a bitter sense of irony that they chose to remind themselves forever after of all that they had left behind by coming to such a barren, lifeless world.

The hills that rose to the west, like the beach upon which they stood, were rocky and hard going. The jagged flint and crumbling shale that covered the landscape was the same hue as corpseflesh, a light shade of grey only a few values darker than the lifeless grey sky which arched over them. The sluggish sea which stretched out to the eastern horizon was not water, but instead a vast ocean of black oil, which surged and slurped audibly against the rocky shore – once the planet had supported an ecosystem of zooplankton and algae, at least, but what life there had been had been reduced to petrochem.

The structure which rose to the north on the shores of the petrochem sea was a massive refinery constructed of corroded black metal, the towering spires and steeples being massive chimneys through which black smoke and excess gases from the refining process were pumped out, the yellow flames of the burning gases above seen only as shimmering waves of heat in the bright light of Vernalis's white sun.

The already-warm air, growing even hotter as the sun rose higher in the sky, was hazed by the smoke and smell of the refinery. But through the haze they could see the rising peak of the mountain that loomed to the west, a few kilometres away over the rolling hills. It was to the mountain that the inhabitants of this region of Vernalis had retreated, scurrying into the chambers and corridors bored and blasted into the living rock itself. And it was to the mountain that Task Force Gauntlet was proceeding.

'Could they not have built a landing strip *nearer* the mountain?' Scout Rhomec complained as the squad mustered at the foot of the hills.

'The Chapter grew muscles for you to use,' Scout Valen said with a grin. He had been raised on a mining world, and the grey flint and shale underfoot and the smoke and haze overhead seemed to remind him of home. 'Surely you're not afraid of a little exercise, are you?'

Rhomec turned his scarred-cheek grin on Valen. 'I prefer to get my exercise with bolter and blade. Shall you offer me a target for my use?'

'Enough chatter,' Veteran-Sergeant Hilts voxed on a private channel to the micro-beads in their ears. 'We're moving out.'

The rocky and irregular terrain meant that mechanised units could not be easily used on the planet, so the bulk of the task force sent to the surface was restricted to infantry elements. Already Captain Lysander was leading the members of the 1st Company in the task force up and over the hills, while Captain Khrusaor stood ready with the elements of the 5th Company to head out in a flanking arc to the south. Orbital surveillance suggested that there were no Chaotic elements between the landing point and the mountain stronghold to the west, but there was no reason to take any chance.

As the last of the Imperial Fists of the 1st Company disappeared over the rise of hills, Captain Taelos motioned to the commanders of the three Scout squads, and they began to climb the hills in a single-file rank, striking a middle path between the 1st Company to the north and the 5th Company to the south, all of them aiming west towards the foot of the mountain.

'I just hope we get some real exercise before this is through,' Scout Rhomec muttered, humping his way up the hill.

Rhomec would have cause to regret that hope, in the coming days.

IN THE WEEKS spent travelling to Vernalis through the warp, the Scouts had been briefed extensively by their squad sergeants, by Captain Taelos and even on rare occasion by the task-force commander Captain Lysander himself. What was known about the opposition they would be facing on Vernalis was not much, based as it was on the fragmentary and sometimes contradictory communications received from the planet's inhabitants. Virtually all communication had been lost with Vernalis some time before Task Force Gauntlet set out from the *Phalanx*, though, so it was possible – likely, even – that the situation on the ground had changed considerably in the intervening time.

Vernalis was a mining world, of a sort, though there were few if any actual 'mines' on the planet. Instead, the mineral wealth of Vernalis was found in the massive oceans of oil that rested on her surface. Settled by Imperial colonists some millennia before, Vernalis was a world entirely dependent on the rest of the Imperium to survive. Though rich beyond the dreams of avarice in theory, given the all-but-endless supply of petrochem that could be leeched off her surface, Vernalis was in practice lacking in virtually all of those things necessary to sustain human life.

Other than a breathable atmosphere, engendered on the planet by early terraforming efforts, and a comfortably standard gravity, everything else on Vernalis had to be brought in via warp from other planetary systems. Food, water, raw materials and so forth – all arrived as regular as a heartbeat at the orbital stations that perched in geosynchronous orbit atop towering orbital elevators. And the refined product of the planet's innumerous refineries climbed those same orbital elevators, to be loaded in the cargo holds of the visiting craft as soon as the delivered goods had been unloaded. Then the craft delivered the refined petrochem to the neighbouring systems, to be dispersed and disseminated, and a short while later the craft returned with more necessities, sundries and the occasional luxury item to Vernalis.

The arrival of the forces of Chaos had disrupted that delicate routine. Their first targets had been the orbital stations, which had either been exploded, or severed from their orbital elevators and nudged out of orbit, sent hurtling away into the void. Without the orbital elevators to send up their petrochem and bring down their food and water, the inhabitants of Vernalis were left without an easy way to resupply. But given that the stations had been destroyed, the cargo ships which normally plied the Vernalis route were in no hurry to return, if for no other reason than that many of them were ill-equipped for atmospheric entry and planetary landing. To say nothing, of course, of the Chaos forces that still ranged over the world and the surrounding space.

And so Vernalis had been cut off, forced to sustain itself with its ever-dwindling stores of supplies. Their interstellar communications having been largely the purview of astropaths based on the orbital stations, Vernalis was left all but deaf and dumb as well, able to squeak out only mundane radio communiqués in the hope that some passing craft might intercept their messages. And then they waited, huddled in their mountain strongholds, praying for deliverance.

THE SCOUTS OF the 10th Company made their way towards the west, descending one flinty hill before climbing the next, their eyes constantly scanning the horizon and their auspex readings in search of any sign of enemy contact.

With the mounds of flint and shale around them blocking out any view of the oil sea or the black-metal scaffolding of the refinery behind them or the mountain which rose ahead, it seemed as though they were surrounded on all sides by an undulating landscape of dead and lifeless grey stone, which recalled to Scout Zatori's mind depictions of the land of the spirits in the traditions of his native Sipang.

Zatori fancied that somewhere ahead, perhaps over the next rise, he might chance to glimpse the spirit of Father Nei, and discover that this *was* the land of the spirits. If he encountered his late master now, what would Zatori say? If asked why he had yet to put his murdered master's spirit at rest, how would Zatori answer?

He glanced over his shoulder at Scout du Queste, who followed him in the advancing line. It was true that he had pledged to see the Caritaigne dead for his crimes, and on those occasions when he had sparred against Jean-Robur he had found it all-too-tempting to lash out with murderous intent. But that was when they were opponents. When they had stood together side-by-side against their enemies, as they had on Tunis and elsewhere, Zatori had not given a moment's thought to his hopes to see Jean-Robur dead at his feet. In battle, the hated Caritaigne was Zatori's ally, and if Jean-Robur fell then it might mean failure for their mission, or death for Zatori himself.

When the day came that he would be able to face Jean-Robur in the Arena Restricta, with no holds barred and a combat blade in his hands, Zatori would commit himself to vengeance. But on the field of battle, with the security of Emperor and Imperium to defend, he would not raise a hand against his squadmate. He hoped that the spirit of Father Nei would understand.

As the stealthy Scouts advanced through the flinty scree, the only sound to be heard behind the muffled crunch of their footfalls was the low keening howl of the winds as they whipped around the curve of the hillsides. In the whistle of those winds Zatori felt like he could almost hear the voices of the dead calling out to the living, demanding justice and revenge.

But gradually, like a descant emerging high above the low wail of the wind, another sound could be heard. Like a distant scream in a pitch-black night, it could have been a high-pitched shriek so faint that the listener was tempted to think he might have imagined it. Could the wailing winds be playing tricks on their hearing? But there it was again, and louder now, though still as high and shrieking.

Ahead of Zatori in line, Scout s'Tonan glanced back, as if seeking in Zatori's face confirmation of what he himself had heard. Zatori merely nodded, remaining tight-lipped and resolute. Taloc returned the curt nod, hefting the bolt pistol in his grip, and turned back to the front.

As the shriek grew louder, more sounds began to fill in the ranges below, first a low bass thrumming like the sound of a massive engine, then piercing shrills that repeated at seemingly random intervals like the beating of an arrhythmic heart.

Louder and louder the sounds grew as they became more numerous, but still it was unclear from which direction they were coming. With the whistling winds baffling their hearing to a greater or lesser extent, depending on their individual mastery of their augmented senses, the Scouts and their sergeants were only able to guess where the sounds might be originating.

But there was no need to guess from *what* the sounds originated, or rather from *whom*. That was something which all of the Imperial Fists knew all too well.

It was their enemy.

The forces of Chaos were out there, somewhere. And by the sounds of it, they were getting closer all the while.

DURING THE BRIEFINGS en route to Vernalis, the elements of Task Force Gauntlet had learned that intelligence about the opposition they would face was patchy, at best.

What little they knew about the forces of Chaos that had descended on the oil-world was derived from the few astropathic communications to make it out of the system before the orbital stations were destroyed, and the grainy visual images which had accompanied the radio transmissions that had been intercepted a few light-days out from Vernalis by a passing ship of the Imperial Fleet, who had then relayed the information astropathically to the Imperial authorities.

'The finest minds of the sector command have examined the visual imagery,' Sergeant Hilts explained to Squad Pardus in their briefing. 'Provisional identification has been made of the enemy elements depicted in the visual images, and conventional wisdom is that there are three principal constituents to the enemy forces.'

Hilts displayed a grainy image that might at first glance have been that of an Imperial Guard army after a long and costly battle. And in some ways, that was exactly what they were.

'Once upon a time these wretches were known as the Righteous Blades,' Hilts explained. 'Long ago, before the days of the Horus Heresy during the era of the Great Crusade, the Righteous Blades were one of the most decorated and respected infantry units in all the Imperium. Vassals to Fulgrim and his Emperor's Children of the Legiones Astartes, the Righteous Blades fought on countless worlds in the name of mankind's Emperor, and won several victories.'

Hilts paused to glare at the figures in the grainy image before continuing.

'But when the Emperor's Children were led by the Warmaster Horus in turning traitor and dedicating themselves to the Dark Gods of Chaos, the Righteous Blades followed behind. The Imperium lost a proud band of warriors that day, but the Righteous Blades lost their souls, becoming sense-addicted acolytes.'

The display cycled, and the rag-tag human army was replaced by a handful of massive figures in power armour.

'And if *those* are the Roaring Blades, it stands to reason that these Emperor-forsaken heretics are the Emperor's Children themselves.' Hilts explained.

He pressed a control stud, and the surveillance image of figures in power armour was replaced by a crisper image of a towering figure, clearly taken in a different setting entirely and from a much closer vantage point. 'Now, this is the arch-traitor Sybaris of the Emperor's Children Legion. Study his features and learn them well.'

In the image, Sybaris's armour was enamelled with garish hues, eye-watering purple and squint-inducing gold, and encrusted with garish decoration and filigree like a tree choked with vines run amok. What flesh that could be seen within the armour was pale white, and studded with piercings, needles and rings of all varieties. The eyes which gazed out of that white skull seemed deadened and numb, the pupils so wide and dilated that scarcely any iris was visible. These were eyes that had seen too much and never quite recovered. It was a condition that was like the opposite of blindness – rather than milky orbs that could see nothing, these were black eyes that could see *everything*, and could never look away.

'There are reports that Sybaris's warband has been sighted in this sector of space, and if so then it is possible that the Emperor's Children on Vernalis may be under his direct command. If Sybaris *is* on Vernalis, locating and destroying him will be one of the primary objectives of Task Force Gauntlet.' Sergeant Hilts paused for a moment before continuing. 'But it isn't just Traitor Guardsmen and Chaos Space Marines that we must account for. It also appears possible that daemons have been incarnated on the surface.'

The display cycled again, and now displayed lithe figures glimpsed only fleetingly, moving so fast that they were seen as little more than blurs of purple-tinged corpse-white flesh.

'It has been speculated that these could be further debased elements of the Roaring Blades, perhaps mutated beyond recognition as human by prolonged and constant exposure to the warp. But it is conceivable that they *might* be incarnate lesser daemons of some stripe, which might account for their apparent speed. It isn't considered a very likely scenario, but it's one we'll have to take into account. In any case, the most likely conclusion based on the evidence at hand is that there are members of the Roaring Blades Traitor Guard on the surface of Vernalis, either in connection with or under the command of some number of Chaos Space Marines of the Emperor's Children Legion, and that the possibility exists of daemonic incarnation.'

He paused, his gaze scanning the faces of his squad.

'What we *don't* know is how *many* Roaring Blades and Emperor's Children are on the planet, how they arrived on Vernalis and what they intend to accomplish in their invasion. There is no evidence of space-faring craft in orbit above the planet, and orbital surveys have found no sign of landings anywhere on the surface. Further, it appears that the indigenous Planetary Defence Forces have been completely routed. There is no indication that any organised resistance remains on Vernalis. We should consider this captured territory, and proceed accordingly.'

UPON EMERGING FROM the warp in the skies above Vernalis, the strike cruiser *Titus* had been able to confirm via orbital reconnaissance that the population centres near the planet's north pole had been deserted, and that the refineries appeared to be running in fully automated modes, crewed by servitors but without any human staff in place. And while the ground-based batteries of the automated planetary defences appeared still to be in fully functional operation, which could explain why the forces of Chaos had not made an all-out aerial assault on the surface, there was no sign of the Vernalis Planetary Defence Force.

With some effort, the *Titus* had succeeded in establishing spotty radio contact with a group of survivors on the surface, who had holed up in the mountain stronghold on the planet's western hemisphere that housed the automated controls of the planetary defence systems. But shortly after contact was established the connection had been lost, though whether the loss was due to interference from the white sun's radiation, or had been caused by some kind of equipment failure on the ground, or was the result of active jamming on the part of the opposition, no one could say.

Captain Lysander and his task force made planetfall with the intent of rendezvousing with the survivors in the stronghold. With the information they would obtain from the inhabitants, they would be able to ascertain the capacities of the opposition, and the extent and range of their control.

It was not expected that Task Force Gauntlet would make contact with the enemy before first reaching the mountain, but still an encounter was a real possibility. Taking that into consideration, when the squads set out from the landing site on the shore, Captain Lysander had put them on a combat footing, and given the squads autonomy to respond to enemy action as their commanding officers saw fit.

SCOUT S'TONAN HEFTED his bolt pistol, resisting the temptation to check the action and rack the weapon for the tenth time since they'd left the shale beach. He felt on edge, his senses strained to their limits, searching out any change in the howling chaos that approached them.

The thrumming and shrieking had grown ever louder, ever closer, without the Scouts or their sergeants getting the first glimpse of the enemy. They had continued on through the rolling grey hills, the flint and shale slipping underfoot as they crunched their way forwards. When they crested each rise, they could see the mountain towards which they marched, looming ever larger in the west, but even the enhanced vision of the Astartes could not see any sign of the enemy.

There were some twenty-nine Imperial Fists in Captain Taelos's column, taking the Scouts and Veteran-Sergeant Hilts of Squad Pardus together with Squads Vulpes and Ursus, both of which were ten-strong, nine Scouts each commanded by a veteran-sergeant.

Squad Pardus was at the front of the column, and Taloc marched right behind Veteran-Sergeant Hilts in the lead. When Captain Taelos called a halt on the leeward side of a hill's crest, and called for the three veteran-sergeants to join him for a quick counsel, Taloc was near enough to overhear.

'Report,' Captain Taelos said, and quickly added, 'and speak freely.'

'Still no sign,' Veteran-Sergeant Hilts said. 'And I'm not getting anything on auspex, either.'

Veteran-Sergeant Karn of Squad Vulpes shook his head, a dour expression souring his scar-cheeked face. 'Nor am I. Nothing but rock and empty air, and the other two columns to north and south.'

'I'm in vox contact with the other captains,' Captain Taelos said, 'but it's proving difficult to maintain the connection. It seems that there's a high degree of particulate matter in the atmosphere, probably mineral and almost definitely pumped into the air as a byproduct of the refining processes. It's scattering our vox-signals badly, and the more air between sender and receiver, the greater the chance of the loss of signal integrity.'

'Could that be what scuttled radio contact between the strike cruiser and the surface?' Veteran-Sergeant Derex of Squad Ursus asked.

'Possibly,' Captain Taelos answered. 'The atmosphere is damned dense, too, which doesn't help.

But that may be the reason we can hear but not see the enemy.'

Scout s'Tonan could remember the tactical indoctrination sessions back on the *Phalanx* in which Veteran-Sergeant Hilts had drilled them on the situational effects of various environments on combat. At the time, Taloc had wondered whether he would ever in his life visit all of the myriad different types of worlds and habitats that Hilts had described, and here he found himself only months later on a world which conformed with one of the atmospheric types that the veteran-sergeant had stressed. And so Taloc recalled easily learning that things in a dense atmosphere could sound as though they were coming from a short distance off, but could in reality be a day's march away, or even more.

But Taloc also remembered Veteran-Sergeant Hilts warning the Scouts of Squad Pardus that the effects of a dense atmosphere on sound propagation could be deceiving. It wasn't that near-seeming sounds *had* to be coming from far off, but that they *could*. And a warrior that convinced himself into thinking that *all* sounds were deceptively far away could pay a heavy price.

Captain Taelos noted Veteran-Sergeant Hilts's expression, and nodded in his direction. 'Hilts, you disagree?'

'Yes, sir. About the enemy's disposition, at least.' He motioned back down the scree to the narrow valley that ran between the hill they stood upon and the hill they had just descended. 'We're going up and over the rises because we've been ordered to value time over stealth.'

'Lysander wants us at the mountain quick,' Veteran-Sergeant Derex put in. 'I think he's still burned that the terrain prevents a nearer landing site.'

Hilts nodded and went on. 'That may be so. But there's no reason to assume the enemy is operating under the same constraints. A sizeable force could easily thread their way through the lowest stretches between the hills, and we wouldn't be able to see them until we were right on top of them.'

'But if they're trying for stealth,' Veteran-Sergeant Karn asked, 'why the clamour and din? That just advertises their position.'

'Not their position,' Captain Taelos said, 'only their presence.'

Hilts gave a curt nod. 'Who can know the Chaos-warped mind of the heretic? But if it were me out there stalking us, I'd look to the noise to disorient and distract my opponent, while using stealth to approach and attack from concealment. The opponent would know that I was out there *somewhere*, but wouldn't know what direction the attack would be coming from, and would be unable to set up adequate defences, particularly if he were on the move.'

Captain Taelos answered only with a steady gaze, looking from one veteran-sergeant to the next. He did not have to say that which they were all thinking. They *were* an opponent on the move, and *were* unable to set up adequate defences as a result.

As if in response, the maddening howls of the enemy seemed to grow even louder, though as the wind shifted it was impossible to say whether the sounds were coming from the east or the west, the north or the south.

For their part, the veteran-sergeants returned the captain's gaze, their silence all the response he required.

'We gain nothing by standing here and waiting for the enemy to arrive,' Captain Taelos said. 'We will continue on in the hope that we reach the rendezvous before the enemy attacks. Be prepared for anything.'

As the other two veteran-sergeants returned to their place in the column with their squads, Veteran-Sergeant Hilts returned to his place in line before Taloc.

'Use well those enhanced senses you've been granted, Scout s'Tonan,' Hilts said in a low voice. 'You'll have need of them soon enough, I expect.'

FROM THE INFORMATION stored in the Imperial cogitators, the leaders of Task Force Gauntlet had known before ever setting eyes on Vernalis what the patterns of settlement and development on the world had been. The majority of the inhabitants resided in a bare handful of hab-domes near the north pole, with a small but functional spaceport situated nearby. Ground and air transportation across the surface of the world was limited, with the only major arteries being the tram lines that connected the hives to one another, and to the transport depots at the base of each of the orbital elevators that dotted the surface. Otherwise, there were no major roadways or other transit paths of note. Large regions of Vernalis's surface were all but untouched by human presence, save for the massive pipelines that crisscrossed the landscape, both those laid above-ground and those which ran through subterranean tunnels. These pipelines carried the finished product of the refineries that ringed the oil seas to the orbital elevator's transport depots, to be lifted into orbit and then ferried out of the system.

Vernalis had, as any Imperial world was required to do, raised a Planetary Defence Force. However, the most recent reports received by the Imperial authorities were that the Vernalis PDF was a relatively small force, a thousand or so infantry at best. The bulk of the planetary defence rested on the servitor-governed systems, consisting of station-to-ship batteries on the orbital stations and ground-to-air batteries at strategic locations on the planet's surface.

The orbital surveillance carried out by the strike cruiser *Titus* when it approached Vernalis showed the devastation wrought on the world by the forces of the ruinous powers. The destruction of the orbital stations made clear that the station-to-ship batteries had been insufficient to the task. And the hives in the north showed considerable damage, the inhabitants having either fled or perished. A number of the transport depots had been demolished, but while the destruction could have been the result of enemy attack or sabotage, the damage could easily have been caused by the impact of the orbital elevator's tether falling back to the surface after the elevator's orbital equilibrium was upset.

However, it appeared that none of the automated refineries had sustained any significant damage, and while it was impossible to say from orbit what the state of the subterranean tunnels might be, the above-ground pipelines did not appear to have been disturbed or disrupted in any way.

The ground-to-air batteries of the automated planetary defences, finally, were intact, and appeared to be fully functional. Each of them was protected by an all-but-impenetrable void shield, each with its own independent generator. Crewed entirely by servitors and with all the defence systems governed by the master controls in the mountain stronghold on the western hemisphere, there were no human crew onsite who might run scared and abandon their posts. So long as the void shields were not deactivated, the batteries were virtually indestructible from any ground-based attack, and had enough firepower to knock any air-based approach out of the sky before an aerial assault could be launched. In fact, there appeared to be evidence of wreckage scattered along the southern edges of the western hemisphere that suggested some number of enemy craft had been shot down in just such an attempted assault, though it was just as possible that these represented the destroyed remains of the craft that had brought the enemy to the surface.

Captain Lysander's best estimate, on receiving the updated intelligence and comparing it against the information from the Imperial cogitators, was that a small enemy force had managed to reach the surface. Then, before the inhabitants knew the enemy was among them, the enemy had infiltrated and taken control of the transport depots, and using the orbital elevators had sent munitions packages up to the orbital stations in the place of the regular petrochem shipments, possibly on timed charges set to explode as soon as they reached the stations. Only then did they launch their attacks on the planet's population centres, when it was already too late for the inhabitants of Vernalis to escape or call for help.

It was a sound tactic, employing stealth to reach the surface and then cutting off the ability of the inhabitants to get off-world or make contact with other systems before even announcing their presence. It was an approach that the Imperial Fists themselves might have employed were the circumstances reversed, and they were cast in the role of invaders rather than reconquering defenders.

If any among Task Force Gauntlet recalled that the Emperor's Children had before their fall to heresy been the most devoted warriors of the Imperium, brilliant strategists and supremely efficient combatants, none of them were willing to mention the fact aloud.

Now THE MOUNTAIN loomed so high in the west that the advancing column did not need to climb the next rise to catch a glimpse of it, but could see its grey peak from the lowest points of the valleys and gullies which snaked between the hills. The Scouts who followed Captain Taelos surely felt that each rise they crested was certain to be the last before they reached the foot of the mountain, but every time there was another valley and another hill before them, and the mountain loomed ever larger.

At the head of the column, Captain Taelos glanced at his auspex again, tempted for the hundredth time today to simply deactivate the device altogether. It was certainly doing him little good as it was. Whatever it was in the atmosphere that was interfering with vox-traffic had begun to baffle the auspex's ability to sense its surroundings as well. In the hour or so since he had called a halt and conferred with his sergeants, he had lost regular contact with the columns of the 1st and 5th Company elements to the north and south, able to send and receive only brief bursts by vox every few minutes.

He knew that Captains Lysander and Khrusaor were advancing steadily to the west, that they expected to reach the base of the mountain within the hour and that they had as yet not made any verifiable contact with the enemy. Only the damnable shrieking and howling that droned ever

on and on gave any hint of the presence of the
Chaotic forces, but as Veteran-Sergeant Hilts had
pointed out there was no solid way of knowing
whether the sounds were travelling a metre or a
kilometre or even more.

The wind shifted, and a gust blew a plume of fine
grey dust into Taelos's face, searing his eyes and
gritting his teeth. His helmet hung at his waist, but
like the veteran-sergeants who followed behind
him Taelos had chosen not to don it. When leading
Scouts who had perforce to march into harm's way
with their heads bare and unprotected, it appeared
to Taelos unseemly that their commanding officers
should not do the same.

His body responded flawlessly to the dust, tear
ducts flushing the irritant from the eyes, and the
grit that had blown into the mouth being simply
swallowed, to be later broken down and isolated by
the preomnor if it proved any kind of threat.

With a glance over his shoulder, Captain Taelos
motioned to Veteran-Sergeant Hilts that they
would continue over the rise and down the next
valley. Hilts passed the signal back to the other
veteran-sergeants with a wave of his hand. There
was no point in employing vox-comms
unnecessarily, after all, and with the howling shriek
rising over the whistling wind, they would have to
shout to be heard from one end of the column to
the other if they were to pass orders vocally.

Sliding down the scree as he descended, the shale
and flint in places not densely packed enough to

support an Astartes' immense weight, Captain Taelos reached the lowest point of the depression between the two hills, and made his way across the narrow gully to the point where the next hill began to rise before them. He could almost hear the thoughts of the Scouts behind him, hoping that *this* might be the last hill before they reached their destination. He glanced back at the column, and saw that the rearguard was now descending the scree, the rest of the Scouts maintaining formation as best they could as they bunched up in the low valley.

And suddenly, silence fell.

Captain Taelos almost reached up to check his helmet's audio intake, before remembering he wasn't wearing it. But the sensation was almost exactly like when the audio from the surrounding environment had been cut off.

But then Taelos picked up the sound of the Scouts' boots crunching on the shale, and the faint rasp of his own breathing. He could still hear the low mournful whistling of the wind, as well.

What he *couldn't* hear was the shrieks and screams and thrumming howls of the Chaotic forces.

Taelos considered, and then immediately dismissed, the possibility that his Lyman's ear might be somehow malfunctioning, involuntarily filtering out the hellish screams of their enemy as background noise. But a quick self-check was all that it took to prove that his implant was functioning normally and at peak efficiency.

And it wasn't as if the enemy had drifted too far out of range for the column to hear, either. One moment the sounds had been as loud as ever, louder in fact, and the next they were replaced with complete silence.

Which could only mean one thing. The enemy had suddenly and unexpectedly fallen silent.

And Captain Taelos had a suspicion he knew precisely what *that* meant.

'Defensive positions!' he shouted, racking his bolter, his gaze sweeping the hilltops on all sides. Raising the firearm in his left fist, he drew his sword with his right. 'Prepare to engage!'

THE SCOUTS OF Squad Pardus stood fanned out in a wide arc, their bolt pistols trained on the hills to the south and to the north-west. The other two Scout squads covered the approaches from the other directions, Squad Ursus covering north-west to east, and Squad Vulpes covering east to south.

Like Scout du Queste and the rest of the members of Squad Pardus, the other squads in the column had seen limited combat since joining the ranks of the Scouts. Isolated firefights, exchanges of fire in skirmishes while on reconnaissance missions behind enemy lines, running exchanges from the backs of Scout bikes with enemy mobile units. Each of them had faced the enemy and survived – though not all of their fellow initiates had been as fortunate – but in every instance the exchange with the enemy forces had been brief and isolated, ending either when the main body of battle-brothers arrived on the scene, or Thunderhawks and other aerial elements took out the enemy from above, or any one of a dozen different reasons. And none of the Scouts of the three squads had ever fought in close combat with an enemy, but had rather exchanged fire only with ranged weapons.

But now, Scout du Queste and his squadmates stood with bolt pistols and blades in hand, ready to face an enemy assault.

Jean-Robur could not help but remember the first time he had gone into battle, alongside his cousins and uncles on the green shores of Eokaroe. But though the sensation was similar, it was not the same. Jean-Robur could remember quite clearly how he had felt that morning on Eokaroe, though he could not now recall the surname of the cousin that had tormented him that morning, or the name of the other officers with whom he had trained. He had felt fear, welling deep inside. But it was not fear that he felt now, but rather something closer to anticipation, almost *exhilaration*.

He was ready to face the enemy, and to test his mettle and his blade against his foe. And he was not willing to wait any longer than he already had.

'Come on, you heretical bastards!' Scout du Queste shouted to the howling winds. 'I tire of waiting!'

Veteran-Sergeant Hilts shot du Queste a sharp look, the kind of hard expression that was typically accompanied by the phrase 'Five minutes in the pain-glove'. But Hilts did not have a chance to speak.

As if in response to Jean-Robur's taunting yell, the enemy came surging over the hills to the north-west and the south-west, howling like the damned as they came, wicked curved swords waving in their hands.

'Finally!' du Queste shouted, and opened fire.

CHAPTER NINE

THE FORWARD-MOST OF the Roaring Blades, a gaunt-faced and skeletal figure who might once have been a woman, took two shots to the chest from Scout du Queste's bolt pistol and kept right on coming. A third shot seared into the Roaring Blade's shoulder, but did not stop the heretic's forward momentum. Throat open and howling a deafening shriek, the Roaring Blade swung a long jagged-edged sabre in a killing-stroke aimed at Jean-Robur's head. He was able to block the attack with his own blade, but the force of the impact jarred his arm to the shoulder, setting his teeth buzzing in his skull. Though the Roaring Blade wore ragged battle-armour which had deflected some of Jean-Robur's shots, at least one of the three bolts that Jean-Robur had fired had bored into the Roaring Blade's flesh itself. But even with one of its arms blown away below the elbow, the injury was not slowing the Roaring Blade down – if anything, it seemed to draw strength from the injuries, even *pleasure*. The cracked and dirt-caked lips of the renegade pulled back in a sickening parody of a smile as Scout du Queste forced it back with a shove of his own sword against the jagged sabre.

The Roaring Blade's shriek turned into something that was almost a song, eyes wide and ecstatic, the rising and falling of its hoarse and croaking voice like the tones of some insane hymn to dark daemonic powers.

Even with his Lyman's ear to filter out the din, Jean-Robur felt the Roaring Blade's song like a knife in the brain, lunatic harmonics that hinted at inhuman intelligences from beyond the veil of the material world. He ignored the noise as best he could, shooting his bolt pistol from the hip, the shot catching the Roaring Blade in the abdomen. Then he thrust forwards with his sword.

Even while blood and viscera pored from the fourth and newest wound in its body, the heretic all-but-swooned in ecstasy, and when it battered aside Scout du Queste's thrust it was with even more force and speed than before.

A headshot would drop the Roaring Blade, surely, but it was also just as clear that the howling figure was not about to give Jean-Robur the chance to take the shot. When he raised his bolt pistol to take aim, the Roaring Blade surged forwards again with a maddeningly fast attack. Scout du Queste barely had time to parry, and any shot he made with his bolt pistol would have gone wide.

Jean-Robur was convinced now that the only sure way to defeat the Roaring Blade was to disarm it, whether by battering the sabre from its hand or removing the hand from its arm or whatever other solution presented itself, and then dropping it with a bolt to the head when the way was clear.

He began to chant a familiar litany of Dorn under his breath to clear his thoughts and counter the enemy's distracting howls. Then a slow grin tugged up the corners of Jean-Robur's mouth.

Close-quarters combat with an enemy swordsman, with no choice but for Jean-Robur to use his superior skills with the blade to overcome his opponent? This was the kind of contest he was *born* to fight.

THERE WERE NEARLY a thousand of the Roaring Blades pouring over the hills towards the column of 10th Company Scouts. The Traitor Guard got their name from their predilection for close combat with bladed weapons of all kinds, and for the fearsome clamour they made in the ecstasy of battle, and the howls they made as they raced towards the Scouts certainly lived up to the name.

The Roaring Blades were so corrupted by their worship of Slaanesh that they found pleasure in all sensation, the more intense the sensory input the greater the pleasure, and so sought out pain as the ultimate indulgence. It was believed by Imperial intelligence that the nervous systems of the Roaring Blades had been altered by their masters in the Emperor's Children, so that their bodies now reacted in the same way to pain that a normal human body reacted to adrenaline. As a result, if a Roaring Blade received injuries on the field of battle, even fatal ones, they would actually be *strengthened* as a result, becoming ever more ferocious and deadly, right up to the point when they finally collapsed from their wounds.

MOST OF THE Roaring Blades were armed only with sabres and scimitars, but a few here and there were equipped with lasrifles and shotguns of antique Imperial make, no doubt scavenged from the bodies of the Traitor Guard's fallen enemies. Had the Roaring Blades kept their distance and attempted simply to exchange fire with Captain Taelos and his Scouts with ranged weaponry, the twenty Imperial Fists in the column would doubtless have made short work of them, even given the Roaring Blades' superior numbers. But heedless of any personal risk to themselves or the potential casualties they would incur, the Roaring Blades instead rushed headlong towards the Scouts and their commanders, swords waving in their hands and yelling themselves hoarse as they charged mindlessly towards their enemies.

It was a tactic of desperation, or so it seemed to Captain Taelos at first, to simply throw superior numbers against the enemy, to bury a better-armed and better-equipped opponent in mounds of your own dead. But as the Roaring Blades ploughed ahead despite the first shots of bolt-fire which exploded in arms and heads and chests like red blossoms, and Captain Taelos saw firsthand the effects of the Roaring Blades' rewired nervous systems, he was forced to admit that perhaps there was less desperation in the tactic than he had supposed. For every Roaring Blade who was dropped by a direct shot from a bolt pistol to the head, or left incapable of advancing when well-placed bolt-fire blew their legs out from under them, there were five more who charged on, ignoring the gaping wounds in their trunks and arms.

And there was always the possibility that this seemingly mindless attack could be only a delaying tactic, or perhaps a first wave to gauge the strength of the Imperial Fists column, with a second wave waiting in reserve to take advantage of any new-found weakness.

Captain Taelos drew his power sword in his right fist, energy coruscating up and down the blade's edge like golden lightning. Already some of the Scouts had worked out that close-quarters would win this engagement, silencing their bolt pistols and raising their blades to close with the enemy.

'Primarch-progenitor,' Taelos whispered beneath his breath while raising the point of his powerblade towards the enemy, 'guide my blade.'

* * *

SCOUT ZATORI HAD holstered his bolt pistol, and now wielded his combat blade in a two-handed grip, after the fashion of the warrior-elites of his native Sipang. In the years that he had lived onboard the *Phalanx*, gradually transformed into a superhuman Astartes, Zatori had studied the Imperial Fists' Rites of Battle and committed to memory the forms and movements set down in *The Book of Five Spheres*.

He had set his foot on the path that would lead to mastery of the Imperial Fists way of the blade, his way guided by Rhetoricus's catechism of the sword. But finding himself in close combat for the first time, Zatori could not help but hear the voice of his *first* master, Father Nei, echoing in his memory. And despite the fact that Veteran-Sergeant Hilts and the other instructors had forced Zatori to unlearn some of that early instruction with the blade when it was deemed incompatible with Imperial Fists philosophy, there was much that Zatori had learned from Father Nei that could be incorporated without difficulty into the teachings of Rhetoricus, and in Zatori's mind the two philosophies had a tendency to blend into one, with the warrior philosophy of his earliest days supplementing and augmenting the rigorous beliefs of his Chapter.

There were three Roaring Blades racing towards Zatori's position, the one in the middle of them a bull of a man who wielded a pair of wickedly curved sabres, one in either hand.

His jaw set and his mouth drawn into a thin line, Scout Zatori slid his right foot forwards, his left foot planted behind him in an aggressive posture, with his sword's hilt in a two-handed grip by his right hip, the blade up at an angle defensively across his line of approach. As Rhetoricus taught, he was adopting an aggressive attitude with his body while maintaining a passive attitude with the blade, to draw his opponent into making the first move.

By inducing the enemy to take the initiative, Zatori would have the advantage of responding accordingly; ironically in such contests it was often the combatant who moved first who surrendered the advantage, and the combatant who remained reactive and passive who prevailed. The warrior-elites of Sipang had employed a similar tactic, which Father Nei had called 'swordlessness'. It was not always necessary to be the first or fastest to move, so Zatori's late master had said, and in fact the unexpected action was often the correct one – such as throwing down one's sword to confuse the enemy.

Zatori found it as difficult now as an Imperial Fist Scout as he had as a young Sipangish squire to accept the idea of discarding one's weapon as a tactic in battle, but he did not question the value of the unexpected. And he had come to accept the maxim that he who moved last often gained the upper hand.

Of course, it did not appear that he would have much difficulty in drawing the Roaring Blade into taking the initiative and moving first.

Little more than a heartbeat had passed since Zatori had slid his foot forwards, his sense of time seeming to slow as the moment of first contact arrived. Though the bull of a Roaring Blade was the largest, he was not the swiftest, and the traitors on either side reached Zatori's position first.

The two Roaring Blades scarcely had time to address an attack when Zatori had cut them down, his combat blade slicing the legs out from under one and taking an arm off the other. They went tumbling to the ground, their blood seeping out onto the grey stones underfoot.

But there was still the largest of the three to contend with, and he promised to be more of a challenge than his fellows. Bellowing like an enraged grox, the Roaring Blade spun his two sabres like the teeth of gears swinging ever towards each other but never colliding. Zatori could feel the wind of the blades' movement just as he could scent the sour stench of the Roaring Blade's breath as the bull bellowed on.

Zatori stood with his weight balanced over both his feet, his sword still held across the line of his body. But as the Roaring Blade closed the distance to him, scissoring the two sabres together at the Scout's head, Zatori suddenly slid his front foot forwards without moving his back foot from its position. His torso dropped lower as his feet spread wider apart, and the two sabres of the Roaring Blade whistled harmlessly over Zatori's head. In that same moment, Zatori swung the tip of his combat blade from left to right with all his strength, pulling the blade's edge across the Roaring Blade's forearms in a powerful cutting stroke.

The force of the stroke after sliding into the splits forced Zatori off-balance, as he had anticipated, and he controlled his fall so that he dropped back down on his hindquarters onto the flinty ground. But even as Zatori was scrambling back to his feet, the two sabres of the Roaring Blade clattered to the shale, along with a pair of severed hands. Zatori looked up into the face of the bull, and saw that the Roaring Blade was awash in ecstasy as the pain of his injuries was transformed by his rerouted nerves into pleasure.

As the Roaring Blade swooned in half-lidded ecstasy, Zatori swung his own sword in a wide arc, bringing the edge of his combat blade biting deep into the bull's thick neck.

It would have taken two cuts for a normal blade to sever the Roaring Blade's head from his shoulder, perhaps three; but like the combat blades wielded by his brothers, Zatori's sword possessed a monomolecular edge, and sliced easily through the enemy's neck in a single stroke.

As the still-smiling head rolled to Zatori's feet, he raised his sword to meet the charge of the next Roaring Blade in line. Perhaps Zatori had not thrown his sword to the ground, but he'd allowed himself to fall in order to win, and he believed that the spirit of Father Nei would be pleased with his mastery of 'swordlessness'.

THE ROARING BLADES were a motley mix of sizes and types, men and women of all imaginable skin colours and facial features, as though they had been selected at random from a hundred different inhabited worlds. And for all that Veteran-Sergeant Hilts knew, that was precisely how they had been assembled. In his experience Chaos cults were insidious, creeping their way into the hearts of civilisations like worms boring their way through the flesh of a fruit, seeking the dark core where they could breed and spread, eventually infecting the whole from the inside out. He had seen it on countless worlds in his centuries of service to the Chapter, as the Imperial Fists had time and again been involved in the attempt to scour the taint of heresy from one world or another.

The clothing, skin and hair of the Roaring Blades were coated with a fine powder of grey dust, the same shade as the flint and shale underfoot. But even through this patina of grey one could glimpse the hues of purple and gold that their ragged uniforms once had been, now dingy and tattered. Most of the Roaring Blades had their bodies and heads completely shorn of any hair, many of them with piercings and elaborate tattoos marking across their soiled flesh, and their wide eyes had the same black stare as Hilts had seen looking out from the faces of Emperor's Children, pupils so large that no iris could be seen, eyes that had seen and experienced too much and could now never look away again.

Veteran-Sergeant Hilts dropped one of the Roaring Blades with a single shot from his bolter, and then cleaved another from shoulder to waist with a single downward stroke of his own sword. He wrenched his blade free, and as the enemy fell to the rocky ground, screaming in ecstasy, Hilts put a bolt-round between the Roaring Blade's eyes.

Another Roaring Blade leapt over the fallen body, either not noticing or not caring that he was landing in a widening pool of his fellow cultist's blood, thrusting a long scimitar at Hilts's midsection. The veteran-sergeant danced back, turning his own blade in a tight arc around the Roaring Blade's scimitar, turning the point away, and then lunged forwards a thrust of his own. His sword skewered the renegade through the shoulder, but the enemy only smiled, luxuriating in the sensation of the cut, and swung his scimitar one-handed at Hilts's side.

Using the sword which was still stuck deep in the Roaring Blade's shoulder as a fulcrum, Hilts levered him to the side, causing the Roaring Blade's swing to go wide. Then, as the Roaring Blade toppled off balance and fell sprawling onto his side, Hilts yanked the blade of his sword out of the enemy's chest, then speared downwards with his sword, driving the point deep into the Roaring Blade's head from ear to ear.

Hilts planted a booted foot on the Roaring Blade's face, bracing the enemy's head while he yanked his sword free once more. Then he turned to face the next enemy to rush towards him.

These Roaring Blades might once have been as human as any of the inhabitants of the Imperium that the Imperial Fists were sworn to protect, but

Hilts did not recognise any kinship with the creatures who lay dead at his feet. These wretches had long ago surrendered their humanity in exchange for the favour of the Dark Gods of Chaos, and they would get no mercy from Veteran-Sergeant Hilts, nor from any under his command.

THE IMPERIAL FISTS made short work of the thousand Roaring Blades, but their victory was only temporary. As the Scouts regrouped, another wave of Traitor Guard came pouring over the surrounding hills, more than a thousand of them in all. Only this time the enemy did not simply hurl themselves against the Imperial Fists, but approached with more caution, targeting those areas where their fallen brethren had been able to inflict the most damage and disruption.

At a signal from Captain Taelos the Scouts of the 10th Company formed into a triangular wedge, with Scout s'Tonan and the other members of Squad Pardus in the vanguard on either side of Veteran-Sergeant Hilts on point, with the veteran-sergeants of Squads Vulpes and Ursus making up the other two points of the triangle with their squads arrayed to either side. Captain Taelos moved up and down the line, temporarily filling positions as Scouts had to fall back to deal with injuries from las-fire or sword-thrusts, then repositioning the Scouts to either side of the gap to free him up to move down the line.

Taloc reached for one of the frag grenades clipped to his belt. But before he'd grabbed one, he heard the voice of Veteran-Sergeant Hilts on a closed-channel vox direct to his micro-bead. 'Remember your valley ambuscade defence tactics, Scout s'Tonan. Bolts and blades only until we put these wretches down.'

Scout s'Tonan nodded, pulling his hand away. He remembered the tactics that the veteran-sergeant referenced, of course. They'd drilled endlessly on the various methods for defending any location or terrain from any potential attack, and Taloc could recite the doctrines of valley ambuscade defence chapter and verse, if asked. But in the heat of the moment, with the enemy bearing down on him, he'd acted purely on instinct, ready to grab the most broadly destructive weapon on hand and hurl it at the enemy without thinking.

He was his father's son, after all. Hadn't Tonan always let his actions in battle be guided by his heart, and not his head? Even on the green fields of Eokaroe where he finally met his end, Taloc's father had rushed in amongst the faithless combatants without any plan or strategy besides 'Kill as many of the enemy as possible before they kill *you*.' Tonan might have waited for the opportune moment to attack, at least in some cases, but once the attack was launched he fought with whatever weapon was close to hand, striking at whichever enemy was within range.

But Taloc wasn't just a clansman of Eokaroe any more. He was a neophyte, Scout s'Tonan of the Imperial Fists. Within five years one of his progenoid glands would be mature, followed in another five by the other. But if Taloc were to die before those initial five years had passed, the line of zygotes implanted within him would die as well, and the Chapter would be robbed not only of Taloc's future service as a battle-brother, but of the service of all those who would have arisen from his gene-seed in future years.

To Taloc's left was a Scout of Squad Vulpes, who grappled with a sabre-wielding female Roaring Blade. The Vulpes Scout managed a flawless parry, spinning the heretic's sword out of her hand, then driving his own combat blade down and to the left, severing her spinal column and leaving her flopping like a headless fish to the ground. Taloc could not help but pause for a moment and admire the artistry and craft of the Vulpes Scout's blade-work. Then in the next instant a sizzling blast of las-fire lanced right through the Vulpes Scout's right eye, punching out the back of his skull.

Scout s'Tonan only had time to glance back in the direction from which the las-fire blast had come, and saw the enemy who knelt near the crest of the nearest hill with a lasrifle aimed and ready, when another Roaring Blade raced forwards. With a blood-curdling scream on his lips and a long curved cutlass in a two-handed grip, he was bearing down directly towards Taloc, with murder in his blank black eyes.

Taloc had no choice but to ignore the sniper on the hill, forced instead to deal with the more immediate threat. Shifting his combat blade in his grip, Taloc sprang forwards one step out of line, thrusting as he did, so that his lunge drove the point of his sword into the soft flesh between the base of the neck and the top of the sternum. Panting in ecstasy but unable to breathe through a severed trachea, the Roaring Blade collapsed to the ground while Taloc yanked his combat blade free.

When Scout s'Tonan looked back to the rise of the hill for the sniper, he could see that the Roaring Blade had shouldered his weapon and was now rushing down to join his fellow cultists in close combat with the Scouts. Most likely the lasrifle's power cells had drained before the sniper had been able to take another shot.

Taloc stepped back to take up his place in the line again, shifting to the left to cover the gap left by the fallen Vulpes Scout.

The Roaring Blades rushed into battle without any apparent thought, it seemed. Scout s'Tonan narrowed his eyes and readied to take on the next attacker. They fought so much like the warrior-clans of his youth. But he was an Imperial Fist now, a proud scion of a heritage of strategic planning and mastery of defence. He would not act without thinking, without planning, but would out-think and out-plan his enemy, like any proud son of Dorn.

'Scouts!' Captain Taelos called over the tumult, bringing his power sword down in a wide arc and cleaving a Roaring Blade's head and right shoulder from the rest of his body. 'Every second Scout, sheathe blades, take up bolt pistols and target the enemy. Scouts on either side, use blades to cover the shooters from close attack.'

It had been some time since Taelos had last had vox-contact with the other captains. If they had not been attacked by enemy elements as the 10th Company column had been, the other columns should have been approaching the mountain stronghold by now, if they hadn't already reached it.

The Scouts had lost three of their brothers in the action so far – one Scout down in Squad Vulpes and two lost from Squad Ursus – but Squad Pardus had not yet suffered any losses and the captain himself and the three veteran-sergeants were still on their feet and fighting.

Despite their considerably greater numbers, and despite the loss of the three Scouts, the fact that the Roaring Blades were relying almost entirely on close-combat weapons meant that they were largely a nuisance rather than any kind of serious threat. Their resistance to pain, and their resilience after receiving wounds that would have put a normal unaugmented human down with the first shot, meant that it was taking more time to deal with the attack than it might otherwise have done, but now that the first wave of the attack had been fended off by the Scouts they had the luxury of using a ranged-weapon defence to thin out the attackers that remained. Put enough bolt-rounds in them and the wretches *would* go down, pleasure centres be damned.

Perhaps more than half of the Roaring Blades had gone down so far, with some fifty or so still upright and attacking. But the growing piles of their own dead that littered the rocky ground around the 10th Company's wedge were slowing down the attackers in the rear, so now it was just a matter of time before the rest were put down, as well.

Then the 10th Company column would make best possible speed towards the mountain stronghold, and they would learn the disposition of the survivors, as well as whether the Imperial Fists of the 1st and 5th Companies had run into any more serious resistance.

'For the primarch and the Emperor!' Captain Taelos shouted, and then drove his power sword to the hilt in the chest of another Roaring Blade.

SCOUT DU QUESTE sheathed his blade with palpable reluctance. He had finally felt that he had got into the proper rhythms of thrust and parry, attack and block, and that the growing number of Roaring Blades who had fallen before him was a testament to that. He recalled the first time that he had found himself in a melee with a blade in hand, facing the swords of the Sipangish on the green fields of Eokaroe, and felt a swell of pride at his evident mastery not only of the blade itself, but of the shifting realities of the battlefield. He had come a long way from the streets of Caritaigne, and in more ways than one.

Jean-Robur had received a wicked cut along his jaw-line from an enemy's blade, but already the special cells pumped out by his Larraman implant had staunched the blood-flow and the healing process had begun. But that slight wound was the only mark on him, and there were four enemy combatants who had fallen to Jean-Robur's blade. As he grappled with the fifth he heard Captain Taelos's call for every other Scout in the line to sheath their blades and open fire, he realised with mounting disappointment that *he* was the second Scout in the line, as the Scouts one man down from him on the left and the right had already begun firing bolt-rounds into the enemy line.

He was tempted to keep on fighting with his combat blade, to continue exulting in the dance that reminded him of his youthful days as a duellist in Caritaigne, that recalled to him the same thrill that he had felt overcoming opponents in the boulevards and salles d'armes alike. But he had been too well trained these last few years to be able to ignore the direct order of a superior, much less the captain of the company – and even if the long hours of indoctrination were insufficient to instil in him a respect for authority, which they most assuredly were not, then the countless hours in the pain-glove had impressed upon Jean-Robur the consequences of failing to follow orders.

But there was still the Roaring Blade before him to contend with.

Tall and lank, looking like a skeleton that had been coated in a thin covering of skin and leather, or perhaps like some kind of ragged scarecrow, the Roaring Blade wielded a long, curved sabre in a two-handed grip. His skull-like head was tilted back slightly, his chapped lips open in a wide circle, and from his thin throat a disconcertingly loud sound echoed, the kind of bellowing roar that had given the Traitor Guard their name. But despite the fact that he resembled a barely animated skeleton, and had his face tilted back towards the heavens, the sound issuing from his raw throat seemingly enough to drain the scarecrow of all his strength, he was fiendishly quick with his blade, and so far had rebuffed all of Jean-Robur's attempts to land a killing blow.

With Captain Taelos's order to sheathe his blade echoing in his ears, Scout du Queste remained in the en garde position, presenting his side to the enemy with his sword in a one-handed grip pointing towards the Roaring Blade, his free hand held out behind him for balance. His bolt pistol was holstered at his waist, and he could almost feel the weight of it through his armour, reminding him that he had yet to accede to the captain's orders.

The scarecrow suddenly blurred into motion, thrusting the sabre two-handed at Jean-Robur's midsection.

Keeping his hand where it was as a fulcrum, Scout du Queste pivoted his blade around in a sweeping motion, turning the scarecrow's attack away. Then, while the Roaring Blade was off-balance, Jean-Robur riposted with a thrust aimed at the scarecrow's throat.

The Roaring Blade jinked to the side just before Jean-Robur's thrust struck home, so that rather than piercing the scarecrow's throat as intended Scout du Queste's thrust drove deep into the Roaring Blade's right shoulder. As the heretic's ululations increased in pitch and volume, his eyes fluttering in ecstasy, Scout du Queste yanked his sword free of the scarecrow's shoulder, intending to press the attack. But before Jean-Robur could bring his blade once more to bear, the scarecrow swung his sabre from side-to-side like a club, the arc aimed directly at Scout du Queste's head.

Jean-Robur barely managed to swing his combat blade up in time to block the scarecrow's blow, the impact jarring his elbow and shoulder. For a moment, the two combatants locked swords, each pushing forwards against the other, Jean-Robur's combat blade and the scarecrow's sabre sliding against one another and sending up a shower of sparks, at last slamming together hilt-against-hilt.

Jean-Robur could feel the Roaring Blade's increased strength, as the scarecrow's tweaked nervous system pumped adrenaline and endorphins in response to the free-bleeding shoulder wound. In another instant, the scarecrow's strength might be even greater. If Scout du Queste was to defeat the scarecrow, it would need to be soon. And there was still Captain Taelos's order to consider.

'Scout du Queste,' came the warning tones of Veteran-Sergeant Hilts buzzing over a private vox channel to the micro-bead in Jean-Robur's ear.

Scout du Queste saw the perfect solution to both his dilemmas. He shoved against the Roaring Blade, pushing his combat blade against the enemy's sabre. The scarecrow was forced back a step, putting his arms out to either side to maintain his balance. In another instant he'd be stepping forwards once more and renewing the attack, but Jean-Robur wasn't going to give him the opportunity.

As the scarecrow lowered his black eyes to Jean-Robur and began to swing his sabre back into an attack position, Scout du Queste simply raised the bolt pistol he'd drawn from his holster as he was shoving the scarecrow forwards, and shot the Roaring Blade down.

As the scarecrow crumpled like a marionette with its strings cut, Jean-Robur began to sheath his combat blade, taking a brief instant to glance over his shoulder at Veteran-Sergeant Hilts.

'A good bolt-and-blade combination, Scout du Queste,' Hilts voxed, and Jean-Robur could see the slightest suggestion of a smile tugging up the corners of the veteran-sergeant's mouth. 'Remind me to schedule two minutes in the pain-glove when we get back to the *Phalanx* for the delay in following orders, but a good combination, nonetheless.'

Jean-Robur smiled, and fired another bolter round at a Roaring Blade a few paces away, the shot searing into the flesh of the Roaring Blade's shoulder. He tightened his grip on his bolt pistol's handle, and planted the next round in the side of the Roaring Blade's skull, right above his ear. The renegade dropped to the ground with an ecstatic grimace on its face.

Two minutes in the pain-glove, Scout du Queste thought with a smile. I'd have expected it to be at least twice that much.

THE LAST OF the Roaring Blades fell in a hail of bolt-fire, as half-a-dozen Scouts turned their bolt pistols on it at once, hitting it with so many rounds that the wretch's head evaporated. It fell to the ground with its sword still gripped in one hand, amidst the piles of its fallen brethren.

The only casualties sustained by the column of 10th Company Scouts had been the three Scouts felled early in the attack, all three of them having been killed by las-fire from an enemy sniper. After the last of the Roaring Blades was put down, Veteran-Sergeant Hilts paused to inspect one of the fallen enemy's lasrifles, and it was revealed that the firearm was an antique that'd had only enough charge in its power cells for two or three shots before it was completely drained. The lasrifle was of use now only as a cudgel or club, its usefulness as a ranged weapon completely lost.

Hilts broke the lasrifle in half with a single foot-fall of his booted foot. 'A few hundred infantry armed only with blades and depleted weapons? This can't be meant as a serious threat, can it?'

Captain Taelos glanced at three lifeless bodies in gold, which were laid out side-by-side at the bottom of the valley. 'Threat enough to cost the Chapter three neophytes,' the captain answered, 'but not much more than that.'

Veteran-Sergeant Derex, whose Squad Ursus was now only seven Scouts strong, scanned the horizon, his bolter still in his hands. 'The reports were that the Chaotic forces had overrun this world, and wiped out the PDF to a man.'

Veteran-Sergeant Karn came to stand beside him. 'Not with troops like these, they didn't. Spirited fighters, I'll grant, but not armed like this. And what of the Emperor's Children?'

'They could be elsewhere, lying in wait. Perhaps these Emperor-forsaken wretches were sent out as a delaying tactic?' Captain Taelos suggested. 'Or possibly they represent a unit that got separated from the main body of the enemy forces?' He looked from one veteran-sergeant to another, studying their expressions. 'Hardly matters now. Form up your squads, sergeants. We're making for the mountain stronghold, best possible speed.'

The veteran-sergeants crashed their forearms across their chests and then raised their fists in salute. Captain Taelos returned the salute, and then as the veteran-sergeants went off to muster their squads, he looked back to the bodies of the Traitor Guard which lay scattered all around.

Three more bodies to add to his count. Three more deaths for which he would one day atone, when given leave to go on his Warrior's Pilgrim-age.

THE SCOUTS OF the 10th Company advanced over the remaining hills and rises marching three abreast, with Squads Vulpes and Ursus formed into single ranks on either side of Squad Pardus, who marched up the middle. The Scouts on either side were given orders to cover the approaches to north and south, respectively, with Squad Pardus concentrating their attention on the horizon directly before them. If they encountered another group of enemy ele-ments, they would already be in position to form up in a defensive wedge and to respond appropriately.

Despite the fact that all of them – Scouts and sergeants alike – were keyed up after the recent exchange and prepared for another fight, as hill after crunching hill passed beneath their boots the col-umn marched on with no additional sign of the enemy.

The mountain stronghold loomed ever larger in the west, until finally they had crested the last hill of shale and flint and stood upon the mountain's foot. To the north snaked a massive overground pipeline that ran from a tunnel blasted halfway up the north-ern face of the mountain and out across the undulating grey hills. A quarter of the way around the circumference of the mountain, facing the east-ward direction from which the Scouts had come, was a wide ledge cut into the living rock a few metres above the surrounding landscape. Ramps were cut into the slope leading down to the right and left from the ledge, and tracks which snaked from the base of the ramp off towards the north suggested the ramps had been used by ground transport at some point in the recent past. Behind the ledge was set the hatch through which the transports had evidently passed, and it was clear to see that even the largest transports would have had no difficulty in entering. The hatch was massive, easily large enough for a Dreadnought to march through without scraping the top or sides.

This hatch was open, it seemed to Zatori against all logic or wisdom, leaving vulnerable whomever or whatever lay within. But he quickly saw that there was no immediate cause for alarm, as a half-dozen battle-brothers of the Imperial Fists were currently standing along the edge of the ledge, their gaze scanning the horizon. On seeing the approach of Captain Taelos and the 10th Company column, one of the Space Marines upon the ledge raised a fist in salute.

Scout Zatori watched as Captain Taelos tilted his head fractionally to one side for an instant, an unconscious gesture that indicated he was receiving a vox transmission to the micro-bead in his ear, and then he turned to Scout Zatori and the rest of the 10th Company with a faint smile on his weathered and scarred face.

'It appears that we are expected.'

* * *

'WITH ALL DUE respect, Captain Lysander, what do you mean, "*gone*"?' Captain Taelos stood with his hand on the hilt of his power sword, his helmet mag-locked against his hip.

Captain Lysander gestured to the trio of Vernalian locals who stood a short distance off, two men and a woman who wore the luxuriant and extravagant clothing of the planet's ruling elite. Each of the three displayed their family crest somewhere on their person, whether on a gold medallion hanging from a necklace, or embroidered on the breast of a tunic, or even tattooed with luminous ink onto the skin of their forehead. The three Vernalians were just at the range of earshot, and kept casting anxious glances at the Imperial Fists, almost as though they were grateful for their arrival but worried that Captain Lysander and his Astartes might turn their weapons on *them* at any moment. It was a common reaction on the part of normal humans on first encountering an Astartes, and Taelos had experienced it himself countless times before.

They stood in a vast, vacant loading bay not far inside the metal hatch on the mountain's eastern face. The smell of petrochem was heavy in the air, and from the corridors that led into the mountain's heart could be heard the distant whispers of a throng of people all talking at once, the huddled survivors discussing what the arrival of the Imperial Fists to their beleaguered world presaged.

'The accounts of our hosts are corroborated by the logs of the automated planetary defences,'

Lysander said matter-of-factly, 'and by our own orbital surveillance. The bulk of the enemy forces appear to have left the planet more than a week ago, and while we don't know precisely how many infantry elements were left behind on Vernalis – such as the Traitor Guard you encountered en route – it is believed that they are relatively few in number.'

'Without the ability to make astropathic contact,' Captain Khrusaor added, 'they had no way of letting anyone know. They apparently sent out radio signals that are even now only a few light-days away, if anyone was in the path of the signal to receive it.'

'Few enough ground forces were left behind,' Lysander said, 'that there's every possibility that they simply missed the last ship out. It seems that, unable to overcome the planet's automated defence systems, the enemy opted to cut their losses and move on.'

Taelos scowled, a crease forming that connected the four golden service studs affixed to his forehead. 'But where did they *go*?'

'I believe that…' Lysander began, and then raised a gauntleted finger for silence as his head tilted almost imperceptibly to one side. He paused for a brief instant, listening to a closed-channel vox, and then nodded. 'As I suspected,' he finally continued, lowering his hand and frowning. 'The *Titus* signals that they have received astropathic communication from the planet Quernum, an Imperial colony a few light years from here. Quernum reports that they are under attack by Chaotic forces, whose orbital vessels match the composition and variety of the craft scanned by the Vernalian defence systems.'

Captain Lysander looked from Taelos to Khrusaor, and nodded.

'Brothers,' he said, 'it would appear we are now bound for Quernum.'

Lysander turned to Captain Taelos.

'Captain, I will take the *Titus* and the squads of the 1st and 5th Companies to Quernum to hunt down this heretical scum, while you and your Scouts of the 10th will remain here to defend the inhabitants against any lingering Chaotic forces, and to hunt down and eliminate any enemy elements that remain.' He paused, and then added significantly, 'And keep careful watch for any sign of the arch-traitor Sybaris.'

Lysander turned to the three Vernalians.

'You and your people are to remain here in the mountain stronghold, under Captain Taelos's direct authority.'

The Vernalians seemed less than pleased with this.

'Do I understand you correctly?' said the Vernalian with the family crest tattooed in gently glowing ink upon his forehead. He was storming over to the place where the three captains stood, his two fellow Vernalians trailing uncertainly behind. 'Weeks we spend occupied by *one* invading force, and now we're expected to remain in the Bastion under the thumb of yet *another* occupying power?'

Lysander looked down at the Vernalian noble, who stood scarcely more than half his own height. The First Captain of the Imperial Fists, the Master of the 1st Company himself, paused for a moment, as though marshalling his reserves of patience and self-control, resisting the impulse to respond to the little man in kind. Space Marines were not used to being addressed in such a fashion, and it took considerable restraint for Lysander not to backhand the man across the floor.

'Our orders are to defend Vernalis and to scour the stain of Chaos from the face of the planet,' Lysander said in calm, measured tones. 'And that is precisely what we will do.'

Taelos was puzzled. Stay behind and protect a group of civilian refugees while Lysander and the others carried the battle to Quernum? This was *hardly* the typical duty of an Astartes. And why was Lysander so quick to believe the enemy had quit the planet, when there was still every chance that a larger force had remained behind in hiding, waiting for their moment to strike?

But he was a dutiful Imperial Fist, and went where he was ordered to go, even if it meant that he and the Scouts under his command would not see any real action.

Lysander must have seen the confusion on Taelos's face, for he paused and regarded him meaningfully. 'Captain Taelos, you have your orders.'

The captain of the 10th Company crashed his arm against his chest and raised his fist in salute. 'In the name of Dorn!'

PART FOUR

'The wise warrior plans out his
actions meticulously.'

Rhetoricus,
The Book of Five Spheres

CHAPTER TEN

SCOUT JEAN-ROBUR DU Queste and his brothers in Scout Squad Pardus mustered in a single rank out in the open air, the mournful wind that whistled past the open hatch sounding like the haunting voices of the damned. They stood on the ledge cut into the eastern face of the mountain slope. The locals apparently called the mountain the Bastion, though the name was not written down in any of the planetary surveys, and if the reports were to be believed every living inhabitant of Vernalis, all of those who had survived the attacks of the forces of Chaos, were sheltered within.

'You should make yourselves at home, Scouts,' Veteran-Sergeant Hilts said dryly, the hint of a smile shadowing the corners of his mouth. 'It doesn't appear we'll be going anywhere, any time soon.'

Jean-Robur had at first been unsure why the locals had remained within the spartan and austere confines of the mountain, which had not been intended for long-term inhabitation by anyone, much less thousands of refugees. But then Veteran-Sergeant Hilts had explained that the hab-domes to the north, which the bulk of the planet's inhabitants had called home, had been left by the Chaos forces in an uninhabitable state, and that the Bastion contained the only facility of a sufficient size to house thousands that was still capable of generating light, heat, water and sustenance.

The living conditions were cramped and uncomfortable, to be sure, but it was the clear choice when the alternative was weathering a cold Vernalian night out on the shale dunes, or sheltering in the refineries down on the shores of the petrochem seas. The interior of the Bastion was at least climate-controlled, heated in the cold of night and cooled in the heat of the Vernalian day, and while the whole place was pervaded by the tangy stench of petrochem, it appeared there was no place on Vernalis that *wasn't*.

'While Squads Vulpes and Ursus are away,' Hilts went on, 'it falls to us to patrol and defend the approaches to the Bastion.'

Captain Lysander and the rest of Task Force Gauntlet left for Quernum nearly a day before, and were still doubtless en route through the warp for the neighbouring world. Taking into consideration the vagaries of calculating the time needed for *any* journey through the empyrean, much less the two legs of the trip outbound and inbound and the uncertain amount of time needed to defeat the Chaotic forces on Quernum, the Scouts of the 10th Company who had remained on Vernalis had no way of knowing how long they would wait until the strike cruiser *Titus* returned for them.

When Lysander had departed the night before, he had equipped Captain Taelos and the 10th Company with a cache of heavy weaponry – flamers, melta guns, plasma guns and bolters – with which they could defend the Bastion, as well as two Thunderhawks at Captain Taelos's disposal. Before the sun had risen on the next day Taelos had already dispatched the two craft on missions. One of the Thunderhawks, carrying Veteran-Sergeant Karn and the Scouts of Squad Vulpes, would carry out a reconnaissance sweep of the planet's northern hemisphere, searching for any remaining enemy elements, while Veteran-Sergeant Derex and the Scouts of Squad Ursus would carry out a sweep of the southern hemisphere. Remaining in vox-contact would be problematic, given the interference from the particulate matter in the atmosphere, but it was hoped that with the added height of the Bastion mountain and the Thunderhawks themselves able to fly higher in the atmosphere, the interference could be largely mitigated.

'It will be tedious work,' the veteran-sergeant continued, 'patrolling the perimeter and guarding the refugees, but we have been given our orders, and we will fulfil them. And always remember that it could be worse. Captain Taelos has his hands full liaising with the local grandees, and I don't think any one of you would want to switch duties with *him*.'

Jean-Robur couldn't suppress a brief grin in response. He had only caught a glimpse of the Vernalian nobles in their sumptuous robes and finery, but he had been reminded of the Caritaigne nobles of his youth, and of self-important wastrels like his cousin. As a young man, really little more than a boy, he'd had no choice but to play their games of etiquette and protocols, and to smile in the faces of fools when his every instinct had been to reach for his falchion's handle. But he was no longer a boy, but was only one step away from his final transformation into a superhuman Astartes.

And though the Space Marine's every training and indoctrination drilled into him the need to protect and defend the citizens of the Imperium, Jean-Robur was not sure that he would be able to resist reacting inappropriately if he was forced once more to endure the kind of simpering foolishness he had once endured. With strength and speed at his command, if the Vernalian nobles were able to drive him to the acts he had only *imagined* committing upon the nobles of Caritaigne, Jean-Robur could do significant damage, to say nothing of bringing shame on himself and his Chapter.

'There are too few of you and too many tasks to perform to operate as a squad, as is typical, so instead I'll be breaking you into smaller teams. Scout Zatori, you'll be team leader with Scouts

Valen and Sandor,' Veteran-Sergeant Hilts called out, indicating the three neophytes with abbreviated nods of his head. 'You are to survey the interior of the Bastion, with particular attention to the defensibility of the inhabited areas. I want a full analysis on the situation with power conduits, air, water and fuel, and in particular an idea of what kind of petrochem reserves we're standing on. The last thing we need is for the oil to explode the mountain out from under our feet if some refugee accidentally strikes off a spark. And get me an accurate headcount on the number of refugees within – we have estimates from the locals, but I don't know how accurate their data might be.'

Hilts turned to the next Scouts in the line.

'Scouts Fulgencio and Jedrek, you're with Scout Taloc. I want you to survey the external approaches to the mountain. We know about the hatch' – he waved a gauntleted hand at the enormous metal door open behind them – 'and the pipeline' – he motioned to his left, towards the northern side of the mountain – 'but are there other points of access above ground? I spied access doors where the pipeline meets the mountain, but constructed of what material? And are they defensible? We've got a good enough view of the eastern approach' – he waved towards the east, and the rolling hills of shale they had marched across the day before – 'but are there concealed approaches from the other directions which an enemy might employ?'

The veteran-sergeant then turned his attention to Jean-Robur and the Scout who stood to his right, the ex-pitfighter, Rhomec.

'I'll be completing a survey of the controls of the planetary defences and the communication systems, located deep beneath the mountain, and I want you two, Scouts du Queste and Rhomec, to accompany me. While I study the systems, I want you to scout the surrounding tunnels. We know there are subterranean passages which link many of the essential locations on the planet, and we have high-level schematics, but I want to know the realities on the ground. What are the dimensions of the passages, and how can they be sealed off? How many passages are there, and where do they lead?'

Jean-Robur cut his eyes to the right without moving his head, and saw the jagged-scar smile on Rhomec's face which left his expression all but unreadable – when he presented a grin to the world at all times, it was almost impossible to see what the ex-pitfighter's *real* emotions were. Rhomec was not Jean-Robur's first choice as squadmate with whom to be partnered, but he was not the last choice, either. Better Rhomec's cruel humour and endless scarred grin than Zatori Zan's murderous glances and simmering anger.

Veteran-Sergeant Hilts stepped back and ran his gaze from one end of the rank to the other, nodding slightly to himself. 'Are there any questions?' Silence was his only response. 'Then you have your orders. To your duty, Scouts!'

While the Scouts began their surveys of the Bastion, Captain Taelos was deep within the mountain stronghold itself, barraged by the questions and protests of self-appointed leaders of the refugee community. He sat at the table in the midst of the high-ceilinged conference chamber, and wished he were anywhere else at that moment.

'This is intolerable,' shouted the man in robes the colour of a Vernalian sunrise, the fiery reds and garish yellows offset by the cool blue of the luminescent tattoo inked upon his forehead. Delmar Peregrine's family crest depicted a raptor in flight, but there was little of the hunter about the man. Corpulent, what muscle he might once have possessed had long since run to fat, the flesh of his fingers verging like the petrochem tide around the edges of the too-small rings he wore, threatening to swallow them whole. 'Our homes lie in ruins, the malefactors still walk freely over the land and we're kept prisoners here in the Bastion by those who should be our salvation?'

Captain Taelos took a deep breath in through his nostrils and held it for a moment, finding his still calm centre and trying not to laugh. If the Vernalian's misplaced outrage was not so aggravating then it might have been comical.

'You are the ruling elite of Vernalis,' Taelos finally said, his tone level and low but with a hint of iron beneath the words. 'And I am charged with defending you.'

'You must forgive Delmar, Captain Taelos,' said the woman in the purple gown, who came to lay a slender hand on Peregrine's round shoulder. Meribet Ofidia's family crest was a golden medallion hung on a chain around her neck, depicting a serpent coiled around the trunk of a tree. 'His holdings in the north were the worst hit of all in the recent unpleasantness, and we have yet to have word of the fate of his sisters and their families.'

Ofidia smiled like a hungry serpent, teeth white against lips the colour of blood, while Peregrine glowered darkly at her, eyes shadowed beneath his thick and bushy brows.

'I sympathise,' Captain Taelos said, nodding slightly in Ofidia's direction, his eyes cutting back towards Peregrine. 'These must be trying circumstances for you' – he paused, and then added – 'and for your people.' It was a calculated addition, as he had yet to hear any mention by the three self-proclaimed 'leaders' of the people they ostensibly were leading. The three Vernalian nobles seemed far more wrapped up in their own immediate concerns, in one way or another. 'But you must understand that while some level of threat remains, you are all perfectly safe now, and that the sergeants and squads under my command will do whatever is necessary to scour any remaining taint of Chaos from your world.'

The serpentine Ofidia's smile faltered, if only for a moment, and Taelos detected the briefest flash of annoyance on her painted features.

'If that is true,' said Septimus Furion from the shadows at the far end of the chamber, 'then why have two-thirds of your... of your *Scouts*, as you say... why have two-thirds been sent elsewhere on Vernalis? If any threat remains to the security of the Bastion and we who harbour within, should the full force available to you not be stationed here in our defence? Or do you simply leave enough guns here to keep *us* prisoner? This hardly seems the sort of task typically given to Space Marines.'

The third Vernalian noble wore a tunic and trousers crafted of a velvet dyed a blue so dark it was almost black, the colour of a moonless Vernalian night. Picked out in gold thread across Furion's breast was his family crest, depicting a small land-mammal reared up on its hind legs, with its forelimbs held out defensively before it. The man had small close-set eyes, and though he was so thin as to appear that he seldom ate at all, when not speaking Furion sucked at his teeth habitually as if he had food stuck between them. Perhaps he was too busy looking dour and unhappy to ever find time to eat, Taelos mused. Was it simply Furion's sour disposition, then, that made it seem that he was raising objections which he himself didn't seem to share? It appeared to Taelos that Furion didn't care a whit where the Imperial Fists went or what they did. It was almost as if Furion was objecting simply because it was *expected* of him.

Captain Taelos turned to address Furion, who had remained sitting at the end of the table that dominated the centre of the chamber since Taelos had entered. As the captain spoke, Ofidia and Peregrine crossed the floor to seat themselves at a pair of empty chairs beside him.

'You are *not* our prisoners,' Taelos said as evenly as he could manage, 'but our responsibility.' But he had to admit that Furion was right about one thing, at least – this was *not* the sort of task typically assigned to a Space Marine. So why *had* Lysander given the order? Taelos paused, considering for a brief moment, and then continued. 'If there *are* enemy elements remaining on Vernalis,' Taelos said, 'as Captain Lysander and I believe, then they should not be allowed to dig in deeper than they already may have done, but should be hunted down and rooted out.'

He did not mention the arch-traitor Sybaris, thinking that perhaps the less they knew of the notorious warband leader, the better.

But Taelos could not help noting that the other two Vernalians also sat on the opposite side of the table, so that now all three sat in a line facing him like some kind of tribunal, with Taelos as the one standing to judgment.

'At the same time, however,' Taelos went on, 'the civilian population should not be left unprotected. Hence my decision to station a third of my Scouts here in a defensive capacity. Even now they are taking a full survey of your security systems and defensive capabilities, and making any necessary alterations or emendations.'

As Taelos spoke he studied the expressions of the three Vernalian nobles. Was it possible that Furion's frown deepened when the captain mentioned changes to the defensive arrangements of the Bastion, or that Ofidia had darted a quick glance in Furion's direction at that same instant?

'We are most gratified by your assurances, captain,' Ofidia said through her widening smile, the gold of her medallion flashing brightly against the rich purple of her gown. 'I know that, with you, we are in capable hands.'

Captain Taelos felt that there was something subtly wrong, but could not put a finger on what precisely it might be. Something in Ofidia's too-easy smile, perhaps, or in Furion's obligatory objections? Or was it simply that Taelos was still uncertain in diplomatic missions after his failure on Nimbosa, the last time he was required to sheath his blade and holster his bolter and use mere words as his only weapons?

Taelos could not say for certain. All he *did* know with any certainty was that he would much rather face the ravening hordes of Chaos with his power sword in hand than fence verbally with the nobles of Vernalis a moment longer.

'If you'll excuse me,' Captain Taelos said, already turning towards the door, 'I must signal my sergeants for status reports.'

He strode from the room, his heavy booted footfalls echoing through the corridors and chambers bored through the living rock itself, leaving the three Vernalian nobles to their own devices… for the moment, at least.

'DO YOU THINK he suspects?' Peregrine said, as soon as the echoes of Taelos's footfalls disappeared down the hall.

Furion only shook his head in disgust, but Ofidia turned to the corpulent noble, her smile replaced with an angry scowl.

'*If* he suspected, you fool,' Ofidia hissed in anger, 'we would all be *dead*. So stay quiet and keep your wits about you. We will not have long to wait now.'

'WHAT DO YOU read on the auspex, Fulgencio?' Scout s'Tonan called down to the foot of the mountain, eyes squinting against the bright noonday sun.

'It's solid rock from here down,' Scout Jedrek called back before Fulgencio could answer, punctuating his words by kicking the heel of his boot against the jagged flint underfoot. It rang out a flat, discordant note, like a drum filled with sand.

'He was addressing *me*,' Fulgencio said, scowling at Jedrek, 'or did all that salt-water as a child rot out your ears?' Then he turned back to Taloc and motioned with his own auspex. 'But he's right, Taloc. Solid rock underfoot, no subterranean passages or chambers that I can detect.'

Taloc nodded, and looked from the pair of squad-mates on the slope below him to the point to the north were the mountainside curved around out of view.

'We'll continue on another dozen paces and take more readings,' Scout s'Tonan ordered. 'We should reach the juncture with the pipeline in another few legs, I estimate.'

The two sailors'-sons nodded in return, and then turned to head towards the north, almost colliding into each other as they did.

'Forget my water-logged ears,' Jedrek sniped, 'did all that unfiltered starlight as a child burn out your eyes? Watch where you're going.'

Taloc shook his head, and headed north. The going was slower higher up the mountain's slope as he was, but at least at a slight distance from the other two he could tune out their near-constant bickering. But while the bond between the two sailors'-sons engendered an almost sibling-like rivalry, in the heat of battle the two were able to coordinate their movements to such an extent that one was almost tempted to suspect them of having psyker abilities, and of sharing their thoughts between them.

After years of training and indoctrination, all of the Scouts of Squad Pardus, and in fact all of the Scouts of the 10th Company in general, were able to complement one another's strengths and skills to some degree in battle. Fighting as a unit and not simply as individuals was a trait that the veteran-sergeants had drilled into them for years, and which

Captain Taelos had emphasised time and again when speaking to the company. When the Scouts had fended off the attack of the Roaring Blades the day before, Fulgencio and Jedrek had stood side-by-side, one with a blade and one with a bolt pistol, picking off enemies as smoothly as if they were both parts of the same machine, like two arms governed by the same mind.

No, Taloc realised, not like two arms, but like two *hands*.

He recalled the words that Chaplain Dominicus had recited whenever one of the neophytes had been helped out of the scouring embrace of the pain-glove by their fellow neophytes.

'The one hand clenched in a fist, to strike your enemies. The other hand held out to your brother, to share your strengths.'

Scout s'Tonan motioned to the other two Scouts to stop and take another set of auspex readings when they'd covered a dozen or so metres. The mountain the locals called the Bastion was easily as large as the biggest peak back on Taloc's native Eokaroe. But the mountains of Taloc's youth had been riven with the scars of ancient lava flows, pocked with caves where pockets of air had formed beneath the molten rock as it cooled, and studded here and there like whiskers on an old man's chin with the green growth of trees and ferns. By contrast, this Bastion was all but featureless, a cone of grey stone that rose to a point high above them, its surface rough and irregular at the narrow scale but when viewed from any distance seeming to be nearly perfectly conical and symmetrical.

When the other two had read off their findings, bickering all the while, and Taloc had recorded them in his data-slate, they continued on to the north, stopping twice more before finally reaching the pipeline on the northern slope.

The pipeline was easily twice as tall as an Astartes in full power armour, and on examination proved to be not a single pipe as it appeared from a distance but several that lay side-by-side and bound together by massive metal bands. Each of the three pipes was perfectly circular and symmetrical in circumference, so that the pipeline altogether was three times as wide as it was tall. The pipeline marched directly north from the mountain, unwavering as it travelled across and over the undulating hills, until it disappeared at last on the far northern horizon.

A blockhouse of metal and stone marked the join between the pipeline and the mountain itself, with a variety of access panels dotted here and there, and a pair of large metal hatches, one opening to the west and one to the east. The hatches and access panels seemed to be locked and secure, but Taloc was not sure how much punishment the materials used in their construction could take before breaking. An Astartes in power armour would likely be able to break through into the blockhouse's interior with only a few moments effort by pounding on the seam between hatch and stone with his gauntleted fists, without even the need to employ any kind of implements or heavy weaponry. And if an Astartes was capable of breaking through, could any less be expected of a Chaos Space Marine?

After Fulgencio and Jedrek had taken full-spectrum sensor readings with their auspexes, and Taloc had dutifully recorded their findings in his data-slate, the trio continued on to the west around the circumference of the mountain. Veteran-Sergeant Hilts would be expecting their report in short order, and they had little time to lose.

FROM THE INDICATOR lights and viewscreens that surrounded them on all sides came a faint reddish glow, giving the control room a vaguely hellish appearance. The gold armour of Veteran-Sergeant Hilts and Scouts du Queste and Rhomec were cast in monochromatic tones, and could as easily have been white and black or any other opposing values. And their eyes seemed to glow with an inner light, pupils dilated wide and reflecting back the instruments' glow.

'Try again,' Hilts ordered, glancing over to Scout du Queste at the next station. 'See if you can bring the controls online now.'

Scout du Queste nodded in reply, and punched in the initialisation sequence yet another time. But when he'd hit the final keys in the sequence, he was answered now with another series of braying tones that made clear that the communication systems were still inoperative.

'No good, sergeant,' du Queste said unnecessarily, shaking his head and scowling.

Veteran-Sergeant Hilts scowled, as well, but could not disagree.

'Scout Rhomec,' Hilts went on, turning from the waist to glance back at the Scout on the opposite side of the small room. 'Anything on your end?'

'Nothing,' Rhomec said simply, turning his scarred visage to look back at Hilts for a brief instant. So many Imperial Fists wore the white nicks of ancient duelling scars on their cheeks, badges of honour from the Arena Restricta, but the young ex-pitfighter had brought his battle scars with him. And lacking the expert hand of an Apothecary or the protective properties of the Astartes implants to aid in the healing process, the chainsword-gashes in Rhomec's cheeks had not healed down to delicate white scars, but were jagged mutilations. Still, the ex-pitfighter seemed to bear them with as much pride as any battle-brother of the Imperial Fists did his own duelling scars.

'Emperor give me strength!' the veteran-sergeant snapped.

Word had come down from Captain Taelos that the self-elected leaders of the refugee community in the Bastion had informed him that they did not possess the access codes needed to gain control of the automated planetary defences, and that they feared the communication systems had been damaged. According to the Vernalian nobles, the codes had been lost when the last officers of the Vernalis

Planetary Defence Force had fallen to a barrage of enemy fire. The refugee leaders had doubted that even Imperial default override codes would suffice, given the modifications made to the system since its installation long years before, but since none of them had access to such codes they couldn't say for certain.

When Taelos had ordered Hilts to survey the controls of the automated planetary defences, and relayed to him the refugee leaders' concerns about the access codes, Hilts had been forced to suppress his immediate reaction. He had served the Chapter as battle-brother and as Scout sergeant for longer than any of these normal men and women had even been *alive*, and he had forgotten more than they ever knew about planetary defence – and considering Hilts's near-perfect recall, that meant that the refugee leaders did not know *much*.

But when he and the two Scouts accompanying him had made their way to the control room buried deep beneath the mountain's peak, and Hilts had entered the most common of the standard Imperial override codes, he had been greeted with disappointment.

Hilts had gained control of the defence systems immediately, and it appeared that the nobles had been correct. The communications systems *were* inoperative, and after hours of attempted repairs remained stubbornly so.

They now had access to the master controls which governed the servitors in all of the defence systems around the planet, but they were unable to use the Bastion's broadcast array to boost their own vox's transmission through Vernalis's atmospheric interference. Any vessel that approached the surface without transmitting the appropriate clearance codes would be fired upon – but the Imperial Fists in the Bastion could still not maintain communication with their own Thunderhawks in the air.

'This is getting us nowhere,' Veteran-Sergeant Hilts said after a pause. 'Du Queste, Rhomec.' He turned to meet the gazes of the two Scouts. 'I'll keep at it in here, but I want you two to get busy with the rest of our survey. I want to know all of the tunnels and other access points that lead to and from this control room, starting with the corridors which we came through and then continuing out until you hit solid rock. Think you can manage it?'

Scouts du Queste and Rhomec both snapped to attention, ramrod-straight.

'Then to your duties,' Hilts said, and waved them away.

As the two Scouts hurried from the control room, the veteran-sergeant turned his attention back to the main control station, and resisted the temptation to draw his bolter and shoot the thing to pieces.

'Very well, you Emperor-forsaken *thing*,' Hilts snarled in a low voice, leaning in close to the controls, 'let's try this one more time…'

THE CAVERNOUS CHAMBERS which had been cut into the living rock of the mountain had evidently been intended for the long-term storage of heavy machinery. Servitors still trundled back and forth along the periphery, squealing to one another in their binary machine-code and tending to the massive mechanical components and drilling apparatuses that were doubtless destined to replace broken or dilapidated elements on the drilling and pumping rigs. But over the sour odour of lubricating oil and the ozone tang of electrics another scent now pervaded, filling Scout Zatori's nostrils entirely – the smell of humanity.

The storage bays and loading docks of the Bastion were crowded with the tattered remnants of Vernalis's civilian population, who huddled with dead-eyed and hollow-cheeked expressions everywhere in sight, alone or in pairs or in clusters of family members or friends. None of them had been able to wash in days, if not weeks, and even with the vaulting roofs of the chambers the air still filled with the sour smell of bodies, intermingled with the palpable scent of fear.

Scout Zatori stood with Scouts Valen and Sandor at the entrance to one of the larger storage bays, dimly lit by fixtures high overhead. The bay was enormous, nearly spacious enough to house an entire space cruiser. But it struck Zatori how quiet the chamber was, all things considered. If he closed his eyes and stopped breathing in for a moment, he would never know that more than ten thousand refugees were crowded into such a relatively small space. Whispers echoed through the hall, slight susurrations of sound so faint that even his Lyman's ear could not pick out their meanings, but there was no shouting or laughing or crying, and hardly anyone even speaking at a normal conversational tone. It was as if tens of thousands of men, women and children had been robbed of some essential vitality, left as hollow husks capable of breathing and blinking and perspiring, but little else besides.

'This chamber's the same as the rest,' Scout Sandor said in evident distaste. He glanced from the dataslate that displayed the Bastion's internal schematics to the ceiling overhead. 'Some ductwork in the walls and ceiling, large enough for a full-grown man to crawl through, and drains in the floor leading to the drainage system.'

Zatori glanced in Sandor's direction and replied with a curt nod. Though they were not especially close, Zatori knew Sandor about as well as he knew any of the other Scouts in Squad Pardus, and knew that Sandor's youth on a sparsely populated agri-world had left him with no real affinity for large crowds. Sandor had grown accustomed to assemblages of Imperial Fists in his years onboard the *Phalanx*, but it seemed that his newfound ability to allow for the proximity of hundreds of Astartes and Scouts did not extend to the masses of unaugmented humanity. Faced with so many refugees in chamber after chamber, it appeared that Sandor was becoming increasingly annoyed.

'I read just over twelve thousand humans in the bay,' Scout Valen said, not looking up from his auspex. 'They're packed in fairly tight.'

Valen had been raised on a mining world, and seemed perfectly at home in the dimly lit subterranean corridors and chambers which bored through the heart of the Bastion mountain. Zatori knew that Valen must have spent his youth in chambers just such as this one. And while the tunnels and vaults of his home world might not always have been as thickly populated, it was surely a difference of degree, not of kind. How else to explain the matter-of-fact way that Valen looked upon each of the rooms and passages through which they'd walked so far, casting a disinterested and clinical eye on his surroundings, hardly affected in the slightest by what he had seen?

'It appears that the entrance to the next corridor is on the far side of the bay,' Zatori said, pointing a finger at the far wall, a considerable distance away. 'We should be moving on. There are many more passages left to survey.'

As the three Scouts picked their way across the floor of the bay, stepping over the bodies of those refugees who lay sleeping and around those who sat huddled or stood in their path, Zatori considered his response to their surroundings. His earliest experiences were not those of his two squadmates, the Sipang of his youth being neither as sparsely populated as Sandor's agri-world or as confined and crowded as Valen's mines. His own reactions to the cramped conditions and the mass of huddled refugees was, perhaps, midway between those of the other two Scouts. Zatori had spent his years as a squire living in one of the largest cities in Sipang, and it was not until he went to live among the Imperial Fists that he learned that his home world was less populated and considerably less technologically advanced than was typical for Imperial worlds, but still Zatori recalled the sense of awe he'd felt on seeing the steepled roofs of the Sovereign's palace towering over the city streets, or the claustrophobic sensation he'd felt when he'd first mingled with the crowds that gathered in their thousands outside the gates of the Royal Court.

So finding himself amongst the hordes of hollow-eyed refugees did not discomfit him as much as it seemed to do Scout Sandor, and yet he was not as clinical and detached as Valen.

If anything, Zatori found himself thinking more about the refugees as *individuals* than either of his squadmates appeared capable of doing. He recalled one of his first experiences with normal unaugmented humans after leaving Triandr and joining the ranks of the Imperial Fists neophytes, when he had gone with the rest of Squad Pardus on an undertaking to the world of Tunis. Zatori had been struck by how the normal men and women of that dry and desolate world had looked upon him, a lowly Scout, with fearful awe, and it had reminded Zatori of his first glimpse of a member of the Adeptus Astartes on the green fields of Eokaroe.

But Zatori saw little of that kind of awe or fear on the faces of the refugees huddled in the storage bay. Instead, he saw on each of the faces that he passed a kind of numb resignation, as though the experiences of the invasion by the Roaring Blades and their masters in the Emperor's Children had already drained the refugees of all horror and outrage, and that they had nothing left over to give.

It was not until he and his squadmates had nearly reached the far wall of the storage bay, where a corridor led away into a still-deeper section of the Bastion, that one of the refugees seemed to react to the presence of the Scouts at all. A young boy, about the age that Zatori had been when he had been sold into Father Nei's indentured servitude, looked up as the three Scouts passed and locked eyes with Zatori.

'Master,' the child said in a voice like the wailing of distant winds, 'how much longer before death comes for us? We've been waiting such a long time.'

Zatori was stopped short for a brief moment, unsure what to say. Then, motioning Valen and Sandor to halt a moment, he knelt and put a hand on the child's shoulder.

'Don't fear, child,' Zatori said, in as comforting a tone as he could manage, 'you shall have a long life ahead of you, and will continue to wait for death for many years to come.'

The child met Zatori's gaze for a moment, and then dropped his eyes towards the floor. 'Oh, well,' the child said simply, seeming let down by Zatori's words. He sighed, his thin chest rising and falling as he did. 'That's all right, I suppose.'

Zatori looked into the eyes of the child, who seemed disappointed that he had not yet died, a child whom life had treated so badly that death would come only as a release. And he could not help but stop and think – We shouldn't be here. This *isn't* what a Space Marine does…

SCOUT DU QUESTE banged his head against the passageway's low ceiling for the fifth time and clenched his hands into fists in angry frustration. Only a day before he'd finally felt himself falling into the sublime rhythms of combat and the blade, testing his mettle against the enemy's swords. But now here he was, only a night and a day later, being forced to crab his way through narrow access passages in the dark and dusty heart of the mountain. To make matters worse he was not allowed to endure this unpleasantness alone, but had to contend with Scout Rhomec the whole time.

'We should have taken the right-hand fork at that last branch,' Rhomec said again, as though Jean-Robur might have escaped hearing him the first two times he said it. 'If we continue this way it will just take us back the way we've been.'

Jean-Robur stopped in his tracks, and after taking a calming breath – remembering all of the times that an ill-considered word to one of his fellow neophytes had landed him once more in the pain-glove – he turned as best he could in the narrow confines of the passageway and glared back over his left shoulder at his squadmate.

'I heard you,' Jean-Robur said with more acid than he intended. 'Of course I heard you. You are

less than a metre behind me and braying at the top
of your lungs in a tunnel in which there is little
place else for the sound to go but into my ears. I
heard you.' He paused, taking another break. 'You
believe we should have taken the right-hand fork,
this way will lead us back the way we've been, and
so on, and so forth, yes?'

Rhomec just treated him to one of his grins, and
nodded.

'Perhaps it would interest you to know that I am
aware of the fact that this will take us back the way
we have been,' Jean-Robur continued, 'and that my
intention in doing so is to determine if any additional passages fork off from it that we aren't yet
aware of.' He pointed with his right hand to the
dim-lit passageway ahead of them, and in particular to the circular shadow upon the wall a few paces
ahead. 'Such as *that* one.'

Rhomec craned his neck to peer past Jean-Robur
down the passageway. Then he slid back on his
heels and treated his squadmate to another of his
maddening grins. 'Ah. Then why didn't you say so,
du Queste?' He waved a hand imperiously at Jean-
Robur. 'Why the delay? Lead on, why don't you?'

Jean-Robur managed to ignore Rhomec's amused
chuckle, but only just. He turned back, the occulobe implanted behind his eyes giving him the
keenness of vision to see in a gloom that would
have appeared pitch black to a normal human.
There ahead, as he had anticipated, another passage
branched off from the main trunk, even smaller

and more confined than the cramped passageway through which he and Rhomec now crabbed.

Pausing at the mouth of the passageway, Jean-Robur held his auspex up and took a full spectrum of readings. 'It continues at a slightly elevated grade for at least a kilometre or more before turning,' he said aloud to Rhomec, who made a show of dutifully recording the information in the data-slate he carried. 'If it continues at that same pitch after the turn, it likely reaches the surface somewhere within a half-dozen kilometres, assuming it doesn't hit another tunnel first. May have been intended as a conduit of some type, but ultimately never put to use.'

Rhomec waved Jean-Robur a step further down the passageway, and came to stand beside him at the mouth of the branching passage. 'Not much more than half a metre in circumference,' Rhomec said, resting a hand on the mouth's edge. 'One of us could likely traverse it, but it wouldn't be easy going. Don't know how much we could gain in doing so, though.'

Jean-Robur nodded, hardly relishing the thought of crawling for kilometres through a cramped tunnel, just to see what might lie at the other end. 'Let's hope Veteran-Sergeant Hilts agrees with you, shall we?'

MEANWHILE, ON THE far side of the world, an Imperial Fists gunship was flashing across a moonless sky, chasing daylight. Veteran-Sergeant Derex and

Scout Grigor had joined the pilot on the flight deck, while the rest of Squad Ursus were strapped into grav-harnesses back in the Thunderhawk's troop transport compartment, where they had been since the gunship had lifted off from the petrochem shores east of the Bastion early that morning.

The Thunderhawk was flying low over the ground just east of the terminus between night and day. Though the skies were dark above them, they could see less than a kilometre ahead of them the trailing edge of daylight. It was as though they were speeding through the moonless night, trying to punch back into day.

Since setting out from the shores near the Bastion, the Squad Ursus Thunderhawk had been hunting for any sign of enemy activity, flying surveillance patterns over huge swathes of the southern hemisphere, alternating low-altitude and high-altitude passes, employing all of the sensor arrays at their disposal. But so far they had found no hint of enemy forces.

They had found countless signs of the recent incursion by Chaotic forces, of course. And not just in the form of ruined structures, no doubt used as low-occupancy habitats for the workers who serviced the southern rigs and pipelines. There were still-burning pyres of the dead, the black smoke curling up into an unforgiving sky. There were countless flayed corpses scattered on the rocky ground, their skin flapping like macabre banners from posts made of human bones. The landscape seemed polluted by the mere presence of Chaos, a taint that would take long ages to scourge, if it were ever to come clean.

But aside from the scars of the recent invasion, they saw nothing that indicated a continued enemy presence.

Not until it was too late.

'Sergeant!' Scout Grigor called out from the monitoring station. 'I'm picking up–'

But before Derex could even respond, the hunter-killer anti-aircraft missile struck home. The charge exploded on contact, blowing a hole clean through the front glacis armour plate shielding the flight deck.

As the howling wind whistled past the vicious wound in the nose of the Thunderhawk, Derex turned and shouted to the pilot. 'Evasive!'

It was only then that the veteran-sergeant caught a glimpse of the charred stub of a neck atop the pilot's unmoving shoulders, and Scout Grigor slumped over the monitoring station.

'Derex to all points!' the veteran-sergeant shouted, reaching past the headless pilot and grabbing the controls, toggling a switch to open a broadband vox channel. 'Taking enemy fire. Repeat, taking enemy fire. Position is–'

At that moment, the second hunter-killer anti-aircraft missile struck the Thunderhawk high on its rear flank, managing to punch a hole through not only the armour-plated hull but the heavy shielding beneath that contained the gunship's fusion reactor.

As the Thunderhawk plummeted like a burning stone from the sky, the automated defence systems of the planet tracked its arc. But as the voxsponder onboard the Thunderhawk was still somehow operational, and still transmitting the appropriate authorisation codes, the planetary defences continued to ignore its passage.

CHAPTER ELEVEN

In the late afternoon of their first full day in the Bastion, Veteran-Sergeant Hilts found Captain Taelos in the chambers in the peak of the Bastion that the Imperial Fists had taken over as their base of operations. The chambers' original use was as onsite accommodations for the technicians who manned the Bastion's control systems, and had before the arrival of the Imperial Fists been taken over as the temporary residence of Delmar Peregrine, one of the three Vernalian nobles who had appointed themselves the leaders of the refugee community. But while the chambers had clearly been originally designed with the same austere severity of the rest of the Bastion's interior – dominated as it was by bare rockcrete floors, exposed duct work and a pervasive smell of refined petrochem – Peregrine appeared to have made significant modifications before taking up residence himself.

'Captain, you wished to see me?' Hilts stood at the entrance, hands at his sides, his eyes assaulted by the riot of colour that surrounded him. But it was not simply the fiery reds and garish yellows of the décor that struck him, but the casual display of so much decadent opulence. For someone who had fled his home ahead of a ravaging army of Chaos, Peregrine appeared to have taken the time to gather up a considerable number of luxury items in his flight – thick-piled rugs covered the rockcrete underfoot, while a menagerie of cushions and pillows of all sizes were scattered everywhere throughout the room. Though Captain Taelos had on arrival extinguished the coils of incense which had hung from the ceiling, the cloyingly sweet smell of the smoke still clung to the room, and whenever one of the cushions was jostled the smoke captured within was wafted out into the air in clouds of scent.

'Yes, Hilts, come in.' Captain Taelos sat at a large dining table, on which were scattered a dozen or more data-slates. He had shoved as much of Peregrine's belongings to the corners of the room as possible, and made of it a somewhat workable space. He waved the veteran-sergeant into the room. 'At your ease.'

Hilts entered, his gaze falling on a low bench that ran along the right-hand wall, opposite the table where Taelos sat. Placed at the centre of the bench was a cut-crystal decanter and a trio of matching glasses, and arrayed behind these like the ordered ranks of a Space Marine squad were a large collection of bottles of various shapes and sizes, no doubt containing a wide assortment of amasec, wine and various other rare and expensive intoxicants.

'This Peregrine doesn't travel light, I see,' Hilts observed, glancing from the makeshift bar to the trunk overstuffed with fine robes and silks, each of them tent-sized in order to accommodate the Vernalian's prodigious bulk.

Taelos hummed thoughtfully in response, not looking up from the data-slate in his hands. 'Perhaps,' he finally said, glancing up. 'He took the precious moments needed to have his servitors gather up all this frippery, but somehow failed to find the time to help his family escape the hive.'

Hilts looked from the noble's extensive wardrobe to his superior, an eyebrow arching. 'Sir?'

'The fat sot claims, or it is claimed on his behalf, that he lost considerable holdings in the enemy attack, and that he left his sisters and their families behind in the north. One wonders at the priorities of such a man, who would take the time to ensure that he himself would flee in luxury, but would cast his own flesh and blood to the tender mercies of the enemy.'

'From what I've seen of the man,' Hilts said with a sour grin, 'he certainly values his pleasures.'

Taelos nodded slowly, a thoughtful expression on his face. 'But enough about these pampered sybarites, I didn't call you here to discuss the failings and foibles of those we are pledged to protect.' He set down the data-slate he'd been reading, and gestured at the others scattered across the tabletop. 'I've been reviewing the reports of your squad. I take it there are three principal approaches to the Bastion that we must concern ourselves with? Two above ground – the main hatch to the east, and the pipeline to the north – and the subterranean tunnel access below ground.'

'That was my assessment, yes, sir,' Hilts answered with a curt nod.

'And your squad is equal to the task of defending those points, with the armoury we have at hand?' Taelos slid a data-slate across the table to Hilts, on which was displayed an inventory of the heavy weaponry which Captain Lysander had left for their use, with notations marking those which had been issued to Veteran-Sergeants Derex and Karn along with the Thunderhawks, in the event that they ran into enemy activity.

Hilts glanced down the list, thoughtful for a moment. 'I believe so, sir,' he said at last. 'Against a force such as we ran up against yesterday, certainly.'

Taelos narrowed his gaze. 'Yesterday we ran afoul of two thousand ill-armed and ill-fed infantry, whose only ranged weaponry were a collection of all-but-useless castoffs. We cannot presume that the only enemy elements remaining on Vernalis will all be so poorly equipped. We must assume that the force is considerably greater, with superior numbers and firepower alike.'

This time Hilts didn't even have to pause to consider. 'Yes, sir. Squad Pardus is equal to the challenge. Though naturally, if the opposing force proved to be *too* much greater or better armed, we would likely request that either Squad Vulpes or Squad Ursus be recalled to assist in the defence. My Scouts are well trained, and know their duty, but there is an upper limit to what we can expect any neophyte to withstand. *Particularly* if the warband leader Sybaris is revealed to be here.'

'Agreed.' Captain Taelos nodded. There were three main reasons why he was preparing the defence of the Bastion. First, and foremost, was that he was an Imperial Fist, and never walked into a location that he didn't first consider how he would defend it. The act simply came as second nature. Second, it was a useful exercise for the Scouts, an opportunity to hone their own siege skills. And last, there was always the possibility that they *would* be attacked.

Taelos noticed the expression on Hilts's face, a twinge of concern that flitted across the veteran-sergeant's features like a cloud streaming across the sky. 'Something bothering you, brother-sergeant?'

Hilts paused before answering. 'Well, it's simply that I don't understand what we are doing here, sir.' He waved a gauntleted hand, indicating the Bastion around them, the Vernalian refugees, the planet itself, all of it. 'Nursemaiding a bunch of spoiled civilians? What sort of duty is that for an Imperial Fist?'

Captain Taelos narrowed his gaze, lips drawn into a tight line. 'Your thoughts echo my own,' he said in a grave voice. 'And if there is a chance that Sybaris is here on Vernalis, why leave only a handful of Scouts to contend with him?'

Hilts was thoughtful. 'One might begin to suspect a larger stratagem at work, sir.'

Taelos nodded. 'You suspect Lysander of laying a trap, with the 10th Company as bait?'

The veteran-sergeant straightened. 'It isn't my place to speculate, brother-captain.'

A slight smile tugged up the corners of Taelos's mouth. 'A prudent answer, brother-sergeant.' He paused, and then added, 'Now, have you had any success in restoring the communication systems?'

Hilts frowned, and shook his head. 'No, sir. I have Scouts du Queste and Rhomec continuing the work, as we speak, but so far we have not made any measurable progress.'

Taelos tapped a finger against the tabletop, thoughtful for a moment. 'Keep at it. But I have another puzzle for you to solve, as well. Despite our hopes, we have been unable to maintain vox contact with either Derex or Karn, and we have not had any report from them since this morning. Even if you can't gain full access to the communication system, perhaps we can employ the broadcast array that the system uses to control its remote bases for our own purposes. It should be possible to use the physical structure of the array itself to boost our vox signal strength, and thereby re-establish communication with the Thunderhawks.'

The veteran-sergeant rubbed his chin with a gauntleted hand. 'We should be able to, at that, sir.' He stood once more to attention. 'If you'll excuse me, I shall get to that at once.'

'Dismissed,' Taelos said, with a wave of his hand. 'And may the Emperor grant good fortune to you, Hilts.'

'To us *all*, captain,' Hilts answered as he made his way out the door, 'if Dorn is with us.'

SCOUT ZATORI ZAN knelt on the ledge outside the main hatch on the eastern face of the Bastion, making careful study of the weapon which lay before him.

'You'll need to watch the build-up inside the coils,' Scout Valen said, standing behind Zatori with his hands on his knees, looking down over his squadmate's shoulder.

'Yes,' Zatori said with a laboured sigh, 'I am well aware.'

'And even if it *doesn't* blow back,' Scout Sandor put in, standing a respectful distance from the weapon, almost as if it would fire of its own accord and boil him to a fine mist, 'the housing assembly is going to get *hot*.'

Zatori nodded again. 'I completed the same training myself, you know.'

Sandor scratched his head, and looked from the bulky weapon to Zatori's face. 'I don't envy you. Give me a bolter and a blade, any day.'

Zatori shot a quick glare at Sandor, then returned his attention to the weapon before him. He had so far completed a full field inspection of the weapon's components, but was doing a final visual survey before powering it up for a systems check.

Is it good fortune or ill, Zatori wondered, that I have the highest accuracy ratios with a plasma gun in all the Scouts of Squad Pardus?

When the Scouts had completed their reconnaissance of the various approaches to the Bastion, and the defensibility of the various key locales on the mountain, Hilts had determined that of all the weapons which had been entrusted to them by Captain Lysander, the plasma gun was the best option for the defence of the Bastion's main hatch. The weapon's combination of destructive capability and long range made it uniquely suited to the main hatch, where the defenders would be able to see any attackers approaching the foot of the mountain from a considerable distance. And whether the attackers were regular infantry, or Chaos Space Marines, or even mechanised units, so long as the gun's operator was able to hit the target accurately, the amount of damage the plasma bolts could inflict would be significant.

So the single plasma gun in the 10th Company's arsenal was the best suited for the defence of the main hatch, and of all the squadmates of Squad

Pardus, the Scout best equipped to operate the plasma gun was Scout Zatori.

Veteran-Sergeant Hilts had called it a signal honour to be chosen to operate the plasma gun, given the weapon's destructive capacities and the complexities of its operation. But at the moment, Zatori was finding it difficult to feel terribly honoured by his selection.

Plasma weapons of any kind were somewhat rare, even among the Adeptus Astartes, but the Scouts of the Imperial Fists had been rated on all of the ranged weapons in the Chapter's armoury as a matter of course. This particular plasma gun was of a somewhat different pattern than that upon which Zatori and the others had trained, though, and the detachable plasma flasks it employed were considerably larger. As a result of the greater quantity of the photohydrogen fuel available for the weapon's plasma reaction, it could be fired for a much longer span of time than a typical plasma gun without requiring refuelling; however, it shared with all plasma weapons the need to allow the core to cool between shots, or else the tremendous heat given off by the reaction would not sufficiently dissipate, and in short order the unit would overheat and, ultimately, explode.

'Hold a moment,' Zatori ordered his squadmates, standing up and hefting the plasma gun. 'I need to cycle the power and fire a test round to be sure.'

Scouts Sandor and Valen stood aside, giving him room to manoeuvre the weapon.

'Initiating weapons check,' Zatori said, and toggled the power initialisation switch on the weapon's stock.

As the plasma gun began to hum, Zatori noted with pride for Squad Pardus that neither Sandor nor Valen stepped back. But he also noticed that neither of them had left their previous positions, when they had been *behind* him. An Imperial Fist was brave, but he was no fool.

'Weapon initialised,' Zatori said aloud, and raised the plasma gun's stock to his shoulder.

The humming from the plasma gun increased in pitch and volume.

'Acquiring target.' Zatori sighted along the back of the weapon at a random outcropping atop a rocky hill several hundred metres away to the south-east. On the bare skin of his cheek, only a finger's breadth away from the housing, Zatori could feel the heat bleeding off the coils and out through the vanes.

'Firing,' Zatori said in calm, even tones. Holding his breath to steady his aim, he depressed the firing stud on the grip.

Zatori's pupils contracted rapidly as the blindingly bright bolt of plasma lanced out of the weapon's barrel. Though not as fast as bursts from a lasgun, plasma bolts had a far greater muzzle velocity than the bolts fired by a bolt pistol or bolter, closing the distance from weapon to target in the merest fraction of an instant.

The rock outcropping vanished in a flash of searing heat and explosive shock, sending a puff of atomised flint into the air, a small black cloud that lingered a few metres over the ground.

'Cycling down,' Zatori said with satisfaction and relief, toggling the switch to begin the cool-down procedure.

He lowered the plasma gun from his shoulder, glancing at the black cloud which was already dissipating into the evening air, only dimly visible in the fading light of day. The sun was setting on the other side of the mountain, and long shadows stretched out before them.

'What's that?' Sandor said, pointing off to the south-east.

Zatori glanced in the direction he was pointing, and shrugged. 'Just a random rock. Seemed as good a target as any.'

Sandor shook his head. 'No, *that*.' He gestured again emphatically towards the south-east.

Zatori looked again, his enhanced vision straining. What he had originally taken to be the debris from his test shot, he now saw, was in fact an even larger black cloud on the horizon, far to the south and east of the Bastion. But what sort of clouds could there be on a planet which knew virtually no weather?

'I'm not sure,' Zatori said, eyes narrowed, 'but we should inform Veteran-Sergeant Hilts.'

FROM THE DARK tunnels far beneath the mountain, Scout Jean-Robur du Queste now found himself dispatched to the mountain's very pinnacle, but while his elevation had increased greatly, it was no less dark for all of that.

At least, Jean-Robur thought, I have a little peace and solitude, for once.

Scout Rhomec was currently a hundred or so metres away, in a similar crawlspace lower down the mountain's southern slope. The two Scouts had been dispatched by Veteran-Sergeant Hilts from the control room at the mountain's heart to the broadcast array threaded through the outer skin of the mountain itself, and there was too much area for the two Scouts not to divide their resources.

The architects of the Bastion had known their business, though, Scout du Queste had to give them that. The automated planetary defences operated countless ground-based batteries and sensor-arrays all over the surface of Vernalis. Communications between the Bastion and the batteries were carried out on several redundant levels, so that if there was interruption or interference on one level the others would be sufficient to continue operations.

The majority of the batteries were connected primarily by buried landlines, either directly to the Bastion or to other batteries or hubs which themselves were. These shielded and armoured cables carried instructions from the Bastion to the batteries, and carried sensor data back to the Bastion from the sensor-arrays. Though they were in the majority of places subterranean, buried at variable distances below the shale and flint of Vernalis's surface, there were a number of locations where the cabling was exposed to the open air, or in which the subterranean cabling passed only a short distance below the surface. And though the chances of any of the lines being cut were remote, given their shielding and positioning, the architects of the Bastion had opted to account for the possibility.

In the event that the landline communication was interrupted, then, the Bastion was capable of communicating with and controlling the batteries and sensors over vox-channels. With redundant relay links located all across the planet's surface, there was sufficient bandwidth on the multi-channel vox to carry hololithic, voice and data communications.

Unfortunately, though, the Bastion's multi-channel vox was a closed system, designed only for the automated defence system to control the disparate parts of its planetary network. It was not intended for the use of the planetary population, or else the strike cruiser *Titus* would have had an easier time of it making contact with the survivors in the Bastion from orbit when first arriving in the skies above Vernalis. The inoperative communication systems had left the planet's surface all but deaf and dumb.

If the Imperial Fists were successful in gaining control of the communication systems, they would gain the ability to reroute some of the communication capacity of the system's vox-network for their own use, and would have an instantaneous communication array that blanketed the entire planet. But without the communication system, that wasn't a possibility.

What *was* possible, though, was that Captain Tae-los and his Scouts could take advantage of the network architecture itself, essentially 'stealing' part of the efficiency of the broadcast array for their own purposes without ever gaining access to the central controls themselves.

Which was why Scouts du Queste and Rhomec were now shimmying around in the arteries of a web of tiny passages that were threaded throughout the bulk of the Bastion a short distance from the outer surface of the mountain.

The architects of the Bastion had known that an external antenna on the outer skin of the mountain would be vulnerable to attack by ground or aerial elements, and the cost in power-consumption of a force-field to shield such an antenna made protecting it from such an attack unfeasible. Which is how they hit upon the notion of *burying* the antenna.

The signal loss due to scatter through the flint and shale on the surface would mean that any antennae buried beneath the surface would be rendered all but unusable. But the signal loss would *not* be complete, and some percentage of the signal would still get through. The architects of the Bastion had reasoned that they could work within this slim margin of throughput, *if* they made the 'antenna' sufficiently large. And thus the Bastion's broadcast array.

The skein of metal and machinery was threaded through nearly the entire surface of the mountain, only a few metres beneath the outer skin. And though the resulting signal strength was only a mere fraction of what an antenna of that size could effect in the open air, the broadcast array was more than powerful enough to reach the overlapping network of relay links which dotted the western hemisphere and rebroadcast the data on to the rest of the planet's surface.

As Veteran-Sergeant Hilts had explained it to Jean-Robur and Rhomec, Captain Taelos's plan was a simple one. The Imperial Fists could attach their *own* vox-communication equipment directly to the structure of the immense broadcasting array buried within the skin of the mountain. That way, even if they were unable to utilise the Bastion's communication systems, they could nevertheless amplify the broadcasts of their own vox-caster through the very same array.

It was nearing evening, and Jean-Robur had been squirrelling his way through the access conduits of the broadcast array since late afternoon. Hours spent squirming through the narrow tunnels to reach the various points where the Bastion's technicians had formerly been able to access the structure of the broadcast array directly. In a pack he dragged behind him through the tunnel, Jean-Robur had hauled a collection of small repeater units, keyed to pick up vox signals of the vox-caster Veteran-Sergeant Hilts was setting up near the mouth of the tunnels far below. The repeaters would then transmit the signals to the broadcast array, which would then, in theory at least, carry the signals out across

Vernalis. They would not be able to make use of the relay network used by the automated defence system, since the Imperial Fists' signals would lack the proper prefix codes, but it was believed they would still be able to blanket most of the western hemisphere with their signal. And if the repeater units functioned as they were intended, and also picked up signals *received* by the broadcast array and transmitted them back down the tunnels to Hilts's vox-caster, it was possible that they would be able to receive return communications from the Thunderhawks, as well.

There was only one more repeater unit left in Jean-Robur's pack. Once it was in place, he would signal readiness down to Veteran-Sergeant Hilts.

And then they would see what they could hear.

DOWN BELOW, A few dozen paces from the control room, Veteran-Sergeant Hilts stood before the jury-rigged vox-caster which had been positioned beneath the largest branch of the access tunnels, listening to the communications device hum to life. Scouts du Queste and Rhomec had signalled that all of the available repeater units were in place on the broadcast array, and the vox-caster was now in the process of initialising connection with each of them. In another moment, they would know if the effort had been successful, and the boosted amplification allowed the vox-caster to punch through the interference of Vernalis's mineral-rich atmosphere.

Scout Rhomec slid out of the tunnel and thudded to the ground a short distance behind Hilts, landing squarely on his massive boots and managing to maintain his balance perfectly. As Rhomec came to stand at the veteran-sergeant's side, Scout du Queste followed, perhaps not as controlled in his landing as his squadmate, forced to pinwheel his arms briefly on either side to maintain equilibrium.

'Good work, Scouts,' Veteran-Sergeant Hilts said without turning around, his attention on the vox-caster's controls. It had now established contact with all of the repeater units, and indicated readiness to begin transmission. 'Now to see if the captain's theory can be put into practice.'

Hilts toggled the vox-caster's controls, initiating a full-band broadcast encrypted to the Imperial Fists Chapter's standard battlefield keys. And though the pickup was sensitive enough to detect a whisper from across the room, Hilts found himself leaning forwards slightly, speaking directly into the pickup's grill.

'Operational HQ to Thunderhawks *Ferrum* and *Pugnus*, Operational HQ to Thunderhawks *Ferrum* and *Pugnus*, this is Veteran-Sergeant Hilts transmitting from the Bastion. Affirmative?'

Static hissed from the vox-caster's speakers.

Hilts straightened up somewhat, thoughtful. 'Perhaps it was too much to expect success on the first try. We should test on short range and then calibrate, see if that affects the results.' Before jury-rigging the connection to the broadcast array, vox-comms between the interior of the Bastion and the surface immediately surrounding it had been problematic, the signal scattered by the dense material of the mountain itself. With the boosted amplification, communication from the control room to the mountain's exterior *should* have been greatly improved. It remained to be seen if it was. Hilts twisted a dial, and spoke. 'Team leaders of Squad Pardus, this is Veteran-Sergeant Hilts transmitting. Sound off by vox.'

Hilts glanced over at Scout du Queste, and could see the neophyte resisting the temptation to reply by vox in jest. Had it been Rhomec in charge of the two-man team, Hilts was reasonably certain that the ex-pitfighter would have sounded off, smiling that scarred-cheek grin all the while, but his visits to the pain-glove had curbed du Queste's sense of humour somewhat more successfully.

'Scout s'Tonan,' came the first reply over the vox-caster, the signal strong and clear and only slightly tinged by static, 'team is present and accounted for.'

Hilts nodded in satisfaction, hands hovering over the controls.

'Scout Zatori,' came the next reply. 'Sergeant, I've been unable to raise you by vox and am en route to deliver a report. There is something you should...'

'...repeat... Vulpes... Bastion... Affirmative?'

Hilts tensed in anticipation, hearing the new voice cutting across Zatori's transmission.

'Scout Zatori, hold silent until signal,' Hilts quickly replied, then boosted the vox-caster's gain. 'Hilts to last unit to transmit, please repeat.'

There was a high-pitched whine and a brief crackle of static, and then the voice came through again, echoing slightly as though speaking from the other end of a long gallery. 'Karn of Squad Vulpes responding, Bastion. Thunderhawk *Pugnus* is grounded, and we...' The voice of Veteran-Sergeant Karn paused for a moment, and in the background could be heard the sound of an explosion, perhaps the detonation of a frag grenade. 'We are engaging an unknown number of daemons a thousand kilometres...' Another pause as a chatter of bolter-fire sounded, and then Hilts could hear the faint strains of something that sounded almost like an ethereal chorus of female voices. '...a thousand kilometres north-north-west from your position. Over.'

'Heeded, Vulpes,' Hilts said, his jaw set and his mouth pulled into a tight line. 'Do you require assistance?' he asked, though he knew there was little chance that any of Squad Pardus could reach them in anything under a few days, and they had still not heard any word from Veteran-Sergeant Derex of Squad Ursus.

The only sound from the vox-caster's speakers was the chatter of bolter-fire, accompanied by the descant of the unearthly singing, punctuated occasionally by the coughing sound of a grenade launcher firing. Then there was another high-pitched squeal of feedback, and a momentary hiss of static.

'Vulpes, do you require assistance?' Hilts repeated as the hiss of static faded.

'Negative,' Veteran-Sergeant Karn replied, his voice sounding strained. 'We are... holding position... and...' The static surged louder, like the sound of a verging tide, and then subsided for a moment. '...continue to the Bastion when able...' The static surged louder once more, drowning out Karn's words entirely.

Then another high-pitched squeal rang from the speakers, and after that was only static.

'Dorn be with them...' Hilts straightened from the vox-caster. He was thoughtful for a brief instant, considering what he had heard, when his thoughts were interrupted by the sound of heavy footfalls fast approaching up the corridor.

He turned to see Scout Zatori slewing around the corner towards them.

As Zatori came to a halt before the veteran-sergeant and arranged himself into something that closely approximated standing at attention, Hilts waved him at ease. 'Report, Scout Zatori,' Hilts said with some urgency.

'Your pardon, sergeant, but I continued on after you ordered silence–'

'Report!' Hilts interrupted. He knew that if it was too important a matter for Zatori to simply wait for the opportunity to vox, there was nothing to be gained from standing on protocol.

Zatori drew a heavy breath, and nodded. 'There is something outside I think you should see.'

* * *

THE SUN HAD set, and a thick blanket of darkness covered the western wastes of Vernalis. But with magnoculars set to view far into the infrared end of the spectrum, Captain Taelos was able to see clearly the column of dust approaching the mountain Bastion from the south-east.

'There's no doubt about it,' Taelos said, lowering the magnoculars and turning to Veteran-Sergeant Hilts and the Scouts gathered with him. 'There's a mixed force of enemy troops approaching, several thousand of them.'

The captain handed the magnoculars back to Veteran-Sergeant Hilts, who trained them unerringly on the points in the darkness he'd scanned a few moments before. 'I make at least four Traitor Marines among their number, possibly more.'

Taelos nodded. 'Agreed. Emperor's Children.'

The figures he had seen through the magnoculars had once been Space Marines, Taelos knew, though it was difficult now to see the resemblance, whether with their armour or with the bodies within. Emblazoned somewhere on each of the suits of armour was a ring surmounted by a cross topped with a crescent – the symbol of the Pleasure Lord, Slaanesh. Taken together with the colouration and barbaric decoration displayed by the figures, the dedication to Slaanesh indicated that these were renegades of the Emperor's Children Legion. And the sonic weaponry they carried meant they were Noise Marines, slaves of Slaanesh who hungered for any and all manner of visceral sensation.

'The rest appear to be of the same Traitor Guard we encountered en route to the Bastion,' Taelos continued, 'though *these* Roaring Blades appear considerably better armed.'

Hilts lowered the magnoculars, for a moment peering with his naked eye out into the gloom, though even the enhanced vision of an Astartes was not equal to the task of seeing so great a distance in such little light. He turned to Scout Zatori, who had been the one to fetch the magnoculars after bringing Hilts from the control room. 'Zatori, when do you estimate that they will reach our position, assuming they do not stop in the night?'

Zatori scanned the horizon with the magnoculars for a moment, and then briefly considered his answer. 'I estimate they will reach the Bastion by dawn, Sergeant Hilts.'

'I agree,' Captain Taelos said, still peering out into the night himself. Taelos turned to regard Hilts and the others. 'It will be dawn.'

The Scouts exchanged glances, their expressions commingling excitement and anticipation over the prospect of the coming battle.

Taelos put his hand on the handle of the sword hanging at his side, and cast his glance over the Scouts of Squad Pardus and their commanding officer. 'As most of you will know, we have received word that Squad Vulpes has engaged the enemy to the north, reporting an encounter with a band of daemons. And that we have as yet not been able to re-establish contact with Squad Ursus. Which means, unless the situation changes drastically in the coming hours, that we ten will be all that stands between the refugees sheltered within the Bastion and the approaching army of Chaos.'

Taelos paused, gesturing towards the open hatch, indicating the chambers and corridors beyond.

'But it will not be merely for the lives of civilians that we will fight,' the captain continued. 'Housed within this mountain are the controls of the automated planetary defences, which are all that stands between Vernalis and a full-scale orbital invasion and assault. It is likely that the only thing that prevented the enemy from overrunning the planet in their previous attempt were those self-same defence systems. Why the enemy has waited until now to launch a follow-up attack I cannot say, but what I *can* say with confidence is that if the enemy should somehow manage to gain control of the automated planetary defences or, failing that, should simply destroy the system from within, there will be nothing to prevent the Ruinous Powers from invading en masse and taking the planet by force. Nothing, that is, except for however many Imperial Fists remain on the planet's surface.'

Taelos raised his hand in a fist, and noted with satisfaction that each of the others balled their own hands into fists at their sides, defiantly.

'But it will *not* come to that,' Taelos said proudly, 'for we will not allow the enemy to gain control of the Bastion! We will stand fast and defend all approaches, and not give a single centimetre to the enemy that they do not purchase with their own unnumbered dead. When dawn breaks, we will stand ready to defend the Bastion and all who shelter within. Which means we've no time to lose!'

SCOUT TALOC S'TONAN stood beneath the starry skies of Vernalis, lit starkly from below by the white-hot glow of the lascutter in his hands.

'Taloc!' shouted Scout Jedrek from the other side of the pipeline, raising his voice to be heard over the sound of Scout Fulgencio's melta gun firing only a few paces away. 'How much longer until you've cut through?'

Taloc thumbed off the lascutter and bent to inspect his handiwork.

'A few more minutes, perhaps,' he called back over his comm-bead. 'Continue working on your end, and we'll see where we stand when I finish with this first pipe.'

'As you say,' Jedrek answered, and went back to cutting.

It was the middle of the Vernalian night, with hours to go before dawn – before dawn and the anticipated arrival of the enemy army. Veteran-Sergeant Hilts and Captain Taelos had been over the data gathered the day before by the three teams of Scouts, and in the final hours remaining before the expected attack the Scouts were being put to work shoring up the Bastion's defences, entrenching in those locations which were most defensible, and barricading those areas which were considered weak points in the mountain's defence.

The blockhouse on the mountain's north face had been deemed by Taloc's superiors to be a weak point, and he and the team that had previously surveyed it, and who were considered the most familiar with the location of all of Squad Pardus, had been dispatched to begin work on fortifying and barricading the blockhouse, in order that it would be better equipped to resist an enemy assault.

Which was how Taloc, Fulgencio and Jedrek had come to be standing out in the frigid night air, cutting and scorching their way through pipeline and panelling, and melting solid rock to molten slag.

'Fulgencio, watch your angle of incident,' Jedrek shouted. 'That last spray almost hit me.'

Scout Fulgencio waved from his position a few dozen paces off and slightly higher on the mountain's slope, and went back to heating up the flint and shale of the upper slope with prolonged blasts from his melta gun. Taloc was sure that Fulgencio knew better than to waste time in bickering with his squadmate, given the time constraints they operated under.

The task laid before Scout s'Tonan and his team was simple. Taelos and Hilts had determined that the hatches and access panels built into the blockhouse were too vulnerable to enemy attack. A Roaring Blade with a lascutter and unobstructed access could make short work of one of the hatches,

and once within the blockhouse could gain entry
into the Bastion itself in a relatively short amount
of time. And the three side-by-side pipes of the
pipeline themselves were likewise a vulnerable
spot, as they were wide enough in diameter for
even a Noise Marine in full armour to traverse; if
the enemy were to somehow breach the pipes further out in the grey desert unnoticed, they could
march unseen right into the heart of the Bastion.

The solution hit upon by Taelos and Hilts would
no doubt be unpopular with the self-appointed
leaders of the refugees, or would be at least assuming they all survived the coming encounter. But
once it had been determined that the pipeline was
not essential to the continued functioning of the
Bastion itself, it had been deemed expendable.
Once the forces of Chaos were scoured from the
face of Vernalis and the petrochem pumping facili-
ties were once more in full operation – and some
mechanism was put in place to get the refined
petrochem *off* the planet, which would not be easy
without the orbital elevators in place – then the
Vernalians could repair the damage the Imperial
Fists were about to inflict on the pipeline. But in the
meantime, it was targeted for destruction.

Taloc felt the lascutter slice through back into
empty air, and then straightened up once more. The
skin of the pipe was wider than his hand was long,
but there was now a gap a little over a centimetre
wide that encircled the pipe completely. Standing
beside the pipe and shining a lume-lamp on the

gap, Taloc could see clear through to the other side, with the stars above and the grey ground below.

'That's one,' Taloc said, and clambered up onto the blockhouse. Jedrek had already cut through the rightmost of the pipes, and was hard at work cutting a similar gap in the middle of the three.

When a gap had been cut into all three of the pipes, the two Scouts would set to work positioning demolition charges around the circumference of the entire pipeline. The wide cuts they had burned through the pipes were intended to act as seams that would guide the energy of the resulting blast, forcing apart the severed sections of the pipes and widening the gap even further.

When the pipes had been blasted open, Scout Fulgencio would set to work in earnest. He was already busy, firing blasts from his melta gun at the slope above the blockhouse, gradually turning the corpse-flesh grey flint and shale of the mountain's skin into white-hot molten slag. When Taloc gave the word, Fulgencio would cut a channel from this molten rock down to where Taloc and Jedrek now stood, and the slag would pour down the channel to engulf the blockhouse completely.

That was the intention, at least. But as the hours remaining until dawn slipped past one by one, the work was proceeding more slowly than had been hoped. By this point in the process, Taloc had originally intended to be finished with the demolition charges on the pipeline, and ready to signal Fulgencio to send the cascade of molten slag pouring down over the blockhouse. But as it stood, they were only a little bit beyond the two-thirds mark in cutting through the pipes, with the demolition charges still to be set.

Taloc resisted the temptation to glance again towards the eastern horizon, to check whether the sun had begun to lighten the sky. He knew that it had not, but had still glanced in that direction already four times in the previous hour, just to be sure.

And if the sun *were* to be rising, and dawn almost upon them, it would hardly matter. He and his team would still have a job to do, and they were already moving as fast as they were able.

A spray of molten rock splashed against the blockhouse near Taloc's feet, but he did not bother to call out any recrimination to Fulgencio. There was work to be done, and no time to waste in idle banter. Bending down and taking measure of where on the pipe Jedrek was making his cut, Taloc thumbed his lascutter on and set to work, slicing in the opposite direction.

DAWN WAS STEALING slowly across the sky, and looking east from the main hatch the Imperial Fists could see the rising sun appearing to set fire to the black oil sea which stretched out to the horizon, a burst of blinding white spreading out across the surface of the petrochem ocean from the point where the sun was rising. And while the previous morning had been greeted only by the low mournful howls of the winds rushing over the undulating landscape, this morning a raucous chorus welcomed the dawn, a lunatic medley of high-pitched shrieks and thrumming booms, of droning chants and ear-splitting screams. And beneath the entire riot of sound the constant refrain of thousands of feet pounding the grey earth again and again and again, the drumbeat of an army on the march growing louder with each passing instant.

Scout Zatori stood behind the waist-high barricades the Scouts had arranged at the lip of the ledge before the main hatch, the plasma gun in his hands and his combat blade sheathed at his side. Beside him along the barricades stood Scouts Valen and Sandor, flamer and bolt pistol in hand. It had been decided that simply sealing the main hatch and sheltering within was too great a risk to take; doing so would give the enemy unobstructed access to the hatch itself, and with time and sufficient amount of demolitions or munitions the enemy would be able to gain access, and would then be free to stream into the Bastion.

Instead, Taelos had ordered that the hatch be left slightly open, with a team of Scouts on hand to defend the breach from behind the barricades, which had been hastily assembled from large bits of heavy machinery brought from the Bastion's interior, with a small gap to allow the Fists to descend the ramps cut into the mountain slope if necessary. The opening in the hatch would allow the Imperial Fists to reinforce and resupply as necessary, and while the Scouts behind the barricades on the wide ledge would be partially exposed to enemy fire, they were not to retreat within the safety of the hatch unless the enemy breached the barricades in numbers sufficient to overrun the defenders. Then and only then were they to retreat within the hatch.

Meanwhile, deep within the Bastion, Scouts du Queste and Rhomec were making the final fortifications to the various tunnels which led from unknown subterranean points into the heart of the Bastion, while Veteran-Sergeant Hilts made a final attempt to gain control of the automated planetary defences in the hope that nearby batteries might be used in the Bastion's defence, or to regain contact with either of the Thunderhawks sent out the day before – they had been unable to re-establish contact with Veteran-Sergeant Derex and Squad Ursus, and as they had received no additional word from Squad Vulpes's Veteran-Sergeant Karn, they were forced to consider the possibility that Karn and his squad had not survived their encounter with the daemons.

On the northern face of the mountain, Captain Taelos stood ready to defend Scouts Taloc, Fulgencio and Jedrek, who were still busy trying to seal off the blockhouse and pipeline to the north. If the forces of Chaos were to reach this point on the mountain's slope before the blockhouse had been completely barricaded and sealed off, they could potentially punch right through into the interior of the mountain, and into the most vulnerable and least defensible regions of the Bastion. Only when Taelos was satisfied that the blockhouse and pipeline had been completely sealed off would he order Scout Taloc and his team to retreat with him to the main hatch, to join Scout Zatori's team in defending that approach.

Wherever the Imperial Fists were in and around the Bastion, they could hear the sound of the army growing ever closer, the constant drumbeat of their marching feet, the discordant sound of their howling songs, the high-pitched whine of their sonic weapons being powered on.

No magnoculars were needed to see the enemy's composition now. Even the enhanced vision of the Astartes was unnecessary. Even the weak and untrained eye of an unaugmented human, if any of the refugees had been brave enough to stand beside their defenders, could have seen the thousand or more Roaring Blades who were even now stepping onto the lower slopes of the mountain Bastion, and the half-dozen or so Noise Marines who marched at their head.

With a roar like the voice of hell itself a blast from a Noise Marine's sonic weapon lanced into the side of the mountain only handspans from where Zatori stood.

Scout Zatori raised the plasma gun, taking aim with a prayer on his lips.

'Oh Dorn, dawn of our being, be with us, illuminate us.'

The blindingly bright bolt of plasma shot through the open air, narrowly missing the Noise Marine but completely disintegrating the head and shoulders of a Roaring Blade standing a metre or so to the left.

The siege of the Bastion had begun.

CHAPTER TWELVE

SCOUT S'TONAN STOOD back from the severed pipeline once the last of the demolition charges was in place. On the far side of the pipes Scout Jedrek had done the same, and now both of them signalled readiness to Scout Fulgencio, who was keeping careful watch on the growing pool of molten slag that he had melted behind a small damming ridge a few dozen metres higher up the mountain's slope.

Taloc could hear the sizzle and pop of the liquid rock as it sizzled impossibly hot only a short distance away, but only barely, the sounds of the battle which was only now beginning around the wide curve of the mountain now growing louder with each passing instant. Even if the enemy *didn't* know about the pipeline and blockhouse, it was only a matter of time before they sent scouting parties to surround the mountain to search for other points of entrance less well defended than the barricaded main hatch.

Fulgencio fired the melta gun at the low ridge which dammed the pool of molten slag, and the searing white-hot liquid began to flow sluggishly down the slope towards the ruined blockhouse. To make sure that the molten rock did not begin to cool and solidify en route, Fulgencio continued to fire blasts from the melta gun into the pool above, ensuring that it remained at the highest possible temperature.

As the molten slag began to pour over the blockhouse, Taloc turned back to the north, where Captain Taelos stood atop the severed pipeline a short distance away. With auspex and magnoculars in hand, the captain was covering all approaches to their position, not only from around the Bastion's curve to the east but also along the western slope, and from the north across the undulating grey hills.

'Sir, it shouldn't be long now,' Taloc voxed rather than called out, to ensure clear communication over the growing clamour from the mountain's eastern slope. 'Given the current rate of flow, we should have the blockhouse and pipe junctions completely sealed off in less than an hour, possibly even sooner.'

Captain Taelos lowered his auspex and glanced in Taloc's direction. 'Very good, Scout s'Tonan. Now I want you and Scout Jedrek to take up defensive positions to the north-east and north-west' – he pointed to either side of the pipeline – 'and cover all approaches. Just because the main body of the enemy forces are approaching from the south, we can't be certain that other elements won't be coming from different directions.'

'Yes, sir,' Taloc and Jedrek replied almost in unison.

As Taloc moved into position, he drew his combat blade from its sheath, and found some comfort in once more having a sword's handle in his fist. Working through the night and morning with lascutter and demolition charges had been a necessary task, and a duty that Taloc had been only too eager to carry out; but in his hearts, Taloc could not help seeing such fortifications as the work of labourers, not of warriors. He knew that the Imperial Fists prided themselves on their mastery of defence and siege warfare, and that by assisting in the fortification of the Bastion he was, in a sense at least, following in the footsteps of Rogal Dorn himself, who had fortified the Imperial Palace on Terra, and led the Imperial Fists in defending the Palace against the onslaught of Horus's heretic forces.

But it was not until he drew his blade that Taloc *truly* felt himself the inheritor of Dorn's legacy. Perhaps it was his upbringing on Eokaroe, and the esteem with which the warrior-clans had held their ironbrands, that led Taloc to identify more with the Chapter's cult of the blade than with the Fists' pride in siege warfare. But there again, Taloc thought, perhaps it was his affinity for the sword that had led him to be selected as a neophyte in the first place.

Taloc's musings were interrupted when he caught a flash of movement off to the north, a few degrees to the east of the pipeline.

'Captain?' Taloc said, drawing his bolt pistol and pointing with the tip of his combat blade towards the movement. 'There's something fast approaching from–'

'Daemons!' the captain said angrily, before Taloc was even able to finish his statement. The captain secured auspex and magnoculars at his waist, and then drew his power sword from its sheath, energy already coruscating up and down the blade.

In the time it took Scout s'Tonan to turn from the captain back towards the north, the faint blur of motion had already grown into a handful of daemons, racing across the grey hills at an impossibly fast speed.

Taloc knew that a significant enemy force was necessary to summon just a single daemon. But to incarnate so many? There was a much larger enemy presence on Vernalis than any of them had suspected.

Captain Taelos raised his bolter in his other hand, and leapt down from the top of the pipeline onto the flinty ground a few paces from where Taloc stood.

'Fulgencio, keep at it,' the captain shouted and voxed simultaneously. 'The rest of you, form on me.'

As Jedrek leapt up onto the pipeline and came to join them, the captain turned to Taloc, gesturing to the bolt pistol in the Scout's hand with a quick nod. 'This strain of daemon is unnaturally swift. Be wary.'

Taloc nodded, jaw set. 'Yes, sir.'

Scout Jedrek came to stand on the captain's other side, and the three Imperial Fists stood together against the onrushing daemons, now just outside the range of their bolter-fire.

'Try to lead their motions with your shots,' Taelos said, 'but even so they may jink or dodge before your bolt strikes true.' The captain lifted his power sword, the energy dancing along its edge. 'But if they should close with us, they'll have our blades to contend with.'

Taloc tightened his grip on his combat blade's handle, and a slow smile spread across his face. Perhaps he was not standing to the tourneys with a named ironbrand in his hands, but still *this* was the work he was born to do.

As THE CAPTAIN had ordered, Veteran-Sergeant Hilts was at the makeshift vox-caster assembly near the control room at the Bastion's heart, making one final attempt to re-establish contact with either of the two Thunderhawks. If this attempt failed, his orders were to join Scouts du Queste and Rhomec who were finalising the fortifications in the catacombs and tunnels beneath the mountain before joining Scout Zatori's team in manning the barricades at the main hatch.

It was quickly becoming apparent that this final attempt to re-establish contact would be no more successful than the previous attempts had been.

'Operational HQ to Thunderhawks *Ferrum* and *Pugnus*, Operational HQ to Thunderhawks *Ferrum* and *Pugnus*, this is Veteran-Sergeant Hilts transmitting from the Bastion. Affirmative?'

Nothing but static hissed from the vox-caster's speakers.

Resolving to make one final transmission before joining the Scouts who were fortifying the tunnels below, Hilts checked the settings and readouts on the vox-caster's controls. And it was then that he noted something unusual for the first time.

Though the communications system of the planetary defences was still in a fully automatic mode, transmitting and receiving routine machine code from the batteries and sensory emplacements scattered all across the planet's surface, it appeared that there was another signal being broadcast from within the Bastion, one which Hilts's equipment had previously been unable to detect.

Adjusting the gain, Hilts was able to tune in the signal, which appeared to be piggybacking on the defence systems' broadcast array in much the same way as his own jury-rigged assembly.

Encrypted comm traffic squealed out from the vox-caster's speakers, discordant and deafeningly loud.

Hilts lowered the volume on the audio output, and picked up his auspex. But the unit was unable to decrypt the communication, registering it merely as unintelligible noise.

So who else was broadcasting from within the Bastion? If it was an automated message and not an active transmission, who had originated it? And to whom was the signal directed?

Hilts scowled, his brows knitted. He suspected that he would not like the answers to any of those questions, assuming he lived long enough to find them out for himself.

SCOUT ZATORI FIRED another blindingly bright burst of plasma over the barricades at the nearest of the enemy, and then crouched down behind the protective cover of the barricades while he waited for the coils to recharge and to cool enough to fire again without overheating.

While Zatori was temporarily behind cover, Scouts Valen and Sandor poured superheated clouds of vapour from their flamers down the slopes at the enemy, while projectile slugs and lasfire pocked the barricades below them and the surface of the hatch behind them.

The sound from the enemy forces massing before the hatch was all but deafening, a mad chorus of shrieks and squeals, booming thuds and thunderous howls. The Scouts on the barricades had long before given up trying to make themselves heard audibly to one another, and were now communicating entirely by micro-beads, the pickups on their throats sensing their subvocalisations.

At the moment, there appeared to be somewhere just north of a thousand Roaring Blades and five Noise Marines arraying themselves in a skirmish line a hundred metres or so from the ramps leading up to the hatch. The army was using its ranged weapons – lasguns, stubbers and the massive sonic weapons carried by the Noise Marines – in an attempt to pick off the three Scouts at the barricades.

Whether by design or by impulse, one of the Roaring Blades broke through the skirmish line and surged ahead of the rest of the Chaos army, racing up the southern ramp cut into the slope of the mountain towards the barricades, waving a long sabre in a two-handed grip. His mouth was open and his head thrown back, but if he was howling the sound couldn't be heard over the din of the army behind him.

'I've got him,' Scout Sandor voxed before Valen could even point him out.

A single spray from Sandor's flamer doused the Roaring Blade in a curtain of fire. As the flames engulfed the heretic, he screamed in agonised ecstasy, his pleasure centres overloading as the sensations of his body being burned alive flooded into his brain.

'Coils are stable,' Zatori voxed, glancing at the status indicator on the plasma gun's stock. 'I'm ready. Targets?'

Zatori asked the question but already knew the answer. The Chapter's protocols for a siege defence of this type were for the Imperial Fist with the longest range and most effective ranged weapon to prioritise his targets on a sliding scale of threat profiles, weighted towards the ability of the target to effect damage at a distance – that is, whether the enemy carried a ranged weapon – the capacity of the target to inflict damage if they reached the barricades – their strength and destructive capabilities, whether they wore power armour or not, and so on – and the distance of the target from the barricades.

Destructive capability at a distance, capacity to inflict damage in close quarters and distance from the barricades – by all measures, the targets for Zatori to prioritise were clear.

The Noise Marines.

'The nearest is on your right, at the trailing edge of the enemy line,' Scout Valen voxed, sending a blast from his flamer at a group of Roaring Blades tempting the defenders by stepping onto the southern ramp. 'Looks like he's making ready to open up with his sonic weapon, too.'

'Preparing to fire,' Zatori voxed.

'Acknowledged,' Valen and Sandor replied.

'Take cover,' Zatori voxed. Then, one fist around the grip and the other on the stock, Zatori leapt up from behind the barricade and swung the plasma gun around to the right, while his squadmates took cover. Taking only a slight second to sight the target Valen had spotted and to aim, Zatori squeezed the firing stud on the plasma gun's grip and sent another blinding bolt of plasma lancing out towards the Noise Marine, a massive figure in power armour enamelled in bright pink and garish gold. At that exact instant, though, the Noise Marine fired his sonic weapon at the barricades, waves of devastating harmonics so loud they could be seen as a visible rippling in midair.

Zatori fell back behind cover as quickly as he was able, letting the plasma gun swing on its tether while he clamped his hands over his ears, but even missing the brunt of the sonic blast he was still hammered enough that his brain felt as though it were vibrating out of his skull, his teeth buzzing like a swarm of angry bees.

As Scouts Valen and Sandor leapt up from cover to lay down suppressing flames, Zatori pulled his hands away from his ears, and saw blood spotting the palms of either hand. He paused only long enough to wipe away the blood which oozed sluggishly down his ear-lobes, and to ensure that his micro-bead was still in place, then got a grip on his plasma gun once more.

'The target isn't down,' Scout Sandor voxed, the sound thankfully transmitting from Zatori's micro-bead directly to the bones around his ears, bypassing his damaged eardrums entirely. Then he smiled, and added, 'But he's reeling. It was a glancing shot, but you appear to have cracked his helmet. One solid headshot, and I think we'll have one fewer Noise Marine to contend with–'

Zatori couldn't *hear* the next sonic blast, but he could *feel* it, vibrating through the ledge beneath him and up his arms and legs.

Sandor stood for a moment like he'd forgotten what he was about to say, a somewhat perplexed expression on his face. Then he began to shake back and forth, slight vibrations from his head and arms to begin with, then wider and wider movements of his neck and torso, until finally his entire body was vibrating like a pearl of water dropped onto a hot skillet. Sandor turned to Zatori for a brief, agonised moment, a confused look on his face, and then his eyes rolled up in his head as torrents of blood burst from his ears on either side. Then, as his body slumped to the ground, Sandor's eyes burst from his skull, splattering in all directions.

The next instant, Zatori felt Valen's hand on his shoulder, and turned to see his squadmate's stricken expression.

'Another Noise Marine, centre of the enemy line,' Valen voxed, clearly trying hard not to look at the lifeless and ruined expression of their fallen squadmate.

The sonic weapons used by most of the Noise Marines were deadly enough on their own, capable of unleashing waves of destructive harmonics at their targets. But the larger variety were even more devastating, focusing a throbbing bass note into an ever-climbing crescendo that could literally shake a target to death inside their own skin and skull.

Zatori nodded, glancing from Valen to the ruin of Sandor and back.

'Target acquired,' Zatori voxed, and bent to consult the indicator on the plasma gun. The coils would be cool enough to fire in a matter of heartbeats. 'Prepare to lay down suppressing fire.'

Valen hesitated, hands clenched around the grip of his flamer. 'But Sandor–'

'Is dead,' Zatori replied simply, still looking at the indicator. 'We are not, at least not yet. So do your duty.' He raised his eyes. 'Coils check out. Preparing to fire.'

Valen was silent for a moment.

'Preparing to fire,' Zatori repeated, pointedly.

'Acknowledged,' Valen voxed in reply.

'Take cover,' Zatori voxed, needlessly as Valen was already crouched behind the barricades. Then he leapt up from behind the barricade, eyes racing to find the Noise Marine with the deadly sonic weapon.

Aiming the plasma gun at the target, Zatori whispered beneath his breath, though his ruined ears could not hear the sound of it. 'For Dorn, for the Emperor and for Sandor.' And then he fired.

SCOUT JEAN-ROBUR DU Queste held a fist up over his right shoulder, signalling Scout Rhomec who followed close behind to halt.

'There's someone ahead,' Jean-Robur subvocalised over the closed vox-comms.

'Not possible,' Rhomec answered the same way, unsheathing his combat blade with the faintest whisper of metal as the blade slid against the scabbard.

The two squadmates were making their final checks of the fortifications beneath the Bastion, where they had the night before blocked up and barricaded the several subterranean passages which led away from the mountain's heart to points unknown through various tunnels.

Jean-Robur and Rhomec had scavenged junked equipment and machine parts from the same storage bays that Scout Zatori and his team had drawn the equipment which had gone into making the barricades before the main hatch. But here beneath the Bastion, there was no need to leave gaps for passage, or to allow the Imperial Fists the option of passing back and forth. These fortifications were more in line with the demolition Scout s'Tonan and his team were performing on the northern blockhouse.

The Imperial Fists didn't care that these tunnels might not be useable after the battle was done. If they hadn't been worried about the stability of the chambers and tunnels above they would have simply turned the entirety of each tunnel mouth to molten rock with a melta gun, or seeing that there was only the single melta gun at their disposal and it was currently in use by Taloc's team, they would have at least blown the tunnels to rubble with demolition charges.

But Veteran-Sergeant Hilts had determined that demolition charges or melting large quantities of the mountain's underpinnings might serve to jeopardise the safety of those who sheltered in the chambers overhead, and had instead ordered Jean-Robur and Rhomec to cram the mouths of the passages with machinery and debris, creating impassable barricades.

The work had taken most of the night, but it had finally been completed. Jean-Robur would have preferred to melt the barricades of debris into solid masses with a few blasts from a melta gun, but Scout s'Tonan's team had not yet finished their work with the group's sole melta gun. And so, however unlikely it might have been, while the slim *possibility* existed that an enemy might somehow be able to force their way through the barricades from the other side, Jean-Robur and Rhomec were required to make periodic checks of the passages, to ensure that the barricades remained in place. As soon as the melta gun was at their disposal they would address the matter once and for all, but for the moment precautionary rounds were required.

So as they made their way through the catacombs, the two squadmates had anticipated the possibility that someone might be trying to force their way through the barricades from the other side, having crawled or crabbed all the way up the underground passages from points unknown in an attempt to break through into the Bastion. What they hadn't anticipated, though, was the possibility that someone might force their way through the barricades from *inside* the Bastion.

Jean-Robur trained his bolt pistol on the trio who were huddled around the fortified tunnel entrance, gracelessly pulling bits of metal and machinery out in the apparent attempt to dislodge the barricade, cursing one another in hushed voices. It was *sabotage*.

'Halt!' Scout du Queste shouted.

The three figures, indistinct in the gloom, sprang upright. From their stances it looked like they might attempt to flee down the other end of the passageway.

Jean-Robur's bolt pistol rang out as he shot the ground a few bare centimetres in front of the nearest of the three, sending up an explosion of rockcrete chips and dust.

'Stand fast,' Jean-Robur ordered. 'Make a move and I will open fire.'

The three straightened, looking to one another. Now that he had a chance to study them more closely, du Queste believed he recognised them.

'Rhomec,' Jean-Robur called back over his shoulder without taking his eyes off the three saboteurs. 'Continue up the passageway and check the next barricade.' There was another tunnel a few dozen paces up the corridor, hidden from view currently by the slow curve of the wall.

Scout Rhomec hustled around Jean-Robur and jogged up the passageway, bolt pistol in hand, steering wide of the three saboteurs.

They were Vernalians, of that Jean-Robur had no doubt. And he had seen these same three in their finery and robes talking to Captain Taelos when the 10th Company had first arrived at the Bastion.

'Please, d-don't…' said the one with the glowing tattoo inked upon his forehead, sounding on the verge of sobbing.

'Oh, stop your blubbering,' said the woman who stood beside him. 'Our Lord will not fail us, if we keep faith.'

'Sergeant Hilts?' Jean-Robur voxed to his superior. 'Du Queste here. We've found a group of locals attempting to remove the barricades.'

Rhomec hurried back down the passageway towards Jean-Robur. 'They've already unblocked the next two tunnels entirely!'

The saboteur with a face like a weasel sneered, and the blood-red lips of the woman beside him curled up in an evil smile. 'Soon,' she said with relish. 'Soon.'

'Sergeant,' Jean-Robur voxed, 'I think you'd better get down here.'

SCOUT S'TONAN REVERSED his combat blade in his grip, and just managed to block the daemon's claw before it skewered him through the abdomen. This close to the creature, Taloc's nose was full of its unearthly scent, a strange musk that was a bewildering mixture of intoxicating and repulsive, and his ears rang with its ululating song.

Or rather, with *her* song. Though he kept reminding himself that these daemons were warp-spawned hellbeasts, it was all too tempting to think of the one he faced as a woman. They certainly resembled human females, in some details. They walked upon two legs, as humans did, with two arms and a head and neck rising above a torso with a very female-shaped silhouette. But the legs upon which the daemons stood were not those of a human, but had an extra joint between the ankle and knee, more like the hind limbs of the goats herded on the mountains of Eokaroe or the lower limbs of the birds who nested in the forest's trees than the legs of a woman. And in the place of hands the daemons had long, dextrous claws, some of them as short as a combat knife, others as long as Captain Taelos's power sword, but all of them capable of rending an enemy's body to ribbons.

The opalescent eyes that peered out from their bone-white faces were mesmerising, and Taloc had already got his attentions wandering when he foolishly allowed himself to meet a daemon's gaze. Rhetoricus had taught that one should always look into the eyes of the opponent when duelling, rather than at their blade or body; the eyes would betray everything one needed to know about the opponent's movements. But in facing the daemons it clearly wasn't an option, if Taloc wanted to avoid being bewitched by that inhuman gaze.

So instead Taloc kept his eyes on the daemon's rending claw. The warp-spawned fiend he now faced had on its right arm a claw as long as his own combat blade, on its left one not much longer than the barrel of the bolt pistol holstered at Taloc's waist. He'd tried to hit the onrushing daemons with bolter-fire when they were first closing the remaining distance to the blockhouse, but their movements were simply too fast and too erratic for even the augmented reactions of a Space Marine

Scout to track. And once the daemons had reached the ground on which Taloc and the others stood, it was clear that firearms would be of little use; the Imperial Fists had a better chance of hitting the enemy with bolt-fire from the closer range, but with the speed and strength of the daemons even the considerable stopping power of the captain's bolter would not be sufficient to completely arrest the daemons' forward momentum.

It was all too possible that Taloc could score a fatal hit on a daemon with a round of bolt-fire, and then fall before its claws as the daemon's inertia carried it forwards and drove its claws into his body. In his first attempt to parry a blow from one of the claws it became apparent to Taloc that even his augmented strength was not enough to block a succession of such blows one-handed, and so he had holstered his firearm and taken his combat blade in a two-handed grip.

The daemon spun around, blurring into motion, and for an instant Taloc thought it was going to rush away to find another target. But instead it feinted with its longer claw, and as he brought his combat blade online to block the attack the daemon drove its shorter claw forwards, aimed directly at Taloc's midsection. Only by dancing back out of the daemon's reach was he able to avoid being disembowelled, and as it was his breastplate was scored by a long gash. A fraction of an instant slower and the blow would have punched through the gold armour and impaled him.

As Taloc recovered his position, weaving a net before him with his blade to ward off another attack, from the corner of his eye he caught sight of Captain Taelos, who was in a pitched contest with the fastest and most fearsome of the daemon band, who had talons as long as the captain's power sword growing from either arm and long purple hair that whipped like an anemone around her head. A short distance off Jedrek was contending with another of the creatures, while Fulgencio had slung the melta gun on his back and was wading in with combat blade in hand. The molten rock was cooling over the destroyed blockhouse, and the Imperial Fists could not retreat until the blockhouse was completely sealed.

Taloc's opponent rushed forwards again, and he managed to turn her longer claw aside, while at the same time driving his shoulder forwards against her upper arm to knock her off balance. In that split second before the daemon regained her footing, Taloc saw his opening and took it. He lunged forwards, driving the point of his combat blade towards the daemon's side, and then plunging the blade up to the hilt in that warp-spawned bone-white flesh.

As the daemon fell to the ground at his feet, a purplish ichor oozing from the wound, Taloc felt a momentary twinge of doubt. Fearsome and ferocious as they were, there was something seductively alluring about the daemons, and as his gaze travelled along the creature's pale, smooth skin and slender curves, he felt the stirrings of strange feelings, deep within. But then he locked eyes with the daemon's gaze, and felt his attentions wander, bewitched by those uncanny eyes even as the life fled from them. He blinked, eyes watering, and with both hands tightened on the handle swung his combat blade down in a killing stroke, cleaving the daemon's head clean from its shoulders.

Only when the creature fell silent did Taloc realise how far its ululating song had wormed its way into his mind.

The daemon began to dissolve into powder and ichor, its very substance being drawn back into the warp. There was no time for self-congratulation, though. There were more of the creatures rushing them from all sides now, eager to mow the Imperial Fists down like overgrown grass and claw their way into the Bastion. Taloc simply picked another target, raised his blade and went to work.

VETERAN-SERGEANT HILTS'S BOOTS pounded against the rockcrete underfoot as he raced through the subterranean passageways which snaked through the heart of the Bastion. Only moments had passed since he'd received Scout du Queste's vox about the Vernalian saboteurs. Who could be mad enough to remove the barricades and risk the forces of Chaos overrunning the mountain sanctuary? Had *they* been the ones responsible for the mysterious signal he'd detected, as well?

Hilts rounded a corner and saw Scout du Queste covering the three Vernalians with his bolt pistol. The suspicions he'd harboured since first hearing du Queste's report were confirmed. The saboteurs were the three self-appointed leaders of the Vernalian refugees, the corpulent Delmar Peregrine, serpentine Meribet Ofidia and weasel-faced Septimus Furion.

'Nice work, Scout,' the veteran-sergeant said as he came to stand beside du Queste.

'Rhomec is trying to repair the damage done to the other barricades,' du Queste said, eyes fixed on his captives. 'But I fear his efforts may not be equal to the task.;

Hilts glanced from the three saboteurs to the partially unobstructed tunnel mouth a short distance off, and then back.

'Why?' the veteran-sergeant said in outraged disbelief, narrowing his gaze at the three Vernalians. 'What madness is this?'

Overfed Peregrine lowered his eyes to the ground, while dour Furion merely scowled, but Ofidia glared at the veteran-sergeant with undisguised malice.

'Our Lord, the Prince of Pleasure, the Despoiler Himself, is come to cleanse Vernalis of the stain of Imperial dominion,' Ofidia said haughtily, her head held high. 'We give ourselves to Him freely, and will deliver the petrochem riches of this world for His holy uses.'

Hilts tightened his jaw, repelled by what he heard.

'It was *you* who summoned the Ruinous Powers to this world, wasn't it?' he said, though he already suspected the answer.

'Lickspittle,' Furion sneered, 'gambolling fool for your parasitic "Emperor". We *entreated* our Lord to dispatch His holy warriors to come to our aid. Too long has the mineral wealth of this world gone to prop up your dying Imperium. Now that wealth will service the undying glory of the Prince of Lust!'

Hilts glanced at Scout du Queste, who was looking with disbelief on the three members of a secret cult of Slaanesh.

'What happened?' the veteran-sergeant prompted. 'Did your plans go awry when you failed to shut down the planetary defences?'

At this Peregrine raised his arm and shook a thick-fingered fist in rage. 'The fools in the Planetary Defence Forces sooner died than reveal the access codes. But it is no matter. Once we have sacrificed the remaining members of the population huddled in the chambers above us to Slaanesh, we will quit the Bastion and the Holy Warriors of the Emperor's Children will level this mountain to the ground.'

Hilts drew his bolter, considering his options.

'Sergeant Hilts!' echoed the voice of Rhomec down the passageway, while his words sounded at the same time via vox over the micro-bead in Hilts's ear. 'Enemy elements coming up the unblocked tunnels, sir!'

Already Hilts could hear the mindless song of the Roaring Blades as they scrambled up the tunnels, the sharp bark of Rhomec's bolt pistol as he fired down into the passages and the clang of metal on metal as Rhomec's combat blade met the sabres of those already emerging into the corridor.

'I can't hold them off for long!' Rhomec added, his voice straining.

'Scout du Queste!' Hilts shouted. 'Go to your brother's aid.'

Du Queste didn't waste time in acknowledging, but raced off down the corridor, his bolt pistol in one hand and drawing his combat blade in the other. With the rest of the Imperial Fists busy defending the above-ground approaches to the mountain, it would fall to the three of them – veteran-sergeant and the two Scouts – to defend the Bastion from within. Whatever the size of the force coming up the tunnels, Hilts, du Queste and Rhomec were all that stood in the enemy's way.

There was no time to lose.

'So,' Hilts said, raising his bolter and aiming at the nearest of the three Vernalian cultists. 'It is to be the quick and simple solution, after all.'

'FOR DORN AND the Emperor!' Captain Taelos shouted, as he swung his power sword in a wide arc, catching the daemon's right claw midway along its length. But while the coruscating edge of the power sword bit deep into the chitinous surface of the claw, it did not cut clear through and sever the claw in half.

Not only maddeningly fleet of foot and swift of movements, the hellspawn were unnaturally *tough*, as well. Or at least the composition of their claws were, which was of principal importance. Had the warp-born substance of which the claws were grown been any less resilient then Taelos could have long before sliced both off at the arm, and then he'd have had the chance to see if the bone-white skin of the daemon's torso was equally as resistant to injury. But as it was, he was forced to parry and block the daemon's attacks, while trying to find an opening for his own killing stroke.

'Scout Fulgencio,' Taelos voxed subvocally, raising his power sword to block the sweep of the daemon's left claw in return. 'What is the status of the fortifications?'

A long moment passed, and Taelos was forced to leap to the left as the daemon suddenly surged forwards, scissoring her long claws together as she ran. If she hoped to catch Taelos between her claws, though, she moved too slowly, as fast as she was. Taelos leapt clear, and as the daemon whistled by at speed the captain was able to lash out sideways with a kick of one of his massive boots, catching her on the right hip and knocking her off balance.

Before Taelos could seize the advantage, though, the daemon simply planted the tip of her left claw into the rocky ground, kicked her left leg up off the ground and spun around like a top on the claw. As she spun around, her goat-like feet lashed at Taelos's head, and while he raised his power sword to bat them away he was only able to connect with the flat of the blade, rearing back out of reach as he did.

By the time he righted himself the daemon had both her feet under her again, and was eyeing him warily from a short distance off.

Taelos took advantage of the momentary lull to glance in the direction of the blockhouse, where Scout Fulgencio stood with his back to the cooling slag, holding off the onrushing daemons with his combat blade as best he could.

'Fulgencio?' Taelos repeated, with growing urgency.

'Sir,' the Scout finally answered, and from the corner of his eye Taelos could see Fulgencio kick sideways at the cooling slag with his boot. The boot rebounded without leaving an impression. 'It has cooled, sir. They won't be getting in this way. Not without more firepower than a few claws, at least.'

'Good,' Taelos voxed in reply. Then he feinted a lunge at the daemon, and when she swung both her claws downwards to block, he shifted the blade and sent it sweeping in a wide arc directly at her head, wreathed in writhing purple.

The daemon attempted to retreat, or to block the stroke with one of her claws, but by then it was too late.

'For Dorn!' Taelos shouted again.

With coruscating energy dancing up and down the edge of the blade, Captain Taelos's power sword swept clean through the daemon's lithe neck.

'…and the Emperor!'

When the daemon's head finally rolled to a stop on the flinty ground, the strands of purple hair which rose in a nimbus in all directions still writhing like worms, her body had not yet begun to fall. It simply stood there for a long moment, headless and unmoving, as though the body were trying to work out what had just happened, but lacking a brain was unable to draw any meaningful conclusions.

'Scouts!' Taelos said, turning and surveying the scene. They had cut down a couple of the daemons, reduced to ichor and powder, but there were still several racing around them, slashing at them with their rending claws and singing their unholy song. And the victories the small band of Imperial Fists had won thus far had not come without a price.

Like Captain Taelos's armour, that worn by Scouts Taloc and Fulgencio were already gored and scared in places, and from the way he was holding his arm it appeared that Fulgencio had been injured. And Scout Jedrek had fallen, his head cleaved down the middle by a downward stroke of a daemon's claw, his arms severed needlessly while his lifeless body had lain on the ground. A daemon, doubtless the one who defeated him, was still standing over Jedrek's body, exulting in victory and singing some incomprehensible song of praise to its unholy master.

Taelos did not hesitate, but drew and aimed his bolter in one swift motion, and planted a searing bolt directly between the dancing daemon's opal eyes.

'Scouts, form on me!' Taelos voxed on an open channel to Taloc and Fulgencio. 'The blockhouse is secured, and our strength and our sword-arms are needed elsewhere.'

'Acknowledged,' Taloc and Fulgencio voxed back, almost in unison.

'There!' Taelos pointed towards the east, around the slow curve of the mountain. 'We make for the main hatch!'

WHEN SCOUT VALEN was hit full-on by a high-frequency blast from a Noise Marine's sonic weapon, Scout Zatori didn't have time to mourn. Instead, while the Noise Marine's weapon was recharging, Zatori simply planted a plasma bolt dead centre on the sonic weapon itself, exploding it in the Noise Marine's grasp. As fragments of the exploded weapon shot like shrapnel up into the face of the Chaos Space Marine, causing him to howl in agonised pleasure, Zatori didn't pause but shot again, and this time the blindingly bright plasma bolt lanced right into the Noise Marine's forehead, blowing the fevered remains of his warp-addled brain out the other side of his skull.

'He should have worn a helmet,' Zatori said under his breath. If he survived this day and lived to become an Astartes, he would always remember that lesson.

But while the question as to whether he would survive the day remained to be answered, Zatori's chances did not look good. Valen had fallen to the rockcrete ground with his eyes burst from his skull and his organs liquefied within his body. He joined Sandor on the ground – had it really only been a few minutes since Sandor had fallen, as well?

Now only Zatori was left to defend the barricades before the main hatch, with only the plasma gun in his hands and the combat blade sheathed at his side.

'Scout Zatori to all Imperial Fists,' he voxed on an open channel. 'Requesting assistance. The rest of the team has fallen, and I alone man the main hatch barricades.'

A pair of Roaring Blades were surging up the southern ramp, and Zatori potted them both in quick succession with plasma bolts.

'…Hilts… overrun by incursion from below…' came the voice of Veteran-Sergeant Hilts, the vox-comm laced with static. 'Roaring Blades infiltrating catacombs… Will send reinforcements… when able…'

'Belay that,' cut in the voice of Captain Taelos, only slightly garbled by static. 'My team and I are already en route. Hilts, you and your team deal with the incursion from below. Zatori, hold out. We're almost to you.'

Zatori nodded, for no reason, then checked himself. 'Acknowledged,' he voxed in reply.

There were a dozen Roaring Blades encroaching on the southern ramp, howling their ear-splitting song, and a Noise Marine following close behind. Zatori chanced a quick glance at the indicator on the stock of the plasma gun. He could fire it twice more, perhaps three times, but then the coils would begin to overheat, and he would be in imminent danger of a blowback and explosion.

But he had no choice. If he fell back behind the barricades and allowed the coils to cool and recharge, the Roaring Blades and their Noise Marine master could climb the rest of the ramp and be at the barricades, and then he would never be able to hold them all off at once. He glanced at the flamer that lay beside Valen's ruined body. From its mangled appearance, it seemed that the flamer had been rendered inoperable by the sonic weapon's blast, just as Sandor's had earlier.

There was no alternative. Zatori would have to continue firing until he could fire no more, and then see what fate had in store for him.

A bolt of searing white lanced out of the plasma gun at the Noise Marine, glancing off his breastplate. Then another cut through the Roaring Blade in the vanguard, the bolt continuing on and searing through the Roaring Blade behind him. As the two burned Traitor Guards fell, Zatori let off another plasma bolt at the Roaring Blade directly in front of the Noise Marine, calculating that it would do the same; the bolt seared clean through the neck of the Roaring Blade and still had enough potency to burn through the greaves on the Noise Marine's left leg.

The Noise Marine still advanced, but he was slowed by a limp as his body struggled to cope with the plasma burn through his lower leg.

Zatori's eyes darted to the indicator on the stock. The coils were already dangerously hot. He could chance perhaps one more shot.

With a prayer to the primarch on his lips, Zatori aimed the barrel of the plasma gun at the Noise Marine's head, pressed the firing stud…

…and missed. The shot went wide, not even striking one of the surrounding Roaring Blades, but instead lancing uselessly into the grey stones on the ground beyond the ramp.

The indicator was flashing wildly now. The coils had heated too far, too fast. It was no longer possible to allow them to cool down, to recharge for another shot. The plasma gun was entering a critical state, and would explode at any moment.

The Noise Marine, as if sensing Zatori's dilemma, raised his sonic weapon and prepared to fire a deadly wave of sound at him.

Zatori tensed, awash in the deafening sound of the Roaring Blades' howls and shouts and the mounting whine of the Noise Marine's sonic weapon. The sounds pounded at him like a physical force that he could feel in his bones.

Then Zatori remembered the words of his former master on Triandr, Father Nei. He recalled the tactic that the Sipangish warrior-elites had called 'swordlessness,' which held that doing the unexpected was often the correct course of action.

Even, in some instances, throwing down one's weapon.

With a final glance at the indicator, Zatori held his breath, and rearing back he hurled the plasma gun down the mountain like an overlarge grenade.

The Noise Marine was about to fire his sonic weapon as the plasma gun hurtled end over end through the air towards him.

Zatori barely had the chance to begin to fall back behind the barricades when the plasma gun erupted in a blinding ball of expanding plasma, engulfing the Noise Marine and the Roaring Blades entirely. The heat from the explosion singed the eyebrows from Zatori's face before he could get to cover, and the sound of the blast was so loud it eclipsed even the deafening roar of the Chaos army.

Zatori sat with his back against the barricade, dazed. He realised that he could hear nothing. Only silence. Whether the shock of the explosion had robbed him permanently of his hearing, or whether it was a temporary condition, he could not say, but for the moment he revelled in the sweet, blissful silence.

But he could not rest. Some of the Roaring Blades or even the Noise Marine himself might have survived the explosion, and be already on their way to the barricades. With the plasma gun gone, the flamers destroyed, and his supply of bolts for his bolt-pistol exhausted, he had no ranged weapons to use. But what did Zatori care?

He had been raised to view such weapons as base and crude, not fit to be carried by noble warriors.

Zatori rose unsteadily to his feet.

Still dazed, he found himself confusing the warrior-elites of his youth and the holy warriors he now aspired to join, but even so he knew that both held noble traditions of going into battle armed only with blades. If he were to die, it would be with a blade in his hand. Then, if he found himself in the land of spirits, he could present himself to his master with pride.

But then, he had not yet avenged Father Nei's murder, had he?

Zatori drew his combat blade and turned to look out over the barricades. Some half-dozen Roaring Blades were stepping over the fallen bodies of their comrades and advancing up the southern ramp.

Stepping into the breach, Zatori raised his combat blade, preparing to meet them.

CHAPTER THIRTEEN

Scout Taloc s'Tonan did not dwell on the larger picture. He did not stop to consider the Imperial Fists' chances of defending the Bastion in the long term with only a handful of Scouts and a pair of officers. He did not even pause to wonder whether he would survive long enough to reach the main hatch, or even the ramp leading up to the ledge. All such considerations were too far in the future for Taloc to waste time bothering with.

All that mattered to Taloc was the present moment, the narrow slice of space and time which was 'here' and 'now'.

There was a daemon's long claw whistling towards his head. Taloc raised his combat blade in a two-handed grip and batted it away, sparing himself a fatal blow to the side of his skull.

Taloc's spatial awareness had narrowed to the area immediately surrounding him, and his situational awareness had shortened to the things happening at the present instant. He barely considered the ramifications of things that might possibly eventuate in another five or ten seconds. A full minute was too far in the future even to speculate.

A daemon was whirling around, preparing to launch another attack, and for the briefest of instants her back was exposed and vulnerable. Taloc drove his combat blade forwards, point first, and buried it in the daemon's back. The momentum of her spinning carried her a partial rotation further, so that Taloc's blade sliced a ribbon of bone-white flesh from the daemon's back before she fell to the ground, spine severed.

Taloc had lost track of how much time had passed since he, Scout Fulgencio and Captain Taelos had set out from the ruins of the blockhouse, heading towards the main hatch. He had no clear notion of how much ground they had already covered, or what distance remained before they reached their destination. Such details had been lost in a blur of claws and blades, of attack and block, parry and thrust, a mindless dance that seemed to have no limit and no end.

Scout Fulgencio was narrowly avoiding a collision with Taloc as Fulgencio fended off the attack of another daemon. Fulgencio had the melta gun slung over his back, the weapon rendered ineffective at such short range against so fleet a foe; instead, he battered at the daemon's claws with his combat blade, wielding it like a club. Fulgencio's gold Scout armour was spattered with blood, some of it the purple ichor of the daemon's but a considerable amount of it his own lifeblood.

At some point along the line, Taloc had received a number of injuries ranging from minor nicks and cuts to fairly severe gashes on his exposed flesh, but the Larraman cells that flooded his bloodstream in response had evidently staunched the flow of blood, and already scar tissue was forming.

A daemon was racing at Taloc with claws out and grasping. Taloc did not bother to prepare to block the attack, but instead lunged forwards unexpectedly, driving his blade up and under the creature's claws, plunging the sword's point deep into the daemon's chest. He crouched low and rolled quickly to one side, avoiding the downward sweep of her claws that was the daemon's dying act.

Taloc's combat blade was nicked in countless places along its edge, where it had met the hard chitinous surface of the daemons' claws. And the blade, too, was gored with the purplish ichor from the creatures' veins, a slow-drying ooze that slicked it from point to hilt.

Captain Taelos was before him as Scout s'Tonan sprang to his feet. A pair of fissures marked the captain's breastplate, his gold armour stained with the blood that had poured out from the wounds within. The injuries were to all appearances grave, the colour drained from the captain's cheeks and the white nicks of his duelling scars all but vanished as the flesh around them were pale from loss of blood. But the captain was not wavering, *but brandishing his crackling power sword as though he had snatched a lightning bolt from the sky to wield against all the enemies of mankind.*

Despite himself, Taloc thought of his father Tonan's named sword, the fabled Lightning. And the naïve musings he'd had when last he stood upon the green fields of Eokaroe, imagining that his own nameless ironbrand might win itself through valour in battle the name Thunderbolt. But while Taloc had not seen Eokaroe, or his father, or either of their ironbrands, named or nameless, since that day, the Scout could not help thinking that surviving *this* battle would surely cover him in more glory than the grandfathers of his warrior-clan had ever imagined *possible*. And even if his clan never recognised that he had attained his full manhood, Taloc would know in his hearts that he was no longer a child, but a fully blooded man.

Captain Taelos batted one daemon aside with a blow from his gauntleted fist, spearing another on the point of his power sword. 'Onwards to the hatch, Sons of Dorn!' the captain called out to Scouts s'Tonan and Fulgencio, his voice booming out even over the daemons' maddening song. 'Fight onwards!'

Thinking of his father reminded Taloc that the one who had killed Tonan still lived.

Another daemon was before Taloc, eyes turning their murderous gaze upon him. Taloc did not hesitate, but surged forwards, swinging his combat blade with all his might.

Taloc recalled that he still had a blood-debt to pay, but he would need to survive the present moment before he could worry about that.

SCOUT ZATORI ZAN stood at the breach in the barricades, the main hatch at his back. He'd positioned himself as far back from the lip of the ledge on the far side of the breach as he was tall, making it all but impossible for the ranged weapons of the Chaos army below to target him. Within this narrow zone of safety, he was able to contend with the enemy as they appeared in the breach, with the combat blade in his hands the only weapon available for his use.

A Roaring Blade crested the ledge's edge, rushing into the breach with a long curved sabre in hand and an animalistic howl of pain and pleasure on his lips. Zatori lunged, keeping his body low to the ground, just as the Roaring Blade's head and shoulders appeared in the breach. He pitted the heretic's head on his sword, driving the blade straight through the enemy's mouth with the point punching out through the back of his head. Then Zatori whipped the blade free as he slid back to the relative safety of the spot a little under two paces from the edge.

The Roaring Blade, the confused expression that had momentarily flitted across his face replaced by a brief flash of ecstasy as the pain of the killing stroke was transformed by his re-engineered nervous system into pleasure, fell in a heap atop the bodies of his slain brethren who already lay at Zatori's feet.

There were already more than half a dozen bodies littering the ground just inside the breach, their blood staining the grey rockcrete black. Another two or three had fallen backwards and tumbled down the ramp, or perhaps even over the ramp's edge and down the steep slope, Zatori wasn't sure which. With another enemy bested, Zatori's tally would come to ten Roaring Blades down, he estimated, and so far he himself had received only the most superficial of wounds.

But Zatori knew it was only a matter of time before the enemy numbers overwhelmed him. Already it had been a close thing on several occasions as the Roaring Blades had burst through the breach armed not only with blades but also with firearms, and it had only been the advantage of the high ground and familiarity with the immediate surroundings that had let Zatori escape a burst of las-fire or a shotgun blast to the face. All it would take for the enemy to eliminate the hatch's last defender would be for a Roaring Blade with a bolt pistol – or worse yet, a Noise Marine with a sonic weapon – to follow right on the heels of one of the sword-wielding Roaring Blades; while Zatori was still involved in dispatching the latter with his blade, the former could fire at him at will, provided they were not concerned with the possibility of also hitting their brethren.

Another Roaring Blade appeared at the breach, but unlike the others who had preceded him by rushing headlong into the breach, this one sidled his way through the opening, his sabre held defensively before him. As a result, Zatori could not simply strike before the Roaring Blade even knew the blow was coming, and the heretic had the opportunity to attempt a block when Zatori launched his attack.

Sure enough, as Zatori's combat blade whistled through the air towards the Roaring Blade's neck, the heretic swung his sabre up in a sweeping arc, turning Zatori's blade aside. Then, as Zatori laboured to bring his combat blade back in line, the Roaring Blade thrust his own sabre forwards, the point aimed unerringly at Zatori's chest.

Zatori leapt to one side, in time to avoid the Roaring Blade's thrust but not quickly enough to completely escape injury. The heretic's sabre dug into the bare flesh of Zatori's sword arm at the biceps, in that narrow band of vulnerability between the bottom edge of his shoulder-guard and the protection of the vambrace that covered from elbow to wrist.

Blood sprayed from the fresh wound on Zatori's right arm before the Larraman cells could seal the gash, and Zatori could feel that the muscles themselves were cut. His grip on the combat blade lessened, and it seemed possible that he might actually *drop* the sword before his system overcame the pain and shock.

Zatori danced back a pace as the Roaring Blade advanced, howling his insane song of praise to the

Despoiler. Not for the first time was Zatori glad that his hearing had not yet completely recovered from the effects of the plasma gun's explosion. Zatori shifted his combat blade from his right hand to his left before he lost his grip on it entirely. He'd been trained to use the blade in either hand, as a matter of course, but was much less comfortable wielding it in his left. He could handle the sword one-handed in his left, but his movements were far less assured, his accuracy considerably lowered.

But it was not as if he had any choice. In another few moments, perhaps, the flesh and muscles of his right arm would heal sufficiently for him to be able to wield the sword in his right hand, but at that instant it wasn't an option.

The Roaring Blade advanced warily, seeking an opening in Zatori's defences.

Zatori could see that the Roaring Blade put far too much faith in the thought that the wounded right arm was debilitating, or that Zatori was in some way overwhelmed by his injuries. After the careful and sidling way that the Roaring Blade had slid through the breach, he now moved with a cocky overconfidence, it seemed, as though Zatori was already fallen.

It would be his final mistake.

Zatori feinted by swinging his empty right hand in a wide arc parallel to the ground, sending the blood that seeped down his arm flinging away in droplets that arced directly towards the Roaring Blade's eyes. Instinctually, the Roaring Blade blinked, and that was when Zatori made his move. He lunged forwards, driving the point of his blade into the meat of the renegade's shoulder, then wrenched the blade sideways and up, slicing back across the Roaring Blade's neck and jawline.

As the Roaring Blade fell to the ground, blood shooting from his shoulder and neck like water from a geyser, Zatori allowed himself the faintest fluttering of self-satisfaction for a duel well-won. But that sense of satisfaction immediately faded when he saw what had followed the fallen Roaring Blade into the breach.

It was Zatori's darkest expectations made flesh. Close on the heels of the sidling Roaring Blade came another, armed not with a blade but with a lascarbine. And the gun-wielding newcomer was not doing Zatori the favour of advancing through the breach into the range of Zatori's sword-arm, but had halted just the other side of the breach and was already taking careful aim with his lascarbine.

Zatori tensed, in that fraction of a second considering his options. If he rushed through the breach and pressed an attack on the Roaring Blade he *might* be able to avoid a fatal shot of las-fire, but by clearing the barricade and emerging out on the ramp he'd be exposing himself to the ranged weapons fire of all of the enemy forces below, to say nothing of the Roaring Blades and Noise Marines currently coming up the ramp. But if he held still he would surely be dropped by las-fire, if not this first shot then the next or the one after that or another to follow.

There was no choice. Zatori began to rush forwards, shifting his weight onto the balls of his feet and lowering his head to the ground. It was the only reasonable option in the circumstances.

But in the next instant, his circumstances changed. Before Zatori had taken even a single step forwards, the Roaring Blade suddenly danced to one side, shaking violently as though he were being rocked by high vibrations, leaning awkwardly towards the southern ramp as bits of blood and gore and scraps of clothing went flying off him in all directions. It was only after another heartbeat had passed that Zatori's damaged hearing picked up the faint sound of bolter-fire.

As the Roaring Blade fell to the ground, his lascarbine clattering down unfired and skidding out of sight, Captain Taelos appeared in the breach, bolter uncharacteristically held in a one-handed grip and a power sword in the other.

'Retreat within the hatch!' Taelos called out as he leapt through the breach, followed closely by Scout Fulgencio, who limped along with sword in hand and melta gun slung across his back, and Scout s'Tonan who backed into the breach covering their flanks with bolt pistol and blade. 'We shall defend the hatch from within, and fill the gap with the enemy dead!'

DOWN IN THE subterranean passages deep below the Bastion, Scout Jean-Robur du Queste was muttering a humble oath to the Emperor and the Primarch

Rogal Dorn and the god of the Caritaigne and any other beneficent agencies that might be listening.

'Please hear me...' Jean-Robur said in a voice scarcely above a whisper.

It appeared that of the two tunnels whose fortifications had been removed, the enemy was only emerging from one. But the tunnel mouth was at the far end of the passageway, and the numbers of Roaring Blades who had so far poured out of the tunnel had already taken up defensive positions up and down the length of the passageway. The fact that the far end of the passageway was blocked by a dead-end meant that the enemy could not go that route and gain access to the chambers and corridors above, but while Veteran-Sergeant Hilts and the two Scouts had so far managed to keep the Roaring Blades contained within the passageway by standing fast at the nearer end, they were not yet having any success in sealing off the tunnel and preventing even more Roaring Blades from climbing out.

'...send us a *melta*...'

Jean-Robur's prayer was interrupted when yet another Roaring Blade came rushing out of the darkness, firing a shotgun blindly into the shadows with one hand and waving a scimitar wildly in the other. Jean-Robur dropped him with a single round from his bolt pistol. Then Scout du Queste dropped back behind the corner to take cover as the Roaring Blades from further up the passageway filled the air with las-fire.

Scout du Queste, Veteran-Sergeant Hilts and Scout Rhomec had taken up defensive positions at a point where the passageway intersected with another. Using the sharp corners as cover, the three were laying down suppressing fire as the Roaring Blades attempted to make their way up the passageway and into the rest of the Bastion. So far, none of the enemy had got past the intersection, the bodies beginning to pile higher and higher on the rockcrete floor of the passageway. But while this tactic was working as a temporary containment measure, it was not a solution.

'We need to seal that tunnel up,' Scout Rhomec voxed. Vocal communication was proving all but impossible, with the echoes of the Roaring Blades' discordant chants and songs echoing up and down the passageway and drowning out all other sounds.

'We need a melta gun,' Scout du Queste voxed in reply. 'We could blast straight up the passageway and mow the enemy down, and then melt the barricade to slag at the tunnel mouth when we get close enough. These Emperor-forsaken bastards might be limber enough to squeeze through gaps in the wreckage now, but I don't like their chances doing so when the metal and machinery are flowing like burning syrup all over them.'

'Good plan,' Rhomec voxed, and across the intersection Jean-Robur caught sight of Rhomec's scarred cheeks and their perpetual grin. But somehow now it looked more like a sneer. 'Except that we don't *have* a melta.'

'But s'Tonan's team *does*, fool,' Jean-Robur shot back.

'Enough!' Hilts broadcast to both of them. 'You are both correct, for all that it matters. A melta is exactly what we need, but we don't have one, and it doesn't seem likely we are to get one any time soon. So are there any more suggestions?'

Jean-Robur and Rhomec exchanged a glance, then broke off as a trio of Roaring Blades came charging up the passageway, swords in hand. The two Scouts calmly sighted around their respective corners and dropped all three heretics with a total of four rounds from their bolt pistols.

In response to the Scouts' silence, Hilts voxed, 'Do either of you have any grenades left?'

'No,' Jean-Robur voxed back, firing a bolt at another Roaring Blade rushing the intersection.

'Neither have I,' Rhomec answered.

The first waves to rush up the passageway had been dropped with frag grenades, which had the advantage of taking out several of the enemy at once as the shrapnel dispersed, but after the grenades had run out bolter-fire seemed to be doing just as effective a job of stopping the Roaring Blades' advance. But again, it was merely a temporary containment, not a permanent solution.

'In that case…' Hilts began, before another vox-communication cut across him and interrupted his next words.

'Brother-Sergeant Hilts, this is Taelos transmitting. Do you receive?'

The two Scouts exchanged another look as Hilts slammed a full clip into the base of his bolter. 'Acknowledged, brother-captain, this is Hilts.'

'The surviving Scouts and I are setting up a defensive position just inside the main hatch. What is your situation?'

'We are holding fast in the subterranean passageways, and have prevented the enemy incursion from spreading into the Bastion. But we have been unable to stem the tide as yet.' A slow grin tugged up the corners of the veteran-sergeant's mouth. 'But if you should happen to have a melta gun on hand...'

'Understood, Hilts,' the captain voxed in reply. 'I'm sending Scout Fulgencio your way now with the melta. He's sustained some injuries, but should be able to assist you with the weapon's operation. We're short-handed here, though, so when you can send one of your Scouts to the main hatch to take Fulgencio's place. Acknowledged?'

'Yes, sir,' Hilts voxed with considerable relish. Then as the vox contact broke off, he turned to look from Jean-Robur to Rhomec. 'Scout du Queste. As soon as Scout Fulgencio arrives with the melta, I want you off the line and up to the hatch quick as you can get there.'

'Yes, sir!' Jean-Robur nodded.

SCOUT s'TONAN HELD his combat blade in a two-handed grip, feet planted at shoulder-width with the right foot slightly forwards, facing the narrow opening of the main hatch. After Captain Taelos and the Scouts had retreated within, the hatch had been partially closed, so that it was just barely wide enough now for one of the Roaring Blades to slip through, but too narrow a gap for a Noise Marine in full power armour to enter. Locked in place with massive bolts housed in the ceiling above and floor below, the hatch could not be forced open wider from the outside, not even with the augmented strength of a Chaos Space Marine. They had not closed it entirely, though, so as not to allow the enemy an unchallenged approach. If they attempted to bore through the hatch itself, the Imperial Fists would be able to fire on them from the narrow gap. It was not a long-term solution, but it served a temporary stalemate, forcing the enemy to approach in smaller numbers.

A Roaring Blade slipped through the narrow gap, his howling song echoing in the vastness of the loading bay. Before he had taken more than three strides into the dim interior of the bay, Taloc swung his combat blade in a downward arc, the blade's edge biting deep into the heretic's neck and shoulder. As the Roaring Blade's eyes rolled back in momentary ecstasy, Taloc yanked the blade free and with a second swing swept the heretic's head clean off its shoulders. The Roaring Blade fell headless to the rockcrete floor to the right of the gap, his head continuing to roll off into the gloom within, disappearing from view.

At Taloc's side stood Scout Zatori, whose stance mirrored Taloc's own, but with his left foot leading instead of his right. And while Taloc gripped his combat blade in much the same way as his father and his grandfathers before him had wielded their ironbrands, with both hands at the hilt, the thumb and forefingers of his left hand pressing tight to the little finger and heel of his right hand, Zatori held his combat blade after the manner of the warrior-elites of Sipang, with his left hand gripping tightly at the hilt and the other holding the end of the handle in a loose grip.

It was perhaps a symbol of the way in which neophytes in the Chapter retained some of their cultural upbringing while adopting the warrior ethic of the Imperial Fists. As was the fact that, while both of them carried themselves as befitted Scouts of the Imperial Fists, Zatori's dour expression made clear that he fought out of duty and a sense of honour, while Taloc could not help imagining the glory that would be theirs if they were to win the day.

Two Roaring Blades pushed their way into the gap, one right after the other. Both bore lascarbines that they fired wildly into the gloom, not yet having even sighted a target, eyes not having adjusted from the bright glare of the Vernalian morning outside to the dim gloom of the loading bay within. Captain Taelos had instructed the Scouts to dim the lights inside as soon as the hatch had been locked in place, for just this effect. Before the two Roaring Blades even settled their gazes on the two Scouts, Taloc and Zatori attacked. Taloc swung his blade

from high over his shoulder, bringing the edge
down at an angle on the forearms of the Roaring
Blade on the right. The renegade howled in ecstasy
as his lascarbine and his severed hands fell to the
floor, and then Taloc ended his delight by spitting
him through the chest on his combat blade. Zatori
dispatched the leftmost of the intruders with considerably more elegance and economy of motion,
batting the lascarbine to one side with the flat of
his combat blade and then thrusting forwards, driving the point deep into the heretic's neck.

In the first few minutes after securing the hatch,
the two Scouts had already dispatched some half-
dozen of the Roaring Blades, whose bodies were
already beginning to accumulate on the floor
before the opening. Blood slicked the rockcrete
underfoot, mixing with the stains of spilled
petrochem and the tread-marks of ground transports stencilled in the grey dust of pulverised shale.

Captain Taelos's wounds were, it appeared, even
graver and more serious than Taloc had originally
suspected. Once they were within the Bastion and
the hatch was secured, the captain had been forced
by his injuries to seat himself on the ground, leaning against the wall a dozen paces from the hatch.
While his implants struggled to heal his battered
frame, even the Larraman cells that crowded his
blood vessels failing to completely staunch the
bleeding from the wounds in his abdomen, the
captain held his bolter in a steady two-handed grip,
the barrel trained on the hatch. Any of the Roaring

Blades who managed to get past the two Scouts would fall quickly in a hail of bolter-fire.

But there were no guarantees that the captain would be able to maintain his vigil, and there was every possibility that his injuries might eventually leave him unable to aim and fire his bolter with any accuracy. For the moment, Scouts s'Tonan and Zatori were the first and best defence for the hatch.

A Roaring Blade rushed through the opening, jinking towards the left while waving a sabre like a fan-blade in the air before him. Taloc stood fast, only glancing over as Zatori blocked the Roaring Blade's inexpert thrust and riposted with a graceful slice of his combat blade that effectively cut the heretic's legs out from under him. As Zatori dispassionately stabbed his combat blade downwards and dispatched the Roaring Blade in a surgically precise killing stroke, Taloc remembered the killing stroke that the Sipangish squire had inflicted on Tonan, chief of Eokaroe's proudest warrior-clan. Taloc had never forgotten that Zatori still held his father's blood-debt. And it was only the discipline of the Imperial Fists, and the threat of a life of endless servitude as a Chapter serf, that prevented him from seeing that blood-debt paid. But if one or the other of them were to die here on this Emperor-forsaken world? What then of Tonan's blood-debt?

Taloc's reverie was disrupted by the appearance of two more Roaring Blades slipping through the narrow opening, the second close on the heels of the first. Both wielded long, razor-sharp scimitars, and as they broke left and right the heretics managed by happenstance to put themselves in good positions to attack the two Scouts, and to defend against the Scouts' attacks.

Zatori shifted forwards to deal with the heretic on the left, while Taloc blocked the first attack of the heretic on the right. But it quickly became apparent, as the one parried Zatori's thrust and the other almost managed to get past Taloc's block, that these two were either more skilled combatants than the half-dozen who had preceded them through the gap, or else the example of the first six to slip through the gap had urged caution on those who followed. After all, while these two howled and shouted like all the rest of the Traitor Guards, they seemed to devote themselves less to their hellish hymns than they did to the business of wielding their blades and staying alive.

While the two Scouts contended with the pair of Roaring Blades, though, a third slipped cautiously through the gap. From his position, Taloc could see that the fact that Zatori had been forced to sidestep his opponent's last thrust meant that the captain could not fire his bolter at this third heretic without hitting Scout Zatori in the process. And while the Imperial Fists were not above sacrificing their own to achieve victory, at this stage of the siege it gained them nothing to sacrifice a defender to put down a single invader.

For a frenzied moment, as his combat blade clanged against his opponent's scimitar, Taloc considered the options available to them, trying to find a solution. But in the next instant, the problem was solved, quite unexpectedly.

As Taloc and Zatori blocked and attacked, thrust and parried, the sound of boots pounding on rock-crete crescendoed behind them, and a figure in gold raced between the two Scouts and flung itself at the third Roaring Blade. The newcomer, who had been eyeing the contests on either side, was caught completely unawares, and went down without a fight.

Glancing over his shoulder with a devilish grin, Scout Jean-Robur du Queste brandished his combat blade. 'I was told you could use some assistance,' he said, and it was clear that he fought not for glory nor for honour, but for fun. 'But I don't know how you got along even this far without me!'

DOWN IN THE catacombs beneath the Bastion, Veteran-Sergeant Hilts sprayed bolter-fire down the passageway while Scout Fulgencio readied the melta gun for another burst.

'Rhomec!' Hilts voxed over the chatter of his bolter and the echoing din of the enemy's infernal song. 'Continue to lay down suppressing fire and prepare to move ahead!'

'Acknowledged,' Rhomec voxed in response.

The floor of the passageway ahead was carpeted with the enemy dead, but still the Roaring Blades hurled themselves at the defenders. Since Scout Fulgencio had arrived with the melta gun and Scout du Queste had gone to aid in the defence of the main hatch, the veteran-sergeant had led his team in pushing the enemy further and further back from the main intersection that had previously served as the defenders' bulwark. If they were to stem the tide of heretics streaming into the catacombs, they would need to seal the barricades in the tunnel mouths, and the Imperial Fists wouldn't be able to accomplish that by remaining safely behind cover at the intersection.

'Ready,' voxed Fulgencio, raising his weapon and preparing to fire another strafing burst of melta-fire down the passageway.

'Rhomec, hold fire,' Hilts voxed. 'Fulgencio, fire at will.'

An instant later, a blast of incredible heat lanced from the muzzle of the melta gun and down the passageway. The weapon itself produced almost no sound as it fired, but Hilts could hear a distinctive hiss as the air through which the blast travelled super-heated to dangerous levels. And when the quartet of Roaring Blades who were rushing towards the defenders with shotguns and lascarbines firing caught the brunt of the blast, Hilts could hear the roar of their bodies' moisture vaporising instantly. In a matter of eyeblinks the four heretics had been incinerated to little more than blackened bone. And even though the blast did not hit them directly, the crowd of Roaring Blades who had been following close behind the quartet fell to either side with fatal burns, howling in redirected euphoria as they went.

'Lay down suppressing fire and advance!' Hilts voxed, and he and the two Scouts scooted further up the passageway, with Hilts and Rhomec spraying bolter-fire as they progressed.

They had been leapfrogging up the passageway in this manner for several minutes, and had already closed half the distance between the intersection and the first of the compromised barricades. The main body of the subterranean invaders was still ahead of them, but no matter how many of the Roaring Blades they put down it seemed that there was still an inexhaustible number of them following close behind.

But while many of the Roaring Blades simply rushed headlong towards the defenders, heedless of any risk or danger to themselves, not in the slightest averse to any potential pain and, quite the contrary, often seeming to seek it out, there were others of their number who appeared somewhat more cautious and calculating in their actions.

Hilts signalled to the two Scouts to take up new positions on either side of the passageway. The veteran-sergeant crouched low against the right hand wall, while Rhomec and Fulgencio crouched against the left, with Rhomec a few paces ahead. When they were in position, Rhomec and Hilts would lay down suppressing fire to give Fulgencio a chance to sidle over to the centre of the passageway, where he would rise up and fire a long melta-burst down the straight passage towards the enemy. Though his movements were slowed by the injuries he'd sustained in the march from the blockhouse, Fulgencio was still able to limp into position given enough time. And while they were not moving as quickly towards their goal as Hilts might have liked, they'd already done this leapfrog manoeuvre several times, and each time without incident.

But their success rate was about to fall. As Rhomec and Hilts lay down bolter-fire while Fulgencio readied the melta gun, they paid little mind to the bodies scattered up and down the passageway between them. Some had been charred and burned by previous melta-blasts, while others had apparently been felled by hails of bolter-fire. But before any of the Imperial Fists realised what was happening, one of the seemingly lifeless bodies suddenly stirred to motion, having only feigned death. The all-too-alive enemy rose, springing up to a kneeling crouch and firing the lasgun in his hands on full-auto towards the left-hand wall.

'Sergeant!' Fulgencio shouted as he saw the las-fire rain on the wall ahead of him, but in the split-second it took Hilts to swivel and clip the Roaring Blade with rounds from his bolter, it was already too late.

Scout Rhomec had been hit from the side by a welter of las-fire, and if the first shot hadn't killed him, then the sixth one had, or the twelfth. Though lasguns were not nearly as accurate on full-auto, at such short range the Roaring Blade had been virtually unable to miss his target.

As Fulgencio knelt over the lifeless body of his squadmate, Veteran-Sergeant Hilts sprayed the nearest of the bodies on the passageway floor with bolter-fire, just as a precaution. Then, as the enemy fire from further up the passageway increased once more, Hilts turned his bolter towards the living enemy and opened fire.

'Fulgencio, take up position and prepare to fire!'

The Scout turned away from Rhomec's body, which even in death wore the same scarred-cheek grin, and nodded in the veteran-sergeant's direction. He tightened his grip on the melta gun and, as Hilts fired his bolter up the corridor, crab-walked into position.

'Fire!' Hilts voxed.

After the melta-blast had hissed its way up the passageway, burning the enemy who stood in its wake, Hilts shifted forwards and motioned for Fulgencio to follow.

'Ahead!' the veteran-sergeant called, and opened fire with his bolter again.

They were halfway to the target, and a man down, with an unknown number of enemy elements between them and their goal. There was no time to waste.

SCOUT DU QUESTE stood with his body perpendicular to the hatch, his right foot forwards and pointing ahead, his left foot planted beneath him and parallel to the hatch. He held his combat blade in his right hand, with his left hand held lightly behind him for balance. The slightest of smiles still played around the corners of his mouth, but in his gaze there was only steel and determination.

The loading bay appeared to be wreathed in silence, and Jean-Robur could hear nothing but the sound of his own breathing and the pulse of his own heartbeat. He knew the Scouts who stood beside him were likely ensconced in silence, as well. All of them had been buffeted by the spill-over of the sonic attacks the Noise Marines on the far side of the hatch had fired into the opening, but given the geometry of the hatch and the narrowness of the gap the Emperor's Children had not been able to fire directly into the bay's interior.

But while the baffling effects of the hatch were preventing the Scouts from suffering the sonic weaponry's full effects, and their eyes had not yet vibrated out of their skulls nor their organs lique-fied within their bodies, the noise was still sufficiently loud to render them all effectively deaf. Every few moments sound would begin to bleed back into Jean-Robur's world as his body struggled to heal the damage to his inner ears, but then a Noise Marine would launch another sonic attack and after a brief thunderous din the world would be blanketed once more in complete silence.

Another Roaring Blade slipped through the gap, and another, and another. The three Scouts stood in a broken line before the gap, with Jean-Robur in the middle and Scouts Zatori and s'Tonan to his left and right, respectively, a few paces to either side and a few paces ahead. The three formed a triangle with Jean-Robur at its peak, just out of the reach of each other's swords, so that they could each fight an enemy intruder without worrying about accidentally striking their squadmates in a parry or riposte. And whether an intruder broke right, broke left or drove straight ahead after slipping through the narrow opening, they would be rushing straight towards an armed defender in every case. So as the three Roaring Blades surged forwards, the three Imperial Fists Scouts were perfectly positioned to deal with them.

One of the three intruders rushed straight at Jean-Robur. It could have been bravery of a sort, or reckless abandon, or simply that the intruder's eyes had not yet accustomed to the gloom and he didn't yet realise that Jean-Robur was standing directly in his path. Either way, though, Scout du Queste stood ready to meet the enemy charge, and as the Roaring Blade got within range, Jean-Robur lunged forwards, his right foot leaping forwards while his left stayed planted, and plunging his combat blade up and into the intruder's belly from below. Then Jean-Robur whipped the blade to the right, slicing outwards through the meat of the intruder's abdomen and spilling blood and viscera out onto the blood-slicked rockcrete as the blade tugged free. The Roaring Blade clutched his side with his free hand, a look of supreme bliss on his face, but continued onwards, his forward momentum deflected but not deterred. And before Jean-Robur could shift out of the way or bring his combat blade back on line to defend, the dying intruder plunged his own sabre into the narrow band of skin exposed above the point where his breastplate met his shoulder-guard. The intruder's sabre drove deep into the soft meat above Jean-Robur's left clavicle.

Jean-Robur shouted in rage and pain.

The Roaring Blade collapsed to his knees, his intestines spilling out onto the ground before him, but his sword was left quivering in place, sticking straight out from Jean-Robur's shoulder. The intruder listed forwards, swooning in a rush of pleasure.

'The warp take you!' Jean-Robur cursed. He reached up, wrapped his left hand around the intruder's sabre and yanked it from his shoulder, heedless of the edge cutting deeply into his fingers as he gripped the blade. Still holding the sabre by the blade, he leaned forwards and stabbed the sabre's point straight down into the nape of the intruder's neck.

'Will you live?' voxed Zatori.

Jean-Robur looked over to his left, and saw his Sipangish squadmate glaring at him with narrowed eyes. It was the same hard look Zatori treated him to whenever they faced each other in sparring matches, or when Zatori seemed to feel that Jean-Robur had spoken out of turn. Jean-Robur had even glanced across a crowded room to find Zatori staring daggers at his back with precisely that expression on his face. Jean-Robur had

never known why Zatori hated him so, unless it
was simply the congenital hatred of the Sipangish
for the Caritaigne that his squadmate simply
could not relinquish. Or perhaps Zatori simply
suspected Jean-Robur was the more skilled with
the blade, and was driven by jealousy to hate him.

'Yes,' Jean-Robur answered with a grunt over the
vox-comms, rolling his shoulder to ease the pain
somewhat. Craning his head, he was able to peer
down past his jaw as the wound scabbed over. It
would hurt, and for some time to come, but it
wouldn't kill him. 'I'll live.'

'Then fight, Emperor damn you!' Zatori voxed
back with a sneer. 'Fight!'

Jean-Robur grinned, and feigned a bow in the
Sipangish's direction. 'As you wish.'

'I CAN'T HOLD them back much longer,' Veteran-
Sergeant Hilts voxed over the chatter of the bolter
in his hands. 'How near are you to completion?'

From the corner of his eye Hilts could see the
flash of the melta gun firing again and again at
the confusion of metal and machinery crammed
into the tunnel's mouth. The makeshift barricade
was gradually melted into a solid, irregular lump
that filled the mouth of the tunnel from side to
side, rendering it all but impassable. But while the
work was proceeding apace, it was taking precious
time.

'Soon, sergeant!' Fulgencio voxed back urgently.
'Another few moments, at most.'

Having left the body of Rhomec far behind along the passageway, the two Imperial Fists had pressed onwards towards the enemy, driving the Roaring Blades ever further back along the passageway. But the enemy was not giving up ground without a fight, and both Hilts and Fulgencio had taken a number of shots, some of which had healed quickly, and some of which had not.

They had already sealed up the first of the compromised barricades, with Hilts holding the enemy at bay further up the passageway while Fulgencio repositioned the salvaged machinery in place as best he could and then melted it all into a single plug of slag. Now, they had managed to push the Roaring Blades even farther back, with judicious application of bolter-fire and melta-blasts, and Fulgencio had set to work sealing up the second of the two compromised barricades, the one through which the Roaring Blades had broken through into the Bastion's catacombs in the first place.

There had been Roaring Blades climbing up though the tunnels and snaking their way around the gaps in the barricade when Hilts and Fulgencio had arrived, but it had only taken a few short blasts with the melta gun to deal with them. Now, Hilts covered Fulgencio's back while the Scout made sure no other Roaring Blades would be following behind.

The invaders who had already made it into the catacombs had retreated ahead of Hilts's bolter-fire all the way up to the dead-end at the far end of the passageway. Even over the chatter of his bolter Hilts could hear the echoing howls and roars of the heretics, and the whistle and whine of their weapons as they fired blindly around the curve of the passageway at his position.

A short distance off lay the bodies of the three Vernalian nobles who had allowed the Roaring Blades into the subterranean passageways in the first place, by removing parts of the barricades that Hilts's Scouts had put in place. Hilts was sorry to have saved the three wretches from the excruciators of the Inquisition. Heretics such as these did not deserve the Emperor's mercy that he had bestowed upon them. But he hadn't the luxury to provide them the justice they so richly deserved.

Hilts realised that his bolter had gone silent, because he had removed his finger from the trigger. The echoes from up the tunnel grew louder, and he knew that the Roaring Blades were approaching. His attentions were wandering, his focus lost. He glanced down at his chest and arms, and saw the countless scorches and pockmarks of enemy fire he'd received in recent minutes. How many times had he been shot since advancing from the intersection? He'd lost count. But the injuries were clearly beginning to take their toll.

'Done, sergeant!' came the voice of Fulgencio over the vox. 'It's sealed.'

Hilts tightened his grip on his bolter, and nodded.

'Then let's move in and take these wretches out, once and for all,' Hilts voxed in reply.

Fulgencio came to stand beside him, looking as unsteady on his feet as Hilts currently felt. The Scout was just as marked by enemy fire as Hilts himself was, if not worse.

'Stand fast,' Hilts said, putting a stabilising hand on Fulgencio's bleeding and burned shoulder. 'You are a son of Dorn, and he is always with you.' Hilts nodded towards the gloom at the far end of the passageway, lit only occasionally by the flash of las-fire from the approaching invaders. 'The primarch will light the way.'

Fulgencio straightened, as best he could, and then he and the veteran-sergeant limped down the passageway towards the enemy, weapons primed and ready.

At the main hatch, the three defending Scouts stood steadfast, their combat blades in hand. They'd filled the gap and the floor within with the bodies of the enemy fallen, but still the Roaring Blades came, wave after endless wave. Captain Taelos still sat along the wall, but he'd not moved or spoken in some time, and the Scouts were beginning to suspect the worst.

Each of the three Triandrians were bloodied and bruised, covered in innumerable cuts from the enemies' swords. But all three were still on their feet, and would remain so until there was no more blood or life left in them.

But with the seemingly endless waves of Roaring Blades still pouring through the gap, and the

continual bursts of sonic attack from the Noise
Marines outside, it was beginning to seem as if
the Scouts' lifeblood would not last long enough
for them to stand against them all.

Their hearing was beginning to return for a
moment, before the next sonic blast of the Noise
Marines beyond. At first, the Scouts thought that the
rumble and roar they could hear from outside was a
trick of the mind, or some new assault the Emperor's
Children were bringing to bear. And when the floor
began to vibrate beneath their feet, sending jarring
waves of vibration up their legs, they could scarcely
imagine what sort of munitions the enemy might
have held in abeyance and only now unleashed upon
them.

'Veteran-Sergeant Karn to any and all Imperial Fists,'
came a voice buzzing over the vox. 'Affirmative?'

The three Scouts were struck momentarily dumb
with surprise, and so it was the wavering voice of
Captain Taelos that was the first to answer over the
vox.

'Taelos receiving,' the captain said, sounding faint
and distant. 'What is your situation?'

'Thunderhawk *Pugnus* is in operation, but barely,
and we are commencing strafing runs on the enemy
positions to the east of the Bastion. We're pounding
them with heavy las-fire and missiles, and the first
pass appears to have taken out a good number of the
enemy elements. A few more passes should be
enough to deal with the rest. Hold fast and we will
join you shortly.'

'Acknowledged, Karn,' the captain replied, and the Scouts could almost hear the pride and satisfaction in his tone.

The Scouts glanced over in the captain's direction, in time to see Taelos hold his arm against his ruined breastplate. Then he raised his fist unsteadily in the air.

'Primarch-progenitor...' Taelos said, his strength fading.

The three Scouts turned back towards the gap, to see a stream of Roaring Blades slipping inside. The Scouts' duty was to defend the Bastion, and that's what they would do.

'To your glory,' the three Triandrians voxed in unison, raising their combat blades against the invaders, 'and the glory of Him on Earth!'

THERE WERE MOMENTS when it seemed to Scout Zatori that the night would never end, and that the Roaring Blades who slipped in their twos and threes through the gap were without number. Through the narrow opening in the hatch could be heard the constant cacophony of heavy-weapons fire as the Thunderhawk poured turbolaser fire and ordnance down on the besieging force, and the Emperor's Children and the Roaring Blades returned with whatever weapons they had at their disposal.

But as the first light of dawn came streaming through the gap, the number of Roaring Blades slowed to a trickle. And it seemed to Zatori that the last few that he and his squadmates had cut down hadn't had much fight left in them, and had made their way through the gap in search of refuge, trying to escape the firestorm outside, and not out of any serious attempt to invade the bastion.

'It's been some time since we've heard from Veteran-Sergeant Hilts,' Scout du Queste observed as he skewered a hapless Roaring Blade through the belly with his combat blade.

Scout s'Tonan nodded. 'If they're not answering vox-hails, one of us should go and ascertain the situation.'

A Roaring Blade staggered through the gap, badly burned by turbolaser fire, but collapsed to the floor before any of the Scouts had even approached him.

'Agreed,' Scout Zatori said. He paused to cast a glance back at Captain Taelos, who still lay on the rockcrete along the wall. He had been slipping in and out of consciousness throughout the night, but didn't seem responsive at the moment. 'I shall go,' Zatori announced, turning back to the others. 'I will vox as soon as I reach the catacombs.'

His two squadmates turned back to the gap, their combat blades raised. They didn't speak, didn't wish Zatori good fortune or warn him to be careful. They didn't have to.

Drawing his bolt pistol, Zatori hurried away from the hatch, heading deeper into the Bastion.

SCOUT DU QUESTE stood before the gap, his combat blade held at the ready in a one-handed grip. He glanced over to Scout s'Tonan who stood a few paces to his left.

'Have I lost my hearing entirely,' Jean-Robur said in a low voice, 'or has it quietened outside?'

Scout s'Tonan shook his head. 'If you've lost your hearing, mine has gone as well.' He gestured with his chin towards the narrow opening of the hatch. 'And it's been some time since any traitors came through the gap, as well.'

Jean-Robur was considering venturing beyond the hatch and conducting a visual inspection when a voice came crackling over the vox.

'Veteran-Sergeant Karn to any and all Imperial Fists. Respond!'

After glancing to where Captain Taelos lay on the rockcrete floor, and seeing that the captain was in no condition to reply, Jean-Robur answered.

'Scout du Queste receiving from the Bastion,' he voxed.

'What is your situation, Scout?' Veteran-Sergeant Karn voxed. 'Is the Bastion still secure?'

'This entrance is, sir. Scout Zatori has gone below to check on the subterranean access.'

'And Captain Taelos?' Karn asked.

Scout du Queste glanced back at Taelos, who was still living but seemed near to death. 'Alive, but out of commission.'

'Acknowledged,' Karn replied. There was a pause, as if the veteran-sergeant were considering his options. 'I won't be able to keep this Thunderhawk in the air much longer. I'm bringing her down just east of the mountain. Provide cover from the ledge, in the event that any enemy forces remain in the area.'

'Is that safe, sir? That is, to land on the dunes?' Jean-Robur shot Scout s'Tonan a look, seeing if his squadmate was as confused as he was. The whole reason that the Thunderhawks had not landed close to the Bastion in the first place was that the ground surrounding the mountain stronghold was uneven and treacherous for landing. And what of the besieging force?

'The landing gear on the gunship is damaged, as it is, so it's going to be a rough descent one way or the other. And we may not have fuel enough to reach the shores to the east. We're going down, either way.'

'And the enemy?' This time it was Scout s'Tonan who voxed in confusion.

'Routed,' Veteran-Sergeant Karn replied. 'But some fled, and might return to take a shot at the Thunderhawk as I bring her in. That's why I want you on the ledge laying down suppressing fire.'

'Acknowledged,' Scout du Queste shot back. When Veteran-Sergeant Karn broke vox-contact, Jean-Robur was already advancing towards the opening. 'Come on,' he called over his shoulder to s'Tonan, as he stepped over the lifeless bodies of the fallen Roaring Blades. 'Let's see if we can't pick off a few more of the wretches before we're through.'

SCOUT TALOC s'TONAN fired a single round from his bolt pistol and caught the Roaring Blade who was creeping towards the Bastion. The traitor dropped like a stone, his rewired nervous system proving no protection against a well-placed bolt.

'A clean shot,' Veteran-Sergeant Karn said, coming up the ramp to gain the ledge, stepping around the barricade that Scout Zatori and the others had assembled in the first hours of the siege. Behind Karn followed two Scouts of Squad Vulpes.

Taloc nodded in Karn's direction, and then went back to his vigil at the barricades. On the other end of the ledge Scout du Queste kept watch over the approach.

In the time it had taken Veteran-Sergeant Karn and the two Scouts to cover the distance from the place where Thunderhawk *Pugnus* lay canted at a considerable angle over the dunes, a handful of Roaring Blades had emerged from hiding and mounted ineffective attacks, but each time Taloc and Scout du Queste had been able to put them down with minimal bolt-fire.

'Where is the rest of Squad Vulpes?' Scout du Queste called over to Veteran-Sergeant Karn.

'This *is* the rest of Squad Vulpes.'

The Squad Vulpes Scouts were badly injured, one holding a still-bleeding wound at his side, the other walking with a pronounced limp.

'The rest fell when the daemons attacked,' Veteran-Sergeant Karn went on. 'We three were all that made it back to the Thunderhawk alive.'

Scout s'Tonan looked from the veteran-sergeant out to Thunderhawk *Pugnus*, which looked as though it might never get airborne again. 'We are grateful that you did, sir. Had you not arrived, I'm not sure we'd have been able to hold out.'

Veteran-Sergeant Karn reached out and laid a gauntleted hand on s'Tonan's shoulder. 'That you lasted as long as you did brings honour to your Chapter, and those who trained you.' He paused, and then glanced around. 'But what of Captain Tae-los? And Veteran-Sergeant Hilts?'

Taloc glanced back at the hatch. 'The captain is this way. As for Sergeant Hilts...' He paused, his gaze darting over to Scout du Queste, who lowered his eyes in response. 'We are still waiting.'

SCOUT ZATORI ZAN made his way through the cata-combs, searching for any sign of his squadmates or their sergeant. The passageways and tunnels were eerily quiet, and he received no replies to his vox-calls, and no answer to his shouts but his own voice echoing back to him.

But he had begun to encounter evidence of his squadmates' bravery. The deeper he moved into the catacomb, the more bodies he found, the fallen Roaring Blades who had infiltrated the mountain stronghold's subterranean passages. The rockcrete floor and walls were pockmarked with weapons-fire, and blackened with the smoke of explosions.

Then he came to the sealed-off tunnel through which the enemy had gained access to the Bastion, and found that Veteran-Sergeant Hilts and Scouts Fulgencio and Rhomec had been successful in sealing it off. No more Roaring Blades would be making their way into the Bastion from those tunnels. And though he found Scout Rhomec's lifeless body a short distance away, he still had not found Hilts or Fulgencio.

He continued on, deeper and deeper into the catacombs, until the bodies of the enemy dead were so thick on the ground underfoot that he could scarcely take another step.

And there he found Veteran-Sergeant Hilts and Scout Fulgencio, lying within arm's reach of each other on the ground, their bolters and blades still in hand. They were surrounded by a ringed mound of their fallen foes.

'Scout Zatori transmitting,' he voxed back up to the surface.

Having sealed off the access from below, the two Imperial Fists had gone on to hunt down and eliminate all of the enemy forces that had infiltrated the Bastion's subterranean passages. And though it had cost their lives to do so, to all appearances the two had been successful.

'The catacombs are secure.'

SCOUT DU QUESTE shoved one last time, and the now-unlocked hatch was finally open wide enough for Veteran-Sergeant Karn and Scout s'Tonan to manoeuvre Captain Taelos out of the opening and into the daylight.

There had not been any sign of lingering enemy elements on the slopes of the Bastion since Scout s'Tonan had picked off the last one some time before. And when Scout Zatori voxed from the catacombs that the underground passages beneath the mountain stronghold were now secure, it appeared that the siege had at last come to an end.

Captain Taelos was still severely injured, but his body's regenerative abilities were gradually finding a state of equilibrium, and he had managed to regain full consciousness. He was still unable to move under his own power, but now that Veteran-Sergeant Karn had propped him up in a sitting position against the jamb of the hatch, the captain was able to survey the situation.

'It would appear,' Captain Taelos said, his voice sounding to Jean-Robur as though it were coming from a long way off, 'that against all odds we have prevailed.'

Scout du Queste stood alongside Scout s'Tonan and the others, listening to the captain address them in a strained voice. The sun was approaching its zenith overhead, and it was nearing midday.

'The Vernalian refugees are safe,' the captain went on, 'despite the best efforts of their heretical "leaders". Finally, and perhaps most significantly, the Bastion has withstood invasion. The defences we prepared were equal to the task, and the enemy was not able to defeat them.'

The sound of echoing footsteps from within the hatchway heralded the return of Scout Zatori, who had voxed his full findings of the catacombs while Jean-Robur still fiddled with the hatch's locking mechanism to get it unstuck.

Zatori glanced at Captain Taelos as he approached, seeming pleased to see the captain more-or-less upright and communicative, but his attentions were quickly diverted to something past Scout du Queste's shoulder, out past the barricades.

'What is *that*?' Scout Zatori asked, pointing.

Scout du Queste turned, expecting perhaps to see a small resurgent force of the enemy appearing from cover, making one last-ditch attempt to storm the Bastion. He raised his bolt pistol in one hand, his other hand finding the handle of his combat blade.

But what he saw instead froze him like a statue, his mouth hanging open in shock.

IT WAS AS if a second sun had risen in the east.

Out past the undulating grey landscape, the shore on which they'd first stepped foot on Vernalis now ended at a towering wall of orange flame. Black smoke curled up into the sky, and even at this distance they could smell the acrid scent.

The petrochem seas to the east had been set on fire.

'Emperor preserve us,' said one of the Squad Vulpes Scouts.

Like a fast-approaching storm front a huge cloud of black smoke came pouring off the burning petrochem sea and roiled over the landscape towards them. And above the sound of the burning oil, which sounded like a chorus chanting somewhere in the distance, they began to hear howls and discordant shouting.

'There!' Scout s'Tonan shouted, pointing towards the northern end of the roiling cloud of black smoke as it verged ever nearer.

'And there!' Scout du Queste added, pointing off to the south.

A teeming mass of figures came surging out of the black clouds to the north and south, making straight for the Bastion.

It was an army of Chaos. But unlike any the Scouts had ever seen before.

There were thousands upon thousands of Roaring Blades, waving their sabres and scimitars overhead, howling at the top of their lungs.

There were Chaos Space Marines in their dozens, wielding massive sonic weaponry and singing unholy hymns to their dark masters.

Daemons, little more than purple-tinged corpsewhite streaks, dashed this way and that, moving almost faster than the eye could see.

The warband was so large that it dwarfed the besieging force that the Imperial Fists had withstood in the previous day and night.

This was an army devoted to Slaanesh, marching straight towards the Bastion, with the petrochem lifeblood of the planet burning to soot and ash in their wake.

'Wait,' Veteran-Sergeant Karn said, narrowing his gaze. He unclipped the magnoculars from his waist and raised them to his eyes. 'So I was right.' He lowered the magnoculars and turned to Captain Taelos, who still sat propped against the hatch's jamb.

'What is it, brother-sergeant?'

'I've spotted their leader, captain,' Karn replied. 'It is the arch-traitor Sybaris himself.'

Captain Taelos struggled into a standing position, using the jamb of the hatch to support his weight. He looked around the ledge at the others – Veteran-Sergeant Karn and five Scouts, two of whom were badly injured. Along with him, a captain scarcely able to stand without assistance, they hardly presented an imposing force. Through a day and a night the Imperial Fists had, at considerable loss of life, barely managed to hold off a besieging force that was barely a *fraction* the size of the warband which now advanced on them.

What chance did they have of standing fast against so large a force, much less one led by the arch-traitor Sybaris?

Taelos's thoughts raced, as he considered their options. Like any battle-brother of the Imperial Fists he was always aware of the defensive possibilities inherent in any position or locale, and did not walk into an area that he did not first consider how to fortify. It was that instinct that had meant for the successful defence of the Bastion, he was sure. But with only a half-dozen Imperial Fists, half of them incapable of operating at full capacity, what possible defensive posture was available to him?

He looked out to the east, where the thousands of the enemy were marching ever closer to the Bastion, the black smoke of the burning sea roiling behind them.

If they retreated inside the Bastion and closed the hatch, the forces of Sybaris would make short work of it, burning and blasting their way in with little trouble. But with the numbers of Roaring Blades, Emperor's Children and daemons now advancing on them a strategy such as they employed in the night, locking down the open hatch to create a narrow defile and then picking off the enemy as they approached, was simply not feasible. There were simply too many enemies that could be thrown into the breach, and with only six Imperial Fists on hand to stand against them it was only a matter of time before Taelos and his Scouts were overrun.

For the hundredth time since he had been left in charge of the Bastion, Captain Taelos again wondered why it was that Captain Lysander had given him the order to stay and defend the refugees. Why had Taelos and his Scouts been handed an assignment so far outside the bounds of normal Space Marine activity? What had been Lysander's reasoning?

Of course, Taelos could find some small measure of satisfaction in the knowledge that he had been correct, and that a larger force of the enemy *had* remained behind on Vernalis. And the fact that the arch-traitor Sybaris had been lured out of hiding to deliver the killing blow to the Imperial Fists in the

Bastion did at least serve to confirm that the war-band leader *was* on the planet.

It would come as little comfort, though, when Sybaris overran the Bastion and sacrificed all within, Imperial Fists and civilians alike, to the greater glory of Slaanesh.

The howls and hymns of the approaching army were now all-but-deafening.

'Brother-Sergeant Karn. Scouts,' Captain Taelos said, turning his eyes to the others. 'You have fought well, and with honour, and have brought glory to the Emperor and the Chapter alike. I am proud to have served as your commanding officer. If only–'

Taelos's words were cut off by a screaming sound that came cutting across the sky, then another that came in answer a split-second later.

'Dorn, be with us,' Taelos said, and looked up to see a flight of Thunderhawk gunships streaking across the sky overhead, the black-fist icon of the Imperial Fists emblazoned on them.

'Captain Lysander transmitting!' came a voice crackling over the vox. 'Brothers respond!'

From the black clouds which gathered overhead a hail of drop-pods came plummeting down, too fast for Sybaris's forces to hit with anti-aircraft fire, retro-rockets blooming like newborn stars as the pods gradually slowed their descent.

'Captain Taelos receiving,' he voxed in reply, feeling a swell of pride from within, combating a mounting sense of annoyance. 'What is your position?'

'The full body of Task Force Gauntlet is on hand, captain,' Lysander replied over the vox-channel.

'And Quernum?'

'We never went,' Lysander answered. 'We have been waiting on the edge of the Vernalian System for this very moment.'

Taelos paused, considering his response. 'Sybaris is leading the warband,' he finally voxed back.

'We have him in our sights,' Lysander answered, as the Thunderhawks unleashed a firestorm of turbo-lasers and missiles on the Chaos army, and the drop-pods disgorged entire squads of veterans in Terminator armour into the heart of the enemy forces. 'Stand fast, and let *us* take care of Sybaris.'

Taelos gripped the edge of the hatch's jamb, so tightly that his gauntlet left the faint impression of fingers in the metal. His suspicions had been correct, then. Captain Lysander had left Taelos and the Scouts of the 10th Company on Vernalis as bait, to lure the main body of Sybaris's warband out of hiding. And the force that had attacked Quernum had clearly been a diversion, too small a force to have been the full warband that had overrun Vernalis.

'Acknowledged,' Taelos replied over the vox.

He turned his gaze back to Karn and the Scouts. Of all of those who had followed him from the *Phalanx* to Vernalis, only this six remained. The rest had been lost, and for what?

Objectively, Taelos understood Captain Lysander's decision. It was a sound tactic, to use the Scouts as bait. And Lysander must have known that the Scouts had the training and the armament to hold their own against the enemy. But while Lysander sat at the edge of the Vernalian System waiting for the warband to emerge from hiding, nearly two dozen of the Scouts under Taelos's command had given their lives in the needless defence of the Bastion. Sybaris had been drawn into the open, yes, but at what cost?

These were questions that would have to plague him on another day. At the moment, he had Scouts waiting for his command.

Captain Taelos straightened as best he could, one shoulder still leaning against the jamb. 'Stand fast, Scouts. We have done our part. Now it is time for our brothers to do theirs.'

EPILOGUE

IN ONE OF the countless exercise halls which dotted the interior of the *Phalanx*, dressed only in a sparring chiton dyed golden yellow, Captain Taelos worked his way through the sword-forms, trying to focus his thoughts.

Nearly two dozen of those under Taelos's command had been lost, Scouts and sergeant included. Nearly two dozen more names to add to the list of those deaths for which he would one day atone, when Chapter Master Pugh finally gave him leave to depart on his warrior pilgrimage. But held in the balance were the lives of the Vernalian civilians who had survived the final assault by the forces of Chaos, huddled with the mountain Bastion. The Imperial Fists had sacrificed their own, but in the end victory had been theirs.

There was no way of knowing whether the arch-traitor Sybaris had been among the fallen on the grey dunes of Vernalis, or if he had once again slipped through the Imperial Fists' fingers. But the fact that the warband had been thoroughly routed was *not* in doubt. By the time Task Force Gauntlet had finished its relentless attacks, there had not even been enough enemy elements left standing to trouble the handful of Scouts who'd waited the battle's end in the Bastion, much less the hundreds of fully armed and able-bodied Space Marines of the 1st and 5th Companies who had descended from on high.

Taelos's reverie was interrupted by a soft chime sounding from the entrance on the near wall. He had sealed the exercise hall when entering, to ensure that there would be no unexpected disruptions to his meditations.

Sighing, Taelos lowered his blade. He had got nearer to finding focus in this session than he had in a considerably long time, but still his thoughts wandered. Still the ghosts would not leave him be.

But no matter. He expected the three battle-brothers to join him shortly, so the session was soon to end, anyway.

Setting his blade in a rack, Taelos tugged a towel from the railing and stepped over to the entrance. He keyed the door to open, towelling the sweat from his face and neck as he did.

'Master,' said the Chapter serf at the door with his eyes respectfully lowered to the floor. He held up for Taelos's inspection a long, narrow case in his hands, and behind him in a single file stood two other Chapter serfs, each carrying an identical case.

'Ah, yes,' Captain Taelos said, and stepped aside to allow the Chapter serfs to enter. He pointed towards the sword rack along the wall. 'Set them there, and then you may go.'

Taelos had set the Chapter artisans to work shortly after Task Force Gauntlet had returned to the *Phalanx*, and he had hoped that the modifications would be completed in time. That the cases were delivered to him now, shortly before the battle-brothers arrived, made his decision seem something like fate.

Once the Chapter serfs had placed the cases and retreated, bowing as they went, Taelos opened the first of them and inspected the contents. The artisans had done their typical work, he was pleased to find, making the Chapter proud.

Taelos closed the case, and retrieving his sword from the rack returned to the middle of the hall. He began again the catechism of the sword, reflecting on Rhetoricus's words about the place where the soul of an Imperial Fist could be found.

As he completed one form and moved gracefully into the next, he was interrupted when the door chimed again. Taelos's first thought was that the Chapter serfs had returned, perhaps having forgotten something. Suppressing impatient irritation, he keyed the door to open.

'Yes?' Taelos asked as the door slid open.

But it was not three Chapter serfs who stood before him, but a trio of newly minted battle-brothers, their gold power armour gleaming and bright.

'Brother-Captain Taelos,' Battle-Brother Zatori Zan said with a slight incline of his head. 'You summoned us?'

Behind Zatori and to either side Brother Jean-Robur du Queste and Brother Taloc s'Tonan stood at attention.

'Yes, brothers,' Captain Taelos said, and motioned for them to enter. 'Come.'

Taelos walked back to the centre of the floor, his blade held in a loose grip at his side. As the three Imperial Fists arranged themselves in a line facing him, the captain resumed his stance and completed the form that had been interrupted by their arrival, his eyes closed. Only when he had finished, and found something like a still centre to his thoughts once more, did he open his eyes and turn to regard the three who stood before him.

Though they had been badly injured in the siege of the Bastion, the three neophytes had remained on their feet and fighting, more than could be said for Captain Taelos himself. When the task force had returned to the *Phalanx*, it had been with pride that Taelos had recommended them for induction as full Initiates of the Imperial Fists, along with the pair of Scouts from Squad Vulpes who had survived under Veteran-Sergeant Karn's command. The two Vulpes Scouts were still in the care of the

Apothecary, recovering from the injuries they received from the daemons that Taelos and his team had eventually wiped out, but Zatori, du Queste and s'Tonan had recovered onboard the strike cruiser *Titus* en route, and when they arrived at the *Phalanx* had been sent to the Apothecarion for a quite different purpose.

'You wear the power armour well, brothers,' Captain Taelos remarked, glancing from one to another. Repaired and refurbished after the previous armour-bearers no longer had any use for them, the three suits of power armour gleamed as if they too were new and freshly forged.

'And I thank you, brother-captain,' Brother du Queste said, acknowledging the compliment with a courtly wave of his gauntleted hand.

'I trust the implantation of your Black Carapaces has been without incident?' Taelos asked. 'Is it as you had been led to expect?'

'It is like *nothing* we could have expected,' Brother s'Tonan said, an undercurrent of wonderment to his words. 'The armour we wore as Scouts was a mere shell, lifeless and unfeeling. But this...' Taloc raised his arms before him, clenching and unclenching his gauntleted hands into fists, marvelling at the action. 'With the Black Carapace, the power armour acts and feels like... like...' He broke off, struggling to find the words.

'Like a second skin,' Brother Zatori finished for him, and Brother du Queste's expression made plain his agreement.

Taelos nodded. It had been centuries since he himself was in their position, having made the transition from neophyte to full initiate and battle-brother, but he still well remembered the sensation of walking around in his power armour for the first time, revelling in the way that it augmented his strength and speed, responding to his barest thoughts.

'You have received your new postings, I take it?' Taelos asked.

The three glanced to one another, and shook their heads.

'You are to report to Captain Khrusaor of the 5th Company,' Taelos answered, 'as soon as we are done here.'

On hearing his words the three battle-brothers seemed to tense, with Zatori flashing a momentary glare at Brother du Queste, while s'Tonan stared daggers at the back of Zatori's head.

'All three of us, sir?' Brother du Queste asked.

'Yes,' Taelos answered. 'I have spoken with Brother-Captain Khrusaor of your service to Emperor and Chapter as Scouts, and of your actions on Vernalis in particular. You have brought honour to the 10th Company, and are to be commended. And on a personal note, I must offer you my own thanks, as I doubtless owe my very life to you.'

Still the captain could sense the tension between the three, and what he could only assume was some level of disappointment that they would not be posted to three different companies.

'Brothers, I do not know the root of the disagreements or animosities that separate you three,' Captain Taelos said, 'but their effects have not escaped my notice. Whatever these personal tensions might be, however, it is clear that they do not impinge on your ability to fight as allies. Had it not been apparent from your actions on Tunis and elsewhere, it was evident in those moments I watched you three stand together before the main hatch of the Bastion on Vernalis. You complement one another, brothers in action as well as name, and the three of you are stronger together than the sum of any one of you individually. Whatever your grudges, one to the other, never forget that you are all Sons of Dorn, and that on the field of battle you have only your brothers to rely upon.'

The three battle-brothers averted their eyes, chastened somewhat.

'But I did not summon you in order to criticise, but to commend.' Captain Taelos gestured with the point of his blade towards the three cases arranged against the wall. 'There you will find three cases, each with the name of one of you inscribed upon it.'

The battle-brothers glanced from the captain to the cases and back, and it occurred to Taelos that he had not yet given them leave to move.

'Go,' Taelos said with a faint smile, gesturing again to the cases. 'See what waits for you within.'

Taelos strode over to the wall and returned his sword to the rack while the three Imperial Fists found their respective cases and opened them. From his vantage a few paces along the wall, Taelos was able to see the look of surprised shock on each of their faces, their mouths hanging open in disbelief as they lifted the weapons from the lined interior of the cases.

'I have kept them all of these years, to remind me what courage truly is. Looking at those blades called to mind the image of three Triandrian youths, all but defenceless and little more than children themselves, who stood their ground against a fully armed and armoured member of the Adeptus Astartes. With only those swords in hand, you three were willing to stand side-by-side against me, and the odds against you be damned.'

Scout du Queste raised his slender duelling sword, admiring the blade. 'My falchion,' he said, all breathless wonder.

'Father Nei's tachina,' Scout Zatori said, drawing the curved sabre-like sword from the case reverentially, as though it were a holy relic of some fallen hero.

'The ironbrand Thunderbolt,' Scout s'Tonan said with pride, brandishing the simple iron blade in a two-handed grip.

'They are not simply the mundane weapons you remember, though,' Captain Taelos hastened to explain. 'At my request, they have been reinforced and enhanced by the Chapter artisans here onboard the *Phalanx*, rendered suitable as Astartes weapons. Though you should prize and cherish them, these will not simply be keepsake heirlooms of your forgotten childhoods, but are combat blades which you will carry proudly onto the field of battle.'

The three battle-brothers found the artisan-crafted sheaths which accompanied each of the blades in the cases, and at Taelos's direction sheathed their blades and hung them at their sides.

'Captain Khrusaor awaits, brothers,' Captain Taelos said. Then he stood to attention, balling his right hand into a fist and crashing his arm against his chest. 'In the name of Dorn.'

The three battle-brothers snapped to attention and returned the salute, then replied with the antiphonal response. 'And Him on Earth!'

'Dismissed,' Taelos said.

As the three newest initiates of the Imperial Fists Chapter filed out of the open door and went off to meet their destinies, Taelos stood alone in the exercise hall with his ghosts. Twenty-three new names for his list, held in the balance against three new battle-brothers to fight for Chapter and Emperor.

A slight smile curved up the corners of Taelos's mouth. The honour of locating and training candidates for the Chapter might not carry the same glory as leading a company onto the front lines, but it was an honour he now felt privileged to bear.

He was not ready just yet to depart on his warrior pilgrimage, it appeared. He knew the day would someday come, but if Taelos was still able to recruit such as these three and train them to be true Sons

of Dorn, it seemed that there was still a service he
could perform for the Imperial Fists.

ABOUT THE AUTHOR

Chris Roberson is a respected SF author whose novels include *The Dragon's Nine Sons* (Solaris, 2007) and *Set the Seas on Fire* (Solaris, 2007). Roberson has been a finalist for the World Fantasy Award for Short Fiction, twice for the John W. Campbell Award for Best New Writer, and four times for the Sidewise Award for Best Alternate History Short Form (winning in 2004 with his story 'O One' and in 2009 with his novel *The Dragon's Nine Sons*.) He runs the independent press MonkeyBrain books with his partner and spouse Allison Baker.

BRAND NEW SERIES
FEATURING SPACE MARINES